SINS OF THE PAST

John A Griffiths, a native of Bangor, North Wales, was born in 1948. He was educated in Friars Grammar School before joining the Gwynedd Constabulary, which later became The North Wales Police.

He was a detective for all but seven of his thirty-three years police service, rising to the rank of detective inspector as head of the fraud squad. In addition to fraud, he also has experience investigating crimes such as murder, kidnapping, sexual assaults and child abuse of the kind that feature in '*Sins Of The Past.*'

Upon retirement from the police service, he worked for a national firm of solicitors engaged in defending civil claims, mostly against police forces and local authorities.

John has been fully retired for a number of years. In addition to writing, he enjoys fly-fishing, hill walking, field sports and cooking.

He lives in Anglesey with his partner, Julia, and their flat-coated retriever, Merlin.

This is his second novel.

SINS OF THE PAST

John A Griffiths

SINS OF THE PAST

Olympia Publishers
London

www.olympiapublishers.com
OLYMPIA PAPERBACK EDITION

Copyright © John A Griffiths 2010

The right of John A Griffiths to be identified as author of this work has been asserted in accordance with sections 77 and 78 of the Copyright, Designs and Patents Act 1988.

All Rights Reserved

No reproduction, copy or transmission of this publication may be made without written permission.
No paragraph of this publication may be reproduced, copied or transmitted save with the written permission of the publisher, or in accordance with the provisions of the Copyright Act 1956 (as amended).

Any person who commits any unauthorised act in relation to this publication may be liable to criminal prosecution and civil claims for damage.

A CIP catalogue record for this title is available from the British Library.

ISBN: 978-1-84897-114-1

This is a work of fiction.
Names, characters, places and incidents originate from the writer's imagination. Any resemblance to actual persons, living or dead, is purely coincidental.

First Published in 2010

Olympia Publishers
60 Cannon Street
London
EC4N 6NP

Printed in Great Britain

To Julia

Acknowledgments

My sincere thanks to Mr Dennis Evans for his advice with regard to the final presentation of this book.

Chapter One

In the hallway of the old farmhouse, the oak-cased grandfather clock struck nine as Emily Parry looked out through her kitchen window. She was barely able to see the outline of the decaying elm trees as they swayed helplessly against the fading sky.

For the first time in her eighty-nine years, she was becoming afraid of the dark, or rather what the darkness brought with it. She wondered if he would call again tonight and if he would finally step out of the shadows so that she could see him properly. Emily had become desperate to know for certain who it was and, if she were correct, why he had returned after such a long time. She was too old now to care much for her own safety, but this presence in her home disturbed the ageing widow for another reason. No matter how she tried, she failed to understand why he was behaving in such a strange and menacing way.

She could hardly recall when it had first started, probably because she had not been conscious of anything sinister in the beginning. A door closing somewhere in the house could easily have been caused by the wind.

Then, in the mornings, downstairs, she became aware of the lingering smell of stale tobacco smoke. Her late husband, Huw, had always smoked a pipe, but this was different and in any event since his death there hadn't been a smoker in the house, not until now. Later, she had found that the ashtray beside the rocking chair in the parlour had been used. This was the chair that hadn't rocked in thirty years. It hadn't even been sat upon during all that time, not even by Huw. One morning the ashtray had contained a cigarette end. She had recognised it as the 'roll your own' kind and that was significant.

It was in the dead of night that she first heard the music. It was Prokofiev's 'Peter And The Wolf', played so quietly in the beginning that she could hardly make it out. At first she thought she was dreaming but, as time progressed, the music had become louder. It had been unthinkable to venture from the relative sanctuary of her bedroom to investigate.

She hadn't told anyone about it. Even now, in her later years,

Emily Parry knew that those close to her still considered her to be a woman of wisdom and strength. Strangely, this was why she couldn't bring herself to tell anybody. She thought that anyone she told might consider that her mind was failing, and who could blame them?

It was getting late and as she warmed the milk in a small saucepan on the single gas burner, she felt for the torch she now carried in the pocket of the overcoat that hung loosely about her frail frame. She had no way of knowing when she might need it and to touch it now and then gave reassurance, for she had no doubt that the darkness imposed by the intruder would soon arrive.

Emily had hardly been out of the same overcoat since the arrival of winter, several months earlier. The farmhouse was damp and cold, but she'd had no inclination to look after it since Huw had died some fifteen years ago. Hendre Fawr had been her home for most of her life and this was where she intended to stay – to live and die there. Not even these recent events could change her mind. She was determined that nothing would drive her out. The old farmhouse was all she had and it meant so much more to her than just the stone walls. There had been the good times, the bad times and the one occasion that was dreadful, but still she and Hendre Fawr were inseparable. Even though she hadn't been able to work the fields for years, the income from renting the land, even in its present state, was more than she needed. But by now she had lost all interest in her income and had come to trust and rely heavily on her accountant.

As she carried the mug of hot milk out of the kitchen, she looked over to the corner, where Betsy, her pet chicken, nestled into the comfort of a hay-filled pillowcase, close to a fading fire. It had done this every night for almost a year, ever since its tangle with a hungry fox one night had provided a narrow escape in favour of the bird.

Emily Parry had never been one to frighten easily, but as she locked and double-checked the doors, her mind returned to the events of the past three months. In the beginning she had attempted to come to terms with the tormenting nature of her night-time visitor, believing that there was no intention to harm her. Now, however reluctantly, she was forced to admit that she was becoming more and more intimidated. It seemed that the occurrences were becoming more frequent and she felt more frightened.

Why should he do it after all of this time? She had loved him – she still did, and she was sure that he had loved her. It was as if the cigarettes and the music hadn't been enough to remind her. 'Peter And

'The Wolf' was his favourite classical composition. It was Prokofiev's gift to the world's children, or in this particular case, to the one whose mind had failed to develop fully and would never allow him to see beyond the vision of a child.

After the music came the knocking on the front door. When she opened it, there was no one to be seen in the darkness, but she would hear a faint cry, 'Mam' – nothing more. Later, she had suddenly seen the face of a middle-aged man in the window, but he was never there long enough, or the light was never strong enough to gain a worthwhile impression. It had, after all, been over thirty years since she had seen her son, but she would never forget him and neither, sadly, would anyone else in the town.

Emily sat upright in her bed and pulled the bedclothes to her chin as she had always done. She opened the family Bible at the place where the white fabric page marker indicated she had finished the previous night – St. Paul's first letter to the Corinthians. On this, her second reading of the Bible, the torch in her right hand provided the small, but essential non-spiritual comfort she needed. On the table beside her bed stood an old oil-lamp and the matches that might be required to light it at a moment's notice.

It wasn't long before Emily Parry froze as the electric light failed. In the torchlight her shaking hands spilled some of the matches onto the floor as she struggled to light the oil lamp. Then, in the dimness of its light, she clutched the closed Bible tightly against her breast and waited.

The silence lasted for what seemed to be an eternity. Then, she heard the faint sound of the music. It would never be, no, never, anything other than 'Peter And The Wolf'. It was such a happy, carefree tune in ordinary circumstances. Slowly, the bedroom door opened and as it did so the musical notes seemed closer than ever. Out of the darkness beyond, the sounds of the strings, the flute, the oboe, the clarinet and the bassoon filled her bedroom. The torch fell from Emily's hand as she pulled her Bible closer, tighter against her breast and she watched the shadowy figure appear, standing there silently, his terrifying bulk filling the doorframe. Grasping tightly, her frail fingers exposed white knuckles against the Bible's black binding as it moved rapidly in keeping with the hurried rhythm of her breathing.

After several minutes, he moved closer to the chair at the foot of the bed. He sat down and his large frame filled it. The light from the oil lamp wasn't bright enough for her to make out any particular feature, but he could see the old lady plainly. In the lamp's light, he could see the fear in her eyes. He wondered how much more the old girl could take.

Emily gasped aloud as he lit the cigarette lighter and she saw the yellow flame beneath his chin, exposing the contours of his face beneath the peak of a cloth cap. He drew hard on the hand-rolled cigarette and as the flame died, the cigarette's red tip disappeared into a cloud of blue-grey smoke. Moments later, the once familiar tobacco-scented air reached her. He had not been so close to her before.

He rose from the chair and walked even closer, slowly coming towards the side of the bed. An arm's length away he stopped and watched her shaking for several minutes, waiting, willing her to die by natural causes. Then, he showed her the cigarette lighter, embracing it in the palm of his hand. Emily gasped loudly again. She had to know. She simply had to know.

'Medwyn. Medwyn *bach*, is it you?'

There was no response. Several empty minutes passed before she found the courage to ask again.

'Medwyn, please tell me. Why are you doing this to your mother?'

Somehow, she knew he was not going to reply, but strangely, the lack of a response seemed to calm her, bringing a curious peace she hadn't anticipated. If she were to be harmed tonight, it would have happened by now.

Once he sensed the change in his victim's bearing, the figure moved back to the chair. It was, to him, an unexpected change and certainly, a change he couldn't understand. Her Bible was not now being clenched in despair, nor was it moving erratically in rhythm with her body, but was rather a part of the whole of the tiny figure that held it.

The old lady watched as he moved slowly, almost gliding, towards the door. Without turning away from her, he disappeared from view, but then she heard the bittersweet music once again and it lasted several minutes. As it faded, she heard the wind cry eerily throughout the cold, dark farmhouse, pulling her bedroom's curtains outside into the dim half-light of the morning. Emily Parry cried, shouting uncontrollably several times as she did so, 'Medwyn, Medwyn'. Then, only then, did the lights return.

The voice woke Emily out of her shallow sleep.

'Auntie Emily. It's me. Where are you?'

The bedroom door opened rather more quickly than it had done so some ten hours previously. 'Auntie Emily, are you all right? It's not like you to stay in bed till this time. The front door of the house is wide open and look at this window. You'll catch your death of cold in a draught like this.'

Elen Thomas moved over to the window, pulled back the damp curtains from outside and closed it to about three inches from the top of the frame. She opened the curtains fully and turned round to face one of her very favourite people. In the morning's light, she studied the old lady's face for a moment.

A number of possibilities raced through her head, all of them bad. She sat on the side of the bed and took Emily's cold right hand in both of hers.

'What's the matter? Are you all right? You're not all right are you? Are you ill? Please, Auntie Emily, tell me. I've never seen you like this before.'

There was silence for several minutes, during which Elen came to realise that her aunt's reluctance to be candid was entirely out of character. There had never been any secrets between them, or so she thought.

Emily took both Elen's hands now. 'I don't want you to worry about me. I'm just an old woman who's at the end of her journey. You've got Geraint to look after and he's a good boy. It's a big responsibility, you being on your own; so you concentrate on bringing him up to be a fine young man like his father was. Don't go worrying about me. What's going to happen to me is inevitable and it's going to happen sooner rather than later, my dear. But I've seen to it that you will be all right, both you and Geraint, so you look after him, do you hear?'

Elen realised that her aunt was not ill.

'Auntie Emily, you should know better than to send me packing with silly talk like that. I'm not going anywhere until you tell me what's bothering you.'

With a hint of a tear in the corner of her eyes, Emily stared at Elen for the best part of a minute. Yes, she thought, Elen was right. She should know better at her age. Elen meant so much to her, far too much to hide the truth and in any event her niece would see through any attempt to hide anything, even though it may have been designed to ease her burden.

'I've been having a night-time visitor.' Reluctantly, the old lady began and slowly she started to tell Elen about the events of the past three months. Step by step, she gave her account of what had taken place, ending with what had happened during the previous night, omitting only the identity of the intruder, or at least the person she thought him to be.

Elen wasn't sure what to read into the story. It was almost unbelievable. This wasn't like the old lady she had known all of her life. Several thoughts occurred to her. Was her aunt hallucinating or dreaming it up? She hadn't shown any signs of mental failure. She'd always been as bright as a button, and still was, or certainly appeared to be. Elen quickly looked around and found no signs or smell of anyone having recently been smoking in the bedroom, but she recalled that the window had been wide open and so had the front door. What significance was there to the music? If her aunt's story were correct, she thought, who would do such a thing – and more to the point, why? Elen felt more than a twinge of guilt before her next move, but it was essential in order to test her aunt's incredible story.

'There's only one thing we can do,' she started. 'We'll have to tell the police.'

'No,' replied Emily. 'I don't want anyone else to know about it.'

'But I know the very man auntie. He's a policeman and a friend of mine. You know Jeff Evans, don't you? He's quite discreet.

'Elen,' she replied. 'I have to insist that you tell no one about this. There's a very good reason why I have to ask you not to, but I can't explain it to you right now. You have to trust me.'

'I've always trusted you, Auntie Emily. I'm not going to stop just because of this. Whatever you say is fine with me for now, but you have to trust me too. I may need to do what I think is best in the circumstances, best for you, but we'll talk about it again. Now come on, get up. I'll make breakfast for you. Let's see if Betsy's laid an egg.'

An hour later, Elen left Hendre Fawr, closing the large oak front door behind her. Still somewhat confused by her aunt's revelations, she decided that she needed time to consider everything she had been told. She did, somehow, find comfort that the old lady had insisted that she should not repeat the story elsewhere. It was almost enough to sway her to think that the whole business was a figment of her aunt's imagination. But still she needed time to consider.

As she was about to unlock the front door of her ageing 'Volvo' estate, she felt a presence close by. She was becoming paranoid herself now, she thought. Nonetheless, she turned round and saw, for a brief moment only, the figure of a man disappearing behind one of the outhouses. He seemed to pause momentarily and then, as if changing his mind turned his back on her and slowly walked away, almost as if gliding out of her view. He seemed to be middle-aged; tall, wearing something like a full-length waxed jacket and a cowboy-type hat rather like a Stetson. Quickly, she ran in that direction, and from where he had stood, looked around the corner. There was no one to be seen. Pausing to catch her breath, inhaling more deeply than usual, she became aware of the smell of tobacco smoke. On the ground beneath her feet lay three discarded, hand-rolled cigarette ends. One was still burning. Whoever it was must have been waiting there for a while, possibly for most of the time that she was inside the farmhouse. Then, in the vegetation, she saw something bright.

Bending down, searching with her hand, she found that it was a cigarette lighter. Elen picked it up and recognised that it was the kind that used to be popular when she was a child. It was still warm to the touch, as if it had been held in someone's hand for a while or perhaps in a pocket, and the warmth of it made her feel uncomfortable. She examined it closely. It was an old 'Ronson'. She hadn't noticed the letters on it at first, but on one side the initials 'M. P.' had been engraved.

Driven by impulse, Elen returned to the farmhouse, but there was something in her mind that made her cautious when she asked her aunt the question that was burning on her lips.

'Auntie Emily, were you expecting anyone this morning?'

'No my dear, why?' Emily's eyes narrowed. 'I thought you were gone anyway,' she added.

'I saw a man outside the house and it wasn't anyone I know. He seemed to vanish as soon as he saw me looking at him.'

There was no response from the old lady.

'He dropped this,' she added, searching for any reaction, urging Emily to respond.

Elen placed the lighter in her aunt's hand. It took a moment for it to register, but when it did, Emily's features changed. First, there was a total lack of facial expression, followed by a show of tears that slowly filled her eyes and flowed gently down both of her pale cheeks.

'Sit down please, Elen. I haven't told you everything. That lighter was a present, an eighteenth birthday present, from Huw and me to our son, Medwyn. It was I who had these initials, his initials engraved on it. You see, I had come to believe, even before last night, that it's Medwyn who has been visiting me.' She paused. 'He's come back. After all of this time, he's come back. Yes, I believed, but now, this lighter,' she looked down into her hand, 'I know.' Her face was quickly becoming a swollen mass of tears.

'But I don't understand,' said Elen, confused.

'I don't expect you do, Elen. You were far too young. Tell me, do you remember anything at all about him?'

'I've got a vague recollection of seeing him when I came here. Then, suddenly, he wasn't here any more. No one in the family would talk about it, but I remember hearing some of the stories that were going around when I was growing up, but that was much later. Why did people call him Peter, not Medwyn? I didn't like to ask Mam or Dad. Even to mention his name was enough to change the atmosphere at home. It was something that was never discussed'.

'Medwyn wasn't like the other boys,' her aunt began to explain; for she realised that the time to be candid had finally come.

'He was simple minded. Do you know what I mean? They wanted to send him to a special school, but I wouldn't have it. In my heart of hearts I don't think I accepted that he needed it, you see, and that is something I have regretted every day since. Maybe he wouldn't have been here on that terrible day.' Emily Parry was speaking slowly now, but her tear-filled eyes indicated that her mind was wandering back through grief-stricken events that she still preferred to keep securely to herself. Even to discuss them with Huw had been impossible.

Elen avoided the temptation to ask questions.

'You know how easy it is for young boys like that to attract a nick name,' Emily continued. 'He enjoyed his music, but he had a particular love of Prokofiev's 'Peter And The Wolf'. So much so that he used to whistle those first few bars all the time – day in, day out. You know; those few repeated bars where the string instruments represent Peter? Such a happy tune, and he was such a happy boy. All the way through his school days, everywhere he went he whistled, repeating the same few notes. Strange thing was, he didn't mind being called Peter. He couldn't see the spiteful side of it, not that you'd expect him to. He had a few friends who came up here occasionally and they would play for hours, either in the woods or in the underground caverns that lead to the sea.

When he left school, he started working on the farm with his father. He seemed to have a special understanding of nature and he knew every inch of this land better than anyone else. Then, it happened. A couple of weeks before his nineteenth birthday, on a Friday night, a young girl was killed, murdered. She was raped and strangled. We ... I haven't seen Medwyn since he went out earlier that evening. Not until now, that is. I didn't tell you earlier because I wasn't prepared to accept it myself. But now, this lighter – you can understand now can't you why it is that I can't tell the police? When it happened, they were here every day, asking questions, more questions, and if they get to know what's happening now, now that he's back, it will be the same all over again.'

Elen was beginning to understand.

'As far as I'm concerned, they still haven't found out who killed that girl. Over the years, the whole thing has gone to the back of most people's minds, but it's never left my heart. Your Uncle Huw took it badly, you know. Took it to his grave with him, he did. Everyone thought it was Medwyn. Elen, I know that Medwyn wouldn't have done anything like that. He was my son, a very gentle boy and I just can't understand why he's doing this to me now. Why has he come back after all this time? It's been thirty years. Why did he run off in the first place? We could have got him the best lawyers money could buy. Oh Elen *bach*, I just don't know what to think any more.'

As Elen drove down the steep farm-track to the road leading towards the town, she thought that these latest revelations had given her an even greater dilemma. Where did her responsibilities lie? Should she keep faithfully to her aunt's wishes that no one should know what was happening at Hendre Fawr, or should her aim be to protect Emily at all costs, even if it meant exposing Medwyn? She desperately wanted to accomplish both, but was it possible?

She had driven down this track thousands of times in the past and had come to know every pothole in her attempts to avoid them. She could remember the countless occasions during her youth when she had walked the same way. Today, she realised how the sinister part of her family's history had been hidden from her. She thought about Medwyn who would have been about thirteen years her senior.

She recalled that he was big and powerful, yet gentle as a lamb, but then she let her mind explore the possibilities. Who knows what might have been going on inside the young man's mind when all of his friends were of an age when they would have been turning their attention to what the town's girls had to offer?

She slowed the car down to walking pace at the right-angled bend in the track, recalling with some pleasure the childhood games played with her parents, counting the number of strides from that sharp bend to the main road. Or on other occasions, from the same bend to the welcoming front door of 'Hendre Fawr'.

She had taken delight in relating the same pleasure to Gareth, her late husband, when she had first taken him to the farm. Emily had immediately treated him as her own, almost as quickly as he had taken to her. Oh, how she wished that Gareth were there to guide her now! The tragedy of five years previously had seen to it that he wasn't, but she wondered how he might have advised her now.

Ten minutes later, by the time Elen had arrived at Llanglanaber town centre, she had decided what she should do – her responsibility was to her aunt and no one else. It was Emily who needed protection, though she knew that her aunt would never leave Hendre Fawr to get it. Neither was Elen about to take up residence at the farm; the old lady wouldn't have agreed to that either – Geraint was far too young to spend his nights in the farmhouse's damp environment and in any event, to expose him to the possibility of danger was out of the question.

By the time Elen Thomas walked into the public foyer of the town's police station, she had decided to give Jeff Evans half a story. Enough, hopefully to afford her aunt some form of protection, or a quick police response if need be, without creating alarm or even a suspicion that Medwyn Parry had returned.

'Is Detective Constable Jeff Evans in please?'

'One moment please, I'll check,' replied the counter assistant. 'I know he's on duty today'.

The attendant picked up the phone, dialled and waited a moment.

'Is 'The Beaver' in?' she heard him ask. He looked in her direction. 'What's the name?'

'Elen. Elen Thomas.'

'He'll be down in a moment. Take a seat.'

A few minutes later, the inner door opened. He hadn't changed much in all the years she had known him. He was shorter than most policemen she had seen, scruffy and unshaven, wearing a duffel coat that seemed to have been fastened in all the wrong places.

Below the coat, a pair of mud-caked, black wellington boots was visible. He smiled broadly, though his red-rimmed eyes betrayed a tiredness that was consistent with a self-induced, irregular lifestyle.

'Elen, what brings a lady like you into a dreadful place like this?'

'How on earth did you get into the police force looking like that?' she asked, smiling.

'Got to look the part you know. A man for all seasons they call me. Besides, I couldn't find my suit this morning,' he joked.

The truth was that he'd been out all the previous night and most of the day before. A number of isolated farmhouses in the area had been broken into in recent weeks. Dozens of sheep had also been killed with what seemed to be a crossbow bolt, and then slaughtered in the fields in the dead of night. It was a matter that was considered serious and the farming community wanted results. Many of the farmers were his friends and the least he could do was to try.

'I heard you being called 'The Beaver' just now. What's that all about?'

'Some people in this town think I'm persistent; that I'll gnaw away at anything until I break whatever it is I'm working on.'

'Do you live up to it?'

'I try, Elen. I'm not always successful, but I try. Now then, what can I do for you?'

Although Elen had practised what she intended to say, she found that she was ill at ease asking Jeff for help by giving him half a story, but for the time being she felt that she had no alternative. What she told the detective was pretty much in line with what her aunt had told her the first time round.

She told him about the strange happenings at night, the music and the presence of the smoker inside the house, but nothing more. By the time she had finished, she felt uncomfortable and more than a little embarrassed, almost wishing she hadn't started. Jeff Evans looked at her in a way that indicated he wasn't paying the attention she would have liked, but who could blame him, she thought? They discussed the possibility that Emily was becoming confused; an option Elen might have considered herself had it not been for the 'Ronson' lighter that was secreted inside her handbag. Then, almost on impulse, as if to induce greater attention, she added the fact that she had seen a man hanging around suspiciously as she left. She described him as someone who looked as if he had just fallen out of a Spaghetti Western. If nothing else, it brought a smile to the detective's face. Then, having considered Elen's tale, he spoke.

'The fact that nothing has been stolen from your aunt's house tells me that this is not connected with the problems we've got in this area at the moment.' He paused and looked at her as she fiddled uneasily with the straps of her handbag, looking away from his eyes as he delivered his appraisal.

'Elen, it sounds to me as if Mrs. Parry is confused. She is almost ninety isn't she? And the man you saw, he was probably a poacher. There's lots of game about there at any time of the year, and you know what they're like round here if there's a chance of a meal. I'll log it down in the computer here, but quite honestly, you can't expect any more than that. You can, of course, call me personally if there's anything else that bothers you.'

Even though he played down his thoughts, he did wonder where these events might fit in the overall scheme of things, bearing in mind what was happening at various isolated farms in the area. It was certainly something he would bear in mind, but there was no need to concern Elen with his innermost thoughts.

Elen left the police station wondering whether she had achieved anything at all. She was still caught between her aunt's wishes and her own judgement. She considered that she should have told the detective the whole story, but had she done so, there was no doubt that 'The Beaver' would have begun gnawing good and proper.

In any event, she had a couple of other tricks up her sleeve that might serve to indicate to any potential intruder that Emily Parry was not alone from now on.

By the time Elen went to collect Geraint from school, the morning's drizzle had returned to Llanglanaber. She had 'phoned Emily Parry twice since leaving 'Hendre Fawr'. On the second occasion, she'd been rebuked for worrying too much, a response that she had almost expected, being typical of the old lady's character. Elen had smiled momentarily, but so many questions remained in her mind, and her concerns grew. There again she tried to look at the alternative – perhaps Jeff Evans was right in that she was making too much of it. She tried to put the whole matter out of her head as she chatted, making small talk with other waiting mothers outside the primary school gates.

In the confusion of running, screaming children, a figure caught Elen's eye. It was a man who was standing alone on the pavement, higher up on a small hill some distance away. He was tall, and wore a long dark coat and a large, wide-brimmed hat. He made no attempt to conceal himself, looking almost as if his presence was intended to intimidate her. As Elen attempted to focus her attention quickly upon all of the implications brought about by this man's presence, the full impact of Geraint's running jump forced itself upon the upper part of her body, his arms wrapped around her neck tightly.

'Mam, mam!' he said, followed by an attempt to relate the events of the entire day in one sentence.

She smiled a little half-heartedly, hoping the eight-year-old would not detect the inexplicable distance between them that might have been apparent to him.

'Hi boy, my little beauty! Let me take you home,' she said, glancing up the hill through the corner of her eye.

The figure was gone.

'But mam, mam, I want to wait for Tommy!'

'No buts today, please, Geraint. Your mam's got a lot on her mind.'

She certainly had.

As dusk once more fell on the inhabitants of Llanglanaber, Elen drew the curtains of her home. This particular evening, she had done so earlier than usual. All of the doors and windows were closed and locked and all of the curtains were drawn tightly, ensuring that no light escaped, but more importantly tonight, she wanted to be sure that nothing inside could be seen by anyone from the outside.

She telephoned Emily Parry again, but got Geraint to do it this time. He spoke to her first while Elen listened on the mobile extension. It would be better for Emily that way and Elen was able to judge her aunt's feelings whilst she chatted with the boy. She thought she sounded fine, but there again, hadn't she always? Emily promised Elen that she would keep the telephone extension by her bed. Elen had already arranged for another car to be parked immediately outside 'Hendre Fawr', left by a neighbouring farmer who, she knew, wasn't going to ask unnecessary questions. A light left on in a spare bedroom also helped to suggest the presence of a guest.

Elen hoped it would work, but the day's events still tormented her. She wondered whether Medwyn Parry was still out there somewhere and if he was, what would he be up to tonight? If he had been responsible for that murder thirty years ago, was he still capable, now, of showing the same tendencies? Presumably, the police would still want to question him. In her stupidity, as she now thought, she had given Jeff Evans half a story, without any mention of Medwyn or the all-important Ronson lighter. She wondered whether there would come a time when she could be held responsible for withholding that information. Elen was becoming well aware that she had put herself in a difficult position. She felt isolated and needed to talk to someone more than ever before.

Elen picked up the phone and dialled the numbers alongside a name in her personal telephone book. Across the Principality, the phone rang several times. Then, to Elen's relief, it was answered.

'Holland.'

'Michael, it's Elen.'

Michael Holland immediately detected an uncharacteristic nervousness in Elen's voice, but the pause before he replied was more a reflection of his own failings.

They had become close friends very quickly, though he recognised that it could have been more meaningful had it not been for the circumstances in which they met. That had been eighteen months ago and he knew that the lack of communication since then had been pretty much his fault. Losing contact hadn't been his intention, but getting too close hadn't seemed right at that time, not so soon after she had lost Gareth. There had only been a couple of telephone calls in the intervening period, both made by Elen and he felt a little embarrassed that he had not called her. This was her third call.

'Oh Elen, how are you? I have been meaning to call. Honestly I have.'

'It's all right Michael, I understand,' she lied, 'but I hope you don't mind my calling you like this because I need your advice. In fact I need your help.'

Holland, sensing her despair, dismissed what he considered to be his own failings. He had seen this woman dealing with the tragedy of her husband's untimely death, only to discover soon afterwards that he had been murdered. While they both struggled to find out why her husband was killed and to expose those responsible, she had also helped Holland to recover from an alcoholic blur following the earlier loss of his own wife and son. He knew that Elen was not only a gentle, but also a strong woman, capable of taking care of difficult situations and if she needed his help now, then that request was justified.

Michael Holland listened intently as she unveiled her burden, interrupting only briefly in order to make sure he understood. Fifteen minutes into the conversation, suddenly, and in mid sentence, he heard a loud sound of shattering glass, followed almost simultaneously by Elen's deafening scream and Geraint's distant cries of terror.

'Elen, Elen. For heavens sake, what's happening?'

There was no reply. The only sound he heard was that of the telephone handset knocking against the hall table as it swung to and fro where Elen had dropped it. The seconds seemed like hours.

'Elen, for God's sake, are you all right?'

Her reply came eventually, but was uttered nervously.

With Geraint in one arm and the telephone in the other, She tried to explain, raising her voice above the boy's cries, attempting at the same time to assess several superficial cuts about her son's head.

'Michael. Someone's thrown a brick through the window. There's glass everywhere. Geraint's hurt.'

'How badly?' Holland's concern was exasperated by the one hundred and seventy miles that separated them.

'I'm sure it looks worse than it is.'

'Now listen Elen, do exactly as I say. Get a torch and put all the lights out in the house and bolt the doors. Go upstairs and stay there until the police arrive. Don't open the doors to anyone else. I'll phone the police from here, now. Do you understand me?'

'Yes.'

'There's little else I can do right now, but I'll come up first thing tomorrow. I should be with you by mid morning.'

Half a brick had been thrown through the lounge window near where Geraint had been playing. Elen saw that what appeared to be a note had been tied around the brick with a strong elastic band. Having quickly released it, she placed the note in her pocket and followed Holland's instructions. Upstairs, by torchlight, she read the note, which had been compiled in traditional 'blackmailer style' using fragments of newspaper. It read, simply: 'YOU'VE GOT SOMETHING OF MINE. I WANT IT BACK.'

Elen's immediate thoughts turned to Emily Parry. She reached for the bedroom telephone and once she had finished dialling, the old lady answered almost immediately. Once again, Emily seemed a little perturbed that Elen had seen fit to telephone her, and so soon, but during the conversation, the perceptive old widow recognised the distress in her niece's voice and Elen was forced, reluctantly, to tell her what had happened. She was reassured by the fact that her aunt was as well as could be expected and that she was not being troubled by anyone. Then, only when the call had ended, did Elen use a damp flannel, gently to clean her son's superficial wounds. In the darkness they held each other, waiting for the arrival of the police. Little did she know, but for the rest of her life, Elen would regret having told her aunt about the broken window.

Detective Constable Jeffrey 'The Beaver' Evans had not been home during that day. He was about to leave his office, but decided to call in at the front desk to phone his wife, just to let her know that he was on his way. Jean always appreciated that. He was still there when Holland's call came through. He heard officers being directed to Elen's home. Abandoning any intentions to fulfil his promise of homecoming, he grabbed the keys to the unmarked car allocated to detectives and ran towards the back door.

'Evans, where do you think you're going in such a hurry?'

It was Detective Chief Inspector Renton and not a voice Jeff Evans wanted to hear right now. They didn't get on well at the best of times. Jeff considered them to be chalk and cheese personalities forced into the same public-serving package. To him, a career detective, his boss, Detective Chief Inspector William Alexander Renton was a young, promotion-seeking hypocrite who made unnecessary changes at a whim and regarded public service as an obstacle in the path of his own ambitions. In his relatively short, seventeen-year police career, he hadn't performed his duty at any place long enough to recognise the needs of those he was supposed to serve. And a good part of that time had been spent in The Police College where, it was widely considered in the lower ranks, men of that ilk went to have half of their brains removed. Jeff Evans paused to tell him what was happening.

'Look here,' came the reply. 'At the moment, this division is being inundated with burglaries in dwellings, petty street robberies, waves of thefts from vehicles and large-scale slaughter of livestock. Kids are selling cocaine and heroin on street corners; half the detective strength is either on sick, annual leave, or attending courses and here you are, prepared to run out in response to a broken window. Where is the uniform staff? Don't you think they're quite capable of dealing with this?'

Jeff Evans tried to explain that Elen Thomas had been to see him earlier that day, giving Renton a brief account of the reason, but the more senior officer's mind was not for changing.

'Look lad, I agree with your initial assessment of Mrs. Thomas's complaint. What's happened at her house this evening is probably the work of children. A couple of uniform lads will already be there by now. That's what they're there for – first response.

If there is anything they can't handle, it will come through to us like it always does. What we've got to do in this department is to prioritise. I know you've been on your feet, working for more than thirty-six hours and I want you back here at nine in the morning, fresh as a daisy. Do you understand me? Now go home and cuddle into your wife's side for God's sake and sleep on it. The concept of prioritisation, I mean.' Renton gave him a wink, took the car keys out of Jeff's hand and walked away.

On this occasion at least, Jeff Evans couldn't really find a way to argue with anything Renton had said.

Chapter Two

Emily Parry was unimpressed with Elen's attempts to make it look as if she wasn't alone that evening. She was almost resigned to having another visit from the intruder. But neither of them had any way of knowing that, for most of the day, he had been watching 'Hendre Fawr' from afar. He found it amusing that anyone should consider that such transparent measures would deter him. Quite the contrary – he was confident that what he liked to call his 'campaign of terror' was progressing perfectly. Even at that moment, his plans were unfolding exactly as he intended and all he had to do was to wait.

Once Elen had told her aunt about the broken window, Emily replaced the telephone onto the bedside table knowing exactly what she had to do next. She had already gone to her bed, prepared for anything the night might bring, but now, unexpectedly, she had something more important on her mind.

The sound of the wind's path through the elm trees and the rain beating against her bedroom window gave no deterrent. She dressed quickly. At least he had not switched off the electricity mains yet, but as she put on her overcoat, she instinctively felt for the torch that she had already placed in its pocket. Slowly, she ventured downstairs hoping that he was not already in the house waiting for her. Ignoring her fears she made her way to the downstairs hall by torchlight, tensely watching the moving shadows created by the furniture and the corners. Her bony hands searched a drawer in the oak dresser until she found her car keys and then she stepped outside.

Torrential rain lashed against the heavy wooden door as she closed it behind her. The night air was chilling and it was so dark that the feeble torch in her tiny hand made little difference. The rain hindered her ability to see very far as she crossed the courtyard, using little more than her instinct to find the lean-to shelter she called a garage.

In a brief interlude, the wind and the rain lessened their deafening noise against the shelter's corrugated tin-roof and she heard that music again. 'Oh no, not now!' she thought. The elements still masked its clarity so that there was no way of guessing from where or from how far away Prokofiev's tones were coming. 'Not now, please not now!' she pleaded again as she fumbled, desperately urging the car keys into the tiny lock. Emily Parry was about to open the driver's door when she sensed the presence of something immediately behind her. She froze, shrieking loudly above the sound of the wind and the rain and as she screamed again something came down onto her shoulders. She dropped the torch as she fell to the ground beside the car, her breast heaving and her heart pounding with fright. She lay there momentarily, motionless, in complete darkness, waiting for whatever was to happen next. Suddenly, something familiar pecked her frozen cheek and, with some relief, she realised that it was Betsy. Emily realised in that split second that the pet chicken must have followed her out of the house. As the old lady's frail, bruised and weakened frame slowly stood up, Emily became conscious once more of the other more haunting presence. The music had returned, but this time it seemed closer and louder, almost as strong as the sound of the wind. 'God, please help me get into the car!' she prayed, as she fumbled with the torch and the keys.

From his hiding place he had been watching Emily Parry – observing her impassively, failing to understand how she could do such a thing. He was puzzled that the events he had just witnessed had not caused the eighty-nine year old woman's heart to fail. But he didn't despair; there was still time, because tonight, events would be on his side.

Emily struggled as she hauled herself into the driver's seat. She turned the ignition key and she pressed repeatedly on the starter button. Impatiently, she waited as the engine misfired three times before coming to life. She was almost afraid to turn on the headlamps, frightened of what she might see. But there was nothing except for the rain that was beating down relentlessly against the windscreen - the car's wipers having little effect against its force. The car jerked forwards as her wet foot slipped off the clutch. Betsy's wings flapped powerfully as the bird attempted to regain its balance on the backrest of the front passenger seat. Emily laboured against the heavy steering wheel, directing the car across the courtyard towards the four hundred yards' downhill track that led to the road into town.

As the lights shone ahead of the car, the rain on the windscreen hampered her vision, forcing her to strain her eyes to see across the yard. Then, the headlamps suddenly illuminated a ghostly figure standing motionless in the path of the vehicle – its huge wet bulk standing out against the lights. It was him!

It didn't occur to Emily to apply the brakes because her mind was focused on one thing only. In an attempt to escape, her right foot pressed the car's throttle, hitting it hard against the floor. She closed her eyes at the very moment she was expecting to collide with him, but there was no impact. When she opened her eyes a moment later, the car was heading down the steep track to safety and when she looked in her rear view mirror, there was nothing to be seen. She breathed a heavy sigh of relief but, in an instant, she realised that something was terribly wrong. She struggled for her life as she fought hard against the car's movement, but there was nothing that she could do as it moved faster and faster towards the sharp bend in the track. There was nothing at all that she could do!

The A470 road was not the best of routes, but it was the most practical way to travel from Cardiff to Llanglanaber. Even at six thirty in the morning, there were several slow-moving vehicles that were difficult to overtake on a trunk road that was no longer suitable for its present volume of traffic. But it wasn't essential to go as fast as Michael Holland did in the primrose yellow 'Triumph Stag'.

He had telephoned Elen late the previous evening, after the police had left and their conversation had eased his immediate concern. It seemed, at least for the time being, that she'd recovered as well as he might have expected and Geraint had been lucky that the injuries caused by the breaking glass were only minor. It was too soon to assess what connection there may have been between that incident and the account Elen had relayed to him. He needed to be there, to get the feel of the place; to experience it first hand before he could make any reliable judgment. He was almost looking forward to depending on that old gut-feeling again!

He cruised in overdrive top gear and, having listened to the first news-bulletin of the morning, he placed a compact disc into the car's newly-fitted audio system. It had meant taking up some of the limited space in the boot, but he had decided that some things in life were more important than others. Holland waited for the beginning of the first movement of Mahler's 'Sixth Symphony'. He needed something powerful to balance his state of mind and had often found that listening to suitable music provided the ideal opportunity to focus while driving.

He thought about Elen, pondered why it was that he felt so much at ease being asked and then leaping to her assistance at such short notice, but why not? He recalled how much she had meant to him and that he owed her a great deal. She was the one who had been the support and the very platform from which his recovery from depression and alcoholism had been made. He had met Elen during his investigation into endemic corruption within local government at Glanaber. He had discovered that her husband, Gareth, had been murdered because he was on the verge of exposing those responsible. It was Elen's strength and inspiration that had led Holland's investigation towards a successful outcome. After the disclosure of malpractices involving government and European grants within the council's finance department, there were those in high political circles who had appreciated the results of his findings. He had regained all the responsibilities that had been taken away from him at the Welsh Office legal department and even the Prime Minister and the Welsh Secretary had voiced their appreciation.

It was unfortunate, he felt, that during the early course of his new-found relationship with Elen, the end of The Welsh Office and the creation of the Welsh Assembly had meant that he had been fully committed and had also had to spend a good deal of his time in Brussels.

He had been putting his life back together again, but at the expense of his relationship with Elen, and he regretted now he had not taken sufficient time to show his gratitude to the one person who had been responsible for the greater part of his recovery. He also considered, with hindsight, that he had been a little anxious about engaging in an emotional relationship that was developing in the shadows of grief – Elen's loss of her husband and the death of his own wife and son. His was a grief that was combined with a guilt, which he was still unable to shake from his memory. He didn't know whether he would ever be able to overcome it. He battled with the question of whether Gareth, or rather the closeness that Elen had enjoyed with him, had been the obstacle, or whether it was his own anguish that had subconsciously suppressed what might have become a closer friendship. As he listened to the third movement of the symphony, the 'Andante moderato', he remembered how much he had come to like and later to respect Elen, her personality and her presence near him.

He also thought about the town of Llanglanaber and how, for the second time, it was some kind of trouble, someone else's trouble that seemed to be drawing him back. It had been Elen's trouble on the first occasion as well, though he hadn't known it from the outset. The main difference this time was that he was going into it willingly. Nothing would keep him away this time and he saw it as an opportunity to be on the giving side of their friendship.

It was approaching eleven by the time he arrived at Llanglanaber. The town hadn't changed much, but there were certainly signs of growing prosperity. Perhaps the marina development idea had been a good one for the town after all. At least it seemed now, more than five years after his investigation, that the discovery of so much criminal conduct entangled in the marina's initial development hadn't affected its progress too much.

Holland made his way directly to Elen's home, but she wasn't in. He spoke to a workman who was repairing the broken window. He handed Holland a scribbled note from Elen indicating that Emily Parry had suffered serious injuries following a car accident.

One of the disadvantages of living in a rural area was that it took Holland more than another hour to reach the county's main hospital and several more time-wasting minutes to get the information he required from the busy reception area.

The Intensive Care ward was about as far away as was possible from the hospital entrance, or did it just seem that way? It was far from the commotion and the confusion of voices he had heard at the reception area, where everyone seemed over-eager to share a particular burden. This was a quiet and tranquil setting where the surroundings had been designed and kept especially comfortable for those visitors forced to experience the deep anxiety always found in such a place.

In the waiting area Elen looked less than comfortable, head bowed, clutching a small white handkerchief close to her cheeks. She didn't notice Holland's arrival until he was almost beside her. Her face appeared drawn as she looked up at him – still beautiful as ever, even in her anguish, though there was no smile to greet him. She stood and they embraced, holding one another for longer than may have been necessary. Then, silently, they sat next to each other. There was no need for Holland to ask any questions. He was in no hurry and he was sure that she would tell him in her own time.

'Michael, it's all my fault.' The tears fell onto his lapel. 'Oh Michael, I just wish I'd handled this whole damn thing differently.'

Holland remained silent, using his hand to cradle her back, rubbing gently.

'I 'phoned her last night, just after we spoke the first time. She knew something was wrong. I told her about the brick through the window. It was such a stupid thing to do. She must have guessed it was connected with everything else that's been happening to her. At her age, Michael, and at that time of night, in that weather, she jumped into her car and she must have been coming down to comfort me when it happened. She hit a stone wall at the side of the track between the farmhouse and the main road. The car turned over and she was there all night until the postman found her this morning. Betsy, her pet chicken was there too. It went with her everywhere, you know – it was all a little eccentric really. Don't you see, Michael, it should never have happened, and it's my fault!'

A number of minutes passed in a silence eventually broken by Holland's voice.

'This is no time even to think about taking responsibility, Elen. You did what you thought best. Was she still used to driving?' he asked, mainly out of curiosity.

'Yes, every day. Well, most days anyway, she would drive down into town for whatever she needed. She had an old 'Morris Minor', a nineteen fifty-nine model, you know, the kind with the divided windscreens. She'd had it from new apparently, older than me it was. She must have been going too fast down that hill.'

Several more minutes passed by.

'Have they let you in to see her yet?' Holland asked.

'Yes, just for a few minutes – she was asking for me. I saw her lying there Michael; there's hardly anything of her, and to think that only a month ago, she was balancing on a stepladder, painting the ceiling. She looks so frail, and she's got all those tubes going in and out of her. Multiple injuries they're calling it, and hypothermia. She was in and out of consciousness, but she kept mumbling something that seemed important to her, as if it was essential to tell me. It wasn't easy to make it out, but it was something about Medwyn wanting her to sell the farm. She said that she couldn't sell it because the farm was mine. She said the farm belongs to my sister, Gwyneth and me – something to do with a will she made after her husband, Uncle Huw, died. It's not something that I know anything about. Is that possible, without my knowing, Michael?'

'It's possible, but there are more important matters to concern yourself with right now.'

Holland left the hospital when several other family members arrived. However much he wanted to stay at Elen's side, he was out of place there then, and he knew it. As he drove back to Llanglanaber, he considered what were extraordinary sequences of events and how, in just two days, everything had all fallen so heavily onto Elen's shoulders.

He was finding it difficult to absorb all the information properly without being able to form a mental picture of the farm and, even though the afternoon was already drawing towards evening, he felt he had to visit Hendre Fawr immediately.

The idea of driving the 'Triumph Stag' along the rough track where Emily Parry's accident had taken place did not appeal to him. He therefore chose to continue along the narrow road passing the farm entrance, following the contours alongside an area of dense woodland. There, within a couple of hundred yards, was a lay by, or rather more of a muddy pull-in on which to park the car. He looked at the farmhouse, an imposing-looking building next to a number of elm trees high up to his right. A foot-stile crossed over a hedge into the field, giving access to a muddy footpath that seemed to lead in the general direction of the house. Holland replaced his shoes with a pair of walking boots from the back of his car and made for the path, pausing momentarily to allow a tractor to pass. The farmer driving it acknowledged his presence with the customary nod of his head.

Hendre Fawr farm showed signs of neglect, which wasn't surprising in such circumstances. It wasn't the best arable land to start with, far from it. Fences had long been in a state of disrepair, the hedges were overgrown and, in the finest tradition of agricultural disregard, gates had been secured to their posts using orange coloured bailing cord. The house itself didn't look much better. A few slates were missing here and there, guttering and down-pipes hung loosely in places or appeared to be totally ineffective and the rotting windows to the south of the property hadn't seen a coat of paint in a decade or more. The property looked to be a shadow of its former glory.

Holland walked around the outhouses, which were substantial, or certainly they had been in the past. Somehow, one of them, the largest, seemed out of place, not in keeping with the structure and style of the others. It had double-sided doors that were chained and padlocked and it seemed it had been built as an afterthought. He wandered round the others. One had the appearance of a makeshift lean-to garage, probably where the old lady had kept the car. Another, an unsecured open shed, looked as if it had been used to store unwanted material and, judging by its contents, had done so for some considerable time, even from the days of horse drawn farming implements. On the ground inside it, Holland found two empty cigarette paper packets and several discarded cigarette ends. There was also food-wrapping material and sweet papers scattered about in a manner that indicated someone's presence over a considerable period of time. Someone had obviously been using the shelter to watch, to wait or to hide. He decided to leave everything as it was for the time being.

Resisting the temptation to enter the house itself, Michael Holland looked through the window, but there wasn't much to be seen. He walked down the track towards the road, to where Emily Parry's car had collided with the dry stone wall. There was no doubting the location when he came to it. Dislodged stonework, broken glass and other debris marked the spot from which the car had since been removed, but Betsy was still there, picking, still foraging away for her food as if little of importance had taken place. Holland examined the track carefully, finding no indication of braking hard or skidding for any distance uphill towards the house. 'Maybe the rain had washed it away,' he thought.

As he surveyed the scene, a strange, cold feeling came over him, chilling the nerves at the base of his neck. He felt as if he had been there once before. Yes, he had, – but maybe not that particular place, but being at the scene of an accident once again brought the memories flooding back. He thought about Eirlys and Neil, his wife and his son, killed by the hit and run driver not more than two miles from that place. If he hadn't argued with Eirlys that night, they wouldn't have been on the road so late. He thought about the way his life had changed since then.

He had compressed a lifetime of drinking into the space of just two years, until Elen had come along. Still, the demons of the night on which they died remained with him. He wasn't sure how long he'd been standing there staring at nothing in particular and thinking. He ran his fingers through his damp hair. Only then did he notice that the drizzle had started again.

The return to 'Gorwel', the cottage where Eirlys and he had once enjoyed so much happiness, didn't hold the trepidation that he had once experienced. He'd got over that, well, most of it anyway. The gardens needed attention, but there was no Dan Lloyd to see to that any more. Daniel's heart had finally given up, six years after his first coronary. Old Dan had had a good innings, but Holland would miss him. He went along next door just to let his widow, Megan, know that he would be around for a few days. Since Dan's death, she had lost much of the enthusiasm she had always shown and Holland knew that he owed them both a great deal too. He ate a light meal that evening to the sound of Ralph Vaughan Williams's 'The Lark Ascending'. Something light and cheerful was just what he needed!

Later in the evening, Holland pulled the 'Stag' up outside Elen's house. As he did so, he saw a man leaving the premises, driving away in a black, well-polished, 'Vauxhall Senator Estate'. He was well dressed in a dark suit and wore a black tie. Michael Holland feared the worst, and he was right. Emily Parry had died that afternoon.

Chapter Three

At nine o'clock the following morning, a dozen or so plain-clothed police personnel – detectives, intelligence gatherers and support staff, assembled for what they called 'morning prayers' – a briefing to review the events of the past twenty-four hours and to plan for the day ahead. Today's meeting was more formal than usual. D.C.I. Renton was present, a rare occurrence, which was regarded by some as interference.

Ten minutes into the meeting, the door burst open with a heavy kick of a boot and Jeff Evans walked into the room. He was unshaven, hair uncombed, chewing aggressively on the remains of a bacon sandwich held in one hand, spilling coffee from a plastic cup in the other and clutching a bunch of papers under his left arm. Jean hadn't been up to making breakfast that morning. Everyone turned and stared. One or two looked at each other, rolling their eyes in mild but cynical rebuke.

'Carry on,' said Jeff, but only then did he note Renton's presence. 'Sorry I'm late,' he added, a little more soberly.

This was not the kind of opportunity Renton could miss. 'Nice of you to grace us with your presence, constable!' he greeted him sarcastically.

One or two laughed as expected. Jeff ignored them, taking a seat to the side of the main party, reaching for a copy of the morning's computer generated briefing notes as he did so, spilling more coffee in the process. Once the meeting resumed, Jeff sensed that one or two were throwing in their 'two-penny-worth' for the sake of it as opposed to making a valued contribution. He'd seen it all before and it was invariably the same ones. Overshadowing the Detective Sergeant, who was supposed to be chairing the briefing, Renton, as always, responded to it enthusiastically.

He had an array of management tools at his disposal, 'but there again, he would have, being a police college boy,' thought Jeff. He considered him to be a man whose own ego came before anything else – including public service.

Glancing through the bulletin sheet, Jeff Evans noted nothing much to warrant his particular interest. The Murphy girl had gone missing again, the fourth time in six months. She usually turned up with friends. Cars had been broken into behind the cinema, and a couple of drug-pusher 'sightings'. Nothing more than what was already at his fingertips. He noted and wasn't surprised that the breaking of Elen's window had been officially regarded as vandalism committed by children and it looked as though there was little hope of finding whoever was responsible. He let his eyes drift down the page. More sheep slaughtered, but no more night-time burglaries in people's homes had been reported. It made a refreshing change. Then he saw the last paragraph under the heading of 'other matters'. '*The sudden death of Emily Parry, 89 years, of Hendre Fawr Farm...*' Reading on, he sensed the agitation in Renton's voice and looked up.

'Are you with us, D.C. Evans, or are you having a meeting of your very own?' Renton was being cynical again.

'Just looking at the sudden death report, boss. Thought there might be something in it.' Smiling inwardly, he knew that he shouldn't have used that term, 'boss', for it was the one title that Renton despised. In the circumstances, Jeff just couldn't help it.

'That, D.C. Evans, is a matter for the uniform department. We, in this office, are concerned with criminal investigation. See me afterwards, will you?'

The last remark provided some of those present with childish gratification. Many of them envied Jeff Evans's crime-solving ability and watching him having to accept Renton's public rebuke was a source of amusement.

It wasn't long afterwards before Renton pulled him to one side. He started by looking disapprovingly at the remains of the breakfast, scattered over the front of his duffel coat. Jeff knew what was coming.

'You're late, you're untidy and you're insubordinate, and, what's more, it seems to me that no one ever knows quite what you're up to. You consider yourself a one-man enterprise that's outside any team activity. Is there anything worthwhile about you – just a tiny hint maybe that you could be an asset to this department?' Renton's words were spat out, delivered in double-quick time, giving the listener little opportunity to reply.

'I'm late because I worked sixteen hours again yesterday,' Jeff eventually interrupted his flow. 'I attended to seven prisoners on my own because other people in this department consider it below their dignity to deal with what they think is mundane crime – and the paperwork's done and dusted,' he added. He was getting on his own 'high horse' now. 'I'm not wearing a suit because I'm going out into the fields again this morning to look for whoever it is that's slaughtering those sheep and there's no justification in calling me insubordinate, just because I like to speak my own mind.'

Backing down, realising that Jeff's response may be understandable – perhaps even justified, Renton considered his reply carefully. 'Look, you're one of the most senior men I've got here, Jeff. I know the hours you put in. God knows how you, of all people, manage to do it, but you and I have got to show these youngsters some standards! Do try and make an effort will you? Become a team member. Talk to your sergeant once in a while. Let him know what you're up to.'

More insincere management tools, Jeff thought, but there was no need to look for more unnecessary conflict. 'Fair enough, D.C.I.'. It still didn't merit a 'Sir' – that would be taking it too far. 'But there is something I don't like about this sudden death,' he added. In fact, there's a hell of a lot that concerns me about it. Remember, we spoke briefly about it, night before last?' Believing that Renton was on the defensive, Jeff was more confident this time.

'Yes, I remember. Something about her seeing things in the dark wasn't it?' Renton was unnecessarily dismissive.

'Let's just deal with reality here shall we? Criminal reality, and let's leave the uniform department and the Coroner's Office to deal with car accidents and sudden deaths. We've got enough problems of our own to be getting on with, and that's an order. Understand?'

'Fair enough.' Jeff gave in for the sake of bringing their discussion to an end. Renton's views on Emily Parry's death didn't seem to reflect a fair or an accurate account of the position as far as he was concerned. He was prepared to let it ride for now, but he couldn't understand why Renton was treating the matter with such disregard. He remained determined, however, to take a look at any matter that pleased him, in his own way, in his own time, just as he usually did.

Jeff Evans went outside the office and onto the fire escape. He pulled out his tobacco tin, rolled a cigarette between his thumbs and forefingers and ran the shiny length of the paper against the tip of his moist tongue. He looked out over Llanglanaber as he put a match to the thin, uneven cigarette and reflected on the morning's events. An uncharacteristic north-easterly wind brought a chill to the morning air. 'Damn this no smoking law!' he thought. He finished the cigarette, flicking the stub down to the concrete yard below, where it joined the countless others he had previously discarded. As he returned into the building, Jeff Evans recognised that he found it almost impossible to take his time – especially when his mind was made up.

Two minutes later, he made for a telephone extension in an empty adjacent office where he could not be overheard and he 'phoned Elen Thomas. The main purpose behind the call was to offer his condolences. Another reason was just to listen to her. He wanted to know what she had to say. He wasn't surprised when she suggested that the events at the farmhouse might be connected with the accident – that her aunt had been fleeing from whoever had been disturbing her and that she had driven too quickly in adverse weather conditions. Jeff considered that it was important for him to evaluate her thoughts, not that they were too far from his own. It wasn't in his nature to disregard anyone's views or concerns, even when he had been instructed to do so from 'on high'. He left the matter open, telling her that he'd see what he could do. They both agreed that the old lady might have simply driven too fast, though it remained a mystery why she would do so at that time of night.

Though Elen had agreed with him, she would have been more inclined to accept Jeff's apparent lack of enthusiasm had it not been for the 'Ronson' lighter she had found. For the time being, however, she was happy to accept it, at least until she'd had the opportunity to discuss the lighter aspect with Michael Holland. Until then, she wasn't prepared to disclose its finding to Jeff, but the decision not to do so still worried her.

Later that morning, fourteen miles away to the north of Llanglanaber, Jeff Evans and a hill-farmer crouched over the carcass of a three-year-old ewe. A short crossbow bolt, capable of tremendous velocity, protruded out of its stomach, leaving a trail of blood from where the animal had been shot, to the spot where it had fled, fallen and then died. There were several blood soaked areas throughout the field where discarded entrails and body parts indicated that other sheep had been slaughtered and then, presumably, butchered and despatched. A dozen times in the past several weeks Jeff had investigated similar instances, almost identical in fact, but no one had been able to provide a shred of information. He watched as a buzzard circled around the thermals high above, rising higher each time. Jeff found it difficult to concentrate properly on the business involving sheep. There was something else that was closer to the forefront of his mind that day.

It was almost eight-thirty by the time he returned to the office to complete his paperwork. He'd spent some time at the farmer's mart, village shops, rural post offices, schools, talking to postmen, visiting anywhere that might produce a lead. He'd called home for a bite to eat – another sandwich – it hadn't been one of Jean's better days. Then, he'd slept for an hour. When he woke up, he was annoyed because sleeping hadn't been his intention. Before he had left, he'd looked in on his wife, kissed her forehead and left before his guilt overcame his need to depart.

It was quiet in the office. All the 'nine 'til five "merchants"' had long since gone home for the day. The Emily Parry business still bothered him. He couldn't get the thought of her lying injured on the track throughout the night out of his mind.

Jeff had always been regarded as being particularly inquisitive, far more even than his professional status demanded – almost to the point of being nosy, some said, but Jeff recognised that this had served him well throughout his service. It kept him alive and attuned to every event, even those that need not concern him. It kept him one step ahead of the opposition, he thought to himself, as he slipped quietly into the uniform department's main office. There was no one about. 'Good,' it was clear. There were several wire trays there housing each constable's work in progress. He looked in the one allocated to the officer dealing with the Emily Parry accident, quickly extracting the relevant file. He began reading, but there was nothing much to take his eye. Then, he suddenly became conscious that he was not alone.

'What in the hell are you doing going through my papers?' There was a touch of anger in the voice.

'Oh, hi Steve,' he said, turning, thinking quickly as he did so. 'I was looking for the papers on that shoplifting you dealt with at the 'Co-op' last week, when I came across this,' he said, holding up the accident report. 'I know the family, you see.'

'Oh yeah!' came the reply, obviously doubting the frankness of the explanation.

'Where's the vehicle examiner's report?' asked Jeff.

'There isn't one.'

'Why not? It's a fatal accident isn't it?' Jeff made his surprise obvious.

'Yeah, but it was on a private road. There was only the one vehicle involved, one old lady driver, who shouldn't have been anywhere near a car at her age. Lewis Hamilton wouldn't have driven down that track so quickly in those conditions,' he added. 'Come on, Jeff, it's an open and shut case if ever I saw one and in any event, I've been told not to bother.'

'Who by?' Jeff asked, raising an eyebrow.

'Someone who outranks me, Jeff, and if I want to get on in this job, I'm going to do as I'm told.'

'The bastard!' thought Jeff. It obviously hadn't taken long for the account of his confrontation with D.C.I. Renton that morning to filter its way along the station's jungle drums.

Steve Pickles took the papers out of Jeff's hands and put them back in the tray, smiling coldly as he replaced it onto the shelf.

'Now then, what did you want to know about that shoplifting?' Pickles was trying to be smart now.

'It's no bother.' Evans was about to leave, but he turned back. 'How did you get along on your recent C.I.D. course?'

'Very well, top of the class actually. I was awarded the course book prize.' The false smile left his face as he lifted his chin slightly in a demonstration of vain superiority.

'Shouldn't be long then before you get a chance at being a detective.'

'Not long at all. The D.C.I. says there may be a vacancy on the department pretty soon.' He was openly grinning now, inferring that he might replace somebody.

Jeff Evans closed the door behind him. No vehicle examination report eh? He's got a lot to learn before he starts catching real villains, he thought as he shook his head. It was Jeff's turn to smile now.

Back in his own office, he pondered why they had not had the vehicle mechanically examined. Maybe it was a cost or resource-saving exercise! That was the way of things these days, but still he wondered what the Coroner might say.

He hadn't been back in his own office more than ten minutes and was looking forward to a reasonably early night. A beer on the way home was on his mind, but then he heard a loud bellow. 'God, doesn't he ever go home?' he thought.

'Evans!' It was Renton. 'In my office, now.'

When he got there, D.C.I. Renton was already back behind his desk, red faced, grinding his teeth in anger. Still, surprisingly, he managed to control his fury. His voice was quiet and deliberate. Jeff's instincts told him that he was about to experience more of Renton's 'management tools'.

'What in hell's name are you doing rummaging around through other policemen's papers?' Renton's cold eyes glared in Jeff's direction betraying his inner feelings.

'Just looking for a file on a shoplifting. The man responsible is a leftover from last year's holiday camp staff. He's been put up in a flat near the beach. He's got a string of convictions for dishonesty and violence and, guess what, he used to be a butcher! The sheep? Worth checking out, don't you think so, boss?' He hoped it sounded convincing, though he half-regretted using that title again. The least amount of confrontation was the better option.

Renton wasn't about to bite. He wanted to remain calm for what he had to say.

'And why did you see fit to delve into the accident report? Do you want to take over that investigation as well? What's got into you, criticising other departments for doing this, and not doing the other? Whatever bee you've got in your bonnet about the late Mrs. Parry or her accident, well, you can forget it. It's just not your responsibility!'

'The papers were just there, and you know very well that I've got an interest in the case.' It would have been a futile exercise to suppress his curiosity now.

'Now you look here, Evans. I have told you more than once to drop this issue. If you persist in ignoring my instructions, I'll give you as many accidents as you like to investigate. I'll even give you a uniform and a pointed hat to go with the job.'

'But damn it, D.C.I., the stupid buggers haven't even bothered to get the vehicle mechanically examined yet! The old girl's died, for God's sake!' Jeff's voice was raised now.

'You, D.C. Evans are not paid to oversee every investigation in this division. On the other hand, I am. Yes, believe it or not, I like to think I've got my finger on the pulse too. Mrs Parry's car was examined today. I arranged it myself when it came to my notice that they hadn't done it. The report won't be here for a few days yet, but I've spoken to the vehicle examiner myself. The car was mechanically sound. What's more, it was serviced regularly and all the paperwork is there to prove it. What more do you want? I honestly don't know what I'd do if I didn't suspect that your motives were well intended, but at the same time, I'm sure, in fact I'm bloody positive that I'm not going to tell you again.

'I want you to mind your own business and I'm going to watch you like a hawk from now on. One wrong move and you're out of this department. This is your last chance, understand?'

Jeff Evans knew when to give up. He couldn't risk being put back into uniform for what Renton would call 'career development'. He knew that the restrictions imposed on him would devastate his style, and the extra salary he earned as a detective had always helped with Jean's medication and the long journeys for special treatment.

It was definitely time for a pint on the way home.

On the following afternoon Jeff knew that Renton and his cronies would have their minds focused on one of the town's most prestigious annual sporting events. The 'Glanaber Charitable Trophy' was a golfing competition played by those who considered themselves to be the town's elite. Thousands of pounds were raised for local charities every year and to be seen at this social occasion was more important to some than the event itself. Cynically, Jeff Evans believed that most of them would look more appropriate in one another's company carrying small black briefcases or wearing black ties and aprons rather than carrying golf clubs and wearing casuals!

Jeff took the opportunity to visit Elen. He knocked three times and the door opened almost immediately. Elen had been expecting him, but Jeff wasn't expecting a third party and Holland's presence took him more than a little by surprise. Elen introduced them. Both men stood face to face, shaking hands firmly, making lengthy eye contact in an attempt to gain the measure of each other. Jeff Evans was visibly guarded. He felt uneasy. He was conscious that they were about to discuss Emily Parry's demise, a matter he had been instructed to disregard. He would have been happy to talk about it with Elen alone, but he had no way of knowing if he could trust Holland.

'You can talk quite freely,' said Elen, noting his demeanour. 'Mr. Holland is a friend of mine from Cardiff. He's here for the funeral.' It wasn't an outright lie.

Jeff Evans still felt far from comfortable, but he began to talk.

What he had to tell them was that the circumstances surrounding Emily Parry's accident had been investigated thoroughly and that the incident warranted no further attention: that the old lady's apparent encounters over the last few months were of little or no relevance. Holland's presence now dictated that he wasn't prepared to enter into a discussion that might generate further debate. Reluctantly, he felt imposed to tell them that a decision had been made that there was simply nothing more to investigate.

'How do you come to those conclusions when Elen saw someone, a stranger, at the farm a matter of hours before the accident? There's a clear indication that someone has been hanging around there for some time.' It was the first time that Holland had spoken. 'That same day, someone was watching Elen collecting Geraint from school,' he continued. 'And that night, half a brick came hurtling through her window. Then, later the same evening, Mrs. Parry had her accident. Is that all a coincidence?'

Privately, Jeff knew it was a valid argument.

'It might be,' said the detective, hesitantly. 'I've seen stranger things happening, but can anyone connect any of those incidents to the accident? That has to be the end of it,' he replied, taking to his feet, though this was not the way Jeff Evans would have wished to end the conversation.

They watched Jeff leaving, searching his pockets as he walked down the garden path. He pulled out a tin, from which he produced a cigarette from a number he had rolled earlier. He placed it in his mouth and lit it with a match as he walked away.

'What did you think?' asked Elen.

'I'm not sure. It was almost as if he was hiding something.' Holland replied.

'I noticed that you didn't tell him anything about who Auntie Emily thought was visiting her.'

'No, and I decided not to disclose the presence or the significance of the lighter either. Let's keep that to ourselves, just for the time being, shall we? I want to see what happens over the next couple of days. See whether Medwyn, Peter or whoever he is, decides to come out of the woodwork.'

Sitting next to him on the sofa, she took both his hands in hers, 'I do so like having you around, Michael. You give me so much strength.'

He drew both her hands to his lips and kissed them, slowly, tenderly. 'Not so long ago, it was the other way around, Elen. Remember?'

'Yes, I do. What happened, that we drifted apart in that way?'
He wasn't able to reply.

Back at his office, Jeff Evans was becoming increasingly uneasy. He wasn't at all happy with the Emily Parry situation. He didn't want to drop it, but he wondered how much the whole nasty business could affect his future. It could affect Jean's future too. He wondered what he should do.

Unbeknown to Jeff, circumstances were about to dictate. Events totally outside his control were already unfolding, creating a situation that would take any such decision right out of his hands.

Chapter Four

Glanaber Golf Links on the estuary of the River Ceirw had more than the usual number of difficult bunkers created by sand dunes that separated the rich farming land from the shore. Mute swans bred their young amongst the reeds that grew along the banks of the river as it flowed slowly towards the sea. Its path twisted lazily, cutting through several fairways, providing a tough challenge to the unaccomplished golfer and the loss of many a ball, not to mention a match or a tournament.

The clubhouse was well used to noisy, even boisterous occasions. The lavish dinners that followed the annual Glanaber Charitable Trophy competitions were never an exception, but this occasion was a particularly jubilant affair. The day's golf had now been forgotten in favour of things pleasurable to the palate. Copious quantities of wine added to the flavour and the atmosphere of the banquet and now the port was about to accompany the prize giving. The mood set the scene perfectly in readiness for the appearance of a promisingly broad-minded comedienne who had been recommended for her ability to provide uncompromising entertainment to an audience of 'well-oiled' gentlemen.

A group seated at one table seemed particularly ecstatic. To the uneducated eye they might have been a bunch of 'hooray-henries' out for a jolly time, but those familiar with the commercial nucleus of Llanglanaber knew differently. Some wondered how, as a relative newcomer, Detective Chief Inspector Renton had made it to that table so quickly, but he was, after all, a man of influence and authority in the area, as indeed were the others around him.

Seated next to Renton was David Beaumont, a man of diverse business interests and a prominent member of the Glanaber County Council, who had done much to enhance local government's credibility following the premature death of the previous political leader. In just two years, Beaumont, with the aid of the Detective Chief Inspector, had engaged in a police-municipal partnership responsible for a vast reduction in street crime. The Chief Constable had been impressed so much that their success was now used as a blueprint to encourage similar co-operation throughout the area. It had also ensured that William Alexander Renton was destined for greater professional heights and status. On the other side of Beaumont sat Rhys Morris, the Chief Planning Officer and Cecil Moorcroft, the County Economic Development Officer, both of whom had climbed the local government ladder at Glanaber, whilst managing to survive an enquiry into corrupt behaviour under the former leader's term of office. Others seated at that table included bankers, a solicitor and two accountants, all of whom were there to flaunt their generous donations to the chosen charity of the day. The quantity and the quality of the wine bottles suggested that they knew how to enjoy themselves. Some regarded them with envy, some with awe and only a few with indifference, but there wasn't anyone in the room who would dare challenge their collective influence. They were rarely seen celebrating together in this way. This group of men was regarded as a tightly woven clique that met behind closed doors and their company was penetrated by invitation only. There were many who had tried and failed to get on the inside.

Passing the port to his left, Beaumont noted Renton's momentary pensive mood.

'Come come now, Alex! After such a good couple of rounds today, you shouldn't be looking as if you're about to make the decision of the week.'

'Yes, David, you're right, but what do you know about decision making anyway?' he joked. 'You get other people to make them for you!' He laughed as he picked up the bottle, pouring a measure of the ruby coloured liquid into his own glass.

'I don't like it when you've got something on your mind, Alex. Is it private or is there something I should know about?' He was speaking quietly into Renton's ear.

'It's just that one of the boys in the office has been shoving his nose where it doesn't belong. This business at Hendre Fawr, you know. Nothing that should concern you, David, nothing at all.'

'Why do you say that, Alex?' Beaumont narrowed his eyes. 'Isn't it my business too?' he asked.

'There's no need for you to worry because I've dealt with it.' Renton's manner was confident. 'I've put him firmly in his place.'

'I'm glad to hear that; and it's just as well, Alex, because I can't have your mind on something else when I've forked out fifty quid to make sure that this comedienne concentrates on taking the Mick out of you for the next hour and a half!'

Renton was dreading the thought, for he knew that David Beaumont was more than capable of arranging an embarrassment of that nature.

Fifteen minutes later, after two of the crudest jokes Renton had heard coming from a woman, his bleeper went off. Glancing at the message, then at David Beaumont, he said almost with relief, 'Sorry, but you've wasted your money, pal! Duty calls.'

He rose to leave the room, passing between tables to roars of laughter at the comedienne's insistence that she would be more than happy to point a particular part of his anatomy at the porcelain.

Once he got to the relative quiet of the outer hall, Renton switched on his mobile, dialled, spoke and listened. The Detective Sergeant's voice was sombre.

'You'd better get down here, Sir. We've got a body on our hands. It's the Murphy girl and it doesn't look good.'

It had already been dark for a couple of hours. Renton could see blue lights flashing in the distance, contrasting with the headlights of several stationary cars. As he drew nearer he could see movement – people casting shadows as they passed to and fro. Some were emerging from the dense woodland close to where the cars were parked. He felt that he was already becoming frustrated. He hoped to God that there was someone present with a modicum of common sense! It soon became evident that his concerns were justified. He spotted more uniformed figures, standing aimlessly by the side of the wooded lane, their lower bodies masked by the undergrowth. Hands in pockets, they were talking, waiting for instructions that weren't coming. One of them was even smoking a cigarette. He saw the Divisional Commander, who appeared to be in a heated discussion with Constable Steven Pickles. A couple of others appeared from the trees behind them. Pickles, clearly relieved at Renton's arrival, was physically restraining the Chief Superintendent, who, in turn appeared to be bellowing uncontrollably at him.

'Sir,' the constable gasped in Renton's direction. 'The body's about fifty yards into the woods. I've tried to stop anyone going anywhere near, but...'

'Yeah, I know,' Renton interrupted him. 'Don't tell me, I can guess. Everyone wants to have a look, including the Chief Super here no doubt. Let me have a word with him in private please.'

Pickles turned his back. Renton looked directly into his own senior officer's eyes and continued.

'Look around you, Chief Superintendent. Has 'scene preservation' entered into your head, or have you deliberately chosen to ignore it? All we need is a Big Top and we've got ourselves a bloody circus here! I've never seen such an awful mess at a major incident scene in my life. What in hell's name are all these people doing here?'

The Divisional Commander was about to offer a reply when Renton cut him short.

'Now, what I want you to do is this. Have these vehicles withdrawn and use them to block the road two hundred metres in each direction. I want the woodlands cordoned off with high visibility tape from those two points, and for a distance of four hundred metres into the interior. No one, except P.C. Pickles, is allowed within this area without my express permission, and that includes you, *Sir*! I want statements from everyone who has been inside that area, detailing their exact movements and I want officers posted on the outside of the cordoned area in sufficient numbers to ensure that my instructions are obeyed. I want immediate enquiries made at the railway station, bus terminus and taxi companies and I want the index numbers of all vehicles seen out tonight, within a fifty-mile radius of here. You can also arrange for a specialist search team, say two units, to be available for a briefing at nine in the morning. If they're not already on the way, I want the Home Office Pathologist, Forensic and Scenes of Crime here now.'

'What about lights, canvas and protective gear?' asked the Chief Superintendent, rather awkwardly.

'The D.S. is seeing to that, and he's setting up an incident room. He's also arranged for 'family protection officers' to attend the girl's home.'

Once the Chief Superintendent had left, P.C. Pickles turned round and half-smiled at Renton, unsure whether or not he should have heard the conversation.

'Okay, Steve, what have we got? Spit it out, chronologically, accurately and clearly.'

Pickles gathered his thoughts, referring to his notes. 'She was found by a passer-by, walking his dog at eight fifty-three. He's in a hell of a state! Jeff Evans is taking a statement from him right now. I arrived here just before nine twenty and I got him to take me to the body using the exact route he had taken through the shrubs. She's partly clothed. Doctor Roberts arrived at nine forty and certified death immediately. I took him in and out using the same route, which I've marked as best as I could. As far as I know, no one else has been near her, but I can't be sure. You saw what it was like.'

'You've done well, lad,' replied Renton, smiling. 'But no better than I would have expected from someone who's just earned himself a C.I.D. course book prize!'

Within two hours, lighting had been erected, turning the cold night into day. A team of four, dressed in white sterile clothing, entered the woodland using the path previously marked by Pickles.

The dishevelled remains of Donna Marie Murphy lay in a natural hollow, beneath a bank. Her fourteen-year-old body was partly obscured by undergrowth and leaves left there in a thick blanket by the previous autumn's winds and re-arranged by several winter storms. Her left leg was bent at the knee, ankle positioned beneath the other calf. Both her arms were above her head, wrists tied together using her own brassiere. She wore only the one shoe. Her denim skirt had been left high around her waist and her torn unbuttoned blouse pushed high, exposing her pale dead body. A pair of briefs had been discarded some distance to the left of her body.

At a discreet distance, the four stood quietly, motionless in a silence broken only by the humming of a video camera. It was several minutes before the pathologist moved forward, taking care as each foot was placed gently, yet closer to where the girl's body lay, disturbing as little of the scene as possible. Several more minutes passed as he continued his visual examination. Then, he removed the dead foliage and looked at what had once been a beautiful face, now bruised and distorted by the dreadful pains of the girl's last moments.

Renton's thoughts were already galloping in several directions. She was a problem child, from a problem family and she was always being reported missing by her mother. Sexual crime had been relatively quiet in the area recently. There had been no attacks on young women or girls, no stalkers and no flashers. Was this a one off? Why here? What had brought her to such a secluded area, a mile from the town? When? Who?

The voice of the pathologist, whose bespectacled eyes were straining to read the thermometer held high against the artificial light in his white plastic gloved hand, disturbed Renton's train of thought.

'She's been dead at least forty-eight hours. That's as close as I can tell you without more accurate data.'

'Anything else you can tell me now?' Renton asked.

'There are severe facial injuries. She's been knocked about quite a bit, Alex. There are more signs of injury around her throat. Looking at the marks on her shoulders and torso, I'd say her bra's been literally ripped away from her body. There are more injuries to the lower abdomen and genital area. It's more than likely that she's been penetrated, but I'll confirm that later.'

At eight o'clock the following morning, Renton stared down at the fourteen-year-old body lying on the mortuary's cold steel slab – lifeless and completely naked. The rest of her clothing had been removed, and so had the sterile plastic sheet that had brought her there. Donna Marie Murphy's body, robbed of its dignity, was there to reveal its secrets to those responsible for caring for the interests of the dead, to expose anything that might have been left behind by whoever had brought about her untimely demise.

The video camera hummed its familiar tune once more as another camera flashed continuously and the pathologist began his examination, knife in hand, speaking quietly and purposefully into a microphone. Once again, Renton's mind wandered momentarily to things outside his immediate surroundings. He wondered how events might unfold from now on and what difficulties might develop in a murder enquiry of the magnitude that this could turn out to be. It was up to him, not only to lead, but also to shine in the process, because he was more than aware that his chief officers would no doubt see it as the first real test of his ability. There would be a great deal to consider in the hours, days or perhaps even weeks ahead.

Detective Chief Inspector Renton stood in front of over sixty personnel gathered for the first briefing held at two o'clock that afternoon. It was immediately apparent that those present were surprised and uneasy to discover that Councillor David Beaumont was there too, standing immediately behind Renton like a trusted gun dog, inseparable from his master. The presence of outsiders at major enquiry briefings was unprecedented and many thought it was taking the police-municipal coalition too far. Sensing this, Renton thought it was an opportunity to stamp his immediate authority on the enquiry.

'Right, sit down everyone and pay attention! I have invited Councillor Beaumont along to this briefing because of the strong links that exist between the local community and the police at Llanglanaber. These links have the support of the Chief Constable. They have been successful, as everyone here knows and in an enquiry of this nature, we need the backing of the community because this, primarily, is a community matter. Councillor Beaumont will attend daily briefings at my discretion. If there is anyone here who can't live with that, then they had better leave now.'

He paused. There was silence, even amongst the sceptics. Nobody left. Renton had won the first battle.

'Good. Now, this is what we've got so far. Donna Marie Murphy was fourteen and she's not from the most caring of families. She was last seen, lunchtime on Tuesday, at her school. She didn't turn up there after the lunch break and didn't return home after school. Her mother reported her missing at eight that evening. She's been missing several times before and she was known to have been sexually active in the past. The body was discovered yesterday evening and death is thought to have occurred forty-eight hours earlier. That takes us back to Tuesday afternoon or evening. She was beaten, possibly unconscious, tied up and raped. Cause of death was asphyxia due to strangulation. It's likely that she was already dead when she was bound and possibly when she was actually being raped. There's no doubt that we're looking for a real animal here. Any questions so far?'

'Any forensic?' one voice asked.

'We're hoping so, but it's too early to say. Everything's gone to the lab but it will be tomorrow before we get the first results. The immediate tasks will be to profile the victim and identify her associates. I want in-depth knowledge in relation to her whole family, including the Social Services file – all of it – not extracts. I want all of the pupils in her school year seen and detailed statements from all of her close friends. I want 'Criminal Intelligence' to identify all known modus operandi suspects and any recent prison releases following conviction for similar offences. The detectives amongst you will interview and eliminate them. If they refuse to co-operate, arrest them, bring them in by force and lock them up if you have to! This is a murder enquiry and we'll use whatever force is necessary.'

He paused for effect, glancing at David Beaumont who, for the benefit of the audience, gave a nod of approval.

'There are two distinct leads at this time,' Renton continued. 'The victim's stepfather, Tony Marino, hasn't been seen since late last night, after the body was found. We've got people out looking for him. Secondly, there was a classic sports car, make unknown, a yellow one, parked on the lane not far from the scene, late on Tuesday afternoon. The timing is significant. We need to find the driver of that car, a man of about forty. Any more questions?'

In for a penny, Jeff Evans thought to himself, raising a hand. 'It's come to my knowledge that a man has been seen in and around Hendre Fawr Farm in recent weeks. The occupier, who has since died, and her niece have both seen this strange-looking character. The farm's only a stone's throw from the scene of the murder.'

Renton, sensing Beaumont's discomfort stopped the speaker before he could finish. 'For the benefit of those present, Detective Constable Evans wants to investigate some kind of ghostly apparition seen by a ninety-year-old lady who has since passed away. Perhaps he would like to join in the *spirit* of our enquiry, once he puts both his feet back on the ground!'

Everyone laughed, except Jeff Evans.

'Next briefing will be at six thirty this evening,' continued Renton. 'There will be two briefings a day from now on. Nine fifteen and six thirty.'

Jeff Evans wasn't about to take Renton's remarks lying down. He hadn't been waiting long when Elen opened the door. His instinct told him not to ignore the Hendre Fawr factor, whether or not it was connected to the murder.

'The kettle's on. Coffee?'

'Thanks, Elen. Sorry to pester you again, but I think it's important.'

He wondered how to broach the subject without causing undue alarm. Noticing his hesitancy, she took the lead, at the same time taking some of the wind out of his sails.

'Don't tell me, Jeff. Now that you've got yourself a murder enquiry right next to Hendre Fawr, you've suddenly developed an interest in my little story haven't you?'

'It's not that I have ever really been uninterested, Elen.' He wasn't about to divulge that he had been steered in another direction. 'It's just that we, or rather that I, have had so much on the go recently and – you know what it's like – I've had to prioritise. Now that this murder has come up, it's taken centre stage.'

'Jeff, I haven't been one hundred per cent open with you so far, but now, the events of the past twenty-four hours dictate that I must.'

'Go on!' She was holding his interest.

'My aunt believed that the person who was visiting her, if that's the right expression, was her son, Medwyn, who disappeared about thirty years ago.'

'So?' he asked, looking for the significance.

'He disappeared during the course of a murder investigation.' She began recounting the story.

'Good God, Elen.' Jeff's brain was racing ahead. 'I'd better take a statement from you.'

An hour and a half later, he left the premises, having taken full account of what she had to say. As he was about to drive away, the primrose-yellow 'Triumph Stag' pulled up. Michael Holland didn't see Jeff looking at him as he locked his car and disappeared towards the house. Passing slowly by, Jeff noted the heavy traces of mud along the sills and on the wheels of the 'Stag'. He also made a note of its number. It would soon be time for the six-thirty briefing.

Back at the police station, Jeff decided that he wasn't going to make a song and dance about the contents of the statement he'd just recorded. He was going to feed it quietly into the enquiry's administration system, knowing that the D.C.I. would learn about its contents sooner rather than later.

By that time, the information would be firmly registered within the computerised brain of the investigation, generating its own further enquiries in the process. It would be too late to interfere with the process then and impossible to erase the data, not that anyone would dare attempt it, not even Renton, however much he had tried to ridicule the Hendre Farm connection. Whatever his thoughts might be at that stage, Jeff was satisfied that the taking of the statement from Elen Thomas would be seen as justified. He also carried out a computer check on Holland's car and fed the sighting into the enquiry's database under the low priority status he considered it merited.

The six-thirty briefing revealed two matters of interest. The Social Services had been reluctant to release their files relating to the victim and had only done so under threat of an application to the Crown Court that afternoon. Once obtained, those files had revealed information alleging that her stepfather, Tony Marino, had sexually abused Donna Marie Murphy. The allegations had come to light over the past several months during interviews connected with a psychological examination of the girl's behavioural difficulties following her school truancy and tendency to disappear. As far as it was known, the activities had been confined to mutual fondling, but had recently been accompanied by emotional threats when the girl had attempted to thwart her stepfather's advances. The briefing learned that Anthony Marino's details had, earlier that evening, been circulated throughout the United Kingdom, informing all police forces that he was wanted on suspicion of having indecently assaulted his stepdaughter.

The second interesting factor was somewhat bizarre. The murder of Donna Marie Murphy had been the first of its kind in Llanglanaber for over thirty years. Many of the townspeople remembered the first murder, though most of those questioned recalled it with some reluctance. It had become evident during the afternoon that a number of people questioned also remembered how the whole town had been divided by that event.

There was a clear indication emanating from the public that many believed that the police, in their eagerness to point the finger at a suspect, had simply got it wrong. Others might easily have taken the law into their own hands had they found the person whom they believed was the culprit – Medwyn Parry, the one everyone had called Peter. It seemed, even now, that those events rekindled strong emotions on both sides of the divide. Enquiry team members were now finding that people being interviewed were showing signs of withholding their co-operation – becoming reluctant to talk.

Councillor Beaumont seemed reluctant as he stood to speak when invited to do so unexpectedly by Renton. Jeff Evans studied his demeanour and thought he looked particularly uneasy. For once in his life, he didn't seem comfortable, let alone assertive, and he wondered why. He was accustomed to seeing Beaumont confidently attaching himself to any successful bandwagon. However, the day's events were beginning to show a lack of cohesion within the community and it may have been that he was keen to distance himself from both sides, at least until an option had been identified as the better one to suit his needs. Indeed, David Beaumont was acting like a man who didn't know on which side of the fence to fall, speaking without the force of words usually associated with his performances. He could only mumble as he gave his assurance that the police had the full backing of the local community.

There was one last revelation to come from the liaison officer appointed to the murdered girl's family. It was that Diane Smith, raped, strangled and murdered thirty years previously, would have been Donna Marie Murphy's aunt. Diane and Donna's mother were sisters. An eerie silence fell over the briefing room.

It was already dark by the time Jeff Evans parked his private car in the car park behind the 'Victoria Arms' Hotel and the woman was already waiting for him. He switched off the interior light so that it wouldn't function when she opened the door. It was quiet and late enough for what he had in mind with 'Midnight Mary' tonight. He smiled as he reflected upon the name that he had given her and how, funnily enough, she had taken to it.

As usual, she wore too much make-up, and her perfume filled his nostrils as she slipped into the car's front passenger seat next to him, carefully closing the door without making a sound. She was wearing a pair of tight black leather trousers with a jacket to match. A distant streetlight cast a shadow within the cleavage exposed by the low cut neckline of her white T-shirt. Dark rooted blonde hair spilled over her shoulders as she fidgeted, betraying her nervous energy.

What an asset she had been since he'd been handling her over the past eighteen months! As was her usual custom, she turned to him, placed the palm of her left hand against his left knee and let her fingers climb provocatively against his inner thigh. She did the same whenever they met and he always responded in similar fashion.

'Cut it out, Mary!' He held her wrist lightly between thumb and middle finger of his left hand and, as if resigned to his wishes, she removed her own hand without resistance. The event was a game that she insisted on playing whenever they met.

'You really are a spoilsport,' she said as if she meant it. 'One day, just one day...'

'One day nothing, Mary! You know very well what I want from you.'

'You're a real bastard, Jeffrey Evans. I just don't know why I bother!'

'You bother because it's in both our interests. Yes, yours as much as mine. Now then, what have you got for me tonight?' he asked.

She sighed. 'You know the cars that were broken into behind the cinema, night before last? It was Dennis Martin the mechanic's boys, Duane and Aston. They sold one of the radios to Colin Webster the following morning.'

'Okay!' He listened and he looked at her profile in the half-light, waiting for more.

'Philip Allen, you know, the one who came out of prison just six weeks ago. He's going off to somewhere in Merseyside tomorrow to see someone he met when he was inside and he'll be arriving back on the five-thirty train carrying eight grand's worth of cocaine.'

'You afraid of the competition, Mary?' he asked her, tongue in cheek.

'Go stuff yourself, Jeff! You know I don't deal in 'crack'.'

He laughed. 'You better hadn't, Mary, because I wouldn't let you. Now, what's the talk about the Murphy girl?' This was his real interest tonight.

'Nothing, just that everyone's shitting themselves. Word's out that Peter the strangler is back.'

'Keep that number one priority, Mary. Concentrate on the murder, but I'll make sure that what you've told me gets the right attention. What else have you got for me?' he asked, slipping five twenty-pound notes into her hand.

She handed him a small package and left without saying another word. Her perfume continued to linger as he sat there without moving for almost ten minutes, watching, listening and thinking. Then Jeff Evans drove home.

It was late. He wondered how Jean would be tonight.

Chapter Five

It was six-forty when Michael Holland awoke. It hadn't been the best night's sleep. Gorwel Cottage still held some of the demons he wasn't able to shake from a past that still haunted him. The most persistent reminders were there in the cottage. It was, after all, the birthplace of his anguish. He would never forget how he and his wife had argued that night and how it had led to Eirlys leaving the cottage, taking Neil, their son, with her. The cottage was where he had last seen them alive, making for the car. He had heard the collision that had turned the car into a tangled, flaming wreck and he had arrived there too late to save either of them.

Away from Llanglanaber, he had learnt how best to deal with what seemed to be a persistent torment. He had learnt to concentrate on his work. He'd thrown everything, all of his energy, into it, but now, back at 'Gorwel', he found that it wasn't so easy. He had awoken several times during the night, always in a cold clammy sweat that he thought he had conquered. He knew that there was only one avenue open to him – to fight it, because he had already known the alternative. He had spent the first two years following their deaths in an alcoholic blur and he was determined not to go down that self-destructing road again.

As he tightened his robe, he walked to the front door, knowing that to focus on Elen's dilemma would give him something to occupy his mind and that, after all, was why he was here. 'Come on, Michael my boy, get yourself into gear!' he thought as he picked up the morning paper, reading the headline. *'No thirty-year link to Glanaber murder'*.

Almost as he turned away from the door, there was a heavy knock on it – heavy enough for him to exercise a degree of caution. It wasn't his usual practice, but he looked through the window first and saw three men in dark suits.

'Bit early,' he thought, as he moved back to open the door. The first intimidating face pushed itself against his, while the other two men rushed past him uninvited into the house. The thought of giving immediate resistance occurred to him, but he doubted that he could have taken all three of them.

'Are you Michael Holland?' asked the one who had remained nearest.

Within that brief moment, one of the others had unlocked the back door to let yet another man in that way.

'What's it to you?' Holland was trying to suppress his anger.

'Who else is in the house?' he asked, ignoring Holland's question.

'Ask your chums. Looks as if they've been through the place already. Who in the hell are you?' Holland asked again, raising his voice.

'He's alone, sarge,' said one of the others.

'I'll ask the questions. Sit down,' shouted the first man.

The same one moved as if about to push Holland into the nearby chair, but Holland saw it coming and with lightning reactions, his massive right-hand grabbed the wrist that was about to shove a palm into his chest. Holland's eyes caught his with fire and he sensed that the weaker man realised immediately that he had met more than his match. In the moment it had taken to hold the man's wrist, and his gaze, two of the others closed in on Holland. He relaxed his grip and the others stood back. At that moment, Holland saw his opportunity to take the initiative.

'You don't act like Jehovah's Witnesses, so I take it you're police,' said Holland sarcastically.

One of them laughed briefly and showed a warrant card to confirm it.

'Now that I've invited you in,' Holland continued, in the same manner, 'if you gentlemen would like to tell me what this is all about, perhaps, just maybe, we'll get on a little better!'

The aggressive one started again.

'Don't get smart, 'sunshine'. I'm in charge here. Whose is the flashy Stag outside?'

He wasn't letting go, Holland realised. 'Haven't you got even flashier computers to tell you things like that nowadays?' He wasn't sure if that was the right approach, but it was too late now.

'Who was driving it late afternoon on Tuesday?' His question was delivered quickly and his conduct remained hostile.

'Why?' Holland asked.

'We're here to investigate the murder of Donna Marie Murphy. I'm sure you must have heard about it,' he said, glancing towards the discarded newspaper. 'Your car was seen no more than fifty yards from where her body was found.'

'Shit, these guys are serious!' Holland thought to himself as he recalled that he had parked just off the lane near Hendre Fawr after he had been to see Elen at the hospital. He remembered the tractor driver's nod. He, and the car, had been there for the best part of an hour. They had every right to ask him these questions, but why were they acting so aggressively? He certainly didn't feel that he could trust these men. He'd tried a reasonable approach, which had fallen on deaf ears, and God knows how they might twist any explanation he might offer! Holland decided he would not enter into a conversation without it being tape-recorded. That would provide him the protection he needed.

'Your manner suggests that you suspect me in some way. In that case, shouldn't you caution me or something?'

'Clever bastard, aren't you!' he said. Then, directing two of the others, he continued. 'Take him in. We'll follow you once we've had a good look around.'

Two of them watched Holland as he dressed, then they handcuffed him tightly behind his back. They took him outside where he saw one of the others taking his muddy walking shoes out of the boot of the car, dropping them into plastic bags.

'These yours?'

Holland made no reply.

They bundled Michael Holland unceremoniously into the back of one of the two Mondeo cars parked next to the 'Stag'. 'Why so heavy?' he thought again. There must be a reason.

The metal gate at the back of Llanglanaber Police station was opened electronically. A closed circuit television camera looked down upon him as he struggled to exit the car, the handcuffs making it difficult to maintain his balance. He was led down a short narrow path enclosed by high concrete walls towards a steel reinforced doorway. One of his escorts pressed a button and spoke into a metal plate. The door opened into a dirty-looking, windowless corridor, dimly lit by grill-covered lights set into the walls just below the ceiling. He looked ahead into what seemed to be a reception area. A sergeant, sitting behind a computer screen, tapped away at a keyboard while a constable emptied a bag containing what looked like the personal effects of a bleary-eyed youth standing next to him dressed shabbily in vomit-stained clothing. A duty solicitor observed the proceedings from a distance designed to minimise the effect of an unpleasant odour that was coming from his new client. The sergeant looked up at Holland and his escorts.

'In there!' he said, nodding towards a reinforced glass-walled detention room. 'Has he shown any tendencies towards violence?' he added.

One of the escorts looked at Holland and then indicated that he hadn't.

'Then off with the cuffs!' said the sergeant, as he turned back to the keyboard and the screen facing him.

As Holland was directed into the small detention room, he rubbed both of his bruised wrists, noting faint traces of blood where the metal had broken into his skin. There were two others in the same room, young lads in their late teens, who seemed to be more than comfortable in that environment. Holland listened as they plotted what to say and what not to say about a car radio they had obviously stolen and sold some days earlier. Within minutes, one of them was taken through to the counter. The other turned to Holland.

'What you in for, mate?'

Holland gave him a look that was sufficient to indicate he wasn't about to enter into conversation.

It was a good half-hour later when Holland was taken through to the counter, by which time the aggressive detective sergeant had turned up. The grey-haired custody sergeant behind the desk was middle-aged and looked as if he was about to retire. He began tapping at the keyboard once again, asking Holland a series of questions about his identity. His fingertips hesitated significantly when the prisoner described himself as a 'Welsh Assembly lawyer'. Holland realised that the detective who had escorted him into custody had also been taken aback. He watched as the constable glanced quickly at the stone-faced detective sergeant, his eyes clearly indicating that that bit of information had been outside his knowledge. The detective sergeant had shown no such surprise. Holland was convinced that he already knew his occupation and that he had not told the others. This posed some interesting questions. Who had briefed the sergeant and why hadn't that information been passed on to the others? Had he purposely withheld this information and if so, why?

'Reason for arrest?' asked the sergeant.

'Suspicion of murder,' replied the detective sergeant, before anyone else could get a word in.

Now it was Holland's turn to recoil at the impact of the words. He fought against what was almost an overwhelming impulse to respond, but he knew that this wasn't the time.

'And the circumstances?'

'I am Detective Sergeant Powell, Major Crime Unit. We're investigating the murder of Donna Marie Murphy. This man's car was close to the scene of the crime for the best part of an hour on Tuesday afternoon. There are five sightings of it, backed up by statements from those witnesses who saw it there. That period coincides with the time the girl was killed. We called to make an enquiry of Mr. Holland at seven this morning. He became argumentative and refused to answer my questions. His attitude led me to believe that he has something to hide and in the circumstances, he was arrested.'

The uniformed sergeant stopped Holland as he was about to speak. He finished feeding the explanation for the arrest and then he invited a response from the prisoner.

'Had the detective sergeant here asked me any questions in a civil manner, he would have received an explanation. He used unnecessary force earlier this morning and his attitude led me to distrust him. I'll be perfectly happy to give a full explanation as long as the questions and answers are tape recorded.'

'You can have it video recorded as well if you like, smart arse!' replied Powell in a way that tended to support Holland's version of the earlier events.

The uniformed sergeant wasn't about to take kindly to that kind of intrusion in his own custody block.

'Detective Sergeant Powell,' he began. 'I don't know how you're used to treating people where you come from, but here in Llanglanaber, even in this custody unit, I insist on treating them with respect. I don't care who they are or what they are alleged to have done.'

'That's got the measure of you!' Holland thought.

Inside ten minutes, Michael Holland had been escorted into a small dark cell, which smelt as if the drunk he had seen earlier had last occupied it. A brown plastic-covered foam mattress resting on a bunk was the only supplement to an otherwise bare room and its only decor was a selection of crude graffiti, drawn by those who had occupied the cell in the past. Holland wondered whether or not those detaining him truly considered all of this to be necessary, or was it part of some 'third degree' tactics designed to soften him up a bit? He was becoming impatient, but soon he hoped he would have his opportunity to present his explanation, after which he was confident that he would be released.

Two hours passed and nothing happened. Maybe he should have asked for a solicitor after all, instead of relying on his own judgement, in which case he would have had an ally on the outside. When the door was eventually opened, he was ushered into an interview room in which Detective Sergeant Powell sat behind a desk with one of the other two who had brought him to the station. There was no preamble, no fancy introduction following the procedural necessities and the formal caution required at the beginning of an interview. At the first opportunity, Holland launched himself into giving the fullest account of the events from beginning to end, starting with the telephone call from Elen and his reasons for travelling to Llanglanaber.

He spent some time describing his movements on the Tuesday afternoon on land belonging to Hendre Fawr. Each time Detective Sergeant Powell was about to speak, Holland preceded the intended question with its answer. It left the interviewer with little to do but listen, something that he would normally have been delighted to accommodate. He was also quickly learning something about the character of his interviewee. Powell had been accustomed to encouraging those he interviewed into talking too much, a ploy that often lead to self-incrimination. This prisoner, however, was clearly placing himself above any suspicion; however tenuous it may have been in the first place. As the interview progressed, the increasingly uncomfortable Powell was also learning that Holland was several intellectual streets ahead of him.

Fully expecting to be released immediately, Holland marched to the counter, only to be greeted by a different sergeant. This one didn't even look at Holland as Powell gave a half-hearted summary of the interview, adding that further enquiries would be necessary to establish the truth, or otherwise, of the account given.

In the cell, another three hours passed before an inspector introduced himself, saying that it was his responsibility to review his detention. It seemed that whatever representations Holland made, he was told that enquiries were being conducted expeditiously and that to release him prior to their completion would prejudice the investigation. 'Balderdash!' thought Holland, but the situation was beginning to intrigue him. He decided not to request a solicitor because he knew the police would be unable to connect him to the murder. Within twenty-four hours he would either have to be charged or, alternatively, a period of further detention would need to be authorised by a superintendent. In the circumstances, he was prepared to sit it out. He tried to figure out whether there was a sinister reason behind his detention and, if so who, was behind it and why? Was it Powell or was there someone else pulling the strings?

Jeff Evans had asked himself several times that day why he had not been detailed to be part of the team assigned to interview Michael Holland. He couldn't understand why it was that detectives from outside the division had been detailed to do it when it was he who had introduced the information into the enquiry. He would have expected to be given the job himself. As he sat in his car overlooking Llanglanaber railway station, he wondered why it had been necessary to arrest Holland in the first place. He was sure that he wouldn't have played it that way but, soon, it would be time for the six-thirty briefing and maybe the reasons for Holland's arrest would be revealed then.

It was already five thirty-five and the train was a little more than five minutes' late. From his position of vantage, Jeff watched as Philip Allen disembarked from the third carriage. He walked along the platform, straight into the arms of two constables who were wearing civilian jackets over their uniform in a feeble attempt to disguise their identity. Feeble it may have been, but there again, Jeff thought, Philip Allen was no drug baron either. He watched the stop, watched the search, and he watched as the secreted package was retrieved from somewhere beneath Allen's clothing and Jeff smiled as he saw the handcuffs being placed on his wrists. No, Philip Allen would never make much of a drug dealer, but still, eight thousand pounds worth of cocaine would have done more than its fair share of damage in a small town such as Llanglanaber.

'Thanks, Beaver,' said Rob Taylor, one of the constables, as he passed Jeff's car. 'That's another one I owe you.'

'I'll remember it,' he replied, but in truth, there was nothing more pleasing to Jeff Evans than seeing young constables making a noteworthy arrest.

'Good old 'Midnight Mary'!' he said to himself.

Jeff Evans sat towards the back of the hall as it slowly filled with murder enquiry team members, eagerly chatting together, each one with his or her own theory as to who was responsible for the premature death of the young Murphy girl. Ten minutes later, Detective Chief Inspector Renton appeared with David Beaumont. The first item was Holland's arrest.

Renton explained that it now appeared that the suspect had a valid reason for being at the scene and that, as yet, there was no evidence to connect him with the murder. He would, however, remain in custody until all avenues had been explored thoroughly.

'Holland is not what he might seem,' he continued. 'He might wear the trappings of a successful government lawyer, but he's got a chequered history. He was suspected six years ago of being involved in a fatal accident when his wife and son were killed. He was arrested in connection with that accident, but never charged. He was an alcoholic then and you all know what they say about reformed alcoholics. My guess is that he's still a safe bet for a breathalyser any time of the day or night. He's not out of the running yet and I'll be detailing a team to profile him, to the extent that we'll know which hand he uses to wipe his back-side by the time we've finished! And, of course, he'll be the subject of the usual, full forensic examination. Keep him close to the forefront of your minds, everyone.'

'What's the present position with regard to the stepfather?' asked one voice from the floor.

'No change,' said Renton. 'The family protection unit has identified several members of Marino's family in different parts of the country. The obvious possibility is that he's with one of them. We've got a slot on national news-time tonight and I'll be appealing to him to give himself up.'

'Are we using the girl's mother for the appeal?' the same person asked.

'Not yet. We'll keep that for another day. The reality is that in the absence of any other theories, and although Tony Marino is our best bet for this murder, I don't think it's the right time to put his wife through that just now. She's best kept out of the limelight for the time being, but we do need to keep that possibility in reserve.'

'What about this 'cowboy' type character who has been seen around the nearby farm and in town?' asked one of the policewomen present. 'We've seen the statement that's been taken from Elen Thomas, but it hasn't been mentioned much yet. How are we treating those sightings?'

Renton caught Jeff Evans's eye before he answered. He hadn't liked what he had seen, but as Jeff was more than aware, there was nothing he could do about it now.

'I'm not treating it with anything other than low priority at the moment. We have to remain focused.'

'More useless management jargon!' thought Jeff, but then the briefing took a turn that caught even him by surprise. It was the same policewoman who spoke again, though rather more quietly and hesitantly this time, knowing that she was about to offer a viewpoint that would be in direct opposition to that of the senior investigating officer.

'But sir, the story's out: this whole town is alive and buzzing and it's even beginning to shake with rumours that this fellow Peter has returned. How can we ignore it? I know there's nothing we can do about the late Mrs. Parry's evidence, but we can certainly take account of it. Elen Thomas has seen somebody, twice, and there's no doubt about that. I've just had a glimpse of Michael Holland's interview, which has just come onto the system, and it seems that his visit to the farm is connected with that same sighting. There are mothers out there who are scared. I could see it in their eyes when they were collecting their children from school today and if we ignore their concerns, we'll lose their confidence. We'll lose the confidence of the whole community.'

The atmosphere in the room changed suddenly. Several people glanced at one another, nodding in obvious agreement with the policewoman's view. Jeff Evans sensed that the events were now overtaking what seemed to have been Renton's planned disregard of the Hendre Fawr connection. Elen's statement had done the trick. Jeff Evans smiled as he wondered how Renton would handle the inevitable u-turn that had to follow. But Renton was a master at damage limitation.

'I hear what you say,' he replied. 'And it's a valid argument, but what I don't want is to open up a thirty-year-old investigation when we've got our own to worry about – one that's no more than three days old yet. While I'm of the opinion that our best bet at the moment is to find Tony Marino, I have never been one for putting all my eggs into one basket. Of course I recognise the need to establish the identity of this so-called 'cowboy' and eliminate him from the enquiry. An instruction has already been given to do just that, but all in due course. What is just as important is to create calm in the community and to assure everyone that we are on top of all aspects of this investigation.'

Although he had backtracked, it was evident that he was still confident.

'I'd like to call now upon Councillor David Beaumont, who has an important initiative to announce. It's an initiative that's intended to enhance the public's response and prevent any potential panic.'

'Another brilliant new idea,' Jeff thought, shaking his head as he watched Beaumont, standing up to address a murder investigation briefing, like a fish out of water, looking as though he was about to attempt to influence his colleagues in the council chamber.

'Detective Chief Inspector Renton, ladies and gentlemen. I'm grateful for the opportunity to address this meeting and do so in the knowledge that you are the investigators and that I am here solely in a capacity to assist.'

'At least he's got that bit right,' thought Jeff.

'We, the elected councillors, both in the community council and the county council, have a responsibility to those who elected us. In circumstances such as we have seen in the past few days we, that is you and I, will no doubt appreciate that not everyone who might have information to offer your investigation will be at ease in coming forward with it. They may feel more comfortable speaking to someone that they have elected to represent them.'

He paused, slowly looking around the silent room, for effect. Jeff closed his eyes in disbelief at the thought of what was coming.

'With the blessing of Detective Chief Inspector Renton, I am anxious to explore a possibility that each elected councillor holds special surgeries so that any member of the public who prefers to do so may disclose information to them first – not directly to the police in the first instance, but through the leaders of the community who will pass it on.'

Rumblings of obvious disapproval echoed throughout the briefing room, but surprisingly no one spoke at first. 'In for a penny,' Jeff said to himself; then reluctantly he began, knowing that once more he was putting himself out on a limb. He just hoped that some of the others might openly share his sentiments.

'We all appreciate your concerns Councillor.'

It was important to start what he had to say in a way that appeared appreciative.

'And we are grateful to you and your colleagues for any initiatives that might increase the volume and enhance the quality of information coming into the incident room. I've got some concerns though, as some of the others present here might have.'

It was also important to throw that in. He saw Renton's eyes engaging his, as indeed so did many others.

'My concerns are these. How do you intend keeping control of the information they receive? Who decides upon the validity or the importance of the information? In addition, how would your colleagues feel about disclosing to the police, information that they might have received in confidence from their public? There might be someone who might feel betrayed if his or her information was disclosed. And isn't it a bit early in an investigation of this kind, to consider such measures, anyway?'

The rumbling voices across the room gave Jeff Evans what he believed was a comforting sense of solidarity.

'If this initiative should take place, an experienced detective could be posted to act as a liaison with each council member,' Renton interrupted, in an attempt to take attention away from Beaumont. 'Each member of the public who approaches a surgery could be told that in the event of his or her information being critical, or even important to the enquiry, it will be passed to the police for further consideration. Each one will then have the option whether or not to co-operate further. As for your last question, Jeff, I'll decide if and when this initiative is adopted, but I already think that its potential benefit is massive, especially where members of the public have concerns such as the cowboy character and a possible thirty-year link. A possibility such as this has never been considered by any police force before and we won't know its full potential until we've tried it.'

'But D.C.I.,' protested Jeff. 'What is likely to happen is that the police will be unable to control the information that's out there, or know its value. No one can assess its potential value to the enquiry until it's been fed into the system and linked to all of the other information that's on the computer.'

'I agree,' said Renton. 'We must take that into account, but nevertheless we have the potential to benefit from information that might otherwise not reach us.'

The room became quiet once more as people began to realise that the whole issue was almost a fait accompli, but what else could Jeff have expected? Renton had the ability to give any policy changes the appearance of having been discussed collectively when he had already made the decision to implement them. At least the matter had received a kind of airing. He still wondered why Renton had taken so long to take the 'cowboy' character seriously when it seemed that everyone else was already in tune with his own way of thinking. 'No matter,' he thought, 'the 'cowboy' was in there now.'

It was almost eleven-thirty before Michael Holland was released from custody, having been bailed without charge to re-appear at the police station in a month's time. He'd agreed to provide a D.N.A. sample, but they had insisted on taking most of his clothing for forensic tests.

Back at the cottage Holland made himself a cheese sandwich and poured out a glass of claret. He found Brahms's 'German Requiem', the first movement of which had always inspired him, and, closing his eyes, he let the choral tones drown the events of the day. Though he listened to the music, it wasn't long before his mind returned to what had taken place earlier. He was certain that the police could have established all of the facts far sooner than the fifteen hours he had been kept in custody. Why had he been detained for so long? One thing was for sure; the whole matter was becoming personal now. The events at or near Hendre Fawr weren't just Elen's problem any more.

Just before midnight, Renton's mobile rang. It was Beaumont.

'Alex, sorry it's so late. The business with the councillors and their surgeries has been sorted. I'll be the liaison on our side. You can kick it off any time you like; all it needs is a press release as we discussed. I'll leave that to you if you like.'

'Do you know? I'm not sure if this is such a good idea after all. It's only going to be a matter of time before someone sees through it,' said Renton, looking for a response that didn't materialise. 'Don't you trust me to look after our interests?' he added.

'I thought that we'd already made that decision,' replied Beaumont eventually, ignoring the last question.

Renton remained silent for a moment, knowing that his reluctance to proceed as planned would not be to Beaumont's liking.

'And another thing, David,' he added. 'You'd better leave the press handling to me from now on. You can see what a mess this morning's headlines have made and how it's forced me to backtrack from our, or should I say your, intention to keep Hendre Fawr and the thirty-year link out of it.'

'Alex, I swear to you that it wasn't me who fed this morning's headlines to the media.' Beaumont was a convincing liar when the need arose.

'If not, who was it? It's a dangerous game we're playing, David, and there's no room for mistakes.'

'I agree, Alex, but I don't like the way it's going. The whole thing's getting too close to the farm. Anything could happen and there's a great deal at stake, for you, me and a lot of other people. Just remember that. I don't envy you or your position right now, but just remember that, won't you?'

'How can I forget it?' replied Renton. 'There's a big cannon ball out there, David. Trouble is, I don't know which way it's going to bounce next, or what it's going to take with it.'

'You just remember where your loyalties lie, Alex.'

Then the phone went dead.

For several minutes William Alexander Renton stared at the wall in front of him in silence.

He poured himself a second large whisky and drank most of it in one mouthful. 'Oh God,' he thought. 'How did I ever get into this mess?'

Chapter Six

On Sunday afternoon, three days following the discovery of Donna Marie Murphy's body, her stepfather, Tony Marino, was picked up for shoplifting food in a service station on the M62 north of Manchester. Within a matter of hours, he had been escorted to Llanglanaber. On the following morning, both he and his solicitor were seated opposite Detective Constable Jeff Evans and another detective in an interview room at the town's police station.

William Paul Anthony Marino had been missing for three days since the discovery of the body. Unshaven and pale, he looked uncomfortable, unable to look directly into the eyes of those who were about to question him.

He was of Italian descent, his grandfather having attained British naturalisation following his internment during the Second World War. Two and a half years earlier Tony had married Claire Murphy, who was seven years his senior. The marriage had followed a twelve-month relationship during which he had cohabited with her in the family home. Donna Marie Murphy had lived there throughout that time, and so had her younger brother, Patrick. The relationship between Tony and Claire had produced another boy, Paul, who was getting on for three. The police at Llanglanaber already knew Tony Marino as a petty criminal, but only to the extent he hadn't cared particularly how he'd earned his money. He hadn't worked much since moving to the area, but there was no previous history of sexual misbehaviour or violence.

The sound of the tape recording machine indicated its readiness to proceed and armed with all the pertinent information provided by the enquiry's computer, Jeff Evans embarked upon an interview designed to elicit Tony Marino's explanation for a number of matters relevant to his stepdaughter's death.

Two hours later, Jeff Evans met with four of the enquiry's senior managers led by D.C.I. Renton. Slowly, methodically, he began summarising the interview, coffee in one hand, interview notes in the other.

'Well, he seems to be admitting it,' he started.

'What do you mean, seems to be? Go on,' said Renton, without hiding the surprise at the tone of Jeff Evans's voice.

'It all started about three years ago when his wife, Claire went into the maternity hospital to have their son, Paul. He was looking after the kids for a few days. There wasn't much to it in the beginning; just a bit of flashing. Then he invited Donna Marie to touch him. It took off from there really, every chance he got, two or three times a week.'

'To what extent?' Renton asked eagerly.

'He maintains he has never had intercourse with her. No penetration; never got anywhere near it.'

Renton looked puzzled.

'That's what he says. The touching went on to masturbation. He says he used to ejaculate regularly by her hand, then one thing led to another – oral sex, that sort of thing, but he says he never had full sexual intercourse with her. "Afraid she'd get pregnant," he says.'

'And was she a willing party?' Renton asked, trying to decide whether or not to accept Marino's account.

'Kind of, well in the beginning anyway, it seems. It was only when it developed from simple touching that she started to object. He threatened to tell her mother; told her she would be the one blamed and that she'd be the one taken into care. Poor girl believed him, so she became trapped: no wonder she was running away all the time.'

'Evil bastard. What does he say about Tuesday?'

'Says he picked her up in his van from school at lunchtime. She ran off. He ran after her into the woods, caught her up and she struggled. She told him she wasn't going to have any more of it, that she had already told her social worker and that the social worker told her that he'd be the one in trouble, not her. That's when he says he lost it. He can't remember the details, says that all he's got from then on is flashbacks. He remembers being on top of her, then standing above her. She was naked and she was dead.'

'What do you think, Jeff?' Renton's question sounded genuine.

'This is the bit you're not going to like, D.C.I., I've got my doubts, you see.'

'Go on, explain. This had better be good.' he replied, searching the constable's face for meaning.

Jeff Evans took a deep breath and it was obvious that Renton didn't like waiting for his answer.

'I don't believe him. I don't think he killed her and what's more,

I've got my doubts that he was even there in those woods on Tuesday.'

'I don't believe this,' said Renton, pushing himself back from the table, his eyes rolling, looking around the room for any sign of reaction from the others. There was none. 'Spit it out, Jeff. Come on, let's hear it.'

'I'm sure that he's telling me the truth about what's been going on over the past couple of years or so. His story is consistent throughout, no matter how many times I go back to individual occasions. I'm happy with all of that, but it's a different story when I come to asking him about the events of Tuesday afternoon. He can't even describe where it happened. He just talks about the woods. He's so vague, you just can't believe him.'

'But he's been missing for three days. How could he have any idea at all where she was killed if he wasn't there at the time?'

'Because he was in the house when our people arrived there to tell them she'd been found. It was only afterwards that he disappeared. Look, I've gone over it in detail with him. He can't even say what she was wearing that day; neither can he describe her state of undress when he's supposed to have left her and he emphatically denies ever having had sexual intercourse with her.'

'Well, his D.N.A. will tell us all we want to know about that,' said Renton, still assessing the bits and pieces – trying to put some logic to it. 'I've already asked for that to be compared with any semen samples found on the body,' he added. 'What does he say about his movements after he killed her?'

'Says he was just driving around with nowhere to go. Then he had to act as close as he could to normal, so he went home and waited. For two days he waited until the body was found.'

"Mmm. Ties in with what we've got already doesn't it? Home all day Wednesday and Thursday, but we can't place him anywhere on Tuesday afternoon from twelve thirty until around seven when he turned up at the house. And that's the crucial time, isn't it? I'd say it's got to be him. I'll have a chat with The Crown Prosecution Service first, but we'll charge him with indecent assault, say half a dozen sample charges and if the C.P.S. agree, we'll charge him with the murder too.'

'Whatever you say, but you know I've got my doubts and why, and I want that put on record. I've still got an uneasy feeling about the Hendre Fawr connection and I want that put on record too. It's too close to the scene to ignore.'

Jeff Evans could see fury in Renton's eyes even though he was trying desperately to suppress his anger.

'I'm the one heading this investigation,' Renton started. 'And I decide on directional policy. That's the last time I want to hear you mention...' He stopped in mid sentence, taking on a calmer tone in the process.

'In any event, I'm grateful for your thoughts, Jeff. No one would have done a better job of interviewing him than you. One more thing please; arrange for every scrap of the girl's clothing to be brought from the house, however old. I want it all examined for semen. Every bit of it.'

It seemed a strange moment for a change of heart, thought Jeff as he left the room. He wondered what the reason might be.

Donna Marie Murphy had lived all of her life in the same house on the same council estate. It was a close community, strong enough to cope with minor behavioural difficulties such as its petty crime and occasional squabbling. That area of Llanglanaber may not have been classed as comfortable by some people's standards, but nevertheless, it was a cherished home to many of its residents.

The events of the past few days had shattered that relative comfort – as indeed had the residents' wellbeing been similarly stunned some thirty years previously. Diane Smith had lived there too.

A uniformed colleague opened the door of the Marino household to Jeff Evans. He was expected. Jeff Evans and Claire Marino had known one another for some time, but it was the first time he had seen her since her daughter's murder. She had always been an attractive woman. She could still have been beautiful had it not been for the harsh years at the mercy of her first husband, Paddy Murphy. As Jeff knelt down beside the chair on which she sat, he noted that in the space of a week, all traces of beauty had vanished.

'I'm so sorry, Claire *'bach'*, so sorry.'

'I blame myself, you know.' Her tears fell again, hands shaking she tore a sodden tissue into several pieces on her lap.

Jeff didn't speak at first, allowing her to open up at her own pace.

'If only I had done something about it earlier. I knew it was happening, or at least I guessed that it was. I just closed my eyes to it:

blanked it out I suppose.'

'How did you know, Claire?'

'It's difficult, it was difficult at the time, but now, looking back,' she paused to blow her nose. 'The bedtime stories he insisted on telling her on his own; the sudden movements between them when I came home or walked into the room unexpectedly. It was my body he was all over in the beginning, but that stopped. I thought that it was me – something that I'd done. Donna became withdrawn, always out late, running away. We were so close at one time, but I just thought it was all a part of growing up. What will happen to him now? I don't want him back here.'

'You needn't worry about that, Claire. Look, we need your help. You know that, don't you? I need to take all of Donna's clothing away with me for examination. All of it.'

Later, as Jeff Evans filled the boot of the car with the girl's clothing, sealed in plastic bags, he looked back at the house. Claire was another victim,

Someone had seen to it that Claire Marino would always remain a victim now, but he still wasn't convinced that her husband had raped and strangled her daughter.

There was an optimistic mood at the early evening briefing. D.C.I. Renton announced what everyone already assumed – that Marino had been charged with murder. Councillor David Beaumont looked especially happy. Renton outlined the various ways in which enquiries into the murder committed by Tony Marino would continue until all avenues had been thoroughly exhausted. The atmosphere was suppressed only when Jeff Evans mentioned that the 'cowboy' aspect was still alive. No one took too much regard of his concerns this time, especially when Renton declared that the drinks were on him, the traditional way to celebrate a successful conclusion to a major incident.

The back room bar of the 'Crown' Hotel was filled to capacity, to the extent that the proprietors had engaged two extra bar-staff. No one put their hands into their pockets for the first hour, but Jeff Evans wasn't comfortable. He didn't think that a murder enquiry was something to celebrate, not even its successful outcome. He looked at Renton who enjoyed being the most popular man in the room and it seemed that everyone wanted to get in on the act – become buddies all of a sudden. 'More management tools,' thought Jeff, as he watched the boss pretending to be one of the boys. He noted that David Beaumont was conspicuous only by his absence, but perhaps this wasn't his scene. Twice, Renton brought Jeff a large whisky, insisting that it was in gratitude for his efforts during the course of the investigation. On each occasion, Jeff returned the toast that was offered and pretended to sip the liquor. Once Renton's back was turned, the spirit was spilled onto the carpet beside him. He never drank spirits. By nine thirty, he'd had enough and left quietly, casting his mind to other, more important, needs.

Mary Catherine Jones, 'Midnight Mary' as he called her, was already waiting for him. She slid into the car like a snake emerging out of the darkness, hissing through her teeth, her hand feeling his thigh provocatively.

'You really are something else, aren't you, Mary?'

'I could be anything you want me to be, my crime-busting friend – your lover, even.'

'Thanks for what you gave me the other night, Mary. It worked a treat,' he said, changing the subject.

'Yes, I heard you arrested Philip. I haven't got anything else for you yet. It's a bit soon.'

'What, nothing at all? Not even a bit of the other?' he smiled.

She looked around the car park then groped teasingly inside her own jacket before producing a package of the usual size. He took it and placed it under his own seat.

'There should be enough there for a week or two,' she said. 'I can't afford any more right now, I have got other clients, you know.'

'Just as long as you never deal in hard stuff, Mary.'

'You know me better than that.'

'How much?' he asked.

'Nothing, the money you gave me the other night will cover it.'

'You're a treasure.'

'I know,' she replied. 'And you know where to find me any time you want it,' she added mischievously, sliding once more out of the car into the darkness. She turned, smiled at him in the half-light, and left.

It had been another long day and it was time to see how Jean was getting along. Jeff hadn't had an opportunity to telephone to let her know he was on his way. He knew how she liked that, but tonight, his homecoming would be a sweet surprise. He lived seven miles from Llanglanaber along a country road he could have driven along blindfolded. He thought about his marriage and the love-hate relationship that accompanied it. The love he felt for his wife and how he hated watching her health deteriorating almost daily.

And there was also the guilt he felt, because he acknowledged that spending so much time at work was the only way he could escape what would otherwise be a dreadful frustration. He was torn between being a carer and a detective. It was a battle that he had played over in his mind on countless occasions, but, alas, it was a battle the carer in him was losing! He was helpless in the thought that there was so little he could offer – apart from the one thing.

Travelling at his usual fifty-five miles per hour, he caught a glimpse of a reflection, suggesting the presence of a vehicle parked fifty yards down a narrow side road to his left. Instinctively, he pressed his foot heavily onto the throttle and watched the speedometer creeping up to seventy-five. He looked into his rear view mirror. He was right. A quarter of a mile behind him he saw the blue revolving lights of a patrol car. He'd consumed three bottles of non-alcoholic beer and normally, it wouldn't have mattered, but tonight he was carrying enough dope under his seat to convict him of 'dealing'. But there again, he knew that that was exactly what he was doing. The consequences of being caught didn't even bear thinking about. A dozen thoughts raced through his mind, but the first and the most important one for now was how to avoid getting stopped. If only he could get to Marble House Farm before those in pursuit rounded the bend, he might stand a chance. Eighty, eighty-five, ninety, he watched the speedometer and as he came up to the sharp left hand bend, he slammed on his brakes, ramming the gearbox into third as the needle dropped to seventy miles per hour. The engine screamed as he pulled hard against the steering wheel, hoping there was enough acceleration at those revs to pull the car safely out of the bend. He came upon the farm track in no time at all. He turned into it a fraction of a second after he had found second gear, bouncing along the unmade surface, round into the farmyard. He turned the car lights off and used only the handbrake to spin the car and stop in a cloud of dust. Heart pounding, he sat motionless, waiting, praying. Then he smiled in relief as he heard the patrol car's wheels screeching around the bend, then past the farm entrance, accelerating into the night. Only the blue lights were visible above the hedgerows a hundred yards away and then they faded into the distance. He didn't wait – there wasn't time.

He returned to the road and quickly disappeared, using a maze of country lanes that he knew so well. It was some time before he returned to the main road, making his way home at a steady pace once more, the best part of an hour later than he had originally intended.

As he entered the village the patrol car pulled out immediately behind him, all lights flashing in similar fashion to the last time he had seen it. He pulled up to the near side, and stopped behind his overtaking pursuers. Then, winding down the window, he waited. He knew he wouldn't have to wait long and he was right. Two uniformed men emerged swiftly from the car and ran towards him. He knew them both well, but they were men with a different set of objectives from his own. Their intentions were certainly different tonight. 'That was for sure,' he thought, as the first one to arrive poked his head through the window, sniffing for any hint of intoxication.

'Quiet tonight, boys?' Jeff asked, provocatively.

'You're an embarrassment to your profession the way you drive.'

'Whatever little game you want to play, get on with it, will you? I've got a home to go to.' Jeff was serious now.

Seething with anger, the patrolman explained what were spurious legal grounds for requesting a breath test and he took him to the parked patrol car to administer the procedure. Jeff smiled, knowing full well that losing the chasing patrol car earlier in the evening would be regarded as the deepest attack on this man's pride. By the time he returned to his own car, it was evident that the other policeman had searched it. Jeff could have asked what he had been searching for, but there was no point. He was more concerned with who had put them up to it, but there was no point in asking that either. He grinned. There would be time enough to recover his package later.

At two o'clock in the morning, Jeff's telephone rang. No one else but the office phoned him at that time, but at least, on this occasion, it was Rob Taylor's friendly voice. The call lasted no more that fifteen seconds, but it was long enough to tell Jeff what he didn't want to hear.

He replaced the receiver and he lay in silence for several minutes, allowing his mind to absorb the whole of the evening's events. Someone had been trying to discredit him, but having failed in his or her attempt to do it directly, were they now resigned to getting at him through Midnight Mary? He got dressed, entered the bedroom next door, and spoke quietly in Jean's ear. He told her it was just the usual nighttime message – that it was work and that he'd try to get back before she needed him in the morning. Jean was used to that kind of message.

It was three thirty by the time he got to the accident unit. The ward was quieter than he had ever seen it. Examining his warrant card, the nurse insisted that the patient should not be disturbed, but the visitor persuaded her that they were friends. It wasn't an outright lie, for they had become quite close during the time he had been handling her as an informant. Mary was awake and conscious. Her face was bruised and she was suffering from mild concussion. She had been attacked by two men, but she had refused to name her assailants. Jeff felt responsible. He was sure that he was to blame in one way or another. There simply had to be a connection.

'Mary, you don't look so good.'

'Tell me about it why don't you? Better still, come closer so that I can grab your thigh.' She tried to smile.

Jeff gave her a half-hearted smile too as he took her hand gently. 'Who are the bastards who did this to you, Mary?'

'It was the Allen twins, Philip's brothers'.

Jeff Evans thought for a moment. 'Do you think they know? How could they have known?'

'Don't know, Jeff. They wouldn't have got to know from anyone on my side, but that's certainly what it was about. When they were sticking the boot in, all I could hear them saying was the word "grass".'

'I'll see that they pay for this, Mary...'

'No, no, Jeff. That's the last thing I want,' she stopped him. 'I'll deal with this in my own way.'

'Will you stay at my place until you're better? Jean won't mind?'

'No, damn it. I couldn't bear the thought of you being under the same roof. Think about it seriously for God's sake, Jeff! That wouldn't do either of us any good, would it?'

She was right and he knew it.

Jeff couldn't get the possible connection between the evening's events out of his mind as he drove home, but still more important were the questions – who did it and why? Why now? He recognised that in the course of his dealings with Mary, he had put himself in a precarious position, but there again, he'd known that all along. He considered that the most important question was whether anyone inside the service knew about his little business connection with Mary, the one that was way beyond a professional relationship. If that was the case, why hadn't there been an internal investigation? In retrospect, it wouldn't have been that difficult to catch him if they were serious about it. The half-hearted attempt a few hours earlier was not the way internal investigations worked. Was there a possibility that whoever was influencing these events was outside the police?

It was still dark, but nevertheless he took several counter surveillance measures before driving to the spot where he had hidden his package a little earlier. Then, before returning home, he placed it in his own, regular, secure place where he was certain that no one would ever find it.

Jean was still sleeping.

Chapter Seven

Michael Holland had decided not to attend Emily Parry's funeral. Although he had never met Emily he would have been perfectly happy to be there to provide support for Elen, but he was conscious that as an outsider his presence might be intrusive.

There was another reason, which Elen had agreed upon without question. Holland had chosen his spot carefully and he'd made sure that he was there in good time. Camouflaged by greenery in a position overlooking the cemetery he watched the cortege arrive following its slow journey from a chapel in Llanglanaber where Emily Parry had worshipped for almost ninety years. He found that spying on a funeral with a pair of binoculars was a strange thing to be doing. At least it wasn't raining, but Holland had something other than the weather or grief on his mind. He believed there was a good chance that Emily Parry's night-time visitor might appear – to intrude upon her memory in the same way that he had disturbed her life in the past few weeks. It was certainly worth a chance that he might turn up.

In the distance, Holland observed upwards of sixty mourners dressed sombrely in shades of black and grey as they walked slowly between the tombstones in the hazy sunshine. Some supported others as they made their way towards the open grave at the far end of the cemetery. It was the one at which the headstone read – *'In loving memory of Huw Parry. Beloved husband of Emily and devoted father of Medwyn.'* Holland watched as Elen stopped, momentarily glancing sideways to the place where her own husband also rested.

He used the binoculars to scour the landscape, covering every inch of the graveyard and the countryside beyond. Nothing seemed to be out of place as the focus of his attention returned to the spot where the Minister now read from the small black New Testament he carried. Everyone was perfectly still; their heads bowed whilst the coffin was lowered into the grave.

At the final blessing, several of the men tossed handfuls of soil onto the surface of the well-polished wood below.

High above them, Michael Holland's attention was diverted to a car that came to a halt close to the cemetery gate. From the back of it emerged a tall, well-built man wearing what appeared to be a dark brown trench coat and a large, wide-brimmed hat. In his gloved hands, he carried a wreath. Holland tried to sharpen the image, but he was too far away to identify any particular features. The 'cowboy' was there. Holland watched him as he placed the wreath on the flat slate that rested on the top of one of the cemetery's gateposts. He made no attempt to move away afterwards, but the car in which he had arrived remained stationary, engine running with the back door open. Several of the mourners had seen the man too and even from that distance it was obvious to Holland that the stranger's presence was having an immediate and disturbing effect upon them.

Holland left his hiding place and ran towards the gateway, but there was too much distance to cover in too little time. There were another hundred and fifty yards between them when the cowboy spotted Holland. Without apparent urgency, he returned into the nearby car, which began moving in Holland's direction, slowly at first then picking up speed. It was obvious that the driver was not about to take account of the oncoming runner's attempt to stop it. Holland caught part of the Vauxhall Vectra's registration number as he continued running towards the hired car he had been using since the police had seized his own. Within seconds, he was in pursuit, but there was considerable distance between them and the Vectra was already out of sight. Moving through the gears Holland picked up speed, conscious that there was only one route the other car could take back into Llanglanaber. Along the length of a straight piece of road, Holland caught a glimpse of it several hundred yards ahead. He changed into third gear before a sharp bend at the end of the straight and rounded it at a far greater speed than was safe to do so, coming face to face with the back of a milk tanker that had emerged from a farm entrance on his right. The engine screeched painfully as he forced the gearbox into second, pumping the brake pedal as he struggled to maintain control of the car.

He began to overtake, but lost his nerve when his offside wheels came into contact with the soft grass verge on his right. He lost time and distance as he anxiously flashed his headlights in a vain attempt to get the driver to pull over. Eventually the tanker driver allowed Holland to pass, but the best opportunity of catching up with the other car had gone.

Holland drove through the outskirts of Llanglanaber at a moderate pace, eyes searching each side-road in turn. He came into the busy town centre, but there was nothing, not a sign of the car. Then, a few minutes later, he saw it emerging from the railway station car park, still carrying one rear-seat passenger. The chase was on again. Shortly afterwards, the Vectra was forced to stop in heavy traffic immediately in front of Holland. He considered his options and made his decision quickly. He jumped out of his own car, stepping hastily to the Vectra's driver door, managing to open it and removing the ignition keys in one swift movement – shouting at the driver in the process.

'Don't even try to move!' Holland glanced to the back seat beyond the driver's panic ridden face.

'Hang on mate, what the hell are you playing at?' asked the taxi driver.

Holland's breath sighed heavily as he saw the look of astonishment on the face of the elderly lady who was now sitting in the back of the car and his anticipation folded immediately into a feeling of acute embarrassment.

'Look, I'm awfully sorry,' he said. 'I thought you were up at the cemetery just now.'

'I was,' the driver replied. 'Are you the one who nearly got himself run over when I was leaving? The 'fare' threw twenty quid at me and told me not to stop. It was your bloody fault anyway, running in the middle of the road like that.'

'Look, I'm sorry,' Holland repeated. 'Was that a big chap, long coat and a cowboy hat?'

'Yes. It was all a bit strange really if you ask me. He said he wanted to drop off a wreath, but he left it at the gate.'

'Where is he now?'

'I dropped him off back there,' he said, nodding in no particular direction. 'And I picked up this lady at the station almost immediately.'

'Sorry for your trouble,' said Holland, glancing to the back seat once more. 'My apologies, Ma'am.'

He handed the keys back and returned to his own car amidst the sound of several other frustrated drivers' car horns.

Elen Thomas and several other mourners looked in astonishment at the wreath, which had been left at the entrance to the cemetery. In Welsh, the card said simply, *'Oddi-wrth Medwyn'*. 'From Medwyn'.

At ten thirty on the following morning, Michael Holland called at the police compound following what had been a thorough forensic examination of his Triumph Stag. Further examination of samples taken from the car was now considered unnecessary following the charges since preferred against Tony Marino. Holland's one-day incarceration had left him in a state of curious bewilderment and he was determined to find out why he had been detained in that fashion. As he crossed the yard at the back of the police station, ignition keys in hand, it also came to mind that no one had bothered to treat him as a possible witness in the murder enquiry; he had been regarded only as a suspect. There was no doubt that he had been close to the scene of the crime when the girl had been murdered. He had enough insight into major investigations to realise that every tiny bit of detail was cross-referenced to such an extent that that kind of slip-up simply did not happen. It was astonishing that no one had asked him if he had seen anything that might assist. It appeared as if the police had no interest other than to intimidate him and he was determined to find the reason for it. As he approached the car he glanced up to a second floor window, where two men looked down upon him. He recognised one of them as Detective Sergeant Powell, the other was a stranger to him. They watched Holland as he opened both doors of the 'Stag', the boot and the bonnet. He lowered the roof so that they could observe the meticulous attention he paid to examining the interior. They had done a thorough job and the upholstery had been replaced with only the slightest evidence betraying the fact that it had been removed in the first place. He grinned as he reflected on the fact that the car hadn't been that clean on the inside for months: at least he'd got a free valet service for his trouble! Although he didn't look again as he started up the motor, he sensed that his observers were still watching as he put the car into first gear and took his foot off the clutch more quickly than usual. He allowed the revs. under his right foot to spin the rear tyres, creating a cloud of dust as he left the compound in circumstances that were akin to pointing his middle finger towards the heavens. 'Grow up Michael my boy!' he said to himself.

Elen was waiting for Michael Holland and within fifteen minutes, they were travelling slowly along the rough track towards Hendre Fawr. From afar, Elen had looked good, wearing denims and a roll neck sweater beneath a trendy red and black anorak, but now, close up, she looked tired. The events of the previous few days had obviously taken their toll. It wasn't just the funeral, coupled with the fact that Emily's intruder had turned up there, but all of the events which had led up to that day. Elen was feeling vulnerable. She was concerned that the 'cowboy' might turn his attentions towards her now that her aunt was dead. She couldn't think of any other reason why he turned up at the cemetery. She showed visible signs of emotion when Holland slowly negotiated the sharp bend where the Morris Minor had collided with the wall and where her aunt had spent the remainder of that night – her very last night.

'Elen, are you sure that you're okay to go through with this?'

'I'm more than happy to do it with you, Michael. If you consider it necessary, that's good enough for me, and I'm anxious to get to the bottom of this. I just can't go on wondering whether or when he might turn up; looking over my shoulder all the time.'

'But is today too soon?' Holland's concern was evident.

'Come on Michael, let's go.'

Elen turned the key in the lock of the front door of Hendre Fawr, opening it slowly. Inside, there was a musty odour that was indicative of the damp atmosphere to which the last occupant had become accustomed. Holland paused to absorb the character and the atmosphere of the place. It was dark inside and as Elen opened the curtains the light exposed a clutter that was akin to eccentricity. The dates shown on brown stained newspapers, stacked in various piles, spanned a decade or more. Calendars hanging on several walls, each displayed the month of December in their particular year. Enough books to fill half a library lay indiscriminately on tables and shelves. Others had been left in piles on the floor as if without a place of their own. An 'Imperial' typewriter dating back to the nineteen fifties had gathered dust as it rested on more books acting as a makeshift table.

Noting that the 'eight day' grandfather clock had stopped Elen opened the case only to find that the weights had not reached their maximum drop. She recognised that something else had obviously caused it to stop. Suddenly, she gasped, her fingertips touching her lips as she looked at its brass face and realised the significance of the day and the time at which the old clock had ceased to function. Tuesday, at three twenty seven – the exact time at which Emily Parry had died!

'I've heard about things like that happening, Michael,' she said, still captured by a sense of astonishment.

'So have I, Elen, but let's not dwell on it, shall we?' Holland was a little more sceptical.

'Michael?' she asked, pensively. 'What exactly are we looking for?'

'I don't honestly know, Elen,' he replied. 'But we'll know when we find it. All we know for sure is that someone was trying to get to her and went to great lengths to do it. Let's keep an open mind about who it was, or who this 'cowboy' character is. What we have to find out is why he was doing it, why he's still doing it. Then Elen, I'm sure that we'll get some real answers. Let's start outside. I want to show you something.'

Holland took her to the open outhouse. He walked around, searching inside the building for several minutes before turning to Elen.

'Have the police been here since the day of the accident?' Holland asked.

'No, I don't think so. Why?'

'I called here after I left you at the hospital. I had a walk around and on the floor just here I found cigarette ends, sweets papers and food wrapping suggesting that someone had been spending some time here. Now it's all gone.'

'Apart from the obvious, what does that mean?' she asked.

'It means that whoever it was is now keen to hide the fact that he was ever here.'

'What do you mean now?' she asked, puzzled – unable to follow his train of thought.

'Because he wasn't trying to hide it earlier, which means that something must have happened to cause him to change his mind.'

'But surely, if this person is the one with the cowboy hat, then he's still not afraid of showing himself is he? How many people must have seen him at the funeral yesterday?'

'Seeing him from afar is one thing, Elen. Leaving something behind that could identify him is another matter. Those cigarette ends and papers I saw could do just that.'

'His D.N.A. do you mean?'

'Yes,' he replied. 'Why is he concerned enough to come back here to clear his mess if all that does is to sever his connection with the farmhouse? That's assuming it's the same person who came back, of course.'

'Is it possible that he may be connected with the Murphy girl's murder?' she asked.

'It's possible I suppose, but haven't I read in today's paper that they've charged the girl's stepfather?'

Noting Elen's expression change suddenly as her thoughts speculated, he looked directly into her eyes.

'Elen, you still think it's Medwyn, don't you?'

'I just don't know, Michael. I'm torn. I can remember him putting a buttercup under my chin, and then telling me that I liked butter. He was so gentle. I can't imagine that he'd hurt anyone – whether it was thirty years ago or now. I just don't know what to believe any more. Everyone in Llanglanaber thinks he's back.'

Holland put his arm around her shoulder, holding her close to him, directing her back towards the house.

'What's in there?' he asked, nodding towards a larger outbuilding that seemed out of place with the remainder of the farm's architecture.

'You mean the one that's padlocked?' she replied. 'I wasn't allowed anywhere near it as a child. A long time ago the farm was taken over by the Ministry of Defence. That door leads to a series of underground passages between here and the sea. Apparently it extends to an enormous cave system – something to do with a wartime submarine base. No one's been down there for years.'

'Would Medwyn have known about it?' Holland asked.

'Of course. As a boy, he'd probably have taken his mates playing down there.'

'Interesting. Let's go back inside. Any chance of a cup of tea, do you think?'

'Yes, why not? I'll get some water from the well.'

'Well? Didn't she have running water, in this day and age?'

'Yes, of course she did,' said Elen smiling. 'Gravity fed rainwater – the house isn't connected to the mains supply. Emily said it was a waste of money having it connected with all the rain we have in this part of the world. There's a big tank outside. The guttering channels the rainwater into it, but apparently something happened a couple of months ago. She told me she'd turned off the water supply because there was something wrong with it.'

She stopped for a moment as the thought occurred to her.

'Oh God, Michael! You don't think that's connected, do you?'

'I don't know,' he replied. 'Show me where the supply comes in, would you?'

Within minutes, they'd found a tap that controlled the flow of water into the house and turned it on. Elen opened the tap in the kitchen sink and looked with disgust at the dirty, brown stained water as it poured into the sink.

The outside water tank was located just below the eaves and it wasn't the easiest location to gain access. Immediately below a broken overflow pipe, a dark patch stained the ground, which Holland did not feel inclined to touch. With the aid of a ladder he climbed up to the tank. It was covered with a heavy wooden board to prevent unwanted debris falling into the water.

The tank's support was also stained and there was an unpleasant smell in the air. Much to Holland's surprise, the wooden board came away freely, almost as if it had been recently moved. As he lifted it, a cloud of bluebottles took flight directly into his face, the impact of which unbalanced him. He turned his head away, aghast at the sight of what he saw. Inside the tank, half submerged in putrid water, Holland was looking at the decaying carcass of a sheep, its head partly severed from the remainder of its body. A sea of maggots moved over the part of the rotting flesh that was above the water level. After he recovered from the initial shock, a closer look revealed something protruding from the hind leg of the sheep. It appeared to be a shortened arrow similar to those fired from a crossbow. There were sufficient bloodstains in the vicinity to indicate that the animal, though injured, was alive when placed into the tank and only then had its throat been cut. There could only have been one reason for that – the maximum possible flow of blood into the water system, an act designed to have a horrifying effect upon anyone who would have opened a tap inside the farmhouse. It had been another step calculated to intimidate Emily Parry.

It took Elen a moment to realise the full implications of Holland's findings and the impact it must have had upon Emily. Why hadn't her aunt told her? She hoped that her aunt had never known what had caused the water to discolour.

'What sick mind could be responsible for this, Michael and why?' Elen asked as she turned to him. There were tears in her eyes once more, but she was also very angry now and the anger was beginning to overwhelm any other emotion.

Two hours of searching each and every drawer in every piece of furniture inside the old farmhouse revealed nothing that seemed to be of significance.

'Where might she have hidden something, Elen? Anything at all,' Holland was showing signs of frustration.

'Wait a minute, Michael. I remember something she did a long time ago. She told me that she hid Uncle Huw's pipe and tobacco once when he was trying to give up smoking. Somewhere he'd never find it. It was a hidden locker somewhere under the stairs.' The memory of the event even managed to bring a hint of a smile to Elen's face.

The cavity within the staircase wasn't that difficult to find once someone knew where to look. The secret opening blended well into the wooden panelling, disguising its presence to the uninformed. Elen reached inside the cavity producing a diary and what appeared to be a number of formal papers in a bound folder. The folder looked to be the most interesting to Holland and he started sifting quickly through the pages, casting his eyes over a number of separate documents.

'Come on, Michael. Tell me, what are they?' Elen asked eagerly.

As he continued looking through them he said, "Congratulations, Elen; you and your sister are the proud new owners of Hendre Fawr. This is a will, signed by your aunt thirteen years ago; leaving everything she has to you both. This is interesting,' he said, looking at another document. 'It's a letter from Estate Agents in London offering nine hundred and fifty thousand pounds for the farm.'

'Gosh, Michael, that's an awful lot of money isn't it?' Elen wasn't quite sure whether to be happy about it or not.

'It seems a bit over the top, Elen, especially when you consider that the offer was made over five years ago. The house and the land is run down to say the least.'

'Then who would pay that much?'

'Your guess is as good as mine, Elen. What's in the diary?'

As Elen looked slowly through the pages, her eyes began filling again. Emily Parry had made meticulous notes detailing each of the occasions on which the intruder had come into her home. The notes had begun as soon as she had realised that something was out of place and the last entry was dated the previous week, documenting the account she had related to Elen the day before she died. The notes covered a span of thirteen weeks, half way through which she had begun referring to the intruder as 'Medwyn'.

They both looked at each other in silence.

Eventually Elen said, 'Michael, I must go. It's almost three o'clock already and it's time to collect Geraint from school'.

Her eyes filled up again. 'Auntie Emily always said that she had looked after us. Now I understand.'

Jeff Evans took to his usual seat at the back of the room in readiness for the six thirty briefing. He was surprised to see that the room was filling up with twice the usual number of personnel when, to all intent and purposes, the enquiry was supposed to be winding down, following the charges brought against Tony Marino. It soon became apparent that a large number of those taking their seats were total newcomers to the enquiry. A sombre-looking Detective Chief Inspector Renton walked in and, for once, he was without Councillor Beaumont. Renton attempted unsuccessfully to hide his weariness. This was another twist in an investigation that was spiralling out of his control and he wondered how long he could contain it in the way that both he and David Beaumont had first intended.

'Right, pay attention everyone,' he started, putting his thoughts together. 'I've got some news for you. Some of the results have come back from forensic. There are traces of Marino's D.N.A. in seminal stains found on Donna's clothing, not just the clothing she was wearing the day she was killed, but virtually everything in her limited wardrobe. There are also semen traces on the vaginal swabs taken from her body. That semen doesn't belong to Tony Marino, but it does match nine entries on the national D.N.A. database from samples taken following attacks on girls in various parts of the country over the past twenty years. Those victims were all in their early or mid-teens and all of them were raped; six were murdered, either strangled using their own brassiere or they had their throats slit. They were cut to the extent that their heads were almost severed. In two of these cases the girls' limbs had been severed too, in one sharp cut using a heavy blade, possibly a cleaver or a similar instrument. Ladies and gentlemen, there's no doubt that we're looking for a serial killer now.'

The atmosphere in the room was tense, but everyone's mind was stimulated. Opinions and speculations were rife across the room, especially amongst those who had been members of the enquiry team since the outset. But the disappointment was also evident, a frustration that the enquiry was wide open once more. Jeff Evans was the only person present who was not entirely surprised.

Pausing momentarily for quiet, Renton continued.

'The first attack was in Halifax in nineteen eighty-eight. There was a gap afterwards until ninety-six and since then he's been active in Merseyside, twice in Bradford, Coventry, Wakefield, Newcastle upon Tyne and Telford. The last one was in Bolton six months ago. Notice how the attacks seem to be in close proximity to motorways.

The M42, M6, M62 and the M1.'

'Then why Llanglanaber?' someone asked. 'It's almost out of character.'

'I'm convinced that the answer to that is connected with Marino. I believe that what we've got here is an accomplice whom Tony Marino is afraid to identify or simply won't identify.'

'Will any of the surviving victims be able to help?' someone else asked.

'Good point,' said Renton. 'But unfortunately that's not possible. One of them died following a car accident a couple of years after the attack. Another hasn't recovered following the trauma – in fact she hasn't spoken a word since the attack and we haven't got the faintest where the third one is. The interesting thing is that the last survivor, the one from Newcastle said in the statement she made following her attack, that she thought her assailant had a Welsh accent. What's more, he had a dragon tattooed on his right forearm, below which there was an inscription she couldn't read. Could this have been *'Cymru am byth'*? – Wales forever: and could the tattoo have been a Welsh Dragon? Food for thought, but my bet is that we're looking for somebody local, a friend of Tony Marino perhaps? Could it be someone who travels about a bit, a long distance driver maybe, whose home is right here? This investigation will be concentrating on that line of enquiry and I want Marino's profile to include all known associates. Don't forget that we're looking for someone who travels – work or social, who knows? From now on, our own database will be linked to each of the databases relating to the other incidents. Members of the incident room staff are preparing a synopsis of each investigation. Make it your business to familiarise yourselves with each one. One more thing; because this enquiry has taken on a different perspective in that it is now a cross border investigation – a serial killer who has struck in other police areas, the Assistant Chief Constable (Crime), Mr. Eric Edwards will be overseeing the enquiry. I will remain in daily control, and I've been appointed Detective Superintendent. Detective Sergeant Powell will be my number two and he will carry the rank of Temporary Detective Inspector.'

Before he finished, he added, 'D.C. Evans, come to my office please.'

Jeff Evans had been waiting for several minutes before Renton and Powell arrived. Renton began in his usual self-opinionated way.

'Right, Jeff, you've heard the score and you know which way this enquiry is heading. You know Tony Marino better that anyone else here and you're the one who interviewed him. Marino holds the key to this enquiry and I want you to unlock it. You've got four days before he comes back from the remand centre. He's appearing before the Magistrates next Monday and I'm giving you all that time to prepare for a second interview with him. D. I. Powell will be your number two in the interview this time. You'll concentrate all your efforts on preparing for that interview. You'll only have the one opportunity and I want it to be our best shot. I want all your research documented as you go along and you'll brief the D. I. once every day so that he knows exactly where you're up to and where you're heading. Understand?'

Jeff Evans, deep in thought, looked at him with more than a suggestion of doubt in his mind.

'I understand you, 'Super'. But what if we're barking up the wrong tree? What if the answer is not with Tony Marino?'

'Let me bark up as many trees as I consider relevant. What I want you to do is to bark up the tree I'm giving you.' Renton was showing his irritation.

'I just hope you've got someone looking at the Hendre Fawr aspect with equal enthusiasm, searching for this 'cowboy' of ours,' said Jeff. He'd have preferred to be participating in that part of the enquiry, but he wasn't in a position to argue. 'Have you heard that he was at the old lady's funeral yesterday?' he added.

Renton breathed heavily, exhaling noisily, hissing through his teeth and looking at Powell in the process.

'Yes, I've heard that too. Now do you think for one minute that a serial killer is going to hang around a Llanglanaber funeral just waiting to be caught? Of course he isn't. He's well away from here by now. I'll stake my reputation on the fact that Marino knows him and that he's got local connections. You also know that on the other side of the coin, I can't afford to ignore any information that comes into the investigation, from whatever source. Bearing that in mind, I won't be ignoring the contents of Elen Thomas's statement or the tenuous link, and yes that's what it is, a tenuous link with a thirty-year-old enquiry. But what I can assure you is that that line of enquiry will carry the low priority it deserves.'

'I'll have to advise you on one matter of caution, Super,' Jeff Evans replied. 'Those people out there, the public, are not fools. You know how they've already made their own connection between our enquiry and the Diane Smith murder. You know what effect that had on the town and how reluctant the majority of the people, especially the older ones, are to speak to us even now.'

He paused to consider how the advice might be accepted in the circumstances. Renton eased Jeff's apprehension.

'Go on, feel free!' Renton gestured with a wave of his hand.

'When the serial killer aspect gets out, and it won't take long, even if it's not out already, the shit's really going to hit the fan. You'd better have a contingency plan ready to deal with it.'

Renton and Powell looked at each other in the knowledge that Jeff's advice was sound.

'I hear what you say,' said Renton. 'That's all for now.'

'Fair enough.'

Once the door had closed behind Jeff Evans, Renton turned to Powell.

'Keep a close eye on him, won't you?'

'Sure thing, Alex,' replied Powell.

Jeff Evans wandered down the corridor, feeling like a bird that had just had its wings clipped. 'Perhaps they intended that he should take on the role of an ostrich,' he thought, burying his head in the sand. One thing was for sure; he was no longer in a position to enjoy the freedom to which he had always been accustomed. The next few days were going to be spent indoors sifting through paperwork, reporting daily to T. D. I. Powell, of all people! He shook his head at the thought.

There was one other job to do later that evening and he was already late. He collected 'Midnight' Mary from the hospital. He still felt responsible; in fact he would always feel responsible. It was quiet and dark, so he risked the possibility of being seen taking her straight home, but just as a precaution he parked round the back. She was already looking better and he was pleased.

'Stay the night, Jeff.' she asked when he dropped her off.

'You know me better than that, Mary.'

'I'm sorry to say that I do, Jeff. Just a hug then.'

He held her for a moment, affording as much affection as he dared. She held him too, but it was something she couldn't have. Even so, she let her hands wander.

'Now, now, Mary!'
She was better all right.
It was time to see how Jean was this evening.

Michael Holland sat alone that evening in Gorwel cottage, mulling over what had taken place during the past couple of days. His thoughts also turned to his wife, Eirlys, and son Neil. The events at the cemetery the previous day had stirred his thoughts in that direction and he had returned there later, carrying fresh flowers for their grave. There were flowers already in the vase, courtesy of Gladys Watkins, no doubt. Yes, he would have to visit Roland and Gladys soon too, but all in good time. After spending several minutes at the graveside, he had left. He wasn't sure if he'd felt any the better for it.

He had paused at the cemetery gate and, looking around, he'd noticed the wreath left there by the 'cowboy', which had been discarded in the waste-bin close by. Picking it up, he'd seen the card and the writing upon it. *'Oddi-wrth Medwyn'*. He had unstapled the card and placed it in his pocket before finally leaving the cemetery.

Now, at the cottage, he was looking at that card once more, trying to fathom its meaning. He poured himself a second glass of Chilean 'Cabernet Sauvignon', walked over to the CD rack and searched down the list of composers' names in alphabetical order until he found what he was looking for – Prokofiev's 'Peter and the Wolf'. He placed the disc into the player, selected the track, adjusted the volume and returned to the chair. The wineglass touched his lips as he listened to the familiar tones of the strings that depicted Peter's walk into the forest, a walk that Prokofiev's boy had made against his grandfather's wishes. Holland remembered his schooldays, recalling his fascination at the composer's ability to represent the characters using all of the instruments at the orchestra's disposal, and how it had been one of his earliest introductions to classical music. Now it had taken on a different meaning.

His thoughts returned once more to the present day. He wondered whether Medwyn was a similar character to Peter – capable of being depicted by the beautiful string melodies – or alternatively had Medwyn become the 'cowboy' who had invaded Llanglanaber? Had he become Prokofiev's big grey wolf that swallowed the little duck – menacingly illustrated by the orchestra's three horns?

Chapter Eight

The early train from North Wales pulled into London Euston just before ten in the morning. Michael Holland was in no particular hurry. He hadn't made an appointment because he considered that surprise visits often produced the best results. He felt good; there was a touch of enthusiasm in his stride as he walked down the Euston Road. Spring was in the air and he felt that he needed the exercise following the train journey. He paused along the way for a large Puerto Rican coffee, which he drank sitting at a table outside in the morning sunshine.

It was eleven fifteen by the time he entered the impressive looking premises of Travis and Bushel, Estate Agents. It came as no surprise that this was no ordinary firm of estate agents. There were no property lists or photographs displayed in the window, but he remembered that he was in London and not Llanglanaber. As he entered the tastefully decorated interior, an attractive woman of Latin origin in her late thirties greeted him.

'Good morning, sir, how may I help you?'

'My name is Michael Holland. I'm a solicitor. I represent the owners of a substantial property in North Wales for which this company made an offer in two thousand and three. I'd like to speak directly to whoever made the offer and I'm looking for an introduction, if that's possible.' It wasn't an outright lie.

'Do you have our reference?' she asked.

Holland produced the letter from his briefcase, showing it briefly, sufficient for note-taking purposes.

'Someone will be with you shortly. Would you care for coffee, sir?' she asked. Her accent was pleasing to the ear.

'Thank you. Strong, black, please, no sugar.'

It was almost fifteen minutes before he was ushered through into a small meeting room.

Inside there was an elegant looking conference table surrounded by six white leather chairs. Standing next to the table was an overweight, flabby-looking man in his mid-fifties. He was immaculately dressed in a grey pinstriped suit and a white shirt. He wore a maroon coloured silk tie with a generous showing of a matching handkerchief, which fell clumsily out of his lapel pocket. His appearance reinforced Holland's view that this was a prestigious company at the top end of the property selling market.

'Will there be anything else?' the receptionist asked politely.

'No thank you, Maria,' he said in a highborn accent exaggerated to the extent that it was difficult to understand his diction.

He turned, extending his right hand limply towards Holland. His right cuff exposed an excess of flesh and a heavy gold bracelet. Holland accepted his hand in the way he was used to greeting people, shaking it firmly and looking directly into his eyes. He was already beginning to change his impression about this man.

'Ralph C. Mortimer, partner,' he said, nose raised in an arrogant manner. 'Black coffee, no sugar, is that right, Mr. Holland? I prefer it with cream myself.'

'Cream? That was no surprise,' thought Holland. 'Black coffee's fine, thank you, Mr. Mortimer.'

He produced a business card from a pocket, placing it on the table next to where Holland stood and he began pouring the coffee

'Please sit down,' he said, unwrapping one of the chocolate biscuits as he spoke. 'Help yourself,' he added, pushing the plate in Holland's direction.

Holland produced a card of his own, handing it directly to Mortimer.

'You'll note that I'm not in private practice. I'm a personal friend of the owners of the property.'

Mortimer took the card and looked at it fleetingly before tossing it into an open file in front of him.

'So tell me, Mr. Holland, what can Travis and Bushel do for you?'

'Travis and Bushel wrote to Mrs. Emily Parry five years ago, making an unsolicited offer for Hendre Fawr Farm. Mrs Parry died recently leaving the property to her two nieces whom I represent, purely on a personal basis. I've been asked to enquire as to the source of that offer.' That wasn't an outright lie, but the next bit was. 'I've also been instructed to say that should my enquiries lead to an eventual sale of the property, then of course your company's interests will be noted.'

Holland smiled inwardly as he watched the money-smelling fat man start to twitch. He adjusted his posture as he tried unsuccessfully to minimise the belch that was only fractionally muffled behind the closed fist of his left hand. With the other he reached for the file of papers, glancing superficially at its content.

'There isn't a great deal I can tell you, Mr. Holland.'

Holland was disappointed. He was convinced that the fee-winning carrot would do the trick, but, in the event, his concerns were unjustified.

'You see, this offer was dealt with by my associate,' he continued, 'who is no longer with the company. I shan't be breaching anyone's confidence if I tell you that the offer came to us from Baldwin, Gate and Waters, Solicitors, New Bond Street, but I haven't a clue who they might have been representing.'

'Might your former associate know?'

'Well, he might, Mr. Holland, but it's rather difficult to talk to him just now. Strange man you know, one of these people who seem to want more than they can have. He left us to do some private work of his own in the Philippines and got involved in some scam or another, apparently. It's my understanding that he'll be remaining there as a guest of the authorities for some time to come.'

'What happened when the offer was made?' asked Holland.

'Here's the reply from Mrs. Parry,' said Mortimer, showing the letter.

As he looked at the one-line, type written document, Holland cast his mind back to the old typewriter he had seen at Hendre Fawr the previous day. The corner of his lips moved only slightly, betraying the smile he couldn't contain as he read a few forthright words indicating that Hendre Fawr was simply not for sale.

'All we did then was to convey the lady's sentiments to Baldwin, Gate and Waters.' Mortimer closed the file, taking another brief look at Holland's business card as he did so.

'Is it usual to make an approach anonymously, through solicitors?' Holland was genuinely curious.

'There isn't a norm in this business, Mr. Holland. Enquirers don't always reveal their identity, certainly not when making an unsolicited offer, but as you will no doubt appreciate, Baldwin, Gate and Waters is a very exclusive firm of lawyers, with even more exclusive clients.'

Michael Holland was getting the picture. It seemed likely that there was someone pretty powerful behind the offer or certainly connected to it in some way.

'I'm grateful for your help, Mr. Mortimer. I'll be in touch should matters develop favourably.'

Michael Holland sensed that he was a little closer now, though he acknowledged that the next step could prove to be a far greater hurdle. He could hardly bulldoze his way into one of the West End's leading law firms expecting the kind of answers he was looking for. He was forced to accept that his next enquiry would require a little subtlety. Perhaps a touch of the 'old pals network' might help.

Matthew Brittain was a tall, fair-haired, good-looking man with the build of an athlete. He and Michael Holland had once worked together in the Welsh Office, but Matthew had been a victim of a pruning exercise at the time of devolution, when the Welsh Office became the Welsh Assembly. At that time an opportunity had presented itself at the Law Society.

'Mick Holland, what the hell are you doing in town?' Brittain's smile was heartfelt.

'It's good to see you too, Matt. Just thought I might be able to buy you lunch?'

'Of course you can, there's a decent pub we sometimes use just across the road.'

Then suddenly Matt appeared to withdraw his enthusiasm as he remembered Holland's drink problem following his wife and son's death.

'Or there's the office canteen if you prefer,' he suggested.

Sensing his unease and the reason for it, Holland quickly put him back on course.

'Don't concern yourself, Matt, having a drink isn't a problem any more: I've come through it, and what's more, I still enjoy a tipple – purely for the taste nowadays, but it must be real ale of course, nothing else will do. Come on, this one's on me.'

'I thought you looked a damn sight better, Mick.' Matt's pleasure was evident.

Over a Shropshire Blue ploughman's lunch and a pint each of Courage Ale, they swept away several years of history in as few as thirty minutes. Eventually Matt couldn't withhold asking the pertinent question that had been on the tip of his tongue for most of that time.

'So, tell me, what brings a country boy like you to London?'

Holland told him, giving him an overview sufficient for his friend to appreciate why his lunch wasn't entirely free. When Holland had finished, Matt Brittain grinned at him.

'You really are something else, mate. You just don't know how lucky you are, do you?'

'What do you mean?' asked Holland, baffled by his response.

'I've just finished doing a job, a disciplinary matter involving a firm of solicitors up north. One of the senior partners of Baldwin, Gate and Waters has been sitting on the Law Society panel. We're on very good terms just now. Come on, let's get back to the office, I'll see what I can do for you, but I can't promise anything.'

'Oh, I understand perfectly.' Holland assured him. It sounded promising at least.

Later, Matthew Brittain came back into his own office where he had left Michael Holland twenty minutes earlier reading a newspaper. His face was expressionless.

'I can tell you this much, Michael. The offer came from another firm of solicitors for which Baldwin, Gate and Waters merely acted as agents and that's all they would really prefer to disclose right now. Listen, Mick, it's my belief that they can smell a rat. They couldn't back then, but they can now, now that you're asking questions and naturally, I've had to tell him some of the story you've told me. They're sensitive about client protection and that sort of thing, and they're even more sensitive in terms of their own credibility.'

'Okay, I understand that, even though I'm disappointed,' said Holland. 'Well, it was worth a try, Matt. I just hope the asking hasn't caused you the kind of embarrassment that might affect your future relationship with him.'

'Not at all, Mick', but Matt then smiled unexpectedly.

Suddenly Holland realised that there was something else coming his way.

'I know you well enough, Mick, and I'm not asking this from a personal point of view you understand.' Matthew was trying to be diplomatic. 'But the precondition I have to ask of you is coming from the third party, not me,' – he paused again, looking for a reaction from Holland, but that wasn't coming. 'As long as you don't use the information carelessly, I've been given permission to tell you that the offer for the farm originated from Williams, Reynolds, James and Co., Solicitors of Llanglanaber.'

Holland's broad smile revealed his delight.

'Any more?' he asked.

'Just that they understood that W. R. James and Co. was fronting another organisation. They've no idea who. Baldwin, Gate and Waters were instructed to make another offer on behalf of the same people four months ago, this time for one million two hundred and fifty thousand pounds. The offer was made in writing directly from Baldwin, Gate and Waters, and they received a reply from the old lady almost by return; same again, no sale.'

'I wonder what prevented W. R. James approaching Mrs. Parry directly,' he replied.

He also wondered why his thorough search of the property with Elen hadn't revealed the existence of the correspondence making the more recent offer. It was strange how the first letter was still there – maybe the more recent one had been removed!

Matt smiled once more. 'I'm sure you'll make it your business to find out Mick,' he paused. 'But hang on, there is one more important matter. I haven't got the answer to it, but it certainly poses a very interesting question.'

'Go on.' Holland had heard enough already to put him on the edge of his seat.

'The guy who dealt with this at Baldwin Gate and Waters was then and still is the head of their corporate sector.'

'So?'

'He only deals in billions, Mick, no kidding, billions. His like wouldn't normally cross the room for a transaction involving a little over the million that they're offering for the old lady's farm.'

Holland understood exactly what he meant.

'You've always been a star, Matt. Now you're a superstar. And yes, you can tell your third party that the information is safe with me. If the way I intend to follow it up should change, I'll speak to you or Baldwin Gate and Waters first so that we can discuss it. Is that good enough?'

'They'll be happy with that.'

Holland's next meeting was closer to home, but he still needed to tread carefully. He was aware that it could prove counter productive to overstep Civil Service protocol. It took twenty minutes to get past the mass of red-tape his tale had created at the front desk before finally getting to see a man who was younger than Holland expected. He looked out of place with punk-style, spiky hair and earrings, not exactly what Holland would have expected at The Ministry of Defence.

'Michael Holland, Welsh Assembly, legal division,' he began.

'Yes, Mr. Holland, my name's Desmond. I've already checked your identity, just as a precaution you understand; can't be too careful these days. Oh, and by the way, in case I forget, would you be good enough to contact Mr. Dominic Chandler in Cardiff when we've finished? Apparently he's noticed your absence from the office.' There was a touch of mischief in the young man's manner. 'Now,' he continued. 'What can we at the Ministry do for our neighbours in the Welsh Assembly?'

Holland smiled. It wasn't just Chandler's request that tickled Holland, but the thought that this efficient and obviously professional young man's appearance had totally deceived him. 'That'll teach you, Michael my boy,' he said to himself.

Holland ploughed into his story, knowing that there wasn't a lot of point in being superficial with this fellow.

'I'd like to know if you have any information concerning a possible wartime submarine base up in North Wales, near a town called Llanglanaber. Chapter and verse please, as long as it doesn't infringe upon state secrets,' Holland smiled.

'If it did, Mr. Holland, I guarantee that you wouldn't have got this far.'

He produced a large box of documents and files, explaining that he'd brought them along when the purpose of Holland's enquiry had been made known to those who had screened him. Holland smiled again. He was becoming quite impressed with this young man.

'Right, Desmond, you've got my undivided attention.'

'This site,' he began, whilst pulling out and opening a set of drawings and plans, 'became of interest to the Ministry of Defence in nineteen-forty. We were looking for a safe haven for submarines, one they could enter for repair, maintenance and re-arming and then leave discreetly, somewhere easily accessible to the North Atlantic, using either The North Channel or St. George's Channel from the Irish Sea and within close proximity to Liverpool Bay. This site's natural cave structure provided the ideal solution, enabling submerged craft to enter and then surface once inside. All they had to do was to excavate the natural caverns sufficiently to provide an underground harbour and workshops. It's large enough to accommodate three submarines of the size they used in those days or perhaps just one of the size of the later

Polaris Class, for example. There's a lot of deep water off the coast there, eight fathoms at low water spring.'

He paused for a moment, referring to the plan, pointing to two locations on the coastline as he continued.

'You can see that there are two caves in fact, approximately three quarters of a mile apart. They join up as they progress inland. One was used as an entrance, the other as an exit.'

'Where does Hendre Fawr Farm feature?' Holland asked.

'Well, that's over here,' he said, pointing to a smaller scale plan on this occasion. 'The tunnel system continues inland towards the farm, requiring very little development to create a supply road into the cavern from the farm itself, which is well inland. They put a railway track in there, actually.'

'You mean from the vicinity of the farmhouse?'

'Precisely.'

Holland's eyes quickly scanned the papers, taking no time at all to evaluate their content.

'The farm is only half a mile or so from the underground harbour where the two caves from the open sea meet,' the younger man continued. 'The Ministry re-accommodated the farmer for a few years until the end of the war, though he continued farming the land throughout.'

'What happened then?'

'It doesn't say here to what extent the site was ever used and in any event, it was of little interest after the end of the war, but the Ministry kept its options open until well into the sixties in case satellite surveillance technology made it useful once more – hiding from the Russians, that sort of thing.'

'And?'

'When the cold war ended, the falling of the eastern block and so forth, well, it was of no use after that. Modern submarines outgrew the facilities and in any event, there are other, more suitable, sites in Scotland. Then defence budget cuts came along making further development out of the question.'

'Any chance of a copy of those plans and drawings?' asked Holland.

'I don't see why not. Mind you, there was no need to have come all the way to London for them.'

'What do you mean?' asked Holland, eagerly.

'We provided copies to Glanaber County Council a few months

ago.'

'Really, to whom?' Holland was astounded.

Desmond looked through the last few pages of documents extracted from a correspondence file.

'Here it is,' he said. 'It's the Economic Development Department. Their reference is CM/ME/03.07.'

Noting familiar names on headed paper a few pages beneath, Holland asked. 'Is that Baldwin, Gate and Waters Solicitors I see there?'

Desmond looked through the document before replying. 'Yes, that's right. I wasn't here then. It looks as if we supplied them with copies of the plans too, going back to early two thousand and two.'

'Mm, interesting. If it's all the same with you, Desmond, I'd prefer to have copies from you, if you don't mind.'

'No problem.'

Michael Holland hailed a taxi, hoping to make it to Euston in time for the five o'clock direct through train. Once inside the cab, he telephoned Dominic Chandler, taking a few minutes to explain his prolonged absence. Holland wasn't sure if Chandler had been any the wiser by the time he'd finished, but at least he'd been able to convince him that he was engaged on a private matter and that there would be no adverse publicity coming the department's way. Chandler liked hearing that sort of thing. It had also provided an opportunity to let Chandler know that Holland was calling in some of his outstanding holiday. The fact was that Chandler didn't really want to know; he was used to Holland's escapades, though he trusted that he would be informed of any development that might concern The Assembly. Otherwise it was very much a case of out of sight, out of mind.

Holland left the train at Bangor and, picking up the Stag, he drove the remaining thirty miles or so to Llanglanaber. It was well after eleven by the time he arrived at Gorwel Cottage. It had been a long day, but worth every minute. He made himself a prawn omelette, opened a bottle of cool Chablis and listened to a Renee Fleming CD. It was just what he needed while he thought about the day's events. Who were Williams, Reynolds, James and Co. representing? Why circumvent the offer through London solicitors and estate agents and why was there such a gap, five years in fact, between the first offer and the second? Who was it that wanted Hendre Fawr so badly, and why? To what lengths would they venture to get it?

Most of all, he wondered what lay behind the interest shown by the authority's Economic Development department and what was that department's connection with Baldwin, Gate and Waters, if indeed there was one? Ms. Fleming's rendition of Dvorak's 'O Silver Moon' was the only influence capable of distracting his attention from what was becoming an interesting puzzle.

Cecil Moorcroft, Glanaber County Council's Economic Development Officer was a man in his late thirties who had shown a great deal of initiative since his appointment. He had been responsible for bringing a number of new manufacturing companies to the area, providing employment for several thousands; the building of industrial estates throughout the region and acquiring European finances at a level well above the national average. Indeed, within six years, he had earned respect as an astute businessman, as a result of which the locality had benefited enormously.

He wasn't expecting a caller from the Welsh Assembly that morning and he found the request for a meeting without an appointment intriguing. His curiosity was such that he was willing to allow the caller a few minutes and asked his secretary to show him in.

'Do we know each other, Mr. Holland? The name sounds familiar.' Moorcroft asked.

'I don't think we've met.' Holland wasn't keen to discuss his past investigations within the authority.

'What can I do for you?'

'I'd just like your thoughts on an issue we're looking into. It's an initiative that's in its infancy at the moment, but there's some support for it, both in the Assembly and in Westminster. Before it's taken any further, the views of people like yourself in local government would be appreciated.'

'I'll do what I can, but aren't such views normally requested formally and submitted on paper with supporting evidence?'

'The PM and the First Minister are keen to get this off the ground, Mr. Moorcroft. That's why I'm here today'.

Holland remembered the promise he'd made to Dominic Chandler to keep the department's nose clean, but it was too late now. He continued.

'What would your views be on whether or not all major industrial development contracts within local authorities, public or indeed private as long as there's a public interest, should be supervised by the Welsh Assembly from start to finish?' He paused. 'But only if the financial threshold is likely to exceed a certain figure.' He hoped the yarn sounded convincing, enough to get him going at least.

'You've caught me on the hop this morning, Mr. Holland, but my initial reaction is that there's enough interference in one way or another from central government already – London or Cardiff for that matter.'

'Here goes – in for a penny,' thought Holland to himself. 'Quite so, but we're thinking about the very largest of contracts only, for example the kind that's under consideration at Hendre Fawr.'

The impact of that statement stopped Moorcroft in his tracks. He rose from his chair and stepped over to the window turning his back on Holland as his mind raced through a dozen scenarios. He decided to play it safe, but he had already seen through Holland's smokescreen.

'Hendre Fawr, Mr. Holland?' It was a question, not a statement.

'It's just a whisper I've heard that there may be a substantial development in the offing.'

'Let's assume for one moment that there is an interest in that property. Do you honestly consider that I would be at liberty to discuss any such issues with you or anyone else? My work is often highly confidential, Mr. Holland, and only one in a hundred ideas come to fruition.'

'But what about the principle, then?' Holland backed off as he recalled his promise not to compromise his department.

'Let me be straight with you, here and now,' Moorcroft turned towards Holland, sensing his retreat. 'You come into this office under an obvious pretext that turns out to be a fishing expedition. If I were to discuss all the possibilities that float inside my head with everyone that walks in here my credibility would fly out of the window. Now, if you'll excuse me, I have an appointment.'

The meeting had been short, but Holland left knowing that the brief exchange had confirmed all that he wanted to know. At the end of their conversation, Moorcroft had attempted to take the upper hand, but the stress in his voice had told Holland that he had something to hide and his only option had been to end the meeting. He wondered whether Chandler would be in touch to admonish him for taking advantage of his position. He was rather hoping that might happen, for it would be interesting to see who from the authority might contact Chandler to complain.

The complexities of Rachmaninov's third piano concerto in D minor pulsated from the car's four speakers as the 'Stag' purred its way along the North Wales coast taking Holland to a quickly arranged appointment with the Special Projects Advisor at the Welsh Development Agency's regional office.

Holland was greeted at the foyer. 'You've been putting a bit of weight on since I last saw you, Michael.'

'You're not looking bad yourself, Guto.' It was an understatement, for there wasn't an ounce of fat anywhere on the man's body.

Guto Wyn Hughes and Michael Holland had known each other a long time, all the way back to college days in Aberystwyth in the mid-seventies. They'd kept in touch for most of the time and their professional paths had crossed twice in the past couple of years. He was a large boned man, not particularly tall, whose constant smile and sparkling eyes portrayed an enthusiasm that was always present. Even Holland's right hand was lost in his as they shook hands firmly.

Over two cups of coffee Holland began to explain the purpose of his visit.

'Guto, do you know anything about a development involving the old submarine base at Llanglanaber?'

'Just a bit, Michael, but it's not current. I had a brief look at it about five or six years ago, but there's been no mention of it since then. It was only a suggestion even in those days and it quickly died a death. The government's policy put an end to it before it even got off the ground.'

'What kind of development was it?'

'A power station – gas turbine,' he added.

'Gosh, that's interesting, tell me more!' Holland's curiosity was aroused.

'There's gas offshore there, Michael. The only trouble is that it's high in sulphur and it's no good for the domestic market. The good news is that it can be used commercially for gas turbines and what's more there's lots of it, enough for thirty years at least, which is the expected life span of a power station. The site at Hendre Fawr is ideal for building it because the existing tunnelling can be used to carry seawater for the cooling system and bringing the gas ashore.'

'I can just imagine the possibilities,' Holland replied, sitting back in his chair, conscious now that the picture was becoming clearer.

'Exactly,' Guto continued. 'The side benefits that were being considered back then included tropical gardens, a trout farm kept at a constant temperature throughout the year, free heating for local schools, you name it – it could even become a tourist attraction – lots of jobs with lots of benefits.'

'Who was providing the financial muscle?' asked Holland.

'I've got no idea. Their identity was never divulged by the front men who were speaking to us at the time – other than in terms of 'our backers' that is, but you've got to be talking about the likes of Carron Energy who are undertaking a similar product down south at the moment. There aren't many people who can provide the kind of financial clout it takes.'

'So what went wrong five or six years ago?'

'The government placed a moratorium on gas turbine power stations for the sake of protecting the coal industry.'

'Is that still in force?'

'No,' replied Guto. 'It was lifted three years later, but as you can imagine, licences to build gas turbine power stations are not easily obtained. There's the question of need as well as employment and environmental issues. Since the moratorium was lifted only a few applications have been granted.'

'What's the present position?' asked Holland.

'Quite simple,' replied Guto. 'The better the case, then the more successful the application is likely to be.'

Holland considered the matter for a moment. 'There are two nuclear sites here in the north – Trawsfynydd, which is closed and Wylfa, which is soon to be decommissioned.'

'Correct,' said Guto with a smile – he knew what was coming.

'Therefore it's likely that an application for a site somewhere in North Wales might be treated favourably just now.'

'It might well be.'

'Would I be right in assuming that it's only a matter of time in any event?'

'There's no doubt about it, Michael.' Guto poured more coffee.

'And if Hendre Fawr should be considered an appropriate site, it's logical that whoever owns that property could ask for a blank cheque?'

'Yes, well more or less. There can't be a better site this side of the Irish Sea and the alternative to using the gas in the UK is to pipe it over to Ireland – after all, it is in international waters. That's a serious option, Michael. Sixty miles of piping wouldn't be a problem to this kind of people – and that would be a huge disadvantage to the U K.' He waited a moment, looking directly at Holland before asking the next question. 'Are you telling me the interest in this matter is surfacing again?'

'There's a possibility, Guto. I don't know for sure.'

Guto held his eye contact with Holland, pausing in thought before he continued. 'Well, if it is, then there's something that concerns me. I move in these circles, Michael and I haven't heard a thing about it. You can't do anything of this nature without the W.D.A. or government backing and support. It's a massive task from beginning to end. If it is under consideration, then they're making a fine job of keeping it quiet.'

'My bet is that's because someone wants to get his filthy hands on the farm before it becomes public knowledge,' Holland suggested.

'Well you be careful, Michael. With that kind of money floating around, some of these characters can be absolutely ruthless.' His concerns were genuine.

'I know,' he replied. 'I think I've seen some of that already, Guto, and it's not very nice – not very nice at all.'

By seven o'clock that evening, Holland had returned to Llanglanaber. It was time to visit Councillor Roland Watkins, though he regretted calling on a friend he hadn't spoken to for some time only when he needed something. He should have called sooner, but he hoped both Roland and Gladys would understand; they usually did. He stopped to buy flowers for Gladys and a bottle of wine for Roland. The least he could do was to show some gratitude to the people who had paid regular attention to the grave where Eirlys and Neil rested.

He knew how close they were to both of them.

The front door opened, revealing Gladys's smiling face behind it.

'Roland, look who's here.' She hugged Holland tightly.

'Good to see you too, Gladys.'

'Now, before you do or say anything else, tell me, will you stay for dinner? Roland came home late from a council meeting this afternoon; it's beef stew and there's plenty of it.'

Holland hadn't put his foot inside the door yet.

'How can I refuse?' He wasn't about to – he knew the extent of Gladys's culinary expertise.

He and Roland sat together, chatting casually while Gladys prepared the meal. It was Roland who changed the subject first.

'Terrible business involving Emily Parry, wasn't it?'

'Yes. I saw you both at the funeral.'

'Really, I didn't see you, Michael.'

Holland told him the reason. 'Coming here this evening isn't just a social occasion, Roland,' he confessed.

'I guessed as much, but no doubt you've been busy. I know you've been here a few days – Elen has told me about it. What can I do to help?'

'Are you still on the Economic Development Committee, Roland?'

'Yes, I've been chairman for the past two years.'

'In the past six months, have you heard of any moves to bring a power station to the locality?'

'Good God no, Michael! Why?'

'There's just a possibility that someone may be planning it.'

'Nothing like that could happen in this county without my knowledge, Michael. If there were any hint of it at all, they would have to bring it before the committee. There are all sorts of implications, not just the economic development itself, but you're talking about planning consent and that's a major issue involving a feasibility study, environmental impact studies and even a public enquiry, more than likely.'

'Roland, I need to take you into my confidence here.'

'You've got it.'

'What if I told you that Williams, Reynolds, James and Co. made an offer for Hendre Fawr Farm six years ago for nine hundred and fifty thousand pounds, possibly for that very purpose?'

Watkins remained silent, pensive, waiting for more. 'Two

thousand and two,' he said quietly.

'Then, about four months ago, they increased it by another three hundred thousand pounds. I have no idea who they represent, but it does seem that the whole matter is being kept quiet.'

Watkins remained silent for a little longer before he answered.

'Sadly, Michael, it doesn't surprise me. As to whom the firm is acting for, my guess is that you needn't look further than the golf club or the Masonic Hall for an answer. Do you think this strange character we've all heard about, the one who's been hanging around the farm and the cemetery, may be involved as well?'

Holland had always recognised Roland Watkins as an astute personality.

'I don't know, Roland, but it wouldn't surprise me,' he replied. 'So who do you think may be behind it?'

'It's only a guess, Michael. Have you heard of Aber Properties?'

'Can't say that I have.' Holland replied.

'It's a syndicate. I don't know who the members are. I doubt if anyone outside of it knows for sure. All I know is that it's very exclusive, but if you go down to the golf club any Friday night, you'll see a dozen or so people together, always the same ones. Give or take, it's any six or eight of them, I suspect, but as I said, no one knows for sure. Within that dozen are also the ones who aren't members, the ones who are trying to get in.'

'Who are they, Roland?'

'Well, there's Rhys Morris, the Chief Planning Officer, Colin Moorcroft, from Economic Development and Edwin James, the solicitor who's the senior partner in W. R. James and Co. Then there's Frank Dobson the accountant, Charles Atkins from the bank and of course, there's our beloved council leader, David Beaumont. Anyone else, well, your guess is as good as mine.'

'They sound a motley crew.'

'They are, Michael, each one with his own particular expertise. Gwynfor Jones was probably one of them too, the founder member maybe and you know how corrupt this council was under his control.'

'What does Aber Properties do?'

'The syndicate apparently started years ago, acquiring properties all over the area. They were private houses at first, and they rented them out, usually bringing unemployed riffraff into the town, destroying the local community for the sake of their own pockets. Then they started getting hold of commercial premises, and not just shops either. They've got so much property now that they've got the whole town in a stranglehold. Hardly anything happens without them being a party to it, influencing it or even controlling it.'

'It seems to me that the group consists of people from specific walks of life who can either make a contribution or exercise influence,' suggested Holland.

'That's how they work, Michael. That's how they've managed to acquire so much, and they're getting bigger and more confident all the time.'

'I would have thought that the corruption exposed when the council was last investigated might have curtailed their ambitions.' Holland was thinking aloud.

'In my experience, Michael, people with that much greed in their hearts often become handicapped by their own success. They get to believe that they are untouchable. That's what sent Gwynfor Jones to an early grave.'

'Dinner's ready, open the wine will you, Roland?' shouted Gladys from the kitchen.

Chapter Nine

The events of the past week had taken their toll on Jeff Evans. His greatest asset was self-motivation, but he felt that his enthusiasm was weakening daily as Acting Detective Inspector Powell thrust upon him what he considered to be a series of futile demands. Creating a profile of Tony Marino and his associates was something Jeff would normally have completed to anyone's satisfaction within a few days, but whenever a glimmer of light appeared at the end of the tunnel, an avalanche of Powell's seemingly pointless ideas filled his in-basket. Every instruction he was given required time-consuming research that Jeff deemed unnecessary for the purpose of the impending Marino interview or indeed for the enquiry as a whole. He had always preferred to work alone and he recognised that he wasn't a team player – a claim that had been made by Renton several times in the recent past. But it now seemed that he was deliberately being kept on the sidelines, given peripheral tasks that were going nowhere. He would have preferred instead to be focusing on the cowboy character, which seemed to be a far more logical way forward. He recognised the need for leadership in any major enquiry, but normally a senior investigator would be pleased to gather ideas from the whole of the team. When he had put his views forward on the need to redirect or re-consider the impetus, those suggestions had been rejected with more than a degree of open sarcasm, even though there were occasions when the passage of time had shown his considerations to be worthwhile. He couldn't ignore a feeling that the investigation just wasn't going right.

That wasn't the only factor that curbed his enthusiasm. His gut instinct told him that there was a link between being stopped by traffic patrol and the beating handed out to 'Midnight Mary'. The two events had taken place within an hour of each other. If only he could work out the connection.

The question was whether the Allen twins had been solely responsible for the attack, or whether someone had put them up to it. The latter of the two possibilities had all kinds of implications. There was no one, apart from D. C. I. Renton who knew that she had been his informant – and that was only because the use of informants had to be documented and supervised at senior level. Could Renton or someone close to him know about his more personal business relationship with her – that Mary supplied him with cannabis? He knew it was a dangerous game he played, but he did have Jean to consider. God, how he was looking forward to having this whole damn business sorted out so that he could return to some degree of normality – if indeed there was such a thing!

That morning at the police station, looking through occurrence reports, Jeff noted that the Allen twins had fallen foul of someone during the night. They had been beaten up by a group of hooded men before being stripped naked and, in a terrifying gesture, made to watch their clothing being doused in petrol and set alight. Then, still naked, they had been hooded and taken to the town centre where they had been left chained to a lamppost outside a nightclub shortly before closing time. The event had provided much amusement to a couple of hundred of Llanglanaber's youngsters as they emerged from the club. Jeff smiled at the thought that it hadn't taken 'Midnight Mary' long to achieve the kind of humiliation the Allen twins wouldn't be allowed to forget for some time. The last thing Jeff wanted, though, was a tit-for-tat retaliation battle of the kind that could so easily escalate. On the other hand, the twins enjoyed what they thought was a revered criminal status in the town – a reputation that had been destroyed within the space of those few minutes – and that couldn't be bad.

It was already nine thirty and time to see what gems of wisdom the Acting Detective Inspector had in store for the day.

Michael Holland spent an hour detailing his findings to Elen. The revelations in connection with the submarine base and the extent of the tunnelling between Hendre Fawr and the sea were all new to her, as was the latest offer made for the farm.

'What do we do now then, Michael, tell the Police?' she asked.

'We can hardly do that,' he said, lost momentarily for a more definitive response.

'Why not?' she asked.

'I have a feeling, Elen, that I've already been warned in no uncertain terms not to look into your Auntie Emily's affairs. That doesn't concern me in the least, but it does lead me to think that there might be a connection between what has happened at the farm over the past few months and my arrest for the girl's murder. There simply has to be.'

'Then why don't you go above them, speak to someone at headquarters?'

'Because I haven't actually got any evidence of wrongdoing on the part of anyone, whether it's against Emily, me or anyone else for that matter. All they would do would be to direct my concerns down the line to Llanglanaber, right into the lap of those I would prefer not to know about it for the moment. One thing's for sure though, we're going to need help from somewhere if we're going to get to the bottom of it. Someone on the inside would be handy.'

'Why don't we speak to Jeff Evans again?' she suggested.

'Yes, those were my thoughts too, but he's already implied that he can't or won't take matters further.'

'That may be, Michael, but if we told him what you've found out in London and at the W. D. A., it might change his mind.'

'Elen, I'm not sure who I can trust. I don't know what involvement he might have had in my arrest or whom he might need to relate our concerns to once he's left us.'

'We don't have much of a choice, Michael. Will you let me speak to him first, just to see how he responds?'

'Okay, but be careful, there's a great deal to lose.'

Elen returned in five minutes having telephoned Jeff Evans.

'He's quite cagey, Michael. He doesn't sound like himself at all. He spoke very quietly, as if he was afraid he might be overheard. He says he doesn't have much work-time to spare, but he'll see both of us this evening at about eight, in the 'Grape Tree', a pub out in the country. He won't come here to the house because he says it's too risky.'

'I wonder what he means by that.' Holland was puzzled.

The 'Grape Tree' was a converted ivy clad coach-house located a short distance from the main road about five miles east of Llanglanaber. It was a popular venue for those wishing to dine in the restaurant or the lounge bar. This night was no exception and the car park was filled to capacity. Jeff had chosen the meeting place for that very reason – two more cars were unlikely to be noticed. There was also a public bar at one end of the building, which had its own entrance. It was normally used by half a dozen or so pool-playing locals and was as good a place as any to meet in relative privacy.

The room was dimly lit and none of the customers inside took much notice as Jeff entered. Placing his duffel coat on a barstool he ordered a pint of 'mild' beer. The aroma emanating from other parts of the building reminded him that he hadn't eaten since lunchtime. He swallowed half of his beer in one gulp and then the door opened.

Elen entered the bar, followed by Holland. She looked buoyant, her footsteps lively as she walked to where Jeff was picking himself up from the stool. She moved close, inviting a cheek-to-cheek embrace, which he accepted. It was a gesture designed to make all three of them feel at ease.

'Thank you so much for coming, Jeff,' she said sincerely.

Holland and Jeff shook hands, but it wasn't a heartfelt greeting. Both men detected a coolness that needed to be overcome if this meeting was to be successful. Holland ordered a dry white wine for Elen, a pint of bitter for himself and 'the same again' for Jeff.

'Just a half, please Michael,' said Jeff, taking a second mouth-full. 'It'll do in there,' he said to the barman, passing his glass over the counter.

The three of them took their places around a table in a dark alcove that seemed ideal in the circumstances. After Holland had taken the initiative, Elen's eyes darted from one to the other, looking for hopeful signs of interest from Jeff. Holland was doing most of the talking.

It hadn't been his intention to tell Jeff Evans everything that he had discovered in the past few days, but he was dealing with a detective who was renowned for his ability to extract information using minimum effort. Holland soon realised that Jeff Evans had the ability to ask exploring questions using minimal vocabulary or by just raising an eyebrow. He realised that he was dealing with a personality of far superior intellect to Powell. When Holland had finished, Jeff began to speak.

'Elen, I want to help you, but you must both understand how difficult it is for me right now. And by the way, Michael,' he added, 'I appreciate how candid you've been in the last twenty minutes. The point is that all of our resources at the moment are being directed towards the murder enquiry. I simply don't have the time to look at these allegations. In normal circumstances I would be more than happy to do it. What you've told me has the makings of an enquiry into allegations of fraud and deep-rooted corruption, but nobody's going to listen to you until we've found the Murphy girl's killer.'

Elen and Holland looked at each other disappointedly, but then it was Jeff's turn to be more open than he had originally planned.

'The truth is, Elen,' he started, 'I was not overly impressed with your story when you first came to see me at the police station two weeks ago. Then, that night, when your window was broken, I was on my way over, but my boss reckoned it was a matter for the uniformed boys and he turned me back. I went out on a limb when I took that statement from you to introduce this 'cowboy' character into the murder investigation and that was frowned upon from on high.'

'Who was that?' asked Holland.

'The boss, D.C.I. Renton, who is now Superintendent.'

'Who was behind my arrest?' Holland grasped the nettle.

'I was, initially,' Jeff said without hesitation.

Holland's eyes narrowed in a manner that indicated his displeasure, but he was also surprised at Jeff's open response.

'You needn't look shocked, Michael. All I did was to put your car number into the system – after all, it had been spotted close to the scene. It needed checking out and so did you. But then something strange happened. I wasn't given the task of eliminating you from the enquiry myself. I would have normally expected to be given that job because the information came from me. I know that Powell went over the top that morning. I don't think I would have gone to those lengths – unless it became essential,' he added, smiling.

'So why did Powell go to those lengths?' asked Holland, ignoring Jeff's last remark.

'Didn't you have a hand in clearing up that nasty business involving the harbour development a couple or more years ago, Michael?' asked Jeff. 'That was a hell of a mess wasn't it, a corrupt local government leader, Gwynfor Jones involved in blackmail, leading to two murders, and a couple of suicides? I'm sorry, Elen,' he added, recalling that Gareth, her husband, had been one of the victims.

'Wait a minute,' Holland stopped him. 'Do you think that what was happening then in Gwynfor Jones's days might have been the tip of an iceberg and that the corruption is still going on?'

'It's possible,' Jeff replied. 'And if that's the case you might be making someone feel vulnerable once more. You'd be the last person they'd want to see poking his nose into Emily Parry's troubles, don't you think?'

'So where is the link between that possibility and my own arrest?' Holland asked. 'There would have to be a connection between whoever is involved in trying to gain possession of Hendre Fawr and Powell, wouldn't there?'

'That's what we've got to find out, isn't it?' Jeff Evans felt it was too early to divulge all of his own thoughts.

'Where does the man who was trying to frighten Auntie Emily come into it?' asked Elen.

There was a moment of silence during which both Holland and Jeff Evans looked at each other.

It was Holland who broke the silence. 'It looks as if he might have been brought in to help facilitate the sale of the farm – one way or another,'

'Well who is he then?' Elen asked anxiously.

'I don't think he's Medwyn Parry,' said Jeff. 'Not after thirty years.'

Elen looked sideways towards Michael Holland who knew what was coming.

'Jeff,' she said. 'I haven't told you everything and I'm sorry. Remember that first day I came to see you when I told you I'd seen someone at the farm that you thought might have been a poacher?'

'Yes.' He nodded, though it seemed a long time ago.

'Well I didn't tell you that he'd dropped something. It was a lighter, an old Ronson with the initials 'M. P.' inscribed on it.'

'Medwyn Parry, you mean?' He paused to consider the implication. 'But those initials could stand for any number of names.'

'They could, but they don't. I showed it to Auntie Emily after I found it. She told me that she and her husband had bought that lighter for Medwyn's eighteenth birthday, and had it inscribed. There's no doubt about it, Jeff. That lighter belonged to Medwyn.'

'God, Elen, that's put me in an awkward position! In fact, it's put all three of us in an awkward position. You'll have to give it to me. It might be a vital clue in a murder investigation.'

'That's always assuming that the man who dropped it is connected with the murder.' Holland suggested.

'You're right, Michael, but the closeness of the farm to the murder scene merits him being treated as a suspect,' said Jeff. 'I'll tell you what,' he continued, still thinking as he expressed his thoughts. 'Superintendent Renton is doing his utmost to steer this murder investigation away from Hendre Fawr. Why don't we let the matter of the lighter rest until we know the reason behind that? But keep it safe, Elen. I've got a feeling it may become important in the future.'

'There's something else we haven't told you about this cowboy's intimidating tactics, Jeff,' said Holland.

'I was afraid of that.' Jeff smiled again in anticipation of whatever revelation that was about to come his way. He felt more comfortable now, sensing that the three of them had become closer in that short space of time.

'I've read something in the local papers,' continued Holland. 'Something about sheep being slaughtered with a crossbow.'

'Yes, it's something I've been looking into for a few weeks and it's still a mystery. Why?'

'I found a sheep, which had been carried and placed into the rain-filled header tank at Hendre Fawr. Its throat had been cut releasing its blood into the water system and there was a crossbow bolt in its leg.'

'That, Michael, provides us with a whole new concept.' Jeff's thoughts were racing ahead. 'What on earth are we dealing with?' he considered out aloud. 'I've seen enough carcasses around this area recently to feed an entire army. I can't get my head round it. What have we got? A long-lost son who disappeared thirty years ago after a girl was killed in the village, returning all of a sudden to intimidate his own mother into selling the family farm at the bequest of someone who wants to build a power station and now he's a frustrated butcher too? It doesn't make much sense, does it?'

'Elen and I appreciate your predicament, Jeff, but we would like you to use every possible opportunity to connect the murder enquiry to the Hendre Fawr business and the cowboy. In that way, we can use the might of the murder investigation to draw him out, whether your Superintendent Renton likes it or not.'

'In the circumstances, it's more than justified,' replied Jeff. He felt himself becoming motivated again.

A few moments later the three of them crossed the car park, still chatting. Suddenly a lone figure walked towards them making his way towards the pub. They hadn't seen him initially, but when they did it was too late to avoid him. Unfortunately, he had noted their presence too. Both Michael Holland and Jeff Evans realised the implications of being seen together with Elen. Every picture told a story. The man, Rhys Morris, was the council's Chief Planning Officer, and he was smiling as he passed them. Morris had been one of Gwynfor Jones's associates and now it was likely that he was one of Beaumont's people – and a probable member of Aber Properties.

'If I wasn't a better judge of character, Jeff, I'd be inclined to think that you'd set me up,' said Holland.

'I was in the process of asking myself the same question.' Jeff felt vulnerable again.

Jeff Evans and Michael Holland immediately felt uneasy in each other's presence once more, privately considering whether there had been a degree of truth in what each of them had said.

Recognising it, Elen said, 'Come on, you two, don't you believe in coincidences?' She laughed. 'You're like a couple of suspicious old women.'

It was late by the time Jeff made his way back to the office, but he had managed half an hour in Jean's company after leaving the 'Grape Tree' Inn. Driving back to Llanglanaber, he pondered whether or not the person who was trying to acquire Hendre Fawr was connected with what he thought was an attempt to steer the murder enquiry away from the 'cowboy'. If it was, then Renton or Powell, or indeed both could be implicated. No, it couldn't be, he decided. He dismissed the idea.

As expected, everyone had left the incident room and as he sat behind his desk, he wondered how he might influence the enquiry so that it focused more directly upon the Hendre Fawr aspect. Searching quickly through his in-tray he also wondered what futile new lines of enquiry Acting Detective Inspector Powell had generated. Jeff almost froze as he saw the computer-created message form lying on the top of a pile of papers. The message had come in at twenty one fifty, received by W.P.C. Harrison. It was from Mary Catherine Jones 'who wished to see Detective Constable Evans urgently with regard to the murder of Donna Marie Murphy'. She would be at the 'usual place' at eleven thirty. The message continued. 'Tell him not to make contact with me first under any circumstances'. 'Damn it,' he thought, 'why the hell hadn't the policewoman telephoned him at home or tried to reach him on his mobile?' He placed the message into his pocket and left.

'It wasn't 'Midnight Mary's' usual way of making contact,' he thought, as he started the car – 'she had his mobile number, why hadn't she used it?' It was eleven-twenty already and there wasn't much time.

It had rained heavily for the past hour and continued to do so as he searched the empty beach car park, his headlights shining in several large pools of water as he steered the car to illuminate the entire area. In the distance he saw the shape of a body lying on the ground and immediately the worst-case scenario came to mind. In his haste he left the car door open, headlights directed on the spot where she lay. 'Oh my God, Mary, not again!' was the only thought in his mind as he approached her. Crouching, he pulled the body towards him, but to his astonishment he found that it was weightless. It was only clothing with a pair of knee-length boots protruding in a way that had obviously been arranged to resemble a body.

Sensing that someone was behind him, he turned around and saw a figure outlined between him the headlamps of his own car. Suddenly, the lights were turned off and in that blinding moment a kick struck the left side of his head with a force that sent him reeling. Stunned, Jeff instinctively tried to get to his feet, but a second painful blow from the right side made contact with his lower ribcage in the area of his diaphragm, emptying his lungs of air. The speed of the second blow and its direction told him that there were two of them. However, as he rose to his feet, staggering and gasping for air, he saw four figures, but one of them was standing further back, just watching. One of the men in his immediate presence, the one in the centre was carrying a pickaxe handle. The ones on both sides closed in on him, attempting to hold his arms, but Jeff had anticipated the move and swung round to his left, aiming a fist at the man who stood there, but only managing a glancing blow. As his momentum threw him off balance he felt the impact of the pickaxe handle across his shoulder blade and he was grounded again. Several more blows rained upon him, but somehow, using all of his strength, he managed to roll away and raise himself to his feet. He sensed that his assailants were happy to allow him this latitude, believing that they could turn the tables upon him at will. Their jibes suggested that they were enjoying their work. Jeff decided he couldn't make a run for it, that they would be too quick for him in his present condition. As he considered his options, the three closed in upon on him again.

The two who held him felt big and powerful as he fought to free himself. Several of his punches made contact, but his attackers' supremacy once more gave them the advantage. They secured his arms on both sides as the third stood directly in front of him. Then Jeff heard the fourth man's voice; he was the one who had until then just been watching the events.

'Right boys, you've had your fun with him: now finish him off.'

Thoughts of his wife, Jean, flashed through his mind as he watched the third man walking slowly and deliberately towards him. He dropped his wooden baton and as he did so Jeff saw the reflection of distant streetlights against the long metal blade of a sword that the fourth man had handed to him. As he moved slowly nearer, Jeff summoned his remaining strength, knowing that his life was now at stake. Then, as if to look into Jeff's eyes for the very last time, the assailant made a mistake and he moved in too close. Using the two men at his sides for leverage, Jeff Evans kicked out with all of his strength, making for the most vulnerable part of the man's body. His foot made powerful contact in the area of his genitals and his cry pierced the night. In that moment of confusion, as he rolled on the ground in agony, Jeff managed to force his left elbow into the solar plexus of the man to that side of him with force sufficient to dislodge his hold. He turned quickly and head-butted the other as he did so, splitting his nose in the process. Thick blood spewed instantly in crimson bursts that covered the man's face and his chest. Jeff continued the turn to his right in a full circle, coming again onto the man who had been on his left side. Using all of his weight behind a right-handed chopping action against the man's throat, he sent him to his knees, gasping for breath. Jeff quickly kicked the sword away and, picking up the pickaxe handle, he held it high and waited for their response, but there was none. He heard a siren in the distance. They all heard it. The three men picked each other up, and half-running, half-crawling, they disappeared into the darkness. Jeff sank to his knees as weakness overcame him. The blood that ran from a scalp wound into a partly closed eye blurred his vision. Then, barely conscious, his body folded chest down into a pool of bloodstained water.

Next to him on the ground, Jeff saw the light-tanned Cuban-heeled boots and realised that the fourth man was standing over him. He was too weak to defend himself. The figure spat down on Jeff Evans and walked slowly away, taking the sword with him. As he did so, Jeff had clearer sight of him. He was wearing a long waxed trench coat and a wide-brimmed Stetson. Even the sound of the siren didn't hurry him as he faded slowly into the darkness.

Moving in and out of consciousness, Jeff tried to recall as much as he could about them. He'd seen so little, but there was something on the fringes of his recollection, as if one of his senses recognised something that was strangely familiar, something he'd experienced before. He lay there, cold, wet and sore, his body aching as he became aware of the blue flashing lights of several approaching vehicles. Thank God someone had raised the alarm!

It was nine-thirty the following morning when Elen telephoned Michael Holland at Gorwel. He immediately recognised the tremor in her voice.

'Michael, have you heard? It's terrible. Jeff was badly beaten up last night, after we left him. He's in hospital.'

'Calm down, Elen. Tell me what happened.'

'The whole town's talking about it this morning, Michael. Someone found him on some waste ground that's sometimes used as a car park. It was sometime after midnight. Michael, do you think...?'

'Let's not think too much until we know more, Elen.' He cut her off in mid-sentence, attempting to discourage the connection she was about to make. 'I'll come down to see you,' he continued. 'I'll be there in fifteen minutes, and then we can talk. How is he, anyway?'

'Pretty badly shaken, so I'm told. They'll be keeping him in for observation for a day or so.'

The question that Elen had been about to ask was also prominent in Holland's mind as he unlocked the Triumph 'Stag' parked outside the house, but it would be unwise to speculate without more knowledge. It was a bright morning and the sun was shining, casting its silver sheen on the ground that was soaked following a night of torrential rain.

He accelerated through a deep pool where flooding often occurred as rainwater ran from the fields about fifty metres before the top of the hill where the road began descending sharply towards Llanglanaber. On the other side, he tested his brakes, but to his astonishment there was no response as the pedal hit the floorboard without resistance. As soon as he realised his dilemma, he was already fast approaching the one-in-eight hill and he frantically tried to find a lower gear at the kind of revs. that would normally be unrealistic for the car's speed. He applied the handbrake, but there was no response there, either. The 'Stag's' engine screamed in discomfort as the car quickly descended towards the hill's first sharp right-hand bend. Holland realised that he would be unable to negotiate it, but then a lifeline presented itself. At the bend, a track led off the road to the left, almost in a straight line with his present direction, turning into a ploughed field and, with some luck, the gate was open. There was no alternative as he pointed the car in that direction and once he was through the gate, his eyes closed in readiness for what lay ahead. Thankfully, there weren't any noises that sounded too expensive. The 'Stag' had come to a stop twenty metres into the field leaving its driver shaking momentarily, soaked in his own perspiration.

Holland telephoned the garage first and then Elen, just to let her know that he'd had a little trouble with the car. There wasn't a need to tell her more.

Later in the afternoon, he walked four miles along the beach taking the footpath that eventually led to Griff's garage in the next village. It had been several years since he'd walked that way. It brought pleasant, but difficult memories, for on the last occasion he'd carried his son, Neil, on his shoulders and Eirlys had made one of her special picnics.

Griff was waiting for him and it was good to see him again. He hadn't changed much – still the same short, stocky frame, ruddy complexion, sporting a welcoming grin the size of a continent.

'Michael *bach*,' he started. 'You know I've come to love this beautiful little primrose yellow treasure of yours and I'd hate to see her getting damaged. A ploughed field isn't the place where she should be driven, you know. Let me give you some advice, next time you want to motor down hill, make sure you've got some brake fluid in the reservoir.'

'What exactly are you telling me, Griff?'

'Just that the brakes don't work too well without it,' he said, smiling, wiping his oily hands on a rag that seemed to be too dirty for the task. 'Come into the office', he said.

Griff cleaned himself up in the half-hearted fashion he always did and made two cups of tea. Using fingers still soiled with oil and grime, he tossed a couple of tea bags into two chipped mugs that had seen years of staining.

'Ever had problems with the brake fluid before, Michael?'

'Never. I had her serviced in Cardiff just three weeks ago. What went wrong with the handbrake then?'

'Cable pin must have snapped: it wasn't there anyway. Could be you put too much pressure on it when the car was moving so fast.'

'Any damage underneath?'

'No, you're lucky. Come to think of it, Michael, you're lucky to be here yourself, actually.'

'If that pool of water hadn't been there, Griff, I wouldn't have tested my brakes at the top of the hill, and God knows what might have happened then.'

'It could have been a lot worse. I've had one of the boys go over her with a jet hose,' he said on the way out onto the forecourt. 'There was no damage. She's like new again.'

Holland glanced to the right of the garage as they walked together, noting what he recognised as the remains of a nineteen fifty-nine Morris 'Minor' next to a number of other damaged cars. Griff could see that he was looking at it.

'That was Emily Parry's car.'

'I thought as much,' said Holland. 'Were any mechanical faults detected following the accident, Griff?'

'I haven't touched it, Michael. The police examined it a couple of days after I brought it here: nothing to do with me now, but I can tell you this much,' he paused, pointing his right index finger at the car. 'I, and my father before me, serviced that car at this garage, right on the button, ever since she had it over forty years ago. I knew that car like the back of my hand and there wasn't a thing out of place with it. And nobody can say otherwise either, Michael *bach*, let me tell you that for nothing.' He was becoming unnecessarily defensive.

'I'm sure no one will,' said Holland. 'Send me the bill for today, will you.'

'You can be guaranteed of that, Michael,' he replied, smiling once more.

Michael Holland saw the curtain move before Elen opened the door and that was unusual. She didn't say anything immediately, but he knew that something was wrong. He closed the door and held her at arm's length, searching for the reason why she looked so worried. He didn't say anything. He pulled her close to him, feeling her body breathing against his.

'He was there again, Michael, at the school, the 'cowboy'.'

'Oh, Elen, you should have called me,' he said disappointedly.

'It was too late, Michael. He just showed himself for a moment, at the top of the hill again. Then he was gone. It's me he's trying to frighten now.'

'I wish I knew what he is playing at.' He hesitated. He wasn't sure whether to tell her, but decided it was in her best interest. 'From now on make sure your car's inside the garage at night, Elen.'

'What do you mean?' she asked.

He told her about his own experience that morning. Then he added, 'When I got back to Gorwel this afternoon, I had a look around the spot where I'd parked overnight. There was brake fluid everywhere.'

'You mean someone tampered with it?'

'There's no doubt, Elen. Someone is trying to warn us off, I'm sure of it. The only thing I don't know yet is who's giving the orders. I'd like to go back to Hendre Fawr too, perhaps I should take another look around.'

It didn't take long for Elen to understand his reasoning. She raised her left hand, touching her bottom lip with her fingertips.

'Oh, no, Michael, not Auntie Emily's car too?'

'We'll see,' he replied. 'Any news of Jeff since we spoke this morning?' He changed the subject.

'I phoned the ward earlier. They said he's as strong as an ox, badly shaken, but that he'll be out tomorrow sometime.'

Holland heard what sounded like a whirlwind behind him as the inner door was opened.

'Uncle Michael, Uncle Michael.'

He picked the boy up. 'Hello, tiger.'

'Can I have a ride in your 'Stag', Uncle Michael? With the roof down, please.'

'Of course you can, Geraint, come on.'

However much Geraint's presence had lightened the mood, Holland's mind continued to drift uneasily towards the cowboy's sinister presence, uncomfortable in the knowledge that he was still out there somewhere.

Chapter Ten

'As you all know, Anthony Marino appears before Llanglanaber Magistrates again today.' Acting Detective Superintendent Renton was addressing the Monday morning briefing. 'We're going to have a second interview with him to clear up a few points that don't match with what we've had back from the lab. Detective Inspector Powell will conduct the interview assisted by D. C. Jarvis in the absence of D. C. Evans.' He paused for a moment as if recalling something he had forgotten to mention. 'Oh, and for those of you who may not know, someone assaulted Jeff Evans late on Saturday night and he won't be with us for a while. He's okay, just badly bruised here and there. Now, back to business,' he continued. 'Everybody knows which way this enquiry is heading and there is plenty of work for everyone to be getting on with. Whatever developments there are during the day, we'll discuss them in full at the six thirty briefing this evening.'

Several of those present noted the lack of compassion expressed when Renton referred to Jeff Evans, but others who were aware of the relationship between them would not have expected anything else. It came as a surprise to those who didn't know, but it was clear to everyone from that moment that the concern, which normally existed when a colleague was injured in the line of duty, simply wasn't there. Astonishment was visible on the faces of those being addressed, but Renton was in no mood to take notice.

Two minutes later, Renton and Powell were alone.

'Richard, there's a great deal resting on your shoulders today,' said Renton. 'You know how important it is that we get results. I want to know who was with Marino when he killed her, who left his semen inside her and I want this enquiry done and dusted sooner rather than later, understood?'

'What's the matter, Alex? You're a bit edgy this morning. This job getting to you, is it?' Powell recognised that Renton was irritated. He hadn't seen this side of him before and he suspected that those attending the briefing had noticed it too.

'Don't push it, Richard. I know that you and I go back a long way, but just don't push it, right,' he replied, then, changing tack, he added.

'Did D.C. Evans leave you an interview package?'

'Yes, it's very comprehensive,' replied Powell. He knew when to leave a question unanswered. 'He's done a good job and I've been through it over the weekend. He's been busy all right; it covers all of Marino's antecedents, family, and work, associates, intelligence, previous convictions, all that type of thing. He's even profiled each of his associates, however distant, and he's looked for links between those people and the names held on the databases relating to the other murders connected by D. N. A.'

'Anything of obvious interest?' The question was simple enough, but the way in which it was said indicated that Renton was still touchy and apparently unimpressed with Powell's sudden high regard of Jeff Evans's preparatory work.

'No, not much, really. Marino's got a brother down south who has a conviction for indecent assault on a fifteen-year-old girl when he was eighteen, but he's already covered that. Jeff got the local police to interview him. They've confirmed that he was in Slough when our girl got killed.' He paused, somewhat puzzled, looking at Renton. 'I don't understand it, Alex. Jeff's done a job and a half here, second to none. Why did you want me to watch him so closely? It seems I've been hassling the lad unnecessarily.'

'You've never worked with Jeff Evans before, have you? He's a loose cannon, Richard, a good detective, but a loose cannon. He needs holding back, firmly at times, or else he'll run off doing his own thing, taking the enquiry in all sorts of different directions.'

Powell was also now learning that there wasn't much love lost between Renton and Jeff Evans, but he realised that this wasn't the moment to explore their differences. He looked at him, meaningfully.

'Like running off in the direction of this character who's been hanging around Hendre Fawr, the farm that's not far from our scene, you mean? That seems to be a perfectly logical line of enquiry to me.' He was willing to push it so far, looking to test Renton's reaction, but Renton stopped him.

'I know what I'm doing, Richard and I don't want this investigation drifting unnecessarily, governed by a figment of some old biddy's imagination and a tenuous notion supplied by the uninformed public that the whole thing's connected with a thirty-year old murder. Look, Richard,' he said, as if unsure of Powell's loyalty. 'I need you to trust me on this one, right?'

'Whatever you say; you're the boss.' He wasn't going to push that issue further, but he was keen to discover more about Jeff Evan's ordeal. 'So, what do we know about Jeff's reason for being in that car park so late on Saturday night?'

Renton looked at him, surprised at the question. 'I understand he was going to meet an informant.' He said it in a manner that suggested to Powell that he should already have known the answer.

'Who, what for? It can't be anything connected with the murder. Well not officially, anyway,' he replied.

'Why do you say that?' asked Renton.

'Because I've looked everywhere on the system this morning and there's nothing to indicate a reason why he should have been there.'

'Like I said, Richard; he's a loose cannon and you know what loose cannons are like.'

'Who've we got looking at it?' asked Powell.

'The assault on Jeff, you mean. I've told the local D.S. to put a couple of men on it for a day or so, that's all we can afford just now.'

It seemed strange to Powell, but the reply was again indicative of Renton's total lack of concern.

It was mid afternoon by the time Powell returned to Renton's office bringing with him news of Marino's interview. His mood was sombre.

'He's withdrawn his confession.'

'He's what?' Renton was unable to hide his irritation. It was way beyond the level of disappointment Powell had expected of him. 'What do you mean, withdrawn it?' he asked, raising his voice, spilling papers onto the floor as he stood up abruptly.

'Simple as that. He says he wasn't there; knows nothing about it. If you remember, Jeff Evans expressed his doubts after the first interview. Perhaps we should have listened to him.' What he really meant was that he, Renton, should have listened to him.

'Why did he run away? Why did he confess?' asked Renton, picking up the papers and throwing them haphazardly onto his desk as he walked round it. 'Come on, Richard, sit down,' he added, regretting his impatience. 'For God's sake mate, I'll get us a coffee and you can tell me about it, okay, chapter and verse.' Even in his despair, Renton recognised that creating unnecessary conflict with his second in command would achieve nothing.

Renton picked up the phone and ordered the drinks.

'He's still admitting all the other abuse,' Powell began again. 'I've put all the forensic evidence to him, the fact that his semen was found on most of her clothing. He still admits the fondling and the masturbation, up to half a dozen times a week. He stands by everything he said in last week's interview, everything except for the murder.'

'Hasn't got much of a choice in the circumstances, has he, not with the extent of the forensic evidence?' It didn't take long for Renton's frustration to surface once more, but it wasn't directed at Powell now.

'When he was told that the girl had been murdered, he panicked.' Powell continued. 'He says that he was already nervous because he knew that Social Services were aware of his antics. Patrick, Donna's brother, had told him as much. He says he knew that the abuse was likely to come out in any murder investigation and so he decided to leg it, knowing that he'd be the main suspect whatever happened.'

'Well he was right there at least, so why confess?'

'He says it was what he thought we wanted to hear.'

'Oh God,' said Renton. 'I've listened to that interview a dozen times and there isn't a hint of oppression on Jeff Evans's part!'

'I know that,' replied Powell. 'But you know as well as I do that, for one reason or another, people will confess to crimes they haven't committed.'

'True, even murder.' Renton brushed his fingers through his neatly combed hair. 'You know where this takes us now, don't you? The whole enquiry's up in the air again, right back where we started.'

'And we haven't got a scrap of forensic evidence to connect Marino with the murder – not the body nor the scene. That was Jeff Evans's concern, remember?' said Powell.

He was emphasising the point, almost making it sound as if he was saying, 'I told you so' – or rather, 'Jeff told you so.'

'Yes, yes, I remember, but that's not what I need right now, Richard.' Renton was becoming increasingly disheartened as all of the implications sank in.

'So, what's the next step, Alex? It's a major decision, whichever way you look at it.' Richard Powell had little notion, in fact, how big a decision it was going to be. 'Do you still think our man's local?' he added.

'God knows, but I think it's time to consider mass D.N.A.

profiling!'

'That's one hell of a job. How would you intend to manage the task?'

'I want a psychological profile of the offender. Contact the Crime Faculty at the Police College. See if they can suggest someone who could do it for us. Everyone living within a fifty-mile radius of Llanglanaber who fits into that profile will be asked to supply D.N.A. We'll start there.'

'What about her school?' asked Powell.

'That's going to be much more difficult to sell, Richard, but we don't have an alternative, do we?' Renton paused, looking at him. 'And it's not only her school we have to consider, there's friends, family even.'

'The truth is, Alex, we'll need D.N.A. from every male person we have cause to interview, whether its as a suspect or otherwise, or any man or boy already within our enquiry system who's between, say, twelve and seventy, and for that we're going to need an awful lot of public support and co-operation.'

'That's right, but first, let's break the news to the teams,' said Renton, rising from his seat again. 'Oh, and I also want more detailed research into each of the databases relating to the other murder enquiries,' he added. 'We'll be looking for any common features – people, vehicles, events, modus operandi, anything. Make sure the people given that task are experienced, Richard. It could be our best bet.'

The disappointing disclosure relating to Marino's interview had already leaked out amongst the men and women who formed the enquiry teams and the mood at the briefing was despondent. Renton found it difficult to maintain the positive leadership attitude he knew the investigation required more than ever now. Much to the surprise of those who knew him, he looked uncharacteristically weary. He quickly ran through the events that had brought the investigation to its present status and outlined his policies for the immediate future. The main concern coming from the enquiry teams was that public co-operation was diminishing and no doubt it would decline further once news broke that the murder charge against Marino had been dropped. Public support would become essential if they were to obtain a voluntary D.N.A. sample from the vast majority of the male population they questioned.

'Any suggestions?' asked Renton.

'Get the School Liaison Officers involved as soon as possible,' suggested one voice. 'Maybe the police should lead by example. Some of the local officers will have their own children in the same school. Let's have the media showing their boys providing the first D.N.A. samples.'

'Gary 'the bomber' Pugh lives on the same estate as the murdered girl,' said another. 'He's a former Commonwealth middleweight bronze medal winner, quite a decent boxer before he got busted up in the professional world. He's a bit of a rough diamond, but he's very popular and I'm sure he'd give us a hand. There's an actor living on the outskirts of town too, quite well known in the soaps. I'll speak to them both if you like, see if they'll lead the way by providing D.N.A. samples publicly.'

'All good suggestions,' said Renton. 'Any more?'

'Yes,' came a third voice. 'What we need is a prominent member of the local community. I'm aware that Councillor Beaumont hasn't attended briefings for the last few days, but he was full of support in the first week and was particularly useful in boosting public confidence then. Why don't we ask him to help by giving a D.N.A. sample publicly as well?'

'Fine, good idea,' said Renton. 'I'll speak to Councillor Beaumont myself.'

It was after nine that evening when David Beaumont opened the door to Renton.

'I understand you're going up in the world, Alex – Superintendent now I hear.'

'Acting, David, it's just a political promotion because of the merging of the enquiry with other police forces.'

'Scotch? You look as though you need one.'

'Yes, just ice, please.'

Renton sat uncomfortably on the 'Chesterfield'. He knew how difficult the next half-an-hour was going to be. He looked around as he waited for Beaumont's return, admiring the tasteful blend of modern leather and expensive looking antique furniture that must have taken him years to collect. Beaumont returned holding two tumblers, passing one to Renton.

'You'll enjoy that – it's a 'Clynelish', a small distillery in Brora,

Sutherland.' Beaumont liked to show off his collection of malts.

'Thanks, but I can hardly say cheers on this occasion, David,' said Renton, indicating the displeasure that was to come.

Beaumont looked at him pensively, raising the glass to his lips as the ice chimed against the crystal. Then he sat down, letting his eyes and his forehead ask the question.

'I might as well tell you before you hear it elsewhere. The murder hunt's wide open again. Marino's withdrawn his confession and there isn't a scrap of evidence elsewhere to connect him.'

'But how does that affect me?' Beaumont's guard was up.

'David, you know I've tried to steer the enquiry away from Hendre Fawr, but I'm not sure that I can continue doing it. Everyone who is involved in the investigation is talking about this character who's been around there in the past three months and they're wondering why he doesn't feature more prominently in the enquiry.'

'How is it that everyone knows so much about him?' Beaumont's bewilderment was evident.

'Jeff Evans took a statement from Elen Thomas in the first couple of days. I managed to keep everyone at bay whilst Marino was charged with the murder, but now, the investigation is on a collision course with this 'cowboy' character whom I suspect is your man.' Renton raised his eyes, inviting confirmation, but it wasn't forthcoming.

'I don't have to tell you how much there is at stake, Alex. Not just for me but for all of us. We just can't afford to let that happen, can we?' Privately, Beaumont could understand his difficulty.

'Damn it, man, can't you see?' Renton clearly felt aggrieved at the nature of Beaumont's response. 'It's not a question of what I can or can't do,' he continued. 'The whole bloody situation is already spiralling out of my control.' He raised the shaking glass to his mouth, swallowed an inch of the golden liquor and replaced it heavily onto the coffee table as he continued. 'It was so easy in the beginning, leading Jeff Evans off the track, then this bloody murder had to happen, and so close to the farm. I thought that we'd managed to frighten that inquisitive Holland off too, but he's like a bad penny that keeps on turning up. At least Jeff Evans is out of the equation for a bit, but Christ, David, I don't know what direction the shit's coming from next, or who might be throwing it!'

'The first thing we can do is to hold our nerve, do nothing, just let things happen and deal with any difficulties as they rise.' Beaumont replied, waiting to assess Renton's response, but realising now that a great deal of what was taking place was indeed outside their influence.

'Difficulties? My God, David, we're up to our arses in alligators already! Do you realise where you could finish up if it was ever revealed that you were behind the attempts to frighten Emily Parry out of her home?'

'Not me, Alex, it was us, remember, and you'd do well to remember that.'

Renton looked at him, fully aware of the significance of his statement. 'Yes, I'm partly responsible – we both know that. The truth is we're all responsible to some extent, but it frightens me how far this has gone, to what I might, unknowingly, have been a party.'

'Pull yourself together, man, and start thinking straight.' Beaumont was beginning to lose confidence in him. 'What I've been able to achieve over the years hasn't been without forcing an issue once in a while. I was born and bred here in Llanglanaber and I started with very little. I've built up a great deal of respect and a bit of security for myself – and a few others in the process. You were quite happy to become a member of the syndicate when everything was going well. Quite content to see your bank balance multiply ten-fold over the past five years, but now, at the first sign of trouble, God knows, Alex, I hadn't put you down as someone who panicked so easily!'

That statement managed to bring him back to reality. 'It's hardly a question of panicking,' replied Renton, gathering his thoughts. 'But rather a question of identifying the need for countermeasures before these annoying little factors present themselves.'

'Now you're talking my language,' encouraged Beaumont. 'Look, we'll just let the whole thing ride then, but I'm grateful that you've told me; it's good to discuss these things. Just make sure you keep it that way; understand? On reflection, I can't see any way in which your murder investigation can hinder our plans, whichever way it goes, especially now that Mrs. Parry is no longer with us. Soon, that farm will be auctioned and the syndicate will be there to buy it, outbidding any potential opposition.'

'I wish I had your confidence,' confessed Renton. 'If only it was possible to clear up this murder without the need to look anywhere near Hendre Fawr. I just don't like coincidences: you see, policemen find coincidences very difficult to believe and virtually impossible to ignore.'

'Are you happy with that, Alex, or is there anything else I can do?'

'Yes, there is something else. As you know, whoever killed Donna Marie Murphy can be identified by his D.N.A.'

'And he's connected with several other murders if what I see in the papers is correct.'

'We're starting a D.N.A. profiling campaign, asking the public to provide samples. This will be limited to certain categories of the local male population, but nonetheless it'll be quite extensive and we'll need public support. I have to convince people that there's nothing to worry about if they provide us with a sample.'

'Do you want me to endorse it publicly?' asked Beaumont anxiously.

'More than that, David, I'm launching a media-led campaign in a couple of days or so. Gary Pugh the boxer, Bleddyn ap Harri the actor and a number of schoolchildren will be asked to give a sample in front of the press and television cameras, you know the score, and we need a prominent leading member of the community to help kick it off.'

'And you want me to provide a sample too?' he asked in a manner that indicated to Renton that Beaumont's guard was coming up again.

'Using you was not my idea; it came from one of the enquiry teams. It stems from your appearances and the support you gave during the earlier briefings. I've already said that I would speak to you.'

Beaumont thought about it for a few moments. Renton watched him taking another mouthful from the crystal tumbler and he wondered what was going through his mind. He studied Beaumont's face, deep in thought as he rubbed his chin between his index finger and thumb.

'I have to decline Alex, for the same reason that I haven't attended the briefings in the past few days. In view of the way your enquiry might progress, towards the Hendre Fawr business, I mean, I believe that the further away I remain the better.'

'I understand, but I don't want to have to go back empty-handed.'

'Leave it with me for a day or so. I'll find an appropriate public figure to give you a sample.'

That evening Jeff Evans discharged himself from hospital against medical advice. He knew that Jean would be cared for as best as possible by members of her own family, but he also knew that she would need him by now – or rather that she would need the kind of help that only he could provide. His brother in law collected him in Jeff's own car, but Jeff insisted driving the twenty-five miles or so back home. It was a long forty-five minutes, during which it seemed that any sudden movement of the car stiffened his body into an aching spasm. He stopped in the village to allow Jean's brother to alight, then he turned the car around and headed back out into the country.

He stopped the car up a track, well out of sight. It was dark and he wished he had a torch, but this was no time for luxury. Normally, he wouldn't have approached the place this way, but tonight there was no alternative because he knew he would never have made it across the fields and through the forest. He came upon the disused mill, admiring its ghostly outline against the moonlit sky as he had done countless times in the past three years. He uncovered the ladder from its hiding place, carrying, or rather tonight dragging it to the familiar spot below where the windmill's blades had once connected to the revolving mechanism inside. As he fought against the pain, it took him all of his strength to lift the ladder onto the structure and his sweat poured as he struggled. Once in position he paused to gather his strength. Then, he climbed the ladder and reached into the cavity for the plastic bag, inside of which there was a tin that had once held Earl Grey tea. He opened the tin, from which he took out one of the dozen foil parcels and he placed it in his pocket. Then he closed the tin, carefully sealing it inside the plastic bag once more before replacing it into the cavity. Within ten minutes, he was sitting back at the wheel of his car, hurting and totally exhausted.

Twenty minutes later, Jeff turned the key in his front door. Jean was alone and though he was thankful for all that her family had done in the past few days, he was glad that they had now left. He knelt down by the side of the wheelchair, stroked her thigh and she woke.

'Oh Jean '*bach*,' I'm so sorry I wasn't able to make it sooner.'

'I've been so worried about you,' she replied. 'They told me what had happened and all I could do was sit here and wait. Your face is a mess, let me look at you.'

'You should see the opposition. But don't worry about me, '*cariad*'. How have you been?'

'Not too good, Jeff – I ran out on Sunday morning.'

'Damn the health service,' he said, searching his pockets,

producing the foil parcel. 'Look what I've brought you.'

'Oh Jeff, you're an angel. Do the honours for me will you?'

'Sure,' he said opening his own cigarette tin. He placed a quantity of tobacco onto the paper and rested it on the table. He unwrapped the foil and using the nearby penknife, he scraped away at the block of cannabis resin, distributing the brown flaky powder along the length of the unrolled cigarette. He rolled it between his fingers, passed his moist tongue over the shining edge of the paper and sealed it. Jeff placed the cigarette between his wife's lips and watched as she drew hard against the flame, holding her breath for maximum effect. She closed her eyes in the knowledge that at last some relief was close at hand, and that pleased him. For the rest of the evening he stayed there, his cheek resting against her thighs, letting her fingers stroke through his black, uncombed, curls, trying desperately to ignore the pain when she made accidental contact with an injured part of his scalp.

Mid way through the following morning, Detective Inspector Richard Powell burst into Renton's office without knocking, clutching a dozen sheets of paper hot off the computer's printer.

'You'll never believe this, Alex. Your mate, David Beaumont was interviewed in relation to the Halifax murder in nineteen eighty-eight. The very first murder.'

Renton looked up confused, but trying not to show undue interest. 'So, tell me about it.'

'One of the researchers picked it up this morning, just by chance.'

'Why has it taken this long to pick up?'

'Because Beaumont's name isn't on our system. He hasn't featured in our enquiry and therefore no amount of searching across the databases would have connected it.'

'Go on,' said Renton, trying hard to suppress his eagerness to learn more.

'In the Halifax murder, the girl was twelve, abducted from a playing field while she was on the way home from school. She was found four days later in woodland, seven miles away. Three witnesses saw a white Ford 'Granada Estate' near the park at the time and a fourth saw her being bundled into the front passenger seat well of the same car. All they got from any of the witnesses was part of the registration number, but they had enough confidence to conduct a massive nation-wide enquiry. They interviewed the owners of over fifteen thousand 'Granada Estates' that fitted into the frame. Beaumont was one of them.'

'That's not much to get excited about,' said Renton, with some degree of relief.

'Hang on, there's more. He was interviewed twice; they weren't happy with the explanation they got from him the first time, so they had a closer look at him.'

'Don't hang about with it, Richard, tell me for heaven's sake.'

'The first time he was interviewed by our people here in Llanglanaber, about four months after the murder – you know, the usual pro forma type of questionnaire. What he said was that he sold his 'Granada Estate' around the time of the murder, he didn't know the exact date and he had no idea to whom. Says he left it to the new owner to notify Swansea, but it seems that whoever it was never did so. That car, Alex, has never been seen or heard of since. No change of ownership, no tax applications and no sightings.'

'Surely he must have had some record of the transaction; cheque, cash deposit or whatever?' asked Renton, somewhat baffled.

'They sent a team down from Halifax to interview him at some length. What he told them was that he sold the vehicle to an unknown antique dealer, you'll never believe this, in exchange for an antique dresser.'

'And were they happy?' asked Renton.

'With his story? Not a hundred per cent. With the car? Not at all.'

'Start with him,' demanded Renton.

'The girl was abducted at four-twenty. He was at a council meeting in Llanglanaber from ten until almost noon that day. Then, his movements can't be verified. He says he was at home, alone until his wife returned from a day out with some friends at eleven that evening. The consensus was that he couldn't have travelled all the way from Llanglanaber to Halifax, then to the place where the girl's body was found and back here in that time. It's possible, but highly unlikely.'

'There was offender D.N.A. from the victim wasn't there?'

'Yes,' confirmed Powell.

'Was Beaumont asked to provide a D.N.A. sample?'

'No, it wasn't done as a matter of routine in those days; the use of D.N.A. was still in its infancy then.'

'And what about the car?' Renton asked.

'His car, whoever's car it was on the day of the murder, is still an outstanding matter. It was never traced. Does this make him a suspect for our job do you think, Alex?'

'Hardly, Richard, he and I were playing golf together that afternoon and early evening. A practice round before the Glanaber Charitable Trophy two days later.'

'How do you want me to handle it?'

'There's not much to handle for now is there?' Renton appeared almost dismissive.

'Not unless the press get to hear about it,' replied Powell.

'Just leave it to me for now,' he insisted.

Renton wasn't the type to wait, especially in circumstances like these. He caught Beaumont between two council meetings, calling him into his car.

'I'm disappointed with you, David. I'm trying to be as open as I can with you and the least you could have done was to return the compliment.'

Beaumont remained silent, inviting Renton to continue.

'Why the hell didn't you tell me that you've already featured in this serial murder enquiry?'

Beaumont remained silent, but this time, Renton followed suit.

'What are the implications, Alex?' Beaumont was introspective.

'Remember what I said last night about being able to deal with potentially difficult situations before they arise, well how the hell am I going to do that if you don't open up on something as important as this?' There was no mistaking his irritation.

'It was a long time ago, for Christ's sake, it's twenty years, and besides, what did I ever do that was wrong?' argued Beaumont.

'Don't give me that bullshit, David, you're not that naïve, far from it. We're not talking about the rights or the wrongs of abduction and murder here – we're talking about you and me and a big ugly mess that is likely to overwhelm us if we're not careful. It's likely to explode in our faces unless I handle this murder enquiry properly. And I don't mean handle it correctly I'm ashamed to say, but rather steer it in a way that protects your interests and mine.'

'I can see what you mean. Believe it or not, I hadn't anticipated this, Alex.' Beaumont was beginning to appreciate Renton's position. 'Where does it leave us?' he asked.

'It means that you're automatically linked between the two enquiries, the Halifax job and ours, to the extent that you'll need to account for your movements on the day the Murphy girl went missing. The fact that you live in Llanglanaber is enough to link you, believe me.'

'So what have I got to hide, I was with you wasn't I?'

'Of course you were, but there's not much point in my trying to make an effort to distance you from the enquiry when there's an issue already known to you that brings you galloping back to the forefront of the investigation.'

'Believe me, Alex; I had no idea this would happen. It's only because I sold my car to someone and didn't do the paperwork properly.'

'I need to know from you, here and now,' said Renton. 'Is there anything else that I should know, anything at all? The Halifax murder, the Murphy girl's death or Hendre Fawr?'

'Nothing, Alex, there's nothing, trust me.'

'There's one more thing, I asked you last night to give us a hand with the launching of the D.N.A. profiling campaign.'

'Yes, well I haven't had an opportunity to ask anyone about that yet. I'll speak with one or two people later. I'm sure that I'll be able to find someone who will be willing to help you.'

'Well you can forget that, for a start. You don't get the point do you, David? My enquiry policy is already in force, timed, dated and well documented. I can't go back on it. Because of your connection with the Halifax murder, your position now requires that you provide a voluntary D.N.A. sample for elimination purposes. If you refuse, you could find yourself being arrested. Now, do you realise the position that you're in? Am I making myself clear?'

Beaumont was visibly shaken.

Renton continued. 'What I suggest is that you volunteer to assist in the media launched D.N.A. profiling campaign and express your support for it. Put yourself forward as a community leader in the hope that that will focus everyone's attention on what a grand chap you are.'

'But I don't particularly fancy the idea…'

Renton cut across him. 'It won't work any other way, David. It's common knowledge within the enquiry team that I was going to ask you to become involved. If it becomes known that you refused, and then your involvement in the Halifax murder enquiry becomes apparent, which it will, my people will be asking some very awkward questions and I want to avoid that at all cost.'

'But Alex…'

'No buts, David; for once in your life, you don't have a choice.'

Chapter Eleven

That afternoon Michael Holland and Elen visited Hendre Fawr Farm. Elen was dreading what they might discover, but Holland was conscious that ignoring the issue wasn't an option and there was no point in prolonging it either.

A keen breeze sent the previous autumn's fallen leaves into spirals as it cut through the elm trees. Anxiously, they walked to the open lean-to shed that Emily Parry had used as a garage. Holland squatted for a moment where the Morris Minor had been parked overnight for almost fifty years and he touched the stain on the ground with his fingers, rubbing their tips against his thumb and lifting them to his nose. He stood and looked at Elen, whose distress was obvious.

'Brake fluid?' she asked, nervously.

'I'm afraid so,' he replied. There was no gentle way to tell her.

'It means that her death wasn't an accident. He killed her didn't he? Elen already knew the answer to her question.

'Well, let's not jump to too many conclusions at this stage,' replied Holland in a vain attempt to soften the blow. 'But it's too much of a coincidence to ignore, I agree.'

'But there's more to it than that isn't there, Michael? He used me.' Her eyes filled with tears. 'He used me to bring it about. He knew what he was doing when he threw the brick through my window. He knew I would make the connection, that I would phone Auntie Emily and that she would be concerned enough about me to leave the farm even at that time of night.'

'We can't rule that out, you're right.' There was no point in dismissing the likelihood, but for Elen's sake, neither was it practical to dwell on it.

Holland placed an arm around her shoulders as they walked back to the car. He felt the need to take her away from there quickly now that he had established his worst fears.

It was Elen who first noticed something different about the large doors of the old Ministry of Defence building and she stopped. It hadn't been immediately apparent to Holland, but Elen's eye was more used to the farmyard and its outbuildings. The chains securing the doors were hanging differently and, on closer examination, they found that the padlock had been removed.

'It wasn't like that on Wednesday, Michael. Do you think he might still be hanging about here?'

'Have you ever seen them insecure before?' he asked, ignoring her question.

'Never, not in all the years I've known this place. Let's have a look inside shall we?'

The metal doors were heavy and the bottom edge of each one housed a series of iron wheels running along rails extending the length of the building's opening. The neglected metal screeched as, with considerable effort, Holland inched one of the doors to one side, exposing unfamiliar daylight into the interior. They squeezed their way inside and remained at the door until their eyes became accustomed to the half-light. It was like going back in time. Heavy lifting gear towered above them, below which an empty, rusting metal truck stood on rails that disappeared into the darkness below. There was a bench where a few tools from a bygone era had been left almost as if discarded in haste.

'A bit spooky, isn't it?' remarked Elen. 'Are we going further?'

'I'd like to, but not now – it's too dangerous. I'd like to take a good look, spend some time down there, but not without proper equipment and plans. Come on let's go – we'll come back some other time.'

'There's somebody still hanging around here, isn't there?' she asked again.

'Looks like it.' Holland answered the question directly this time.

It didn't take much for their thoughts to gel on the most likely possibility.

Griff, his ruddy face beaming as usual, was crossing the garage forecourt as Holland drove the Stag into the parking space to the right of the fuel pumps.

'What's the matter with her this time?' he shouted across to him.

'Nothing that a good burn-up on some of these country roads wouldn't sort out.' Holland replied.

'The driver or the car?' He grinned some more.

'I'd like you to do something for me please, Griff. It may sound a strange request, but would you check the braking system on Emily Parry's car for me. Please don't ask too many questions. I might not be able to answer them.'

'I know you well enough, Michael. You wouldn't ask me unless you had good reason. The police have finished with it anyway – it's only a heap of scrap in the condition it's in and nobody's likely to pay me for collecting or keeping it here. I don't see any reason why I can't do as I like with it.'

As they walked over to the nineteen fifty-nine Morris 'Minor', Griff's curiosity got the better of him. 'What am I looking for?' he asked.

'Anything that looks out of place,' Holland replied. 'After my narrow escape the other day, I decided to check the drive up at Gorwel and I found traces of brake fluid. I was at Hendre Fawr earlier today and I found the same thing there, on the ground just where the old girl kept the car.'

Griff gave Holland a look that asked a thousand questions, but he knew better than to ask. He opened the door of the car, released the bonnet catch and lifted the damaged bonnet as high as it would go. He took several minutes examining the brake fluid reservoir and the connecting pipe. He poked his short fat fingers here and there, first from above and then on his back from beneath the car. He returned inside the vehicle and pressed the brake pedal two or three times with his foot, muttering something beneath his breath which Holland wasn't able to decipher. He jacked up the car, removed all four wheels and asked Holland to press the brake pedal. As Holland quickly realised what little resistance there was beneath his foot, Griff emerged from beneath the car.

'Well, I've got your answer for you,' Griff said, scratching his head. 'I think you're right, but there's something I still don't understand. The brake fluid reservoir is fine and it's full; no problem, but there's very little fluid in the system.'

'How can that be?' asked Holland.

'Come here and I'll show you,' he said, leaning over into the engine compartment. 'Look at the pipe emerging from the reservoir, it's not the original pipe and it's certainly not meant for this car. There's been a crude attempt to try to blend it in with grease and dirt.'

'Could it have been fitted as a repair in the past?' asked Holland.

'Never – remember that this car hasn't been touched by anyone outside this garage. No one here would have carried out a repair as badly as that, but that's not all. When you pressed the brake pedal, there was little resistance, right? I'll tell you why, Michael. No pressure – no fluid in the system, just pockets of air.'

'What does that mean?'

'It means that someone's messed around with the brakes and tried sometime later to repair them so that on first glance, no one would notice. Someone's put the new pipe in afterwards and re-filled the reservoir, but the system hasn't been bled.'

'Wouldn't the police examiner have noticed that? You did.'

'Yes I did, Michael, but only because you pointed me in that direction.'

'Tell me, where was the car parked after you brought it in following the accident?'

'Inside the garage until the police examined it, then I brought it out here.'

'Did anything suspicious happen about then?'

'It's strange that you should ask me that; wait a moment.' Griff left Holland for the best part of a minute and returned having checked his facts. 'The night after I recovered the car, that would be two weeks ago today, we had a break-in here. There was nothing stolen, so I put it down to some of the village children. It happens once in a while. Might that be connected, do you think?'

'I think there's a good chance it was,' replied Holland. 'I'll bet a pound to a penny that someone's tampered with this car, then after the accident they've tried to hide whatever was done, in the hope that the police examiner wouldn't discover it.'

'And didn't bother to bleed the system, Michael, because they wouldn't have time or they thought no one would look that far,' added Griff, his eyes meeting Holland's as he said it.

'You've got it, Griff and I think you're right. Now, not a word to anyone about this, okay? It's not my intention to hide anything from the police or anyone else for that matter, but there's a lot at stake and the time's not right to release the information, not just yet.'

'You can count on me, Michael *bach*,' you can count on me.'

Michael Holland drove slowly back to Llanglanaber. There was no doubt about it now. Emily Parry's death was no accident. She had been murdered.

Chapter Twelve

The evening's fresh southwesterly wind brought a penetrating drizzle to the south-facing coast as Michael Holland left Llanglanaber, heading north. There were several matters he needed to discuss with Jeff Evans and he hoped it wasn't too soon to call upon him. He parked in a side street close to the village square in order to avoid the Stag being seen outside Jeff's home and he walked the remaining five hundred metres to the address Elen had given him.

Jeff Evans lived in a modest-looking property on the corner plot of an estate that seemed to be about twenty years old. The garden was immaculate, with springtime flora emerging at the front while at the side and rear, a vegetable plot had been turned over in readiness for warmer soil. Holland couldn't help but wonder where Jeff found the time to do it all. He pressed the doorbell, stepped back and waited. When the door opened, Jeff's immediate reaction didn't look particularly inviting, prompting a cautionary response from Holland.

'I'm sorry for calling without invitation, Jeff; if it's too early, we can always meet again.'

'No, it's not that,' he replied, sensing Holland's hesitation. 'It's just that work and home don't cross paths where I'm concerned, but in your case I suppose I'll have to make an exception.' He smiled, attempting to soften the remark. 'Come in,' he said and then he looked around cautiously, adding. 'Did anyone see you arrive?'

'No, I've parked well away. Here, I heard that you could do with a little medicine,' Holland said placing a bottle of whisky into Jeff's hand.

'Malt too,' Jeff remarked with obvious pleasure as he looked at the label. 'Just what the doctor ordered. Thanks Michael. Let's go through there,' he said, pointing along the hall towards the rear of the property.

While Holland was being ushered through, he noted a chair-lift fitted to the stairs and a hoist was also visible through a partly opened door leading to what he presumed was a lounge.

'Mind you don't trip over the wheelchair, there isn't much room here.'

'Your wife?' Holland asked, apprehensively.

'Jean? Yes. Multiple Sclerosis,' he replied, showing him through into a kitchen diner.

'I'm sorry.'

'So am I, believe me. That's the main reason why I don't mix work with my domestic circumstances – we're a little vulnerable, if you know what I mean. Drink?" he asked, gesturing with the bottle that was still in his hand.

'Just a beer if you have one, please. I've already consumed enough of that stuff to last me a lifetime, but don't let me stop you.'

They sat down facing each other across the table in a moment's silence. A great deal had happened to both of them since they parted company at the 'Grape Tree' Inn a few evenings previously and it was Holland who broke the ice.

'You getting over it?' he asked.

'Yes thanks, I'm still a bit stiff here and there, but another couple of days and I'll be right as rain.'

'Who did it?' There was no point in beating about the bush.

'I wish I knew, but one of them was wearing a Stetson, blue jeans and cowboy boots.'

'That doesn't surprise me,' replied Holland. 'Have you told anybody?'

'The hell I have!'

'You're beginning to sound like a cowboy yourself now!' They both laughed, then Holland continued. 'But seriously, that's not all our cowboy friend's been up to.'

Jeff looked at him, somewhat perplexed. Holland sipped his beer and then continued.

'He tried to sort me out too; and would have succeeded had it not been for a bit of good fortune. Let's just go over it together, shall we? See if we come up with some answers.'

'Go on.' Jeff stared back at him in tense concentration through eyes that were still partly closed and bruised.

'What do you see as the most significant factor prior to the attack on you?'

'That I was set up for it,' Jeff replied. 'There are two significant things. Rhys Morris, one of Beaumont's men saw us together with Elen when we left the pub, right?'

Holland nodded.

'You don't need to be a genius to guess what we were doing

together, right? Morris has to be one of the syndicate, Aber Properties, but what beats me is how quickly they got their act together. When I got back to the office later that night, there was a message in my tray asking me to meet with an informant who claimed that she had something to tell me about the murder. I went to the meeting place and that's when they jumped me. I've spoken to the informant since and she knows nothing about it.'

'That leaves two possibilities doesn't it? Holland said. 'Either someone phoned in claiming to be her, or...'

'Someone on the inside fitted me up, but I find that so difficult to believe, Michael. The message was apparently received by a policewoman called Harrison, but I haven't ventured to ask her about it yet.'

'Nevertheless it's obvious, isn't it, that whoever was behind the message knew the identity of your informant. Isn't that confidential?'

'Yes, highly confidential, it's known only to senior C.I.D. management. What's even more intriguing is that whoever it was also knew where I usually meet up with her.'

'And whoever it was, was also able to summon the 'cowboy',' suggested Holland.

'Quite resourceful isn't he? I've refused to believe it so far, but sooner or later, I'm going to have to face up to the fact that it must be someone on the inside.' Jeff shook his head slowly, not wanting to believe it.

'Any idea who?'

'Not for sure, but I had 'traffic' chasing after me with a breathalyser all over the place a few nights ago. Your mate Powell has been giving me all sorts of pressure recently and I've never got on well with the boss, Renton. There are all sorts of possibilities.'

'Do you remember anything about the others who attacked you, the ones with the 'cowboy'?'

'Only that they weren't local and that there were three of them. The 'cowboy' was the one giving instructions. He didn't take part himself, but there was something else about the other three that I can't quite put my finger on at the moment and it's something important. If only I could bring it to mind, maybe it's the bump on my head that's stopping me.' He paused. 'So what happened to you?'

Holland told him about his own experience; the failure of the 'Stag's' brakes – how it led to Griff's examination of Emily Parry's car and what he discovered.

'You know what this means, Michael, don't you? It isn't just that we're looking at another murder. Bearing in mind that Aber Properties has an interest in Hendre Fawr, the implication is that members of that organisation are implicated or might even be responsible – and they are all prominent people within the community.'

'Yes, by all accounts pillars of society. In addition, there may be an involvement on the part of someone inside the police force,' Holland added. 'Should we report it further up the line? I can make some official noises through the Welsh Assembly if you like. They could pass it on to The Home Office and then we'd see some fireworks.'

'No, well not yet anyway – we haven't got enough proof. Hang on. Let's just stand back a minute and look at it from another angle. Who is the only one involved in all of this that we haven't got a clue as to his identity?'

'The 'cowboy' character,' replied Holland.

'Precisely. In all probability brought in to intimidate Emily Parry – and by whom?'

'Aber Properties?'

'And he's someone capable of murdering Emily Parry and possibly making an attempt on both our lives.'

'Correct,' said Holland. 'But we haven't just got the one murder have we? There's two – the Murphy girl. We can't ignore the fact that we've got two murders within a stone's throw of each other, all within a couple of days.'

'Yes,' agreed Jeff. 'But they are two very different kinds of murder; one a professional hit for want of a better term and another that's sexually motivated. That doesn't add up, Michael. I have difficulty imagining a professional hit man also being a serial killer who's careless or rather brazen enough to leave his semen, his own identity, at various murder scenes over the past fifteen years.'

'That's always assuming that he is a professional killer,' suggested Holland. 'Are we in danger of forgetting the significance of the Ronson lighter? Medwyn Parry disappeared thirty years ago in the middle of a murder investigation. The 'cowboy' turns up here three months ago to intimidate Medwyn's mother, and he's in possession of Medwyn's lighter.' Holland paused to emphasise the fact. 'The 'cowboy' is roughly the same age as Medwyn would be now and perhaps we should consider the possibility that he has returned, having committed these other murders during his thirty-year absence from

Llanglanaber.'

'And maybe countless others,' Jeff knew there was a likelihood that Holland was right. 'What you mean is that we haven't got a professional killer, but a psychopath who would even kill his own mother? Okay, it's a plausible theory we can't afford to discard.'

'Taking it one step further, who do you reckon is the link between Aber Properties and the 'cowboy'?' asked Holland. 'Could it be Cecil Moorcroft, Economic Development or Rhys Morris, Planning perhaps? He's the one who saw us with Elen and it didn't take whoever it was long to get their act together.' Holland was fishing now.

'No way,' replied Jeff. 'They are men who take instructions, they don't give them and they're not ruthless enough either. We've got to go higher up the Aber Properties chain of command, but I think you know the answer to that question already, don't you, Michael?'

'Beaumont?' Holland had been leading the conversation in that direction, but both men were in tune with each other's thoughts.

'Now you're talking,' said Jeff, rolling a cigarette between his fingers.

'And who's he got inside the police force, Renton?' The implications were greater than ever.

'Like I said, I've never got on with Renton,' said Jeff. 'He and Beaumont are close all right, but Renton is a career man and I don't see him getting mixed-up in something like this. Besides, I remember pointing out to him that Emily Parry's car hadn't been examined immediately after the accident. I later discovered that Renton himself had arranged for it to be done. In my book, that doesn't fit in with someone who doesn't want the car examined.'

'Not unless he was arranging a delay so that whoever broke into Griff's garage could cover his tracks.'

Jeff Evans was silent for a minute before making a suggestion. 'Shall we watch Beaumont's home for a few nights, just to see what goes on; who knows what might turn up?'

'How do you propose to do that?'

'Just sit tight. Not in a hurry are you?'

'No.'

Jeff Evans left the room and Holland heard him speaking to someone on the telephone. After he had finished, Holland heard him going through into the lounge and he heard voices being raised. Then the lounge door was closed with a little more force than he would have expected. When he returned, Jeff Evans was visibly anxious, his mood clearly more edgy than it had been just moments before. Soon, the scent of her cigarette smoke filtered through to Michael Holland's nostrils, but this was different from the smell of Jeff's own tobacco. It had its own distinctive fragrance. Then, Michael understood the man's anxiety, and why Jeff Evans was reluctant to allow anyone connected with his work into his home.

'I've asked a friend of mine to come along,' said Jeff. 'But I'm not sure if it's a good idea right now.' His uneasiness was growing.

Holland ventured to interject. 'Jeff, listen to me.' He spoke solemnly and sincerely. 'I once had a sister who suffered from multiple sclerosis and I watched her too. I told her that I would welcome any opportunity to experience the pain on her behalf, but all she said was that she would never give it to me. Had I been able to help alleviate her pain in any way possible, then believe me, I would have done it.'

'I've asked Jean not to use it when there's someone else in the house. I mean, God, Michael, in my position I can't afford to get caught.'

Holland leaned in close, not only making a point of looking directly into Jeff's eyes as he did so, but making sure also that Jeff was looking back at him.

'I can understand that, Jeff, but trust me, please. It'll go no further.'

'I have to do it Michael. Ever since I first read about the possibility, I've just had to do it; it's as simple as that. You've got no idea how it helps her. She relaxes and she functions so much easier. She couldn't get her hands on any of it while I was in hospital. She ran out, and the effect was dramatic, but now she's ten times better again, the spasticity is reduced, depression and anxiety are lessened and so is the pain generally. There isn't a conventional drug to touch it and the ones that are used have a host of side effects – depression, and weight gain – that sort of thing. Using cannabis may be wrong in the eyes of the law, but as far as Jean and I are concerned, there's no alternative.'

'You don't have to convince me, Jeff. I've lost my own wife and I'd do anything to bring her back. All I can say is that you should continue to do as much as you can for her and for as long as you can.'

'I just wish I could do more, Michael, but I hate to watch her deteriorating. The only way I can cope is by being busy, which often means that I'm absent from the house. I just have to be elsewhere, however much the guilt of that hurts me in another way.'

'So come on, tell me, who's this mate you've got coming?' Holland changed the subject.

'His name's Esmor Owen, the local head water-bailiff – he's a bit of a character – you'll like him.' Jeff's tenor was already improving. 'He owes me a favour or two. I gave him a hand with some forensic evidence at the back end of last season when some poachers put lime in the river, destroying every living thing over half a mile of it. Now, any time I want to borrow image intensifiers or any other nighttime surveillance equipment, I just see him. It saves filling in all those ridiculous forms for the authority I would need from our lot.'

'You mean we can borrow his equipment?'

'No, he'll do better than that. Beaumont lives down by the river. Esmor and his boys have plenty of reason to be out there all night if they have to. It'll make a change for him to be watching someone other than poachers and he'll love it.'

Holland was intrigued. Suddenly, there was a knock on the back door and it opened without invitation.

'I could smell the beer from outside and I wondered where it came from,' said Esmor loudly. He was smiling broadly as he reached for a tankard from the shelf, exercising his familiarity with the kitchen.

Jeff introduced them and they shook hands firmly.

Esmor was a man in his late forties, not particularly tall, but strong, wiry looking, carrying not an ounce of fat. His dark hair parted on one side and flowed backwards in abundance with sideburns that reached the bottom of his protruding ears. Dominating a lean, weather-beaten face his eyes sparkled each side of a Roman nose, betraying a sense of humour and enthusiasm. His nicotine stained fingers searched the pockets of a well-worn waxed jacket, producing a packet of 'Woodbine'. He pulled one out, tapping both ends against the packet, more from habit than necessity. He placed a cigarette in his mouth, allowing it to dance between his lips as he chatted away.

'So, what have you got for me then?' he asked, inhaling deeply, then exhaling the smoke through his nose and mouth simultaneously.

They told him more than enough to hold his interest and sufficient to ensure that he exercised caution. Esmor didn't have a problem with that. He guessed that he hadn't been given the full picture, but he knew that whatever he hadn't been told wasn't necessary for the task in hand. When they had finished outlining what was required, Esmor spoke.

'If there's a chance it leads us to the buggers who put you in hospital, Jeff, I'll be more than happy to spend every night there for a week. As it happens, being around that part of the river doesn't present a problem at the moment. Aber Ceirw Angling Association put a couple of thousand stocked brown trout into the river not so long ago, two to two and a half pounders, real beauties, and we're getting complaints that someone's poaching them out already.'

'Just be careful,' said Holland. 'Beaumont's a powerful man and this 'cowboy' friend of his has already shown that he can be as evil as they come, and he's the man we're after – well, the one we're after first of all, anyway.'

'Don't you worry, Michael, I won't get caught. With the equipment I've got, I won't have to go anywhere near them to find out what's happening,' he said with a sparkle in his eye. 'And if he has a piss a hundred yards away in the dark, I'll be able to tell you whether or not he's circumcised – get a few pictures as well if you like!' Esmor grinned.

Holland knew what he meant, but in the circumstances decided not to seek a deeper understanding. 'Sounds good enough for me, and please, not a word to anyone except Jeff or myself.'

'You can count on it. Bloody good lager that Jeff, thanks mate. See you in a couple of days, or sooner, depending how it goes. Nice to have met you, Mike.' He stood, emptied his tankard, stroked his lips with the back of his hand and left.

'Like you said, Jeff, quite a character, I hope he's trustworthy,' he added.

'One hundred per cent; I'd stake my life on it.'

Holland believed him. 'Going back to this 'cowboy' chap and the possibility that it's Medwyn,' he said. 'How can we find out exactly what happened thirty years ago – in what way he was connected with the murder, I mean?'

'That's going to be difficult,' replied Jeff. All undetected murder enquiry files are kept alive, but my people looked for the papers relating to the Diane Smith murder last week and they can't be found. There should be boxes of them, but they seem to have disappeared.'

'What?' exclaimed Holland, attempting to fathom how significant their disappearance might be.

'Exactly. You can read into that what you like. They're always kept at Headquarters, but this force has amalgamated during that time and the storeroom has moved more than once. They could have got accidentally lost I suppose.'

'Any other suggestions?' Holland asked.

'There is one actually. I was going to do it myself this week, but now that I'm out of action, you can have a go yourself if you like.'

'Fire away,' said Holland, straightening himself up enthusiastically.

'We could try Raymond Rogers, the town's former Chief Inspector who's been retired twenty years or more by now. He's getting on a bit; in his late seventies, but he's bright as a button. I'll introduce you. Tell you what, I'll phone him now.'

Jeff Evans was away for a little longer this time.

'He took a bit of convincing, Michael, so you'll have to go softly with him. You probably know how uneasy the town is about this whole business. Mr. Rogers is taking it personal because there was a bit of criticism of the police over the Diane Smith murder and it's all coming back to him now. Is ten-thirty tomorrow morning okay with you?'

Mozart's Requiem seemed fitting music that evening as Holland contemplated the identity of the person or persons who had been responsible for two murders thirty years apart, and the demise of Emily Parry. He particularly enjoyed this version of the requiem, performed by 'La Grande Ecurie et la Chambre du Roy.' He'd opened a bottle of Australian red wine, which was a little too spicy for his liking, but it was a fine excuse for tasting what was left of a Roquefort cheese that had long since reached its maturity.

The plans provided by the Ministry Of Defence detailing the underground complex of caves and artificial tunnels between Hendre Fawr and the sea covered the lounge floor. The system of caverns was well documented and Holland was amazed how many there were. In addition to the main system there were dozens of smaller inlets that seemed to lead nowhere in particular. There was no doubt that they would take a great deal of careful searching. Holland couldn't understand why someone, presumably the 'cowboy', was still hanging around the Hendre Fawr entrance to the underground system. He wondered how familiar the 'cowboy' was with the place and whether he, Holland should concentrate his efforts on the former submarine base while Esmor kept watch on Beaumont's activities. He decided not to do so for the time being; it wasn't a priority when there was so much else that needed his attention. The caves would certainly merit a visit sooner rather than later and he decided to draw up a list of what he might need for the task.

Holland was five minutes late for his appointment with retired Chief Inspector Raymond Rogers. It brought a smile to his face when he saw the elderly gentleman purposefully looking at his watch as he opened the door. He looked well for his age. Holland guessed he had been a little taller in his prime, but still he stood almost as if to attention as he gazed down in a pompous fashion at Holland from the stepped entrance of his front door. He had a silver, tidily trimmed moustache matching his thinning hair, neatly brushed away from his forehead in a series of natural waves. He was dressed in a fawn cardigan over a check shirt, sporting what Holland guessed was a police tie of some significance or another. His brown, baggy corduroy trousers had once been quality garments, but were now too long for the old man's stature and fell clumsily over the top of his favourite brown brogues.

'Come in, Mr. Holland,' he called out in a military sort of fashion, extending his right hand as he did so. 'Ethel will make coffee for us in a moment, won't you my dear?' he continued in a voice loud enough for his wife to hear from somewhere in the background.

This man seems to be living in a past age, Holland thought to himself. 'Black please, no sugar,' he said, equally loud, following him into the lounge. There was no reply from elsewhere in the house.

Holland accepted the invitation to sit down and watched the retired gentlemen pacing up and down in front of him, hands held behind his back.

'Now then, Mr. Holland, I'm not entirely sure how it is that you're involved in this business. Murder is a matter for the police, is it not?' he asked, coughing in a manner that was not indicative of a cold.

'What murder are you referring to?' Holland asked in a way that was designed to bring him down a peg or two.

'Diane Smith, of course; why else would you want to see me?' He looked and sounded surprised.

'Well we could examine the possibility that Diane Smith's murder is connected with this latest killing, but my interest is related more to the anxiety that's been experienced recently by Mrs. Emily Parry's family. It seems that someone may have been visiting her, masquerading as her son, Medwyn. The police don't seem to be particularly interested in that theory and, on behalf of the late Mrs. Parry's family, I'd just like to ask your opinion.'

'The lack of interest by the police doesn't surprise me, Mr. Holland,' he said self-importantly. He cleared his throat again, unnecessarily. 'They're too busy staring into their computers these days, not getting about patrolling the streets as we did in my day. You never see a uniformed constable when you want one these days.'

'So tell me about Medwyn and Diane Smith,' insisted Holland.

Raymond Rogers coughed again, brought his right fist up to cover his mouth and paused a moment in thought. 'There was a dance on a Friday evening in the town hall. We usually had a constable somewhere in the vicinity in case there was a bit of fighting, as indeed there was now and again. Several youngsters had seen Diane in Peter's... I mean Medwyn's, company on and off during the evening. He looked as though he fancied his chances with the lass, if you ask me, and later, the same constable saw them leaving together.'

'What, just the two of them?' Holland asked.

'There may have been others with them, Mr. Holland, I can't be precise after all this time, but Medwyn Parry was definitely there. Diane didn't return home that night and her body was found under the bridge the following morning. She'd been raped and murdered – strangled with her own neck scarf in fact. Medwyn's cap was found at the scene, Mr. Holland, in her right hand.'

'How did you know it was his?'

'Simple, his name was inside it and it was identified by his mother, Emily Parry.'

'Was there any forensic evidence?' Holland asked.

'I expect there was, I can't be certain at this stage exactly what, but we never found anyone to compare it with, did we?'

'So what do you think happened to Medwyn?'

'He disappeared off the face of the earth. We looked for him everywhere. There were several supposed sightings of him up and down the country, but they never came to anything significant.'

'Could he have been hiding closer to home?' Holland paused. 'In the cave complex between the farm and the sea perhaps?'

'There was no evidence of that, on the contrary most people

believed that he just left the area to evade the consequences.'

'Was he capable of that, Mr. Rogers?' asked Holland. 'Did he have the mental capacity to run away and survive on his own?'

'I don't have the medical qualifications to answer your question, Mr. Holland.' Rogers was being defensive.

'Was he capable of murder, do you think, or was he just a mildly retarded gentle young giant incapable of hurting a fly?' Holland paused. 'I'm simply posing the question, no more.'

'The whole town was divided on that very issue; the whole community was split for months, years even. A very nasty business it was too. There were strong feelings on both sides. I can feel it out there, even today. It's surfaced again following this latest killing. Some of the townsfolk believe he's back, some think he's dead and others believe he didn't do it in the first place. Everyone's talking about it.'

'Into which category do you fit, Mr. Rogers?'

'I don't have to fit into any category do I, Mr. Holland? What we had to do back then was to conduct an enquiry, examine the facts as thoroughly and as impartially as possible.'

This was Holland's opening. 'Just the same as the police are doing all over again now, I suppose.'

'Huh! I often wonder if they know what they're doing these days. They're too busy trying to bring everyone into the policing arena. Are you familiar with what's been happening around here over the last few years? It's difficult to know who's running the show. You'd think Mr. 'high and mighty' David Beaumont was the Chief Constable and that 'sidekick' Renton was his deputy.'

Rogers had taken Holland's bait and now it was important to give him some freedom with it.

'I'm not with you,' Holland lied.

'Renton's letting him poke his nose into every aspect of policing and Beaumont is manipulating the whole of this community, getting rich in the process just like his father before him. He was a right little tearaway in his youth; spoilt little brat on the periphery of every bit of trouble that was going.' Rogers's shoulders shook at the horror of the thought. 'Then, he left to go to college, made his name and some money – by dubious means no doubt, and then came back to Llanglanaber twenty years ago. Since then, he's been slowly taking over the whole town.'

'Would he have known Medwyn Parry?' asked Holland.

'Yes, of course he would, but I can't say how well. Beaumont was a born leader; even in his youth he was the leader of the town's young gang of lads. He could always find use for anyone if it suited him, but Peter, I mean Medwyn, it's unlikely that David Beaumont would have chosen him for company.'

'Just as a possibility, Mr. Rogers, could Beaumont have found Medwyn Parry and brought him back here to Llanglanaber to intimidate his own mother?'

'Assuming that it was to Beaumont's advantage, anything is possible.'

At least Holland had established that Beaumont had known Medwyn Parry, but that in itself confirmed very little. Perhaps it opened the door to more questions as opposed to providing any answers.

Holland considered there was no point in prolonging the meeting with Raymond Rogers. He was convinced that he had learnt about as much as the retired Chief Inspector had to offer. The coffee hadn't materialised – perhaps his wife had something else on her mind.

Moments later, Holland thanked him and left.

Chapter Thirteen

On the following Wednesday Jeff Evans was able to move about comparatively free of pain, though his bruised face still told the tale of his harrowing encounter. Shortly after nine-fifteen that evening, he parked his car in a town centre car park and walked a few streets towards the police station. He slipped unseen around to the rear car park and used his plastic pass card to gain entry through the back door. He had walked this way many times in the past, but on this occasion the circumstances were different. He could trust no one and didn't want to be seen. Head bowed, he passed the security camera, attempting to act as normal as possible, hoping that whoever was manning the front desk was otherwise engaged. He tiptoed silently upstairs, making his way to the part of the building that was used entirely for the major incident investigation. The long second floor corridor was well lit as usual. He stopped and listened, but heard no sound coming from the semi-darkness of the incident room itself. The door was ajar, and as he pushed it further open he was pleased to see that there was no one inside. The light from the corridor shone through the frosted glass of the upper part of the partitioning wall, making it unnecessary to turn the lights on inside the room. A dozen monitors and keyboards stood on several purpose-made computer stations with papers lying untidily next to most of them. He walked to his own desk and found it much the same as he had left it four nights earlier. He pulled the crumpled message sheet out of his jacket pocket – the one he had found on his desk indicating that 'Midnight Mary' had wanted to see him. He sat there for a moment in quiet contemplation that was disturbed only by the humming sound of the only computer terminal that had been left on. He moved over to that computer station and tapped away at the keyboard. 'Naughty, naughty!' Jeff said to himself, finding that the user hadn't logged off the machine, inadvertently allowing him access without having to use his own password. Unauthorised access was what he wanted right now – the kind that couldn't be traced back to him. He searched the database for a message timed at twenty-one fifty the previous Saturday from 'Midnight Mary', but to his surprise, it didn't exist.

There was no such message. Jeff wasn't particularly computer literate, but he knew enough to realise that H.O.L.M.E.S. computer-raised messages generated their own consecutive numbers. The database showed that there was no break in sequence and once more he looked at his own copy to check its number, which was eleven hundred and forty seven. He brought that message up on the screen and found that it was also timed at twenty-one fifty hours on Saturday and also recorded by W.D.C. Harrison, but that it related to a completely different matter. There was no doubt that the computer's printer had produced the fictitious copy left in his tray. It must have been typed and printed, then deleted without having been saved on the database. It was the only way it could have been accomplished, but these findings concerned Jeff all the more. Someone with intimate knowledge of H.O.L.M.E.S had done it. More important, it was someone from within the service and someone who knew that 'Midnight Mary' was his registered informant.

As he considered the significance of this discovery, he heard footsteps coming up the stairs. He quickly exited the page he had been viewing, but there was no time to shut down the computer. The footsteps came closer and with seconds only to spare, Jeff Evans slid behind a filing cabinet before the door to the room was opened wide. It was Renton. Of all people, he was the one he least wanted to see. Jeff held his breath, searching his mind frantically for a reason to be there, realising that any excuse would be worthless now that he was hiding in the semi darkness. Without daring to look, he heard Renton's footsteps walking over to the computer terminal he had been using moments earlier. Heart racing, he listened while Renton closed down the machine and turned it off. 'Whoever had left it logged on would feel his wrath in the morning,' he thought. Then, Renton left the room, making for his own office two doors further down the corridor. Jeff breathed a sigh of relief and was more grateful still when he realised that the door to the room had been left ajar. He tiptoed towards it and stayed there a few moments while Renton settled down to whatever he was about to do. He heard him pulling at the chair from behind his desk and then he heard his mobile ring. Jeff listened to Renton's side of the conversation.

'Yes, it's all right; we can talk.'

There was silence as Renton listened for a few moments.

'Happy or not, David, we've already discussed this haven't we and I thought we both agreed that you don't have a choice in the matter, remember?'

Jeff assumed it was Beaumont and suddenly he was intrigued.

'But I've explained that there's nothing I can do about it. What's the big deal anyway? What have you got against it?'

Following a short period of silence, Renton continued.

'Yes, I know that we've all got a great deal to lose, every one of us, but I've told you that in the circumstances, the best way by far to deal with this is to make a big show tomorrow. That way, everyone will see you at the forefront of the community, supporting the police in a major investigation. No-one is likely to connect you with the Hendre Fawr business just because of that, and after tomorrow, you can drift back into relative obscurity.'

Jeff knew it was unusual for Beaumont to be obscure or to purposely distance himself from any aspect connected with the area's policing, but in the present circumstances it made sense, confirming Holland's belief that he and Aber Properties were intending to acquire the farm. However difficult it was to evaluate this one-sided conversation, it was providing the best indication yet that both Renton and Beaumont were collaborating in one way or another and that the farm was connected.

'No, there isn't a way round it.' Renton answered another question. 'If you don't volunteer to provide D.N.A. tomorrow, you will be asked to provide it by virtue of the fact that you featured in the Halifax enquiry. I can't keep you out of it, David. It's impossible. If the right hand doesn't get you, the left one will. It's that kind of scenario; surely you can understand?'

Jeff was astounded as he listened. Waiting for more, he felt his heart pounding beneath his shirt. There was a longer pause before Renton spoke again.

'You're asking me to do what? You must be joking. My career would be over if anyone found that out.'

There was another pause before he continued in a voice that was unaccustomedly shaken.

'Do as I'm told? Don't threaten me, David.'

There was another pause.

'Yes, I'm well aware of what I've done for you in the past, but the past is behind us and you settled that score – very handsomely, but it was my understanding that we were quits.'

Jeff could hear Renton breathing harder as he listened. As he heard him getting up from his chair, striding about the room, Jeff became concerned that his own presence might be detected.

'You're putting me in a very difficult position, David.'

He listened again.

'It seems that neither of us has a choice. So what happens if I don't?'

Renton was sounding increasingly vulnerable.

'I never expected this from you, David. You of all people,' he continued. 'Business? Business indeed: sounds more like another threat if you ask me. Yes, I'll do it, though I don't understand your motive. You were playing golf with me when the Murphy girl was murdered – remember? The D.N.A. on her body matches the D.N.A. from the Halifax murder, so it's obvious that the same person is responsible for both their deaths. I don't understand your concern about it. I just can't fathom your reasoning.'

Beaumont connected in some way with the Halifax murder? This was another revelation to Jeff Evans. He listened harder, trying to catch as much meaning as possible, attempting to interpret the full conversation.

Renton continued. 'Trust you? How can I trust someone who's holding a gun to my head?'

He paused yet again as he listened.

'All over? The sooner the better, David, believe me. Yes, I certainly hope so. I'll see you in the morning.'

Jeff Evans heard Renton's sigh of desperation as he fell back heavily into the chair.

Taking this opportunity to leave, Jeff made his way down the corridor as quietly as possible, remembering that the soles of his boots were making the same noise against the tiled flooring as had warned him of Renton's approach just a few minutes earlier. When he was half way down the long corridor, he heard Renton's chair being moved again and he realised that he'd been heard. He looked towards the door at the end of the straight corridor and tried to judge whether or not he could make it to the other side of it before Renton reached the door to his own office. It could have gone either way, but there was no room for error. The damaging content of the conversation he had over-heard meant that he couldn't risk Renton knowing or even suspecting that he'd listened to it. He was only half way down the corridor and guessing that Renton would be almost at his door, he realised that there was only one thing for it. Jeff turned round quickly and with relief, he found that Renton wasn't within sight. Walking briskly in the direction from which he had come, Jeff had only taken three strides before Renton's head appeared.

'What are you doing here?' he asked, his voice still shaken and sounding unsure.

'Just passing, I saw the light on in your office and thought I'd come in for a chat. You know how difficult it is for me to keep my nose to myself.' Jeff was still striding towards him, hoping that the whole act looked and sounded convincing.

'Well in that case you'd better come in, hadn't you.' Renton still regarded his presence with some suspicion.

He sat behind his desk again and in an unnecessarily nervous manner, his hand felt for the mobile phone. He switched it off and placed it into a drawer. His action spoke volumes, thought Jeff.

'I just wondered how the enquiry was coming along.' Jeff tried to sound casual, but genuine.

'Well, Marino's withdrawn his confession,' Renton started to flow before Jeff interrupted him.

'I don't mean Donna's murder. I mean the attempted murder on myself.' It took Renton by surprise.

'We're not treating it that seriously. You've been bruised a little here and there and now you're up and about again. I've put a couple of men on it, but there aren't any leads as yet. You know what a strain this murder enquiry is putting on manpower. How are you recovering anyway?'

'Well I'm grateful for your concern, boss,' he said sarcastically. 'I'm a hell of a lot better than I was a couple of days ago, but one thing's for sure, I'd be lying in a mortuary right now if I hadn't got my boot into the knifeman first.' He wanted to let Renton know exactly how serious he was taking it.

'So who do you think they were and what was their motive?' Renton wanted to know what he was thinking, whilst paying little regard to the extent of Jeff's injuries. Jeff realised that little effort was being made to find those responsible.

'Obviously someone I've crossed in the past,' he replied, pausing for a moment, then adding. 'Or someone who believes I can damage their plans, now or in the future.' He was looking intensely into Renton's eyes, but they showed no obvious signs that might have reflected his thoughts, one way or the other.

'Such as?' he asked. Renton began fidgeting nervously with a pencil in his favoured left hand.

'No idea, but one thing's for sure, I'll find them, even if it takes the remainder of my service and beyond. Not just the ones who did it, but whoever put them up to it as well,' he paused again, still staring. 'Know what I mean,' he paused. 'Boss?' he added, knowing Renton's dislike of that title.

'What makes you think someone put them up to it?' asked Renton, for once ignoring Jeff's arrogance. His breathing was more shallow and quicker now.

'They weren't from town; I'd have known them if they had been. They knew what they were doing and they enjoyed it. It was a job of work for somebody; I'm convinced of it.'

'What were you doing there in the first place?'

'Someone who said she was 'Midnight Mary' 'phoned in. She said she wanted to see me – had some information about the Murphy girl's murder. It wasn't Mary; they were there waiting for me,' Jeff replied, waiting to see whether Renton would ask the next obvious question – how did he get the message to meet Mary. In the event, the question wasn't asked and that, to Jeff, was the most significant pointer of all. He wondered whether he was staring into the eyes of the man who had sent him to his intended death.

'The first thing you must do is get better, and then you can get back to the sharp end, Jeff. Don't hurry back. Make sure you take a couple of weeks off. There's enough of us here to keep the enquiry moving.'

'Yeah, sure,' Jeff replied, knowing that the brief encounter had been a conversation dominated by mistrust, though neither side could see the other person's full playing hand. Still, the main purpose had been achieved, which was to minimise Renton's suspicion that Jeff might have been present long enough to have heard his conversation with Beaumont.

Driving home, Jeff wondered to what extent Renton was implicated and in what exactly he was involved. He found it difficult to believe that he could have been responsible for sending him to the beating, but that possibility was looking increasingly likely now. He wondered where Powell fitted into the equation. What was the true nature of Renton's relationship with Beaumont and what was Beaumont's involvement with the 'cowboy', if any? Even that was no more than speculation and probably Esmor, his water-bailiff friend was still the best hope of finding any such connection. More to the point perhaps, was what it might be that Beaumont feared in relation to the Halifax or the Llanglanaber murders and what was Renton likely to do so reluctantly for him on the following morning? Why was it that Beaumont was apparently unwilling to provide a D.N.A. sample? It seemed that whatever concerned Beaumont about the murder of Donna Marie Murphy applied equally to the Halifax murder and, by implication, each of the other murders connected by D.N.A.

Later that evening, having been home for no more than ten minutes, Acting Superintendent Alex Renton emptied his heavy tumbler for the second time and poured himself a third large whisky. Sitting in an armchair he began reading through the latest batch of statements recorded in connection with Donna Murphy's murder. It wasn't long before the alcohol flowed through his veins, making concentration difficult. As his glazed eyes wandered away from the papers his mind began reflecting uneasily on his earlier meeting with Jeff Evans, a man for whom he would normally have had a great deal of time and respect. But the situation in which he now found himself wasn't normal. Inwardly, he recognised it hadn't been normal for years. Not that he'd been too concerned when everything was going well, but even in the early days he knew that what he was getting into was wrong. Wrong? He asked himself in disbelief – it was much more than that. He realised that he'd got himself into a position where he was completely out of his depth and now he was drowning. If only he had been able to see it coming, but the situation in which he found himself had grown like some hidden disease, becoming apparent only when it was too late! He recalled how pure his intentions were when he began his career. The neat golden liquor burned his gullet as he swallowed and poured again from the bottle. The alcohol was beginning to depress him, but even in his despair he recognised that it wasn't just a desire for wealth that had destroyed his youthful vision, it was also his uncontrollable greed for status – his need to move in the right circles.

Early in his career it had been predicted by some that he would reach chief officer rank. His academic achievements had been recognised, as had his performance on the streets where he always considered that it really mattered. His law degree had served to place him in contention for rapid promotion and he had excelled at the Police College.

Then, six years ago, he had met David Beaumont, and how he wished that he could change much of what had happened since! Somehow, the world looked different from the inside of Beaumont's pocket. It had been quite innocuous at first. A chance round of golf to make up a foursome and drinks at the bar afterwards had led to a number of dinner parties hosted by Beaumont. Later, Beaumont found Renton's wife an excellent job at the council offices. Even though she was less qualified than some of the other applicants, Beaumont's contacts on the interviewing panel had ensured that none of the others stood a chance of being appointed. Neither Renton nor his wife had realised it at first, but Beaumont wasted little time in letting it be known, once it favoured him to do so.

Then came Renton's planning application for the erection of a bungalow, outside of the town, in a designated area of outstanding natural beauty, well beyond the recognised settlement area. The application had sailed through what was normally a tedious process, the planning committee ignoring that it was in complete contravention of their well-established policy. Beaumont had been the chairman of that committee and Renton recognised that he was indebted to him.

Even then, Renton would have been prepared to argue that he had done nothing wrong, but three months later the re-payment of the debt was called upon. Beaumont had been involved in a minor car accident, following which a breath test had shown that he was marginally over the limit – a borderline case where a blood sample was required for definitive purposes. Beaumont's blood sample had disappeared from the police station prior to being sent for examination. There was an internal enquiry, but who would have suspected that the person responsible for its disappearance was the senior officer leading that investigation? Beaumont had shown his gratitude in generous terms – a holiday for four in the Seychelles, which their wives had enjoyed enormously. From the moment the blood sample had disappeared, Renton recognised that he was well and truly under Beaumont's influence. He had committed an act that was to the detriment of his office and an affront to his own self-respect.

He sipped from the glass again as his thoughts drifted towards the benefits their relationship had produced. He had accepted membership of Aber Properties and over the past three or four years, as a member of that syndicate, he had become the joint owner of several houses. These joint acquisitions had provided a useful second income and as they acquired more properties, his personal wealth increased considerably, an income far in excess of that which the police service could provide. Renton had closed his eyes to the grants that had become available from whatever quarter in order to upgrade those properties and the last thing he wanted to consider was the creative accountancy used to support each application. There had been some rumbles heard and public innuendo voiced in that respect, but he had used his influence to thwart any possibility of an investigation. It was just as well that no one knew he was a member of Aber Properties, but now, bearing in mind all that had taken place during the past two weeks, his secret was in danger of becoming common knowledge. Beaumont was right; each member of Aber Properties had a great deal to lose.

He stared again at the empty glass lying in his lap, as he recalled that he had known about Aber Properties' interest in Hendre Fawr for the best part of twelve months. He had attended a syndicate meeting during which the matter was first explored, and later when Emily Parry's refusal to sell the place was discussed. Those present on that occasion had smiled knowingly when Beaumont suggested that 'the stubborn old lady needed some gentle encouragement that might help persuade her to sell' and that he, Beaumont, had the very man to do it. How Renton regretted being a party to that discussion! He hadn't a clue what Beaumont was up to! He preferred not to know, but he was perfectly happy to reap any benefits resulting from the acquisition of the farm as long as he could not be connected with any pressure brought to bear against Mrs. Parry. That decision had since returned to haunt him and the extent of Beaumont's antics had been made known to him publicly, meticulously recorded by Jeff Evans in a statement taken from Elen Thomas. They hadn't foreseen that Elen Thomas would bring in Michael Holland, who could still pose a danger. He doubted that even the day he had spent in custody had deterred him and neither would his experience of driving his car without brakes. Holland was a capable adversary and the fact that he was still out there, exploring Emily Parry's misfortune was discomforting to say the least. It was as if the cards were stacking up against them. He wondered how long it would be before Beaumont acted again to safeguard their interests and what would be the extent of his malicious trickery next time?

When Beaumont told him to have the examination of Emily Parry's car delayed overnight, Renton recognised that he was too deeply involved to argue. In suppressing what had obviously been some kind of tampering with the car, he recognised that he had become a party to the old lady's murder – even though he had not known about it beforehand. It hadn't been difficult to steer Jeff Evans's interest away from what had taken place at Hendre Fawr, but by coincidence, Donna Marie Murphy had been killed close to the property and Jeff had quite justifiably brought Beaumont's facilitator, the so-called 'cowboy', into the frame. However much he had tried to guide the investigation towards the stepfather, Tony Marino, in the desperate hope that he had been responsible, he couldn't ignore the increasingly strong possibility that this 'cowboy' character might have murdered the girl. Whether or not that was the case, he had to be eliminated from the enquiry, but doing so was likely to expose 'the cowboy's' connection with the farm and that he was acting on behalf of Aber Properties. In that case, there would be a full investigation into the activities of Aber Properties' and everything would be lost. In reality, that was now the least of Renton's worries.

His thoughts turned to Jeff Evans and the way he had looked searchingly into his eyes a couple of hours earlier. If only he'd listened and kept out of the way! He tried to convince himself that he had meant Jeff no harm. Beaumont had decided that Jeff needed a lesson that would 'help to deter his enthusiasm'. Renton knew from experience that he should have known better. The most he wanted was to create his temporary absence, but the attack had indeed been an attempt on Jeff's life.

Even in his intoxicated state, Renton could see how easily and cleverly he had been brought under Beaumont's influence and how difficult or rather impossible it would be to escape. He was leading one of the largest murder enquiries the area had seen and his hands were tied to the extent that he had nowhere to go. All paths open to him led to his own destruction. Was there a career, a life, or anything to safeguard any more? Who was Beaumont's facilitating 'cowboy'? Was it Medwyn Parry, the man suspected of the thirty-year old murder of Diane Smith and what was behind Beaumont's reluctance to provide a D.N.A. sample?

It was almost three in the morning when he woke up, still in the armchair, his joints stiffened by a posture he had not intended. He half crawled, half stumbled to his bed, dreading the thought of what the next day might bring.

A number of local and national media people gathered at Llanglanaber police station in readiness for the press conference at ten o'clock that morning. Several boys from Donna's school were present, many of whom were police officers' sons. Gary 'the bomber' Pugh was clearly enjoying every minute of it; a welcome contrast to the lack of personal limelight that followed the end of his boxing career! The actor, Bleddyn ap Harri was taking matters a little more in keeping with the nature of the event, while Councillor David Beaumont was unusually reserved. He tried several times amid the pre-conference mayhem to attract Renton's attention. The dreadful thought occurred that Renton was trying to ignore him, but as it was about to begin, he breathed a sigh of relief when their eyes met. In addition to the slight nod of Renton's head, Beaumont noted a comforting half wink that no one else would have detected. It told him everything he wanted to know.

Beaumont hadn't expected what happened next. It unsettled him, but only Renton noticed. The team assigned to Donna's family entered the room with Claire Marino, the victim's mother. Beaumont looked nervously at Renton as she was escorted to the seat next to him behind a table on which stood a number of microphones. Renton's face was without emotion as he began to speak and, after thanking those attending and a brief introduction, he introduced Claire Marino, who made the kind of emotional appeal expected of a grieving mother. It was clear that Beaumont was getting more uncomfortable, but the worst was yet to come. Claire Marino, however distressed, wasn't slow in coming forward, and without warning, she began adlibbing. To everyone's surprise, she connected the murder of her daughter to that of her sister thirty years previously, adding a plea that Medwyn Parry, 'the boy they called Peter – the one everyone was referring to as the 'cowboy'' give himself up to the police. It threw the conference into chaos and Renton had difficulty making a convincing statement in answer to the many questions from the press. He insisted that although this possibility could not be disregarded, it was not a major line of enquiry.

Beaumont listened as he fiddled nervously with a copy of the conference agenda in front of him, hoping that the subject of Hendre Fawr would not emerge. In the event it didn't, but he knew that much of the potential damage he feared was likely to surface sooner or later and there was little he could do about it. He was disturbed by the way the conference was going. He simply couldn't afford to be connected with the farm or 'the cowboy'.

It was another twenty minutes before those attending were led into a hall elsewhere in the building. There, a number of uniformed police officers prepared to take D.N.A. samples from Beaumont, Gary Pugh, Bleddyn ap Harri and the schoolboys. The procedure was televised and photographed for the benefit of local and national media. Each person's mouth-swab saliva sample was sealed and placed into a refrigerator, whilst their details were logged onto a database prior to sending the samples to the laboratory. Acting Superintendent Renton then appealed for equal co-operation from all members of the community who would be asked to provide similar samples in the coming days. The appeal was endorsed by Councillor David Beaumont, Bleddyn ap Harri and the shadowboxing Gary 'the bomber' Pugh.

Jeff Evans was well aware of the procedures adopted when taking samples for examination from Llanglanaber to the Home Office Forensic Science Laboratory at Chorley. Alex Renton's media show had made interesting watching on lunchtime television news. He had particularly enjoyed the reference to Diane Smith's murder and Renton's unsuccessful attempt to deflect the issue. The telephone conversation he had overheard the previous evening had left him in no doubt that he should establish whether or not Beaumont's D.N.A. was included with the others on the 'forensic run' that day. He knew the civilian driver responsible for transporting the samples to the laboratory well and there was no difficulty when they met at the back of another police station some fifty miles up the road where other materials for examination would be collected for the remainder of the journey.

'How are you doing, Jeff? I heard that you'd had a bit of a hiding.'

'Not bad, Tom, thanks. That was last week; can't keep a good man down, eh? Listen, I'm glad I caught you. I have to check on some of those samples you took from Llanglanaber earlier. There may be a bit of a problem with the log. Just let me have a look will you? I won't keep you a moment.'

'No problem,' he replied. 'I'm ahead of schedule today.'

Jeff searched the container from Llanglanaber. According to the printed copy of the database enclosed, there were twenty-seven D.N.A. samples submitted in connection with the Donna Murphy murder enquiry. David Beaumont's name wasn't on that list. Nonetheless, he searched through each of the samples and without difficulty; he found those provided by Gary Pugh and Blethyn ap Harri. The schoolboys had provided the remaining samples, but there was nothing from Beaumont.

'Thanks for your help, Tom. There's no problem, it's all fine.'

'Keep your guard up next time, Jeff!' he shouted as he drove off.

Chapter Fourteen

Jeff Evans was anxious to get back to Llanglanaber to share his thoughts with Michael Holland. He also recognised that he was getting close to the position where he would feel morally obliged to report his findings at senior level in the force – somewhere above Renton's head and beyond his influence. He had enough evidence to do so now, but he wasn't sure what the consequences might be. Renton was highly regarded by chief officers, but if his story was accepted, Renton would be suspended immediately, Beaumont would be rattled and the 'cowboy' might disappear. That was the last thing Jeff wanted. He telephoned Holland and arranged a meeting later that evening.

By the time Jeff got home, he discovered that Esmor had been trying to contact him throughout the day. Jeff 'phoned him and found that Esmor was excited. Watching Beaumont's home the previous evening and into the night had produced some useful information and he couldn't wait to tell him.

Holland arrived first and it didn't take long for Jeff to explain all that had taken place since they last met. They both agreed that their priority should be to identify the 'cowboy' before reporting the matter to someone at Headquarters. There was a sudden knock on the kitchen door, which opened almost immediately. Esmor's weather-beaten face peered around the doorframe, his eyes sparkling enthusiastically as usual.

'Come in and grab yourself a beer,' said Jeff, pulling up a chair for him.

Esmor took his coat off first, which was unusual for him.

'He thinks he's staying the night,' joked Jeff.

'You might well be asking me to stay for supper when you hear what I've got for you,' replied Esmor, hanging his waxed jacket on a coat hook behind the back door. 'But lager will do fine for starters,' he continued, opening the fridge door. 'You ready for another, Mike?'

'Why not?' replied Holland, looking at his empty glass.

'Bloody fellow's taking over my house now! Make that three, why don't you?' added Jeff, laughing.

Esmor complied, handing a can to each of them and lighting a 'Woodbine' before sitting down.

'Well boys,' he started. 'You're going to like this. I went round to Beaumont's house on Tuesday night, after I left you two. I waited until it was dark and then I had a good look around, just to get the feel of the place. There wasn't much doing, couldn't even say if he was in or not, but the lights were on. Then I went back last night and that's when the trump cards came up,' he smiled, swallowing a mouthful as he did so.

Holland shuffled his feet, somewhat frustrated at the pace of the delivery. He took a sip of his beer in an attempt to hide it.

Jeff didn't feel the need to be quite so polite. 'Come on, Esmor, get on with it,' he said, knowing how his friend always enjoyed stretching out any yarn he'd ever told.

'There was a meeting there last night; there were three cars there when I got to his house at nine o'clock,' he continued at last. 'They came out at ten to ten, four of them, Rhys Morris, Colin Moorcroft, Edwin James, the solicitor, and Dobson, the accountant. A fifth, Charles Atkins, the banker, appeared ten minutes later; Beaumont came out with him and saw him to his car.'

'You know what that means, don't you, Michael?' asked Jeff.

'I think I'm with you," he replied. 'Do you mean that they were all present when you overheard the telephone conversation on Renton's mobile?'

'Either they were there, or the call was made immediately after they left. Interesting isn't it?' The implications continued to unfold as Esmor resumed.

'I thought you'd like that, but there's more. David Beaumont went back inside the house and the whole place fell into darkness. I decided to stay for a bit and it paid off. About ten minutes later, Beaumont left the house by the back door, in darkness. It's a bloody good job I didn't miss him. He left on foot, went down the drive, crossed the road and took that path down towards the river. You know the one I mean, don't you, Jeff?'

'Yes. Did you follow him?' asked Jeff anxiously.

'Of course I did, but I thought I'd blown it, I'll tell you. Fortunately I could see his torchlight in the woods ahead of me. He wouldn't make a poacher, that's for sure. Then, the light went out and I couldn't see him, even with the night sights. The vegetation was too thick, so I picked up the pace to try and catch up with him. That's when I heard someone coming up behind me; it was just by the fishing hut that's on the bank there in a bit of a clearing. God, I panicked for a second because I hadn't heard him coming! Then Beaumont's light came on again and only a few yards in front of me, but only for a moment or two. I jumped into the trees for cover and I saw both of them go into the hut; right next to me they were.' He paused, swallowing some more of the lager.

'Who was the other fellow?' asked Jeff. "Did you see what he looked like?'

'I've got no idea who he was,' he replied. 'It wasn't easy to make him out, even though we're not far off a full moon just now, but I can tell you that he was a hell of a big man, broad shoulders and wearing a cowboy hat.' He paused again. 'I thought you'd like that too.'

'Were you close enough to hear what was said?' asked Holland.

'I tried, Mike, but it wasn't easy. In that sort of environment, even the sound of the river can distort a conversation and I couldn't risk getting too close. One thing I do know is that Beaumont was angry about something that this other chap had either done or hadn't done and he kept saying that he wanted him to get something back to him at any cost and that he didn't care how he did it. Does that make sense?'

Both Jeff Evans and Michael Holland looked at each other, shaking their heads. Jeff got Esmor another lager from the fridge. He gave it to him and watched him pour out the golden fluid into a smooth white head as he continued his account.

'They weren't together long. It sounded as if Beaumont was giving him instructions. He was definitely the boss; you could tell that. Beaumont left and I stayed with the other one. Now he's more of the poacher type – knows his way about in the dark. He moved quickly and I followed him for about half a mile to the lay-by near the junction with the old Roman road. Know where I mean? His car was parked there. I think it was an old Jaguar, but I couldn't be sure from a distance.'

'That's a shame,' said Jeff.

'Not so quick, boy "*bach*",' he continued, his grin betraying that there was still more to come. 'Don't be hasty.' Esmor took another sip.

Holland was beginning to learn that patience was indeed a virtue in this man's company.

'Remember I said that we were having a problem with poachers in that area?'

Jeff nodded, indicating that he remembered.

'One of my lads, Trefor, was out on the river a few nights ago. He saw the same character that night, talking to three 'gyppos' who are camping up the road. I think they're a bunch of itinerant antique dealers on the knock in the area. There are a couple of dozen caravans there. We think they're the ones poaching the river, but we haven't caught them yet. Anyway, they left with him in two cars. Here's the Jaguar's number,' he said, passing a piece of folded paper. 'The number of the pickup belonging to the tinkers is there as well.'

'Any more?' asked Jeff. Holland noted that his interest was increasing by the minute and he had a good idea why.

'You're getting greedy now, Jeff Evans, aren't you? Esmor smiled. 'Well yes, there is actually. Trefor stayed on the river until past midnight. Only one vehicle returned. It was the pickup and there was bloody pandemonium there then, women screaming and men shouting. God knows what was up, but Trefor left in a hurry.'

'I think I do,' said Jeff. 'What night was this?'

'Last Saturday, early Sunday morning,' he replied.

'The night they tried to sort you out,' added Holland.

'Yes, that's right,' said Jeff, pensively. 'Do you remember, I said that there was something about my assailants that I couldn't put my finger on? Well it's just come to me. It was the smell about them that I couldn't bring to mind, but I knew there was something. Anyone who's ever had to deal with itinerants like these will know what I mean. It's a kind of unwashed odour that's mixed with the smell of smoke from an open fire for months or years and it lingers on their clothing. It's unmistakable and that's what I remember.'

'Turning back to this cowboy character,' said Holland. 'I believe that for some reason or another, he may be going back to Hendre Fawr now and again.'

'Why do you think that?' asked Jeff.

Holland told him the reason.

'If it is him, why do you think he goes back there?' asked Jeff.

'I don't know, but I'd like to have a look round inside and I've got the plans if you fancy coming along. Are you fit enough for a trip down there yet, Jeff? I've got no idea what we'll find, but we'll need to be well prepared. Strong footwear, ropes, good lighting gear, bolt cutters, that sort of thing and it might take some time, judging by its size and number of tunnels.'

'I've got everything you need, boys,' said Esmor. 'And all for the price of another lager, Jeff,' he said looking over to the fridge. 'I'll bring it all round later,' he added.

'Try and stop me coming,' said Jeff, with a touch of devilment in his eye. 'Esmor my old mate,' he added, opening the fridge door, 'here's your lager. I don't know where you put it all in that little frame of yours, but if you want it, you've just earned yourself some supper too.'

'Well, I'm off out again later tonight, but if there's a bacon butty going, I won't say no.'

'Fair enough; what about you Mike?'

'Why not?'

'Right, you two get things started,' said Jeff. 'I've got a quick telephone call to make and then I'll be right back.'

He returned in five minutes, discovering that the other two had found all they had been searching for in the kitchen.

'We're in luck,' he said. 'I've just 'phoned the office. The two till ten shift that's on this evening is on again at six in the morning. I've just spoken to the sergeant and they've got a full complement of men. He'll get one or two of the night shift boys to stay on late and they'll hit the tinkers' camp at six-thirty tomorrow morning. We can't risk them moving on. Don't upset them on your travels tonight will you, Esmor?'

'That's where I was going, but it looks as though you've just given me a night off, Jeff,' he replied.

'In that case help yourself to another can!'

He didn't need to be asked twice.

Turning the bacon over in the grill-pan, Holland turned to Jeff asking, 'Will the Acting Superintendent Renton know what's likely to happen tomorrow morning?'

'No chance; well not until after it's happened anyway.' Jeff gave him a knowing grin.

'Good. That's the way I like it. How would you like your bacon, gentlemen?' asked Holland.

'Well done, crispy,' they both replied.

'Then it's three crispy bacon butties coming up,' he said, rather enjoying his recent appointment as head chef.

Suddenly, the door between the kitchen and the remainder of the house opened and without initially seeing who it was; Holland noted the immediate look of concern on Jeff's face. When he turned round, he saw the woman standing in the doorway, aided by aluminium

177

elbow crutches on each side. She wasn't tall, but Holland guessed that she had once been taller. She must also have been a beautiful woman at one time, but the years of pain had obviously taken their toll and her hair had turned prematurely grey. In that brief moment, it looked as if Jeff had been caught in a time warp where everything else in the world moved except him. Open-mouthed, it took him several seconds before he responded to her presence.

'Jean "*bach*," my darling. What, well... how on earth...?'

He wasn't allowed to finish.

'I couldn't help but smell that lovely bacon, so I had to come and see for myself,' she said. Her voice was stronger than her feeble frame might have suggested. 'And you must be Mr. Holland? I've heard a lot about you.'

Jeff looked uncharacteristically hesitant as he started to move towards her.

'I can do this, Jeff,' she stopped him.

The three of them watched her progressing slowly inch-by-inch towards them. She took her right arm out of the aluminium clasp, extending it towards Holland. He took it, gently.

'I know he won't mind my saying so, but Jeff has a great deal of respect for you, Mr. Holland.'

'And I for him,' he replied. 'We seem to have hit on a good partnership, but I'm afraid that we've made quite a mess of your kitchen. The least we can do is offer you a bacon sandwich.' Holland smiled.

'I'd love one,' she replied, as Jeff helped her into one of the chairs, his eyes filling at the sight of her. She had walked unaided for the first time in many months.

'I hope you don't mind, but the bacon's burnt, Jean,' said Esmor, joyful as ever, for he was also aware of her achievement. 'Looks like this new chef we've got only works part time.'

They all laughed.

The following morning's early light reflected against the dew left behind by a cold and clear moonlit night. A fire still smouldered in the centre of the encampment, its smoke rising upright in the still air. A dog barked once, as if disturbed in a dream. Odd pieces of furniture in various stages of being stripped and polished littered an area directly in front of several caravans, and items of clothing lay untidily on the hedgerows waiting for the wind or the heat of the mid-morning sun. At six twenty-five, the sirens of seven police cars and a personnel carrier broke the tranquillity. Young men and women in combat gear and helmets, batons drawn, rushed in pairs to each of the caravans. Several dogs barked aggressively and one yelped in pain as it retreated from the point of the baton brought down against its nose. Women and children screamed vulgar abuse while most of the men stood in quiet opposition.

It wasn't long before those inhabiting the caravans had been brought out into the centre circle where they stared in silence at the dark blue uniforms that surrounded them. Without much delay, three of the men amongst them were singled out and handcuffed, placed into a vehicle and driven away while the others shouted more abuse. The remainder were made to stay where they were. One young woman who was breast-feeding a child that appeared almost old enough to attend school, spat contemptuously at one of the women officers in an act of bitter defiance. Some of the officers were delegated to carry out a thorough search of the caravans and the surrounding area. It lasted an hour; during which time a number of items from inside and outside the caravans were photographed in situ and removed in plastic bags. Within an hour and a half it was over. To more angry protests, the remaining men were driven away by personnel carrier to Llanglanaber police station. Stones, a block of wood, saucepans, soiled nappies and anything detachable that came to hand bounced off the vehicle's protective grill and windows as it departed.

Jeff Evans had found it difficult to withhold a need to telephone the police station that morning, but he realised that there was nothing worse than unwelcome interference from the outside. Bearing in mind the whole picture, he knew he was better placed on the outside of police activities that day so that he and Michael Holland were free to concentrate on other aspects. Still, the waiting game wasn't an activity 'the beaver' was used to playing and he hadn't been far from the phone all morning. Holland, who'd phoned Jeff twice, wasn't any better. The second time be rang was ostensibly to talk about what Beaumont and the 'cowboy' had been discussing at the fishing hut two nights previously. They were both intrigued as to what Beaumont wanted back from him.

When his 'phone rang for the third time, it was almost twelve-thirty. Jeff caught it before it rang more than once. It was Bob Taylor, the young constable to whom he'd given the Philip Allen drugs collar almost two weeks previously.

'Jeff, you'd have loved it today. Talk about a job going to plan!' he started. 'We've got them. They're not admitting to anything at the moment and there's not enough to charge the three who assaulted you, but I'm sure we'll get there. But there's more to it than that. They've been up to all sorts of tricks since they've been in the area,'

'You've got the three? How did you single them out?'

'We didn't have to; you did it for us.'

'What do you mean?' Jeff was intrigued.

'Well, out of fourteen men, one of them had two black eyes and his nose was split, splattered all over his face. The second has a severely ruptured larynx and wouldn't be able to talk to us even if he wanted to.'

'No cough coming from him then!' Jeff joked. 'What about the third?'

'Remember the limerick about the man from Devizes, who had two balls of two different sizes?'

'Something about him winning several prizes, wasn't it?'

'That's the one, but in this fellow's case, both of them are huge and black and he certainly won't be fathering any more little "gyppos".'

'That'll be the knifeman. Perhaps I've done the world a favour. What else have you got on them?' he asked.

'Each one had a roll of banknotes in his possession. Five hundred in twenties, not unusual maybe, bearing in mind what they do, but these notes are new and the numbers run in sequence. The cash distribution centre in Manchester is doing a trace on them as we speak,' replied Bob.

'Blood money. Good, anything more on the 'cowboy'?'

'Yes, but I'll come to that in a minute. By the way, we've taken their clothing for forensic tests; looks as if there may be some traces of blood here and there. Can you come in sometime this afternoon to provide a blood sample of your own?'

'No problem.'

'You'll never guess what else we found there, two crossbows and the remains of enough sheep to feed half the nation! Looks like they've been living well on Welsh lamb ever since they've been here!'

'Yes, makes sense, and Esmor Owen's trout for starters, if 'gyppos' do that sort of thing,' he added, laughing at the thought.

'Seems they've been up to the same tricks in Cumbria before they came down here. Penrith C.I.D. officers are coming down to see us in a day or two. We've cleared two 'antique' burglaries in Mid Wales. They stole a desk and a dresser from one place and a grandfather clock from another. We found both in a pick-up ready for market.'

'Sounds like a good job all round. Any idea where they are getting rid of the furniture?'

'For once, I'm ahead of you, Jeff,' replied Bob with a degree of pleasure in his voice that Jeff didn't mind at all in the circumstances. 'I've run the registration number of the Jaguar through the computer. Would you believe it, the keeper comes out as a Medwyn Parry, with an address in Toxteth, Liverpool!'

'Christ, Bob, you've waited until now to tell me that?' he exclaimed.

'Well, hang on; it's not that straightforward. I couldn't sit on that bit of information, could I? I passed it on to the major incident room upstairs at eight this morning and your mate Powell sent a couple of teams to Liverpool almost immediately.'

'Anything back yet?'

'Apparently they 'phoned in about a quarter of an hour ago. The place is almost derelict and the neighbourhood isn't the most helpful in policing terms, but they did manage to speak to someone next door. He remembers the last occupant, not as Medwyn Parry, but as Marcus Payne. 'Bloody big bastard who thinks he's a cowboy!' is how he described him, but he hasn't seen him around for a while.'

''M. P.' same initials,' commented Jeff.

'Our teams, together with Merseyside Police, are executing a warrant on the house later this afternoon; it seems they can't do anything there without consulting the local community first.'

'Let me know how they get on, will you?'

'Of course,' replied Bob. 'But listen, I've done a bit more digging of my own and this is interesting too. I 'phoned 'Criminal Intelligence' in Merseyside and Cheshire. They know Marcus Payne. He came to Merseyside's knowledge way back in the early to mid-seventies. Apart from some minor convictions for dishonesty, he served five out of an eight year sentence for the attempted rape of a twelve year old girl.'

'When did he come out?' asked Jeff.

'Eighty one, and he hasn't been in trouble since.'

'Or hasn't been caught, you mean?'

'Right.'

'So there's no DNA?'

'No, all this was before D.N.A., but he's been on the National Paedophile Register since they decided on retrospective inclusion of names. It was a pretty nasty job apparently. The girl was lucky to survive, but he was acquitted of attempted murder.'

'Is there a current description of him?' asked Jeff.

'No, nothing since he came out. Twenty years is a long time and people change, but he did have a tattoo on his right forearm – a Chinese dragon.'

'Same as the man who committed the rape and attempted murder in Newcastle!'

'Don't tell me that's just a coincidence, it can't be, can it?' asked Bob, looking for a reaction as opposed to seeking an answer to the question. 'He's got to be our man.'

'What do they think he's doing now, apart from rape, murder and intimidating old ladies?' Jeff didn't believe in coincidences either.

'There's a suggestion that he's in the antiques trade, but that leads me on to what I learnt from the Cheshire Police. One of their crime cars stopped and checked the Jaguar on the Wirral in the early hours of Wednesday, nineteenth of this month.'

'Two weeks last Wednesday.'

'Yes. It was heading towards Birkenhead and the driver gave his name as Marcus Payne, producing a driver's licence in confirmation. I've spoken to the lad who stopped him and, interestingly, he says that the driver's hands were covered in oil. In fact the driver said that he'd been working on the car. There was nothing out of place – no reason to detain him and so off he went. Oh, and he also told me that there was a Stetson on the passenger seat!'

'Never leaves it behind does he? Did you know that there was a burglary at Griff's garage that night, Bob?'

'Yes, but is that connected?'

'Probably,' replied Jeff. 'But keep that under your hat for now. Tell me, what's D. C. I. Renton, the Acting Superintendent making of all this?'

'Strange that, Jeff, very strange. You'd think he'd be elated wouldn't you, but he seems to have become withdrawn; and that's something a few of us have noticed in the past few days. Everyone else is on a high today, but not him. It even looks as if Powell is running the show now. It's not at all like the D.C.I. we know.'

'Do you think that this Payne fellow is disposing of the antiques on behalf of these itinerants?' suggested Jeff.

'Looks like it.'

'And he'd be travelling up and down the country doing that, wouldn't he?'

'Presumably, why?' replied Bob, somewhat puzzled.

'Up and down the country – places such as Halifax, Bradford, Coventry, Wakefield, Newcastle, Telford and Bolton.'

'Could be, Jeff, but listen, I have to be off. I'll keep you posted.'

'One last thing,' said Jeff. 'That collar, Philip Allen and the drugs – the debt's well-paid.'

'No problem mate, my pleasure.'

Within half an hour, Jeff arrived at the police station to provide a sample of blood for comparison with bloodstains found on the clothing taken from the three itinerants suspected of the assault. He shared a joke with the police surgeon, who had never before had the dubious honour of extracting blood from a policeman. Jeff bared his left arm and watched the needle enter his vein. The doctor pulled slowly against the syringe as they watched the crimson fluid fill the barrel.

'You be careful with that now, doctor. It's precious stuff you've got there,' teased Jeff.

'I hope you haven't got any skeletons in your closet, Mr. Evans,' he replied. 'No sins in your past, I hope, or this will surely find them out.'

Jeff Evans was notably unresponsive for a few moments after that comment. He was quiet enough to prompt another question from the doctor.

'Are you all right – not feeling a bit faint are we?'

'No, I'm fine, thank you, "doc".' He might have been quiet, but his brain was in overdrive.

Pressing the cotton wool against his arm as the doctor filled the appropriate receptacle, Jeff looked hastily around the medical room, quickly taking account of what he needed.

'We're a bit short upstairs of some of this kit you've got here, doctor. You seem to have plenty, mind if I help myself to some of it?'

'Not at all. It all belongs to the Police Authority, anyway.'

He picked up a box of sterile swabs in sealed plastic tubes, together with sterile plastic bags, and left. He thought it wasn't the time to be hanging round the police station, and he made his way directly to Gorwel cottage, having first phoned Holland to confirm that he was in. Holland was equally pleased at the news of the morning's events, but there were still important questions that remained unanswered: there was one question in particular.

'So which one do you think he is?' Holland asked.

'Payne or Parry? Marcus or Medwyn, you mean?'

'Yes, but let's ask ourselves another question. Could he be the same person? One man using two separate identities.'

'Marcus Payne became known to the police about twenty-five years ago; he was convicted in the mid seventies under that name. His fingerprints will have been taken and they'll be on record against that name,' said Jeff.

'But there's nothing to say he might not have been Medwyn Parry before then. After Medwyn disappeared from Llanglanaber, he could have moved to Liverpool or wherever and assumed a new identity.'

'True, we can't ignore that possibility, but Elen would disagree. She sees him as a character who wouldn't hurt a fly.' Jeff paused a moment and then continued. 'So why should he have a car that's registered in Medwyn Parry's name?'

'Confusion?' Holland suggested.

'In case the car was seen over here, you mean?'

'Maybe,' replied Holland. 'But let's examine the other possibility. If he isn't Medwyn, just plain and simple Marcus from Liverpool, an antique dealer who's into rape and murder, how does he know so much about Medwyn, a youth who disappeared from Llanglanaber over thirty years ago? He knows so much about him that he was able to convince Emily Parry that he was her son.'

'Someone must have fed him with all the information he required.' Holland suggested.

'Precisely.'

'And who is the person most likely to have done that?'

'David Beaumont,' said Jeff.

'Because Medwyn Parry and David Beaumont grew up together, here in Llanglanaber. Medwyn was on the periphery of the group of young lads led by Beaumont in the sixties and Beaumont would have known everything there was to know about him. The retired Chief Inspector told me that much.'

'But there was something else the 'cowboy' needed, wasn't there? Something that would convince Emily Parry beyond doubt that he was her son. It's the lighter, and it's the only material thing that could connect David Beaumont with the man who I think we now agree has to be Marcus Payne, and not Medwyn Parry.'

'That is likely to be what Esmor overheard between them the night before last,' said Jeff. 'Beaumont is angry that Payne has lost the lighter and he wants it back, at any cost.'

They stared at each other as the full implications penetrated.

'Oh my God, Jeff!' said Holland anxiously. 'Elen! She's got the lighter and she's in danger. I hope we're not too late.'

'Want me to come with you?' asked Jeff.

'No, it's okay, but if there's a problem, I'll call you.'

'Good, because I've got an important call to make. I'm going to pay David Beaumont a visit,' he said, knowing that it would provoke the reaction that followed.

'You're going to do what?'

'Don't worry; he won't know I'm there. It's just a hunch and you'll be the first to know if anything turns up, I promise. You've got my mobile number, haven't you?'

Holland, somewhat confused, confirmed that he had.

In half an hour, Jeff had met up with Esmor Owen on the outskirts of Llanglanaber. He spent five minutes briefing him, and then he tested his understanding just in case something went wrong.

'Are you sure you've got it?' Jeff asked.

'When did I ever let you down, boy "*bach*"?' he replied. 'There's just one thing that bothers me, though,' he added. 'What if he comes back when you're inside the house?'

'Then I'm in the shit good and proper, aren't I? And if that happens, I'm on my own, Esmor. I want you to disappear. If everything goes well, I'll give you a call on your mobile in about fifteen minutes and you can pick me up here.'

'Fair enough.'

Within a few minutes, Jeff Evans watched from his hiding place behind the cover of the hedgerows as Esmor drove onto the forecourt of Beaumont's home. He knocked on the front door and rang the bell on the pretext of making an enquiry about the recent poaching in the area. He waited and there was no reply. Good! He watched Esmor walking around the back of the property, emerging from the other side a minute later. Even better: now it appeared that not only was the house empty, there was nobody in the grounds, either. He continued watching while Esmor returned to his van and drove off. Without wasting a moment, Jeff ran from his hideaway straight to the detached garage at the side of the building. He hoped it would be unnecessary to risk an entry into the house. He knew he wouldn't have to do so if he were lucky enough to find something suitable elsewhere. He looked in through the garage window. Beaumont's car was there: that was strange.

It looked like the inside of any average garage. A number of tools were visible on a workbench together with gardening equipment that was neatly stacked up against the walls and on shelves. His golf clubs stood neatly in a tanned leather golf bag next to the folded trolley, waiting for their next outing. The bag was marked 'D. Beaumont' in bold gold lettering. 'That will do,' he thought. The garage door was locked, just as he expected, but 'in for a penny', he said to himself as he reversed his elbow through the pane of glass. 'No time for a warrant,' he thought as he smiled, knowing that he would never have got one for the purpose he had in mind.

The glass of the window shattered noisily. He inserted his gloved hand, opened the catch and climbed through. Once inside, he unlocked the door in order to ensure his quick unobstructed exit if an emergency arose. He had enough experience to know that that was how all the best burglars behaved. Having opened the door, he collected his bag from the outside and took it over to where he had seen the golf clubs. First, he searched the bag's pockets and found Beaumont's left-hand golfing glove. He pulled it out and placed it in one of the sterile plastic bags he had brought with him. Next, he took one of the sterile swab sticks out of its container and carefully swabbed the handle of one of the putters. He replaced it into its container, labelled it and repeated the process with several other clubs, concentrating on the other putter, the sand wedge and any of the other clubs that were likely to have been used without a glove. Then, he moved to the car. He wouldn't have been too concerned if it had been locked but, as luck would have it, it wasn't. It took him no time at all to swab the steering wheel.

Afterwards, he took great delight in making a bit of a mess inside the garage, so that it appeared that a search had been made for something, anything that may have been of interest to the town's young criminal element. 'All in the interest of justice,' he tried to convince himself as he left the property the same way as he had entered.

He met Esmor as arranged and, within twenty minutes, he was home. He pulled a can of lager out of the fridge for Esmor and placed the samples he had obtained inside.

Chapter Fifteen

Michael Holland tried 'phoning Elen, but there was no reply at the house or her mobile and he was concerned. As the 'Stag' pulled up outside, he saw her Volvo 'Estate' in the drive, but there was no sign of life. He rang the doorbell and listened to their chimes. He stood back looking at each of the windows and he waited. There was nothing. As he stepped closer to the door for a second time, a neighbour emerged from a garden on the opposite side of the road.

'I'm sure she's in,' she said. 'She hasn't been out since she took Geraint to school this morning.'

Holland rang the doorbell for a second time, knocking the door anxiously with his knuckles at the same time. Again there was no response. He found that the wooden gate at the side of the house was bolted from the inside. Climbing over it, he gained access to the back garden where he saw recently washed clothing on the line. The back door was unlocked. He opened it and walked in cautiously, listening for any sound. From the kitchen, he stepped slowly into the hallway, glancing into the dining room as he passed. The lounge was empty too, but there was no sign of a disturbance. Steadily, he climbed the staircase, but once again there were no signs of life and nothing could be heard from above. At the top of the stairs he spoke quietly.

'Elen, are you there?'

It took him by surprise as a figure suddenly appeared in front of him on the landing. Momentarily he lost his footing on the top step and he fell back against the banister. Whilst trying desperately to regain his balance, he saw the cricket bat above his head and instinctively used his left arm to shield himself from it.

'Elen!'

'Michael, what on earth are you doing here? How did you get in? You frightened the life out of me.'

'I'm so sorry,' he said, embarrassed, regaining his balance and some of his composure. 'I didn't mean to alarm you Elen. I thought you were in danger. You may still be; come downstairs, I'll explain.'

She took him into the lounge and they sat next to each other on a sofa. Elen looked at him, still unsure what had led to his unusual behaviour.

Holland saw the uncertainty in her eyes.

'I'm so sorry, Elen. I rang the doorbell and I knocked and banged the door. When you didn't answer, I thought I was too late.'

'I was in the shower, Michael. I didn't hear you. I'd just come out when I heard someone moving around downstairs. What do you mean 'too late' anyway?' she asked, still breathing heavily. 'Too late for what?'

In the excitement of the moment he hadn't noticed that she was dressed in only a white towelling bathrobe with a small matching towel wrapped around her head in turban-like fashion, and she was still shaking.

'That'll teach you to leave the back door unlocked, won't it? Now listen, this is important,' Holland explained. 'I think you may be in danger. Have you still got the lighter, the one that belonged to Medwyn?'

'Well, yes, Michael, in a manner of speaking. Jeff said it was such an important piece of evidence that I took it to the bank a few days ago and had it put into a safety deposit box.'

'Good,' he replied. 'Because Jeff and I think that the 'cowboy' may be after it and we don't know what harm he might do to get it back. That's why I was worried about you.'

He began telling her about the developments of the past couple of days. As he did so, she became conscious how much he cared for her. The shock of someone entering the house unexpectedly was past now and she had quickly become the relaxed woman that Holland had always known. It even seemed that she was paying too little attention to his apparent concerns about the 'cowboy'.

She was wearing nothing beneath her robe. He could see the lapels of the garment opening slightly, exposing her collarbone as she twisted to face him. Holland's eyes couldn't help but follow a path downwards as her skin darkened into the shadows of her cleavage. His attempts to continue the account of recent events were hopelessly distracted as he gazed at the beautiful woman beside him. Beneath her bathrobe he could see the shape of her thigh and her calves. Her slim ankles and delicately toenail-painted feet were the only parts protruding below the gown. She looked at him in a way, which showed that his distraction had been noted. She parted her lips slightly as she removed the towel from her head, tossing it onto the floor. Shaking her head, her hair fell in long, wet, raven-black coils, contrasting sharply with the white towelling that covered a little less of her tanned neckline.

'Michael?' she asked. 'Do you know how I feel about you?'

'I wasn't sure, Elen,' he replied. 'Not until now that is, but perhaps I am being presumptuous.' It sounded as if he was afraid to answer her question.

She moved closer and kissed him gently, the fullness of her lips caressing his.

'What about Geraint?' he asked, breaking off.

'Don't worry, he's gone straight from school to a friend's birthday party. We've got all the time in the world.'

He drew her closer, returning her kiss, harder now, their tongues probing, searching passionately and uncontrollably. He could smell the peachy perfume of her hair and the fragrant freshness of her body.

Suddenly, the telephone rang and he broke off again.

'Let the answer-'phone take it,' she said. 'It can't be that important.'

She felt his right hand moving inside her open gown, searching along the outside of her thigh, over the slender roundness of her hips, cradling the small of her back and pulling her firmly towards him. They kissed even harder. Her clothing parted, exposing her breast, which he kissed tenderly.

Elen stood up, taking both Holland's hands, urging him to his feet.

'Not here, come upstairs,' she said.

She led the way through to the hall and stopped unexpectedly by the telephone. It was as if a deep maternal instinct prevented her from passing it.

'I must do this,' she said. 'I don't want anything else on my mind once we're upstairs.'

She dialled the answer-'phone service and listened for a moment and he saw the immediate change in her – from perfect calm to desperation.

'Geraint!' she screamed.

Holland took the phone from her trembling hand and he listened to the message himself.

'Listen to me very carefully. I've got your boy. He's all right at the moment and he'll stay that way as long as you do as you're told. If you fail or delay in complying with my instructions, he'll start to lose his fingers, first his left hand, and then the right: one finger every two hours. All I want in exchange is the lighter. That's not too much to ask, is it? Don't be foolish enough to contact the police, not if you want to see him alive again. I'll be phoning you at six o'clock sharp. Be there.'

Holland saved the message, turned to Elen, holding her firmly by her shoulders and asked for the telephone number of the place where Geraint was supposed to be attending the party. Holland dialled the number and spoke to the woman at the other end. Geraint was not there. She told him that he hadn't been at school after the lunchtime break and she had assumed he'd been unwell. Holland then called Elen's sister who arrived a few minutes later. It was already five to six; he used his mobile for the next call.

'Jeff, it's Michael. Payne's got Geraint, Elen's boy, and he's holding him to ransom in exchange for the lighter. He's making all kinds of threats unless he gets it back.'

'Good God, Michael, we've got no choice but to report it officially now.'

'No, Jeff,' he replied. 'If we do that, Renton will get to know and so then will Beaumont. We can't risk Payne knowing that we're on to him.'

'So where does that leave us?' asked Jeff.

'There's only one place Payne would take the boy. Did Esmor leave that equipment with you last night?'

'Yes, I've been through it. It's more than adequate.'

'Payne's phoning back shortly. As soon as he's finished, I'll meet you up at Gorwel.'

On the stroke of six o'clock the phone rang. Elen picked the handset up apprehensively, her hands shaking and voice trembling. Gwyneth, her sister, was at her side while Holland made the best use of the limited equipment at hand in an effort to tape record the conversation. The voice on the other side was indistinct, muffled by some means or another in an attempt to disguise it.

'If you want your son back in one piece, hand over the lighter.' The voice demanded.

Her response had already been discussed with Holland. 'I can't get my hands on it until tomorrow. It's in a safety deposit box in the bank.' she replied.

'You're a liar.' The statement was spat out angrily.

'You're a damned fool if you think I'd risk my son's welfare for the sake of a lighter.' Elen was showing her anger as well as all the other emotions the crisis was producing.

There was silence at the other end as he considered his options.

'Damn you, speak to me!' she demanded.

'You have until ten tomorrow morning,' he replied. 'You will go to the bank at nine thirty. Take your mobile with you. I will telephone you at nine forty-five with further instructions. Give me your mobile number.'

She gave it. 'Don't harm my baby,' she added anxiously, but the line was dead.

Ten minutes later, Holland arrived at Gorwel. Jeff was already there and so was Esmor. Jeff explained that Esmor would drop them off close to Hendre Fawr so that no vehicles would remain in the area. Within fifteen minutes, Michael Holland and Jeff were walking along the public footpath to the farm. Elen's last words echoed in Holland's ear. 'Please bring him back safely'. They got to the farm and found that the old Ministry Of Defence building door was chained and padlocked once again. Jeff was carrying the bolt croppers, which made quick work of cutting through the padlocked chain.

'How confident are you that we're looking in the right place, Michael?' asked Jeff.

'I wasn't sure before we got here, but now that we've found the place locked up once more, I'm hopeful' he replied. 'I just hope that we get to him in time. Payne's a psychopath and I doubt that he's got any intention of letting the boy live. Do you know whether he's got any history of using firearms?'

'I've got no idea, Michael, but it's a bit late to consider that now.'

He was right.

They took the miners' helmets out of the rucksacks Esmor had provided, placed them on their heads and switched the lights on. Replacing the rucksacks over their shoulders they walked into the darkness. Holland studied the plans as they walked. It seemed that the rail track was detailed accurately on the plans, and if correct, those tracks followed the main tunnel system all the way down to sea level, a distance of about three-quarters of a mile. There were several offshoots here and there on both sides and they decided to search each one in turn as it was encountered. It looked as if no one had been near the place for years. Suddenly, the stony ground beneath their feet gave way to a softer surface, which showed signs of recent footmarks. They were encouraged to see that the tracks indicated that something or someone had been half carried or half-dragged along the way. Soon, this surface was replaced once more by rock, but the indication that they were on the right trail was encouraging. There wasn't a great deal to be seen in the main passageway, but two of the three first side tunnels appeared to have been used for storage. A number of cartons had been left there, some of which had been opened, exposing tools and equipment belonging to a time long past. They continued following the rails and they were now quickly descending. It was also becoming quite apparent that the tunnel walls were getting increasingly wet. Moisture was also dripping from the roof of the cave onto the plans that Holland had stopped momentarily to examine.

'There should be another passageway to the right again in a few yards,' he said.

'I can see it just ahead,' said Jeff.

They turned into it. It seemed longer than the others. Metal shelving ran along one wall at a height of about eight feet and, at the end of the passage there appeared to be another smaller opening at the same height as the shelves. It was barely visible from ground level and accessible only by climbing the shelving first.

'I'll go,' said Jeff, taking off his rucksack.

'Be careful,' urged Holland.

Holland helped by pushing him as far as he could and waited for the commentary.

'It's like another little room, about sixteen by eight,' he shouted. 'And there are bunks to sleep in, I'd say enough for four.'

'Probably for the workforce.'

'Maybe,' Jeff replied, but there are candles here too and a box containing some comics and books – football annuals from the early and mid sixties.' He paused a while, then added. 'And there's a sack here too with something bulky inside it.'

'Open it and see,' suggested Holland.

Holland waited a moment, and then he heard the last thing he wanted to hear. Jeff shouted, loudly, almost as if startled.

'Oh! Oh my God, Michael, it's a body!'

'Geraint?' Holland shouted, as he jumped upwards using the shelving for assistance. As he dreaded what he might see, Elen's last words filled his mind amid thoughts that he had failed to accomplish the most important mission.

'No, thank God, this isn't Geraint.' Jeff was crouching over it as Holland's light caught him and the body. 'There's nothing that we could have done to save this one,' he continued.

They both knelt together, their lights shining as their hands parted the sacking to expose more of the body. The clothing they saw had long since decayed, along with the flesh of the man who had worn them. Though years of decomposition had bared the skull and the face of most of its skin, some of the hair was still visible in parts.

'Look at the deep indentation mark here against the back of the skull,' said Holland. 'It must have been fractured, and there's another one; there must have been two blows at least.'

'I see them,' replied Jeff. 'Those blows surely would have killed him.'

'How long do you think it's been here?' asked Holland.

'Several years, God knows,' replied Jeff. 'But judging by the literature that's been left around here, it looks like a hideout that was used by a boy in the sixties. Are you thinking what I'm thinking, Michael?'

'Yes, I guess it has to be him, doesn't it?'

They looked around, finding tins of food and other empty containers, which had once held more of the same. Then Jeff spotted an old mechanical gramophone, the type that required winding by hand. There was an old 'seventy-eight' record still on the turntable. He picked it up, and rubbing his fingers against the label, he could just manage to read it.

'Prokofiev's 'Peter and the Wolf',' he said, turning to Holland. 'Do you think he could have been hiding down here when the police were looking for him all those years ago?'

'Could be, until someone clubbed him to death. I wonder why?' Holland thought, aloud. 'Come on,' he continued, 'Medwyn's beyond saving; let's find Geraint.'

They returned to the main passageway, and followed the rail track as it continued to descend, but more gradually again now. Soon, they could smell the salt in the air, but there was mustiness about it, unlike the smell normally associated with the seashore. Before long, the passageway opened out into a huge cavern where they found the remains of several workshops. The inadequate lighting of their head torches prevented them from seeing all of it. Oil drums, hoses and smaller pipes were piled high against one wall and a large generator rested below heavy lifting gear on the roof above. Elsewhere, workbenches looked almost as if they had been left at the end of any working day.

Suddenly Jeff looked down. 'Michael, look,' he said as he picked up and examined a shoe. It was a child's sandal of the size that would fit a six-year-old.

'It must be Geraint's. It has to be.' Holland said, more in hope than certainty. He looked at the plans again. 'How the hell do we search this place with this limited lighting?'

'Hush,' said Jeff, placing the palm of one hand against Holland's shoulder. 'Did you hear that?'

'Hear what?'

'Listen.'

There was silence. For the best part of a minute they waited and listened in the cavern's silence.

'You must have imagined it,' suggested Holland.

'No, listen. I'm sure I didn't. Wait,' Jeff pleaded.

Another minute went by before it was heard again, this time by both of them. It was a faint, muffled whimpering sound, almost like that of an animal in distress, but it was definitely the cry of a child.

'Geraint!' they both shouted, their voices echoing against the rock face.

'What do we do if Payne's down here somewhere?' asked Jeff.

'The doors were locked, remember, but do we have an alternative?' replied Holland. 'We'll just have to deal with that if and when it happens,' he said, hoping that Payne hadn't followed them down.

They listened again and almost immediately, they heard the cry, loud enough this time to gain an impression of its bearing. They moved cautiously in that direction and after twenty paces, they listened again. There was nothing.

'Geraint, it's Uncle Michael,' he shouted. 'I've come to take you home.'

This time the cry that came out of the darkness was in response to Holland's voice and it was louder still. The next two or three paces made all the difference, but what they both saw below them was a chilling sight. Geraint was standing on a ledge half way down a set of stone steps that disappeared into the sea water below, his arms fastened in front of him to a heavy iron coupling positioned above his head. The seawater, seemingly still as a stagnant pool, covered his feet. But this was no stagnant pool. This was the Irish Sea that was flooding into the underground cave. When they reached him, they found the boy shivering from the effects of hypothermia and distress, his reddened eyes squinting in light that was breaking the darkness of several hours. Jeff shone his beam on Holland's face so that the boy could see him.

'Uncle Michael, my arms hurt,' he said.

His bruised wrists were handcuffed to the metal coupling and there was blood where the tightening ratchet had cut into his flesh. There had been occasions when his legs had given up and the metal had taken his weight. Holland supported the boy's weight while Jeff attempted, in vain, to free the metal restraint. The coupling through which the handcuffs had been placed had been intended for tying vessels to the underground quay wall and any attempt to dislodge it would have been futile. Their despondency was quickly overtaken by alarm when they saw the tidemark left by the previous high water a clear two feet above the boy's head.

'Tonight's tide will be higher, we're coming up to a full moon – a spring tide,' said Jeff.

'Did you see any tools about that might help?' asked Holland.

'No, but I can look,' replied Jeff.

'Don't!' Holland snapped back in frustration. 'If you look and find nothing, it won't give us a hope in hell. How long will it take you to get back to the entrance and return here with the bolt cutters?'

'A good fifteen minutes each way, but it's our best chance.'

The water was climbing, even as they spoke.

'Leave your rucksack here; you'd best travel light. Now go like hell, Jeff, and don't let anything stop you.'

Jeff Evans took a deep breath and disappeared into the darkness. Holland tried desperately to think of anything that might assist, but his anxiety grew as he watched and felt the water rising. He held Geraint tightly in his arms, whispering a tune in his ear, promising every material thing in the world that he could offer the boy. – A warm bed, fizzy lemonade, chocolate ice creams, a ride in the open 'Stag' and fishing – indeed all of the things he knew that Geraint enjoyed and talked about and all of the things Holland had been looking forward to doing with him and his mother. Everything was possible, but only if he could achieve his freedom. His thoughts drifted towards the memory of his son, Neil, who had been close to Geraint's age when he had died along with his own mother.

Ten minutes had gone since Jeff's departure. The water was

already level with Geraint's waist and it didn't seem as if Jeff was going to make it back in time. He couldn't bear to consider the consequences of failure. Had he made the wrong decision? Could Jeff have found something, any tool closer to hand, anything that might have been of use? Holland suddenly remembered that he'd seen some lengths of hose and tubing about fifty metres away. It might just buy them enough time until Jeff returned, but he would have to leave the boy for a few minutes. He told him what he was going to do and the boy cried. Holland heard him calling for his mother and crying again as he left him in the terrifying darkness. With a knife from his rucksack, Holland cut a two-foot length of tubing that was about an inch in diameter and he rushed back to where the boy now stood, chest deep in the rising water.

'You and I are going to play a game, Geraint,' he said, taking off his helmet and battery, placing them on top of the quay wall above so that the light pointed towards them. He inserted the tubing in his own mouth and it tasted foul. 'I'll show you how we can breathe under water. Look!' he continued. He submerged himself, leaving the tip of the tube above the surface. 'Easy, now I want you to try.'

He placed the tube into Geraint's mouth and squeezed gently but firmly on both sides of his nose, forcing him to breathe in that fashion for a minute or so.

'Can you do that when the water comes up?'

'Yes, I think so, Uncle Michael' he replied.

'Good. I know you're going to be a brave young man.'

Jeff was out of breath when he reached the entrance, but he had managed it in a little under the fifteen minutes that he had estimated it would take. He looked for the bolt cutters he had discarded earlier, but he couldn't find them. He was sure that he'd dropped them by the door as soon as he had cut the padlock. Quickly, he turned, sensing that there was someone behind him. Jeff was staring at the silhouette of a figure, towering above him in the moonlight. The man was wearing a Stetson.

'Are these what you're looking for?' he asked, holding the bolt cutters in his left hand and the long blade of what looked like a Samurai sword in the other. 'Well, you'd better come and get them, hadn't you?' he taunted him, tossing the bolt croppers to one side and waving the sword above his head with both hands as would a gladiator of Eastern origin. Jeff remembered that this was the second time he had been threatened with the same weapon.

Jeff realised that there was no time to waste and the big man wasn't expecting such an immediate response as he lunged quickly at him. Although Payne swung with the sword, Jeff had been quick enough to get on the inside of it. As Jeff pushed him heavily against the door, his helmet was thrust into the pit of the man's stomach with all the strength he could muster, and he heard the wind being forced out of his lungs. He gave a loud cry and dropped the weapon as he did so. Attempting to take full advantage of the bigger man's temporary incapacity, Jeff moved sideways and picked up the bolt cutters, but he had underestimated his adversary's resilience. He felt the kick of the cowboy's boot crashing against the side of his chest cavity and now it was his turn to be winded. As he fought for his breath, he realised that the other man was reaching for his sword once more and Jeff made another dash for the bolt cutters. In the nick of time, he lifted them high enough to stop the blade as it came down upon him, creating sparks like a flash of lightning in the night sky. As Marcus Payne raised the sword for another attempt, Jeff twisted himself in a circular motion, aiming his own weapon at Payne's torso. It caught him heavily in his ribcage and was enough to ground the man.

Jeff realised that he had no alternative but to run. It didn't matter that Payne might recover or what he might do once he regained his ability. He would have to cross that bridge if need be. Getting the bolt cutters to where Holland waited with Geraint had to be the first priority and so, reluctantly, he left Payne there, groaning on the ground. As he ran, often stumbling, Jeff realised then how little he had recovered from the first beating a few days earlier. As he made progress downhill he also realised that his light was beginning to fade, and he remembered that his spare battery was still in the rucksack he had left behind with Holland. Before his journey's end, the light gave out completely. He fumbled in complete darkness, using the railway line as his only guide. His body ached as he fell against the bruises that hadn't completely healed in five days and the rib injury inflicted just moments earlier. At last, he saw the dim light of Holland's helmet in the distance and he knew it wouldn't take long to reach them.

The cold water of the Irish Sea continued to rise in St. George's Channel as it flowed northwards to fill the Menai Straits and Liverpool Bay beyond. Inch by inch, the level became higher inside the old submarine base. Holland watched as its surface reached Geraint's chin and eventually, his mouth. He felt helpless at the mercy of a tidal force that was beyond anyone's control and, for the first time in years, he prayed. He stroked Geraint's head; not knowing how much the boy could take. When the time came, he stopped stroking his head. One hand now held the tube firmly in his mouth while the other squeezed his nose to prevent inhalation of water. He had no way of knowing how the boy's exposure to hypothermia might affect his consciousness and his ability to breathe. Another two or three minutes saw the boy totally submerged. Geraint's arms now pointed down towards the coupling where they were fastened, his body supported by Holland and the water. He wondered how long he would be able to continue sustaining him, for the water level would eventually reach well over his head too and he would be unable to continue holding the tube and the youngster's nose and remain afloat himself. Had the tube been any longer, the boy would have been in danger of inhaling too great a portion of his own exhaled carbon dioxide.

Holland felt for the knife he was carrying. The last resort would be to sever the boy's arms above the wrists and he was surely only moments away from making that dreadful decision.

Suddenly, he heard movement somewhere above him, but there was no light to be seen but his own.

'Jeff, is that you? Jeff, for God's sake, hurry!'

'Hang on mate, I'm here, my battery's gone, I had to be guided by your light.'

'Have you got them?'

'Yes.'

'Take your fleece off before you get it wet. We'll need it to wrap him up as soon as we get him out of the water.'

There was no need to say anything further – both knew exactly what was required. Jeff quickly submerged, taking the bolt croppers with him. Working blindly, he felt for the chain between the metal bracelets around the boy's wrists and he guided the blades of the bolt cutters against them. He squeezed the handles together and he felt the cutting of the metal. Was the boy still alive?

Holland pulled him free, threw away the tube and, before even taking him from the water, he pushed his head backwards, opening his airway as much as possible. He held his nose once more and exhaled sharply into Geraint's lungs. Even in the dim light of the helmet, his face appeared blue. They placed him on the ground, but Holland wasn't sure if he could feel a heartbeat or pulse. He continued mouth-to-mouth resuscitation while Jeff performed cardiac massage. Soon, Geraint coughed and vomited. He was definitely breathing now. They wrapped him as well as they could and gave him small doses of a warm sweet drink from a flask Esmor had provided.

Geraint's first words were, '*Ble mae Mam*? (Where's Mum?)'

Holland lifted the boy into his arms while Jeff carried the rest of the equipment as they followed the railway track uphill towards the farm.

'Thought you weren't going to make it in time,' said Holland.

'I'd have made it sooner if I hadn't come across our 'cowboy' friend,' replied Jeff.

'Payne?'

'Yes, he had the bolt cutters and a bloody big sword and I had to take them away from him. I left him lying up there. There wasn't time to do anything else with him, so we'll need to be careful when we get out.'

When they got to the entrance, Holland stayed back for a moment while Jeff looked around. Marcus Payne was gone and so was his sword. The front door of Hendre Fawr farmhouse felt the force of Jeff's boot, and within minutes, Holland had undressed the shivering boy, replacing his clothes with anything of Emily Parry's he could find. Finally, he found a wide roll of kitchen foil he had seen while looking around the property with Elen a few days earlier and he used it to wrap Geraint up. He held him next to the relative warmth of his own body and they waited.

Jeff had made several telephone calls by then and within fifteen minutes, the cars began to arrive and the night sky was tinged with the reflection of blue flashing lights. Soon afterwards, a police helicopter hovered overhead and in ten more minutes, Geraint, accompanied by Holland, was airlifted to hospital. Jeff had already spoken to Elen to let her know that the boy was safe and that police transport had been arranged to take her to the hospital.

By the time Elen got there, the handcuffs had been removed and Geraint's injured wrists were bandaged. The boy was sleeping when she first saw him. His face had regained some of its colour but his dark brown curls remained damp against the white pillow on which his head rested. She glanced at Holland who was sitting in the corner of the room. Geraint's head turned and he smiled at his mother. It was the biggest, most wonderful smile she had ever seen and, as she held him, her tears poured in abundance. Holland waited a moment and then made to leave the room.

'Where are you going?' Elen asked.

'I thought you might want some time alone with him.'

'Please don't go,' she replied. She stood, walked up to Holland and held him tightly. 'Michael, thank you for bringing him back safely. I'll never know how to thank you.'

'There's no need,' he replied.

They continued in an embrace for some time before Elen moved away from him.

'You're wet,' she said.

'Soaking actually,' he replied. 'And so are you now.'

'What happened?' she asked.

'I'll tell you sometime,' he replied. 'Not now.'

They both smiled as she pulled him close again.

Acting Detective Inspector Powell had arrived at Hendre Fawr shortly after the police helicopter had left. Jeff spent ten minutes briefing him on the events that had taken place, though he was careful not to mention anything outside the kidnapping, the finding of the decomposed body and his contact with the man he believed to be Marcus Payne. Having finished, Powell looked at him.

'You're suspended from duty until further notice.' It was a statement uttered completely without emotion.

'Suspended?'

'Yes, on the instructions of 'Superintendent Renton, for acting in an unauthorised manner, neglecting your duty and no doubt a host of other charges when the time comes. I'll have to take your warrant card now and you're prohibited from entering any police premises. Is that understood?'

'Perfectly, but you can tell the Acting Detective Superintendent that I'll be going to Headquarters tomorrow to see the Assistant Chief Constable and the head of the Professional Standards Department. I might even drop in on the Chairman of the Police Authority on the way,' he paused, 'and I still have my citizen's power of arrest and I know how to use it. Just tell him that and you watch his reaction.'

Without waiting for a reply, he left.

Chapter Sixteen

At eight thirty the following morning, Jeff Evans picked up the telephone at his home, dialled and waited a moment.

'Good morning, Home Office Forensic Science Service, how may I help you?'

'May I speak to Dr. Poole if he's in today please?'

'I'll check. Who shall I say is calling?'

'Detective Constable Jeff Evans, Llanglanaber CID.'

He waited a couple of minutes.

'Jeff, how the hell are you? You're damned lucky to find me here on a Saturday morning, I'll tell you,' he began. 'We're hearing some disturbing stories over here about you being beaten up, in addition to everything else that's happening down there in Llanglanaber.'

'I'm okay thanks, Brian. How are you?'

'Fine. Hey, what about that result we had in Chester Crown Court last week? That's what I call teamwork, Jeff. He had to plead guilty in the end, didn't he? There was no way he could dispute the forensic evidence – a bit disappointing he only got four years for a job like that, though.'

It seemed to Jeff that Brian's enthusiasm never waned.

'Yes, it was good, Brian; saved a three-week trial too,' he replied. Then Jeff told him the purpose of the call. 'Listen, Brian, I'd like you to do something for me, please and I'm not going pretend that I feel totally comfortable in asking you.'

'You're not going to ask me to jump the queue for you again, are you, Jeff?' he replied, light-heartedly.

'Yes I am, but there's a hell of a lot more to it than that. It's in relation to the murder we're investigating down here. There's something very strange going on in connection with one of the D.N.A. samples taken for screening purposes. It's gone missing, but what's more, the fact that it was taken in the first place has been erased from our records. There's no trace of it on our database or the printout you've received at the lab.'

'Good God!' His mind raced through a number of possibilities. 'It's got to be someone on the inside.'

'Unfortunately you're right and if I'm correct,' he hesitated, unsure how much he should reveal at this stage. 'I think, well, I believe, it's a senior ranking officer who's responsible, Brian. There has to be a reason for it and I just don't feel confident enough to tell anyone else down here, not just yet, not until I know a little bit more about the reason,' he explained. 'There are other implications too.'

'So what do you want from me?'

'Well, I've managed to get my hands on some articles that might carry the same person's D.N.A. and I'd like you to have a look at them, please, as a matter of urgency.'

'You know how to give a man problems first thing on a lovely morning like this, don't you, Jeff? Especially when I should be on the golf course. Go on, I'm listening,' he said encouragingly.

Jeff told him about the swabs he'd taken from Beaumont's golf clubs, the car's steering wheel and the golfing glove in his possession.

'Could be difficult,' the scientist said when Jeff had finished. 'The swabs from the golf clubs and the steering wheel are likely to be what we call Low Copy Number, the kind of sample you might get from a suspect's watch, hair root or perhaps a door handle or the trigger of a gun. It would be most unusual to go to the lengths required to get a result for the reasons you've just given me, just for the benefit of a screening process, I mean.'

'But there's much more to it,' Jeff interrupted.

'I understand that,' replied Dr. Poole. 'But the difficulty is that the samples would probably have to be cultured under laboratory conditions and it would take up to twelve, perhaps fifteen weeks to get a result. This is fairly new technology and it's in great demand.'

Jeff was becoming a little disappointed, but he listened as the doctor continued.

'That's in respect of L.C.N. samples of course. Now the glove could be a different matter. If your man has worn it often and it isn't new, there might be sweat secretion as well as tiny skin deposits inside it and we may be able to do something in the usual three or four weeks. It's possible in forty eight hours, but there's a cost implication and it would need to be authorised by someone in charge of your forensic budget.'

'It's an old glove all right, so if it carries enough sweat deposit and skin particles, identification would be beyond doubt would it?' asked Jeff.

'Near as damn it, now that we're working to S.G.M., Second

Generation Multiplex.'

'Explain, please.' Jeff asked.

'In the early days, we used four strands for D.N.A. comparison. We've been working to six strands and the subject's sex gene for some time, which gives us a one in fifty million comparison. Now we work to ten strands plus the sex gene and the chances of there being two of the same is one in a thousand million. Unless of course you're looking at identical twins, who have the same D.N.A.'

'There aren't any twins as far as I know, Brian.' Jeff hesitated again. 'Look, I understand the implications and I have to tell you that there's much more to it than I've mentioned.' He paused again, thinking how much he could afford to reveal. 'But I don't feel happy discussing it over the phone.' He desperately wanted an examination, but he was afraid that his request would be rejected if he asked for too much too soon.

'I was afraid of that,' Dr. Poole replied. 'You're asking me to overstep the mark, you realise that, don't you? For a start, it doesn't sound to me as if your samples have been obtained lawfully, but for the moment, you needn't answer that question. What you're doing may be justified; only you know that, but if you want me to go along with you, Jeff, you will have to give me chapter and verse. I don't think that's asking too much of you, is it?'

Jeff knew that he was right.

'Look, Brian, can I come over to see you, now? There's another aspect to this whole affair that's been niggling me for the last couple of days, something that goes way back in time, and I've told no one. It's very important, Brian and I need you to trust me.' He was almost pleading with him.

'Very well, Jeff. How long will it take you to get here?'

'About two and a half hours.'

"Make it after lunch would you please, Jeff? That means I'll get my round of golf in before we meet.'

'No problem and oh, Brian, not a word to another soul please. That beating they gave me was an attempt on my life and it's probably connected.'

'You'd better be careful then.'

Jeff made himself a good breakfast and a lighter version for Jean.

He took Beaumont's samples from his refrigerator and placed them into a 'cool bag'. He left at ten thirty, but the M6 was busy as usual and it was almost two by the time he got there. The laboratory seemed lifeless and the only car in the car park was situated in the space marked specifically for Dr. B. Poole. Jeff parked next to it in the director's allotted parking place and he waved an acknowledgement at Brian Poole, who was unlocking the front door as he walked towards it.

It took two hours for Jeff to unload all that was on his mind. He was glad to have seen Brian Poole face to face in order to judge his reaction and hopefully, the visit had also served to demonstrate his own sincerity. Dr. Poole had listened with all the interest Jeff had hoped for, asking pertinent questions at various points. When they parted at the front door, they shook hands.

'I can only thank you, Brian,' said Jeff. 'I just hope it's all going to be worthwhile, but whatever the outcome, I'm convinced it's something that needs to be done.'

'Like I said, Jeff, we are both sticking our necks out and you know I can't promise anything in relation to the other business. We'll be lucky if we still have any exhibits from that enquiry left here by now, but I'll get someone to search through the old store rooms in the cellar just in case. Even if we find anything, it's hit and miss after all this time. You understand that, don't you? If you are right and it comes up trumps, like I've already said, I won't be coming back to you. I'll be contacting the A.C.C. directly.'

'I've got no problem with that, Brian.'

Acting Detective Superintendent William Alexander Renton's promising career had been torn apart in the space of three weeks. He hadn't turned up at work that day, which had added weight to the account Jeff had related to Assistant Chief Constable Eric Edwards at Police Headquarters on his return to North Wales. It hadn't been difficult to persuade the A.C.C. to allow Detective Constable Jeff Evans an audience, even on a Saturday afternoon. Renton was unofficially regarded as 'missing' and his absence was causing a great deal of concern at chief officer level.

Alex Renton had left his home early that morning after a sleepless night. He knew that the game was finally up, but he was still thinking – trying desperately to salvage something. As he drove aimlessly around the countryside, ignoring his ringing mobile 'phone, he recognised that the chance of coming out of this predicament scot-free was virtually impossible. He listened to the recorded messages on his 'phone. Most were from Powell, who seemed to be becoming increasingly anxious as the day progressed. Renton learnt that he was to be replaced as head of the investigation and that his absence was already becoming a matter of media speculation. The body recovered from the cavern had been identified as Medwyn Parry by virtue of his dental records and additional police resources were being drafted into the area to search for Marcus Payne.

Renton recognised he had to think about his own welfare first, but he realised that damage limitation was all that was left to him now. He might have to be candid about his relationship with Beaumont and he considered that it might be to his benefit if he could arrest Payne single-handed. Maybe that would be regarded favourably enough to reduce whatever sentence his transgressions might attract! God, he hated the thought of going to prison, but was he over-reacting, he thought? Surely there was something he could salvage? Somewhere far out in the countryside, he sat in his stationary car in deep contemplation, but he wasn't even sure he could trust his own judgement any more.

He picked up the mobile again and dialled Beaumont's mobile number. Half an hour later, they met in Renton's car. In silence Renton drove off and parked in a disused quarry half a mile up the road. He sensed that Beaumont was subdued as well. They were both acutely aware that they were no longer in control of events and that anything could happen from now on. It was Renton who spoke first.

'You've got us into a right mess, haven't you, David?'

'You seem to be anxious to place it all on my shoulders.'

'How long have you known Marcus Payne?' asked Renton.

'Years.'

'How?'

'Antiques. He's an antique furniture dealer.'

'No matter where he gets it from, is that it? He's been filling your house with stolen antiques for years hasn't he?'

'How should I know where they came from?'

'I don't suppose you gave a damn, did you?' asked Renton. 'I suppose it was with him that you exchanged the Granada 'Estate' for the dresser in nineteen eighty eight wasn't it?'

'Yes.'

'And you lied through your teeth when the police from Halifax came to see you in connection with the girl's murder, didn't you?'

'I had to, Alex. The dresser was probably stolen. It had to be for what I paid for it.'

'Even though you knew there was a chance, a strong chance that you were covering up for a murderer?'

Beaumont bowed his head in silence.

'And then you used the same man to do some more of your dirty work at Hendre Fawr.'

'Our dirty work, Alex,' he replied. 'Never forget that I was acting for the syndicate. We all knew what had to be done to get her out of the farm. None of you protested when there was a chance of buying the property and selling it on to the power generating industry. No one batted an eyelid when I proposed that the stubborn old bitch be persuaded to sell. You and the others were happy to sit on your fat arses as my motivation increased your bank balances.' Beaumont was showing signs of anger.

'Was Emily Parry's murder part of the plan too, just another little killing to help things along the way?' Renton was raising his voice now as well.

'I, I just lost control of him, Alex.' Beaumont was clearly frustrated as well as angry. 'He was acting outside my authority. The man's a psychopath and I was as surprised as anyone else when I heard about her accident, but it was too late then. I assumed immediately that it was no accident, Alex, but as I said, it was too late.'

'I suppose Emily Parry's death by natural causes would have been easier to contend with? He tried to frighten her to death first, but that failed, didn't it?'

'Yes, but don't forget the part you played in covering it up. You delayed the car's examination and we're both in this together.' Beaumont wasn't slow in reminding him.

'I don't need you to tell me that.' Renton snapped back at him. 'If only I'd ended it all there and then, maybe the Murphy girl would still be alive. Tell me what you thought when you heard about her murder so close to where your man, your facilitator was operating. How long did it take you to make that connection – especially when you knew about the Halifax murder?'

'I thought about it, of course I did, hoping it wasn't him, but there still isn't a shred of evidence to connect him with it, is there?'

'Don't talk so bloody daft, man. There's more than enough circumstantial evidence to pull him in any time. The man's so bloody arrogant he's never used a condom in any of his attacks. Shoots his bloody load into all of his victims as if he thinks he'll never get himself caught. As soon as he's arrested, his D.N.A. will connect him to every crime he's ever committed.'

'How long has this D.N.A. technology been in existence, Alex?' Beaumont asked, looking concerned.

'Long enough to put him behind bars for the rest of his life. It's only a matter of time until we catch up with him now that his identity is known.' Renton was still talking the part of a policeman. It was difficult to get out of the habit, though he acknowledged that in reality he was now the hunted and not the hunter.

'What I can't understand, David,' he continued, 'is why he had to kidnap the Thomas boy yesterday.'

'I don't know the answer to that question, Alex. I really don't,' he lied. Renton watched him touching his nose, nervously. 'So what do we do now?'

'We've only got one option,' said Renton. 'Our only hope is that we turn him in. Me that is, of course. I've got to arrest Payne, take him in and hope for the best outcome.'

'Is that wise?' Beaumont asked. As always, he was thinking about his own position.

'It's our only chance. Once I've done that, I can claim that I've flipped, a nervous breakdown or something, make believe that the enquiry was too much for me and that's why I made so many wrong decisions.'

'But what about Payne?' Beaumont asked. 'If he gets cornered he's likely to expose everything.'

'Look at it this way, David.' Renton replied, willing Beaumont to listen and be convinced. 'How much does Payne really know and who's going to believe him; he's dishonest, he's a rapist and a proven serial killer. No jury will listen and believe what he might say.'

Beaumont turned and looked at Renton in a way that showed he was becoming interested.

'He knows very little, you're right,' he agreed. 'But don't forget it was me who brought him into this and it was me who paid him to threaten Emily Parry and Jeff Evans. I'm the one at risk.'

'But listen to me,' insisted Renton. 'Now, where's the independent evidence to connect you with him or him with Hendre Fawr? Any potential case against you will require evidence a jury can believe beyond all reasonable doubt and, at the end of the day, Emily Parry's dead – she can't give evidence. Elen Thomas has seen Payne twice from afar and it's only his clothing she can recognise, nothing more.'

'What about the tinkers?' suggested Beaumont. He was becoming enthusiastic now.

'They aren't likely to give anyone the time of day, let alone give evidence against you, me or anyone else.' Renton was sounding positive. 'No one can connect them with you, only with Payne and no one can connect me with sending Jeff Evans to meet them, either. I can assure you of that.'

'What about the other members of the syndicate?' The possibility that they might talk concerned Beaumont.

'They are the last people who would want to become involved or even distantly connected with any of this. Believe me, they'll run a mile given half a chance! Their hands are dirty too, remember; and I'm sure that you'll remind them of that fact when the time comes.' He recalled how many times Beaumont had threatened him in some way.

Beaumont knew Renton was correct again. He had put forward a plausible argument.

'That leaves us with one more important matter to consider,' said Beaumont. 'Where do you and I stand?'

'We have to trust each other, just as we always have done in the past, only that trust has to run deeper now than it's ever done before.' He paused. 'Do we have that understanding, David?' he asked, looking directly into Beaumont's eyes.

'Yes.' Beaumont replied. 'Yes, of course we do, Alex, my friend. If we stay together we can recover from this situation. It's our only hope.'

'That leaves one last question,' Renton said, still looking directly into Beaumont's eyes.

'What's that?' he asked.

'Can you deliver Marcus Payne to me? It had better be sooner rather than later.'

'Leave that to me,' replied Beaumont. 'Will later this evening be soon enough for you?'

After they parted, Renton checked his mobile again. There were another two voicemail messages from Powell. Renton learnt that Jeff Evans had been to Headquarters and that all hell had broken loose. He learnt that his own absence had given weight to whatever story Jeff Evans had told them. The A.C.C. had taken personal charge of the murder enquiry, Powell had been relieved of his duties and Jeff Evans's suspension had been withdrawn. The second message told him that there were rumours emerging that a high-ranking officer from the Greater Manchester Police, supervised by the Independent Police Complaints Commission, had been appointed to conduct an investigation into Renton's role as senior investigating officer of the Donna Marie Murphy murder and all associated matters.

There was more reason than ever now for him to arrest Payne and take him into custody personally. He also wondered where his loyalties should lie in relation to Beaumont. He decided that he would keep his options open, no matter what agreement Beaumont thought they had.

Renton hadn't been home during the course of the day, believing that his former colleagues would be watching the place. He knew his wife would be worried, but he had more important matters to occupy his mind. It was eight thirty by the time Beaumont contacted Renton's mobile, telling him that he would be in a position to deliver Payne in thirty minutes, at Hendre Fawr. The meeting place Beaumont had chosen had taken Renton by surprise. Initially he felt uneasy about it, but as he became accustomed to the idea, it grew on him. There was nowhere more appropriate, and in any event, he wanted Payne badly enough not to argue about where they should meet.

Twilight was approaching and the pale white moon was already visible over the horizon as Renton approached the farm on foot. Cautiously, he entered the farmyard, which was deserted apart from Betsy, the solitary chicken that pecked away in the dirt, seemingly oblivious of his presence. Beaumont called him from one of the outbuildings, the one that had once been Emily Parry's garage. Renton followed him inside, his eyes taking a moment or two to adjust to the faded light. His right hand felt for his baton and the pouch on his belt that held the handcuffs hidden beneath his jacket. This was going to be his greatest arrest even if it was the last one he was to make in a distinguished career.

Beaumont was alone.

'Where is he?' Renton asked, anxiously.

'He'll be along shortly,' replied Beaumont.

'How did you sell it to him?'

'Same as always, Alex – money. I told him I had another job for him, cash in advance as usual.'

Beaumont looked confident again. It seemed to Renton that the chat they'd had earlier in the car had changed his attitude. He was back to the usual self-assured David Beaumont that Renton had always known and often admired.

'And I suppose he's going to do exactly as I tell him, is he?' Renton replied, testing Beaumont's allegiance.

'That isn't going to be a problem, Alex. I've brought some insurance along, just in case.'

Beaumont took two steps backwards, and without turning his head away from Renton, he reached into the shadows for the thirty-inch barrels of a twelve-bore, hammer action shotgun he had brought with him.

'This will ensure that you have the freedom to do whatever you want. When you've got him where you want him, give me time to disappear. I've got my alibi set up, just in case he starts shouting that I was here helping you. We can both deny that later.'

Yes, he thought, Beaumont was certainly back to his usual positive style, but in the fading light, he had failed to see that Beaumont was wearing a pair of disposable rubber gloves.

Renton was unaware of the movement behind him; it was Beaumont's manner that betrayed Payne's presence. He turned and it felt as if his heart missed a beat when he saw the Stetson-wearing figure standing motionless in the doorway, his arms folded in front of him. A leather belt hung diagonally across one shoulder and beneath the opposite armpit. His sudden appearance and his physical presence had taken Renton by surprise. With what appeared to be supreme confidence, Marcus Payne took three slow steps further into the building and stopped. It was as if he was seeking some advantage. His eyes held Renton's as they became visible below the rim of his hat. Renton's heartbeat was racing as he also re-positioned himself so that he could see both Beaumont and Payne without turning.

'I don't think you two have met.' said Beaumont. 'Alex, this is Marcus Payne. Mr. Payne, this is Detective Superintendent Renton.' Beaumont sounded sure of himself, but there was something in his tone that made Renton feel uncomfortable.

Beaumont was holding the shotgun across his chest, both hammers were cocked and the barrels pointing upwards at a forty-five degree angle. Renton tried to disguise his anxiety as he stepped closer to the man he was about to arrest. As he did so, he ensured that he did not disturb Beaumont's uninterrupted view of Payne. Renton was tall, but Payne was taller and by far the bigger man. There was barely enough light to see clearly into Payne's eyes. They didn't look as if they belonged to a psychopath or a serial killer, but how could he tell? How could any of his victims have known until it was too late? He moved close enough to smell the stale tobacco smoke on his clothing and on his breath. Payne seemed extraordinarily calm, and as Renton drew nearer he saw that his eyes had fire inside them. Payne was concentrating entirely on Renton, paying little heed to Beaumont or the gun he was carrying.

In those few seconds, the world belonged to the two of them, but a feeling of uneasiness overcame Renton as he told Payne that he was being arrested for the murder of Diane Murphy. He wasn't allowed to finish. Payne smiled, showing his yellow-brown tobacco stained teeth. It was a smile that came from the darkest side of Payne's character. Renton could only watch as Payne quickly reached behind his head. In the blinking of an eye, he released the Samurai sword from its scabbard, its blade flashing in the semi-darkness as he brought it down to within an inch of Renton's head. Stunned, Renton sought comfort from Beaumont as Payne held the blade, above him, but in disbelief and sheer horror, he saw that Beaumont was not pointing the weapon in Payne's direction but at him. As he stared down the barrels of the shotgun, Renton recognised that the tables had been turned. He realised too late that Beaumont could never have faced a future that was dependent on his trust.

Beaumont showed no remorse as his eyes turned to Payne and he nodded just once. He showed no sentiment as the blade was lifted and brought down like a thunderbolt. It removed Renton's left ear as it passed, cutting deep into his shoulder, splitting his collarbone in the process. Bright red blood spewed out as it cut several inches into his flesh. Renton's bowels moved involuntarily. Beaumont didn't flinch. To him, this was a commercial decision, a sacrifice that was necessary so that his affairs could proceed unhindered. Renton was still as Payne removed his weapon, raising it sharply above his head again. Captured in the pleasure of the execution, Payne's second blow in as many seconds was buried deeply into his right shoulder. Renton's mouth opened and his eyes widened for the last time as he fell to his knees, his body remaining upright. Once more, Payne lifted the sword above his head and using all of his might, he brought the blade down a third time. It split Renton's skull in two, before finally being imbedded deep into his chest cavity. It was only Payne's grip on the bloodstained Samurai sword that kept Renton's body upright. Once disengaged, the body fell backwards and sideways into a cloud of dust that consumed it on impact with the floor.

Beaumont showed no reaction – not even the gory manner in which his plan had been executed had shaken him.

'Quick,' he said to Payne. 'Help me move the body. We're going to take it into the cave. There's a canvas bag here that we can put him into.'

Beaumont moved behind Renton's body, dropping the shotgun onto the ground beside him while he struggled to lift the body from behind. Payne, discarding his sword, moved to the other side to carry Renton's feet. Beaumont raised Renton's body into a sitting position and waited for Payne to get into place. Still supporting the body, Beaumont quickly picked up the gun, ensuring that its lock and as much of the stock as possible was in front of Renton's body and he pointed the barrels at Payne. Before Payne became conscious of what was happening, Beaumont pulled the trigger, discharging one of the barrels into his groin at point blank range, blowing away the very part of his anatomy that had violated several of his victims over two decades. Payne gave a loud scream as he recoiled, but he was still standing when Beaumont fired the second barrel from the same position, ensuring that Renton's clothing would bear the powder marks left behind by the firearm's discharge. He aimed the second barrel at his stomach, intending that Payne should not die immediately. The big man collapsed to his knees and fell forward. Beaumont watched his vain attempt to crawl to the place where his sword lay a few inches away. By the time he reached it, he was motionless but for the movement of his shallow breathing.

Beaumont operated quickly. He could still hear Payne's groaning as he placed the untraceable shotgun in Renton's hands, ensuring that his fingerprints were credibly transposed onto the stock, the barrel and in the area of the trigger guard. The gun was left beside Renton's body and by the time he was ready to leave, Beaumont was satisfied that Payne had bled to death.

Beaumont, having checked and double-checked his actions, left hastily, cutting across fields he had known so well since the days of his childhood.

In forty minutes, he was home. He stepped into his garage and in the darkness he stripped naked, changing into the clean clothing he had left there earlier for that purpose. He placed the clothing he had removed and the disposable gloves, into a plastic bin bag and made his way to the bottom of the garden. In a corner used by his gardener for burning waste, he emptied the bin bag and doused its contents with petrol. He struck a match and threw it at the clothing and he watched the flames burn until he was satisfied that there was nothing left but ashes. Once inside the house he showered, and, using a brush, he carefully scrubbed his entire body. Afterwards, he put on a bathrobe, went downstairs and poured himself a brandy. He sat quietly in his armchair as he brought to mind each detail of the evening's events. He was confident that he had taken care of everything, and convinced that he had committed the perfect crime. What little evidence there had been to connect him with Payne was non-existent now and, in the process, he had taken care of any risks that may have been posed by Renton. Now, all he had to do was wait and see how events would unfold. As a leader of the local community, he would need to comment publicly on the tragic demise of the late William Alexander Renton. He had no doubt that he would dream up the most praiseworthy annotations to honour the sad loss, and in such brave circumstances, too.

Not long afterwards, Beaumont's wife came home, greeting him with a kiss on his cheek.

'Drink, darling?' he asked.

Chapter Seventeen

Early the following morning, a farmer who rented the land at Hendre Fawr discovered the two bodies. He had also been a wholesale butcher and a slaughter-man for most of his life, but nothing could have prepared him for what he saw that day. The sight had been enough to make him physically sick. In a state of shock he had driven to Llanglanaber Police Station where he half-stumbled to the counter and stammered uncontrollably whilst giving his account of the finding.

Later that day, four men dressed in white sterile suits entered the outbuilding. Three of them, the pathologist, the forensic scientist and the scenes of crime officer had walked a similar path three weeks earlier to the place where Donna had been murdered. But it was Assistant Chief Constable Eric Edwards who now accompanied them, not William Alexander Renton. It was virtually impossible at first to identify the bodies, but Eric Edwards was ready to deal with a discovery that would cause intense media coverage and inevitable speculation. He wasn't surprised when he saw a pair of handcuffs and a police baton strapped to a belt around one of the bodies, but Renton's identity was confirmed only when a police warrant card and a number of credit cards bearing his name were found in a wallet on the same body. The disfigurement was such that scientific identification would be necessary at a later stage, but Edwards had seen enough to know that he was dealing with the murder of a colleague. 'What on earth had the man been up to, coming out here on his own?' Edwards thought.

The position of the bodies suggested that Renton had fired both barrels of a shotgun, severely injuring the man they assumed was Marcus Payne. Fatally wounded, Payne had struck three deadly blows before he had also perished. A more considered opinion would be available following closer examination of the bodies.

Later that day, after the post mortem examinations, Eric Edwards returned to Llanglanaber and summoned Jeff Evans to his office. Jeff knocked and entered. He stepped in front of the desk looking as if he was unsure of himself.

'You wanted to see me, Sir?'

'D. C. Evans,' he asked. 'Are you fit enough to return to duty?'

'Well, yes Sir, I am,' he replied, still a little hesitant. 'But am I not supposed to be suspended?'

'That's already been rescinded. The decision to suspend you in the first place was quite improper. As far as your personal record is concerned, it never happened.'

There was another knock on the door.

'Ah splendid, I've asked Mr. Holland to join us, that's probably him now,' said the A.C.C.

Holland stepped into the room extending his right hand.

'Hello Eric, how are you? It's good to see you again.' He smiled.

'And you too, Michael. Please take a seat.'

The heartfelt greeting confused Jeff. 'Do you two know each other?' he asked.

'Our paths have crossed in the past.' Edwards explained. 'Now, sit down Jeff, please,' he continued, using his Christian name this time. 'You'll return to duty as from now and the first thing I want you to do, is to give me a full run down of everything that's happened – from your perspective, no one else's. I know you've both been working together, Jeff. Michael's told me all about it.'

Jeff looked at Holland and smiled. Holland allowed him to take the lead, interrupting only occasionally to emphasise a particular point. That morning's macabre discovery meant that Jeff's briefing was required in finer detail than the account he had given the previous afternoon at Police Headquarters. When they had finished, the A.C.C. began to probe.

'Do we have any evidence which shows that David Beaumont was connected to what happened to Emily Parry?'

'Not a great deal at the moment, Sir,' Jeff replied after he had considered his answer. 'What we've got is circumstantial, but a lot of it is no more than speculation or gut feeling.'

'And if he is implicated, what exactly is he involved in?'

'We do have Esmor, the water bailiff's evidence. He saw Beaumont and Payne together,' Holland interrupted.

'But it was dark then and we have to concede that identification could prove to be a difficult factor,' began Edwards. 'Gentlemen,' he continued, 'I'm playing the devil's advocate for good reason, as I'm sure you'll be aware. I don't believe we have sufficient evidence at the moment to apply for a warrant to dig into the affairs of Aber Properties. There is little or no evidence to show that the syndicate has been involved in criminal activity and we would have difficulty in demonstrating that Mr. Beaumont or his colleagues have had interests in acquiring Hendre Fawr at any time. We must remember that it was W. R. James and Co., Solicitors who made the offer for the farm and they are under no obligation to reveal the identity of their clients. So there goes your evidence that David Beaumont, or any other member of the syndicate had a motive for intimidating the late Mrs. Parry.'

'So you don't think we've got enough to arrest Beaumont, Sir,' asked Jeff. 'I appreciate that we're lacking in proof, but our suspicion is reasonable enough and surely we have to act quickly if we're going to do anything at all. He must have been involved in the conspiracy to intimidate Emily Parry, or blackmailing her into selling the farm at the very least. If he wasn't, then why else was Payne brought in?'

'It's more than likely that Beaumont told him to murder her too,' added Holland.

'I agree, but we can't arrest him on the kind of inkling we have at the moment,' replied Edwards. 'Certainly not yet, so let's treat him gently but shrewdly – we'll see if he'll make any mistakes. Remember that he's a fine upstanding member of the community who has worked alongside the police for the past five years, and with a fair degree of success, I might add. The Chief Constable has publicly praised him for the work he's done with Alex Renton and applauded their success in reducing crime. They accomplished a great deal together and we can't be too careful. I don't want to arrest him now and later be forced to make a public apology. What I want you to do is this, Jeff. We'll question him as a witness, treat him as you would anyone who may have something to offer any murder enquiry, and we'll take a statement from him. He was close enough to Alex Renton to justify interviewing him in that way, don't you think? When he signs the written statement, he will be committed to whatever he says in it. That will give us an opportunity to test his truthfulness and, if he falters, we'll expose those lies and that, I believe, will strengthen any plans we might have to arrest him in the future.'

'We have the lighter too, remember,' said Holland.

'Yes,' agreed Jeff. 'But we can only connect that to Payne. It's only by implication that it's linked to Beaumont.'

'I want that lighter in police possession as soon as possible,' insisted Edwards.

'Yes, of course,' replied Holland. 'But I'd ask your indulgence for a little while longer, please, Eric. There's something I've been working on for the past couple of days that might help us. It's not something that you need know about just yet.'

Edwards gave Holland a knowing look, recalling that he wasn't the most renowned rule keeper in history. 'Twenty four hours then,' he conceded. As they parted, he added, 'I want you close to me for the remainder of this enquiry, D.C. Evans. I don't want you to discuss this case with anyone else but Michael Holland and me. Is that understood?'

'Yes, Sir,' replied Jeff, but he remembered that he'd deliberately failed to tell him about one particular matter. He'd thought long and hard about revealing what he had asked Dr. Poole of the Forensic Science Service to do, but he decided not to say anything on the grounds of its unlikely eventual bearing on the investigation. He did, however realise that his failure to tell the A.C.C. had the potential to cause him problems if the result went his way, but he decided that he would have to deal with that if and when it arose.

On the following Monday morning David Beaumont was purposeful and confident as he considered the day ahead, even though he would have preferred not to have been asked to meet the Assistant Chief Constable at such short notice. He picked up the newspaper and the letters that had been pushed through his letterbox, flicking quickly through the envelopes, separating the junk mail from those that might be of interest. There was one jiffy bag that had not been franked. 'Strange,' he thought. He placed it with the other letters, preferring to read the newspaper as he ate breakfast. The front page contained nothing more than a sketchy account of the events at Hendre Fawr. The story was fuelled by speculation that Renton had been murdered while attempting to arrest the man who had raped and killed Donna Marie Murphy and countless other girls throughout the North Of England and part of the West Midlands over a period of two decades. Renton was becoming a hero, but a dead hero. A number of inside pages gave an account of his career in the police service and his life as a man who was devoted to his family. Beaumont's own photograph appeared next to his splendid tribute to Renton, a man of visionary qualities who had achieved so much for the benefit of the local community.

Beaumont poured himself a second cup of coffee and began

opening his mail. Lastly, he came to the package that was addressed to him 'personally'. Though his home address was written on the package, there were no stamps or other indications that it had been delivered with the rest of the mail. He used a knife to remove the four staples that sealed it. He emptied its content on the table and was stunned when he saw the 'Ronson' lighter that lay on the table in front of him. He picked it up and his hands trembled uncharacteristically as he looked at both sides, staring uncomfortably at the initials 'M. P.' that had been engraved upon it so long ago. He tried, but couldn't understand why it had been delivered to him that morning. If it had been in Elen Thomas's possession, why had she parted with it? He tried to work it out, but he simply couldn't understand the reason. Every possibility he considered was at odds with the fact that Elen Thomas was now the owner of Hendre Fawr and that she had delivered to him the one item that could connect him to Payne. She was obviously making some kind of statement and the only credible, or perhaps incredible explanation in the circumstances, was that she was offering some kind of partnership. The possibility of her as the owner and him as potential developer coming together suddenly appealed to him. While at first he had been unsure how to react, he began to realise how important the reclaiming of the lighter was and that without it, no-one could prove his connection with Marcus Payne. There was no hurry to decide how he might yet pursue the issue, but suddenly he felt more buoyant still as he prepared for his meeting with Assistant Chief Constable Eric Edwards. There were, however, two things he needed to do first as a matter of urgency.

He drove towards the town and left the main road, taking the alternative narrow, unclassified lane running along the cliff tops. He stopped at a well-known beauty spot on the edge of cliffs that descended a hundred feet to the sea where the water remained deep even at low tide. Ignoring the danger signs, he crossed the barrier and stared at the white crested waves as they crashed relentlessly onto the cliff face below. He turned around, looking in all directions to make sure that he wasn't being watched. He pulled the lighter out of his pocket and looked at the engraved letters for the last time, rubbing them with his thumb for a moment as his eyes became glazed in a distant memory. With all his energy, David Beaumont threw the lighter as far as possible over the cliff edge, watching it fall until it disappeared from view. Then, he felt for his mobile 'phone and threw it equally far in the same direction. Having done so, he turned his back on the water and made his way towards his car. No one would connect him with that lighter ever again. Should there be a need to disassociate himself from his mobile phone, then that had also been accomplished. It was better to be safe rather than sorry.

At ten-thirty Beaumont was shown into a small interview room close to the front desk at Llanglanaber police station. He had been expecting a better reception. He had been used to more considerate treatment in Alex Renton's day, but now he was being kept waiting. Several minutes passed before the Assistant Chief Constable entered the room.

'Good morning, Mr. Beaumont. My name's Eric Edwards. Good of you to make it at such short notice.' The formality with which the occasion was to proceed was immediately apparent. There was no offer of hospitality.

'It's the least I could do in the circumstances. It's a terrible business. How's Alex's family? I haven't been to see them yet – too early I think.'

'Devastated.' Then Edwards changed the subject. 'I've asked you to come along because of the wonderful working relationship you enjoyed with Alex. The Chief Constable is well aware of your achievements together over the past five years and of course the valuable support you've generated over the past three weeks since this ugly mess began. Primarily, I've asked you here to introduce myself, in the hope that the relationship between the police and the community here in Llanglanaber can continue to flourish, even during this difficult time.'

'It goes without saying, Mr. Edwards, that my support and that of the whole council is yours and will remain so. You need only ask and I'll do whatever I can to help.'

'Good, I was hoping I could count on your co-operation.' This was the opening Edwards wanted. 'The first thing I would like from you is your help in answering a few questions.'

'Me? Why me?' Beaumont was taken aback. It wasn't what he had been expecting.

'Purely routine,' explained Edwards. 'In any enquiry of this nature, we need to interview a number of people who knew or worked or might have been associated with the victim. As far as Alex was concerned, you fit into that category.'

'Yes, that's understandable of course. Are there any particular facts emerging from your enquiries so far, Mr. Edwards?' Beaumont was fishing. 'My belief is that co-operation and mutual understanding works on a candid exchange of information.'

'Nothing more than you've no doubt read in today's newspapers, Mr. Beaumont.' He wasn't about to be drawn by Beaumont. 'Just a few questions then?'

'Yes, of course.'

'Some refreshment perhaps?'

'Coffee please.' 'About time – that was more like the treatment to which he had been accustomed,' Beaumont thought. He was expecting the coffee to be requested from elsewhere, but then Edwards stood and moved towards the door. As he departed he spoke.

'One of my officers will be along shortly to take your statement.'

Beaumont was somewhat dejected at the thought that someone else would take over. He had come here to meet The Assistant Chief Constable, which was fitting for a man of his importance. He waited for several minutes before the door was kicked open and his heart sank as Jeff Evans entered the room. He was the last person Beaumont was expecting – Evans of all people. Jeff had made sure that he looked as scruffy as possible, not that it required a great deal of effort! His duffel coat looked as if it had been thrown over his body, his hair was a mass of uncombed curls, and he looked as if he hadn't shaved that morning. Beaumont became visibly uneasy when he saw the fading yellow bruise still evident across the detective's face. Jeff had a rolled-up newspaper beneath one arm. In one of his hands he held a number of blank statement forms while in the other he balanced a small tray on which were two paper cups half-filled with vending machine coffee. Beaumont would normally have expected the station's best silver, but his ally, Alex Renton, wasn't there any longer – no 'silver service' and no back-up – not that he needed Renton's support to deal with the likes of Jeff Evans, he thought.

Jeff placed the tray on the table in front of him and the forms by its side. He threw his duffel coat unceremoniously into a corner and the newspaper on top of it. It landed in a way that partly showed the front-page headline: 'Police chief slain...'

'Coffee, wasn't it? There aren't any biscuits. We've run out in the office.'

'Can we get this over and done with, Mr. Evans, sooner rather than later, please? I do have some other important business to attend to.'

Beaumont was clearly unhappy about the position in which he found himself, but he recognised that he had committed his assistance to the Assistant Chief Constable. To pull out now would be unwise, but he remained confident in that no one, least of all this Detective Constable, had the ability to endanger his position.

The interview began with an account of his first meeting with Renton and the way in which their relationship had progressed from a casual one to friendship and eventually a working partnership. Beaumont told Jeff Evans about the dinner parties, holidays together and the golf. The first indication of stress came when Jeff touched upon any business relationship they may have had together. Beaumont had finished his coffee and was now fingering the empty plastic cup nervously. He refused to be drawn on questions relating to his business activities, especially when asked whether or not he was a member of Aber Properties – doing so on the grounds that the police had no business investigating his private affairs. As Jeff continued to write down the statement, he noted Beaumont's increasing agitation, but he decided to drop the issue for the time being. There would be time enough to explore that avenue. The interview continued.

'When did you last see Acting Superintendent Renton?'

'At the news conference the other day.'

'Have you spoken to him since then?'

'No.'

'So you haven't seen or spoken to Mr. Renton since last Thursday morning?'

'Correct.' Beaumont was exhaling heavily, eager to demonstrate his lack of enthusiasm.

Jeff's next question served to focus his attention.

'What connection have you had with plans to develop Hendre Fawr into a gas-fired power station plant?' Jeff had changed tack. Again, Beaumont fiddled uneasily with the paper cup.

'None. I'd heard that there was some possibility of it a few years ago, but the government's moratorium put a stop to it. That's all I know and I fail to see the connection.'

'Oh there is, Mr. Beaumont. You see, I know that's what brought Marcus Payne into this area.'

'And who is he?' asked Beaumont, thinking quickly, conscious that the newspapers hadn't released 'the cowboy's' name.

'He was the man whom Mr. Renton was attempting to arrest. Don't you know?' Jeff was equally aware that no name had been published or released.

'How could I?'

'But the whole town's been talking; everyone's been aware of his presence for the past two or three weeks. – The man in the cowboy outfit.'

'And how would I have connected him with the man mentioned in this morning's papers or the name, what was it, Payne, you say? I wouldn't be able to, would I?' Beaumont dismissed what he considered to be Jeff's childish attempt to trick him.

'For the record, do you know him or have you ever met or spoken to him?'

Beaumont looked angry, yet confident. 'For the record, Constable Evans, no I certainly haven't.'

'We know why he has been here and we even know why it was he who tried to harm a young boy he kidnapped a couple of days ago.'

'Then I'm sure that you'll tell me if it becomes relevant,' Beaumont replied, looking away from Jeff's eyes.

'For the record once more, Mr. Beaumont,' Jeff continued. 'Where were you between seven and midnight, night before last?'

'The night Alex was killed? You might as well be blunt about it, Constable Evans. I was at home, and, before you ask, no one can confirm it. My wife was out all evening. She came in at about eleven. After that, we were together.'

'One last question on this matter, Mr. Beaumont,' said Jeff. It was to be purely speculative and without a grain of substance. 'Mr. Renton was a very meticulous man wasn't he?'

'Yes, I believe he was.'

'Were you aware that he was in the habit of making copious notes of every event that he felt was important to him, either business or personal?'

The question had done the trick. Beaumont fiddled nervously with the paper cup once again, knocking it over and spilling the remaining tiny drop of coffee it still held. He righted the cup and leaned back in his chair, crossing his legs and his arms in a way that revealed everything the question was designed to elicit.

'No, I wasn't. Is that it, constable? I'd like to go now.'

'Yes, that's it as far as that incident is concerned, but as a leading member of this community, I'm sure you won't mind assisting us with the other murder that we've just begun investigating.'

'Other murder? What other murder?' he asked; his astonishment was apparent.

'The murder of Medwyn Parry. His body was found on Saturday. He was obviously murdered, and the fact that it happened such a long time ago has little bearing on the issue. It's a matter that has to be investigated just the same.'

Beaumont moved uneasily in his chair once more.

'Why should you ask me about something that happened such a long time ago?'

'Because you were at the dance the night he disappeared. The night Diane Smith was murdered.' Jeff paused, but there was no immediate reply from Beaumont.

'Weren't you?' he added.

'Was I? And how could you possibly know that?' Beaumont was looking anxious. He thought the papers relating to that murder had long since disappeared. Renton had told him as much.

'There are some retired police officers still around, and even if there weren't, there are others in Llanglanaber who still remember that night,' replied Jeff, as he began recording a new statement. 'Were you ever interviewed by the police in relation to those events, as indeed were most of the town's youngsters?'

'No. I went off to college within a couple of days of it happening. No one came to see me there.'

'Tell me about that night, Mr. Beaumont. How old were you?' asked Jeff.

'Nineteen, and yes, I was there, not that I remember much about it now. I remember seeing the Smith girl, not that I knew her well. She and Medwyn were two of a kind you know, both a bit simple, certainly not in my circle of friends. I saw Medwyn there, too, Peter we used to call him. The girl's body was found with his cap in her hand or something pretty conclusive like that if I remember,' he said confidently, as if delivering a well-prepared speech.

'When did you last see her?' Jeff asked, ignoring the statement and his demeanour.

'I can't remember. In the dance I expect, but I can't be sure.'

'And Medwyn?'

'I remember seeing him later. I think it was a good hour after the dance had finished, say twelve thirty to one.'

'Where?'

'He was running like a bat out of hell in the direction of Hendre Fawr.'

'Where?' Jeff repeated the question.

Beaumont bowed his head. 'He was running from the direction of the river, from the direction of the bridge where she was found.' He paused. 'And he wasn't wearing his cap then either.'

'And you never considered telling anyone about it until now?'

'Like I said, I was away. It wasn't my business.'

'I wonder who killed Medwyn Parry,' said Jeff.

'Probably the girl's brothers. They were a hard lot, they still are. Now there's a line of enquiry for you.'

Beaumont shuffled in his chair once more, making it apparent that he wasn't happy being kept there for this line of questioning.

'How well did you know Medwyn?'

'We played as children.'

'On the farm?'

'Yes, but it didn't last. You know what young fellows are like. It wouldn't have done my credibility any good – messing around with a simpleton like that. I saw less of him once we reached our teens.'

'Did he ever take you down into the tunnels beneath Hendre Fawr?'

'No. I knew about them, but no, I've never been down there.'

Jeff invited Beaumont to sign both statements, which he did.

'No doubt you'll give us further assistance should we need your help again, Mr. Beaumont?'

'Like I told your Assistant Chief Constable, I'm always glad to be able to help.' Now that the interview was over, his confidence seemed to be returning.

Beaumont stood to leave the room, but as he did so, Jeff placed himself in front of the door.

'There is just one more thing,' he said. 'Would you believe that of all the D. N. A. samples we took from several volunteers the other day, and in front of the media people too, yours seems to have gone astray – the only one to have done so. Strange, isn't it? Now, I'm sure that you won't mind giving us a replacement sample would you, Mr. Beaumont?'

Beaumont was momentarily speechless. When he recovered, he said the first thing that came into his mind, which he realised was not a particularly good response.

'I certainly do mind. If you have lost it, you'll have to do without it.'

'Who said anything about losing it, Mr. Beaumont? But never mind, we'll use this'.

As Beaumont moved in the direction of the door again, he looked at Jeff in disbelief as he produced a sterile plastic bag from one pocket and a pair of tweezers from another. With the tweezers, he picked up the paper cup that Beaumont had been using, placed it into the plastic bag and sealed it. It had been a performance intended for the benefit of the onlooker and Beaumont glared angrily at him.

'What's the meaning of this?' he asked.

'Oh, it's nothing to worry about, Mr. Beaumont. There'll be enough of your D. N. A. on this paper cup to put things right.'

Beaumont was cornered and they both knew it.

'Or perhaps you would prefer to provide a proper mouth swab,' he continued, 'which of course, would demonstrate the continued support you promised the A.C.C.'

Jeff was starting to enjoy this.

Reluctantly, Beaumont supplied a sample and, having signed the label, he finally left the room. Hiding his anger was something that Beaumont was barely able to achieve. As Jeff escorted him to the outside door he smiled secretly, knowing that he had lawfully obtained a sample of Beaumont's D.N.A. – one that could now be used lawfully by Dr. Poole and used in court if necessary.

Moments later, Beaumont crossed the rear car park of the police station to where he'd left his car. He couldn't have missed seeing the severely damaged nineteen fifty-nine Morris 'Minor' which lay on a trailer next to his own car. There were two men dressed in white overalls standing over the Morris – and they didn't look as if they were mechanics. He also recognised the ageing Jaguar on the other side of the compound, which was being dusted for fingerprints by two young men. He recalled that not long ago, he had been in that car giving instructions to Payne. Beaumont's confidence was waning once more.

He called at his office at the civic centre to tender apologies for his absence from the day's earlier meetings. Someone had left a package on his desk. It was a jiffy bag of a similar kind to the one he had received earlier that morning. He closed the door to ensure that he was out of sight and he opened the package. He was stunned, but it was a feeling of anger that dominated his emotions as another Ronson lighter fell onto the desk. He picked it up and on closer examination he found that this one had been engraved with the words 'Medwyn Parry' on the one side and 'Marcus Payne' on the other. It didn't take him long to realise that someone was playing a game. It put a whole new perspective on his receipt of the first lighter. As he left the building, his fury was raised to fever pitch.

It had barely subsided by the time he reached home and as he pushed open the front door, he realised that a small object was obstructing the door's path. It was a cassette tape. He took it over to the stereo system and played it. He closed his eyes and clenched his fists as he recognised the first few bars of Prokofiev's 'Peter And The Wolf'. In his fury, he slammed his fingers hard against the controls, switching off the tape player. Not only was David Beaumont feeling angry now, he was aware that he was extremely vulnerable and someone was keeping up the pressure. The receipt of the first lighter had given him confidence. The appearance of the second one had taken it away again, but the arrival of the tape had served to demonstrate that someone was now intimidating him. The more he thought about it, the more Beaumont's rage grew.

Chapter Eighteen

Mid-way through the following afternoon, developments required that key personnel met to discuss the enquiry's strategy. Jeff Evans listened as the pathologist, forensic scientist and the fingerprint expert outlined their findings and conclusions.

As expected, fingerprints taken from the second body had identified him as Marcus Payne, who had a history of several court appearances in the sixties and seventies. His whereabouts had been unknown since his last release from prison in nineteen eighty-one, following a conviction for the attempted rape of the twelve year old girl. A D.N.A. sample taken from his body had matched samples taken from each one of the nine victims in his fifteen-year reign of terror. His were the only fingerprints on the sword found next to his body and all of the bloodstains on it belonged to Renton. There were no powder-burn marks to be found on the sword. There were other clear indications that Payne had been responsible for Renton's slaughter. Blood had been sprayed in a direct line with the sword's upward movement between blows. There were two distinctive blood paths on the building's wall and ceiling as well as on Payne's face and his hat.

Payne had been shot at almost point blank range, but his injuries were such that he may not have died immediately. It was feasible that he could have inflicted the injuries upon Renton after Renton had shot him, but the experts agreed that they would in that case have expected the sword to be stained with some of Payne's own blood as well as Renton's.

The examination of the firearm had created some interesting questions. The shotgun was not registered to anyone's shotgun or firearms certificate anywhere in the United Kingdom. It was an old hammer gun in poor condition, which had been manufactured in Spain sometime during the first half of the twentieth century and although it carried a serial number of sorts, the maker couldn't be identified. It was unlikely that the gun would ever be traced. Renton's fingerprints were the only ones found on it, but there were no prints on the spent cartridges inside its chambers. Renton had not been wearing gloves.

The fingerprints on the gun were bloodstained, but none of Renton's blood that had been sprayed elsewhere at the scene had been deposited on the firearm in the same fashion. Renton's bloodstained palm and fingerprints from his left hand had been found on the barrels, whereas his right hand had left similar marks in the area of the lock, the stock and the trigger-guard. The triggers themselves carried too small an area for the purpose of identifying any such marks. It was also revealed that powder burn marks were evident on Renton's clothing, concentrated in an area close to his ribcage on the right side of his body. All these findings gave an indication that he had fired the gun from the hip area.

'That's not unusual given the circumstances, I mean firing in a hurry when someone's coming at you with a sword,' said Jeff. 'Except,' he continued, 'that Mr. Renton was left-handed. Any powder-burns would have been on the opposite side of his body and the fingerprints would be reversed, right hand on barrels, left hand near the stock area.'

'Precisely,' said the Assistant Chief Constable. 'No left-handed man would use a shotgun in that way and certainly not in that situation. The lack of any fingerprints without bloodstains also lends weight to a possibility that a third person may have put his prints on the gun.'

'Have we found any prints on Payne's Jaguar that aren't his?' asked Jeff.

'Just some that can't be identified,' replied Edwards. 'But we have found a tape player and a tape recording of 'Peter And The Wolf' and, interestingly, some small gauge metal piping that looks as if it's part of a braking system from Emily Parry's car. The lab boys are confident they'll be able to match it up. A bit careless of him really to have left that kind of evidence behind.'

'Not careless as much as arrogant,' suggested Jeff. 'We've found Payne's mobile 'phone as well. He was carrying it when he died. We're working on that too.'

'Jeff, in the light of what we've discussed, will you tell us about your interview with David Beaumont yesterday and the results of your subsequent enquiries, please?' asked Edwards.

'He's been lying through his teeth, that's for sure,' he replied. 'He denies knowing Payne or ever having met him. We can make a connection between them through Esmor Owen. Beaumont also says that the last time he spoke to Mr. Renton was at the press conference of last Thursday. We can show that he's lying in that respect too. There was a call from Mr. Renton's mobile to Beaumont's late on the afternoon of Mr. Renton's murder, at twenty-three minutes past five. The call lasted fifty-three seconds and the 'phone companies can pinpoint the caller's 'phone to an area approximately seventeen miles outside Llanglanaber. The two mobiles spoke again at seven fifty-two the same evening. Beaumont made the call to Mr. Renton and this time, the 'phone company people can place him in an area that is within a few hundred yards of Hendre Fawr. It's only circumstantial evidence because we can't show who was using the phones. We're working on any calls made between his and Payne's mobile.'

'That call was made in the vicinity of Hendre Fawr a matter of an hour or so before the deaths took place,' Edwards said. 'So we have to ask what Alex Renton was doing there with a shotgun. What was he up to? I would suggest, gentlemen, that we already have the answer to that.'

'For some reason best known to himself,' said Jeff. 'He wanted to bring Payne in on his own. The only way to do it was with Beaumont's help. The other possibility was that Beaumont set him up for Payne.'

'I prefer the first,' replied the A.C.C. 'because Alex Renton was carrying his handcuffs at the time. He wouldn't be doing so for any reason other than to make an arrest.'

'And the evidence relating to the gun suggests that he may have been set up. If that is the case, then by whom?' asked Jeff, knowing that the answer to the question was obvious.

'The question is not necessarily by whom, but how do we prove it?' said Edwards. 'We don't have enough evidence to convict him, and if he should choose to say nothing, then without more evidence, the case is weak, agreed? However, the time has come when we need to act positively. My decision is that we arrest David Beaumont, search his property and question him thoroughly, putting his lies and all of our evidence to him as it now stands. Bearing in mind the connections we've established between Beaumont, Renton, Payne and Emily Parry, we have enough evidence now to apply for a search warrant to look for any material held anywhere on behalf of Aber Properties and that includes the offices of Williams, Reynolds, James and Co. Solicitors. That should provide evidence of offers made for Hendre Fawr by Beaumont and the syndicate.'

'Specifically, what do we arrest David Beaumont for?' asked Jeff.

'Let's hit him with the whole lot – suspicion of being involved in a conspiracy to defraud Emily Parry and being implicated in her murder and also on suspicion of murdering Payne and Alex Renton. Provided that we find evidence to connect Aber Properties, we'll arrest other members of the syndicate for conspiracy to defraud and intimidating Mrs. Parry. That should give them all enough to chew on for a while. We'll ruffle their feathers and see what happens. Want to handle Beaumont's arrest, Jeff?' he asked.

'You bet, Sir.'

'I want that done tomorrow morning at six. The other search warrant in respect of documents and records of Aber Properties at W. R. James and Co. can be executed at the same time. Take as many people as you need and brief me on your operational plan by seven this evening.'

Michael Holland was waiting for Jeff Evans when the meeting came to an end. They discussed the latest developments over a couple of Jeff's paper-cup coffees. When they had finished, Jeff asked him a question.

'Did you bring the lighter with you? I'll need it for the interview with Beaumont tomorrow.'

'It's here,' he said, laying it on the table between them.

'What did you want it for?'

'It may be better that you don't know. Let's just say that I've spent the last few days going around every car boot sale in North Wales. I bought a couple of similar looking lighters, which I had engraved in various ways and sent to Beaumont just to see how he likes being intimidated a little himself.'

'You're right. I don't need to know that,' Jeff replied. 'But I like your style.'

'There is one thing you should know,' continued Holland. 'I found an old jeweller in town here who sold the original lighter to Emily Parry. He can recall the transaction and he can identify his own engraving on this lighter,' he said, pointing to the one he had placed on the table.

'There's no doubt, therefore, that the lighter in Payne's possession is the one that was given to Medwyn by his parents. That's interesting, thanks. I'll let you know what happens tomorrow, as soon as I can.'

David Beaumont was in a shallow sleep after another restless night. He heard several cars coming to a stop on the gravel drive below his bedroom window and, as he pulled back the curtains, he heard the doorbell ringing and heavy knocking on the front door. A feeling of trepidation weighed heavily in the pit of his stomach as he looked below the window and saw Jeff Evans looking up at him. Several men were running towards both sides of the house. This was no courtesy call. He tied the cord of his dressing gown and walked anxiously down the stairs and opened the front door. Jeff Evans and two other men he didn't recognise invited themselves into the house and followed Beaumont into the lounge. Beaumont listened as Jeff Evans detailed the reasons for his arrest. A request to make a telephone call was granted. Beaumont picked up the receiver and dialled without having to look up the number. Edwin James, the solicitor, wasn't at home. His wife told Beaumont that the police had taken her husband to his office – something to do with Aber Properties and a search warrant. Beaumont's thoughts were racing ahead as he replaced the receiver and Jeff wasted no time in telling him that it was all a part of the same operation. Beaumont was taken to the police station whilst other officers began a methodical search of the house and the grounds in the presence of a distraught and confused Mrs. Beaumont.

It was ten-thirty by the time Beaumont's interview began in the presence of a solicitor who was unconnected with Williams, Reynolds, James and Co., or Aber Properties. Beaumont didn't look directly into Jeff Evans's eyes as the tape-recording machine bleeped, signalling its readiness. He seemed to disregard the preamble that Jeff Evans was obliged to deliver before questioning began. Then, he produced copies of the witness statements made by Beaumont two days earlier, giving him and his solicitor an opportunity to read them through.

'Do you confirm that these are the statements you made?'

'I do,' Beaumont replied.

'Will you confirm that you are a leading member of Aber Properties, a syndicate engaged in property and business development in this area?'

'I have nothing to say about my business affairs.'

'And that Mr. Alex Renton was also a member?'

'Mr. Renton's affairs were his own.'

'For the record, a search warrant was executed at Williams, Reynolds, James and Co. this morning. We have found sufficient evidence to connect both of you to that organisation.'

'Then why bother asking me?' Beaumont replied arrogantly.

'Last time you were interviewed, you distanced yourself from having made an offer for Hendre Fawr as a potential development site for a gas-turbine power station. Papers found this morning show that Aber Properties made an offer for that property in two thousand and one and yet another one four months ago and you, Mr. Beaumont, are the leading member of that syndicate.'

'Local economic development on that kind of scale is a matter that often involves private negotiations. Bringing big business into this area is my responsibility as the leader of local government and it is a matter that requires tact, diplomacy and secrecy. It is not a matter I care to discuss with anyone, either then or now. I'm not sure you're capable of understanding how issues of that nature work.' There was an air of superiority in Beaumont's tone.

'Explain to me the difference between economic development on that kind of scale and accumulation of personal wealth at anyone's expense would you?' asked Jeff.

'I see nothing out of place in trying to make a buck or two. We live in a capitalist society and there is nothing wrong in making a perfectly good offer for a property, Hendre Fawr included. I should have thought that even you could appreciate that.' he replied.

'What, even if an owner who is unwilling to sell is intimidated in an attempt to get her to change her mind?'

'I challenge you here and now to produce any evidence that someone connected with Aber Properties, myself included, has done anything of the kind.' Beaumont was on the offensive, leaning over the table in Jeff's direction, pointing his right index finger at him as he spoke.

'Mrs. Emily Parry was intimidated over a period of ten weeks or more. Her collision with the wall was not an accident. We can show that someone tampered with her car, causing its brakes to fail.'

'Why are you telling me?' Beaumont laughed, moving about in his chair, glancing at his solicitor, eyes rolling upwards in their sockets as he did so.

'Marcus Payne was responsible for that. The remains of Mrs.

Parry's car braking system was found in Payne's car.'

'You've asked me about him before and I've told you that I don't know the man and I've never met him.'

'Mr. Beaumont,' said Jeff. 'You were seen with Marcus Payne in a fishing hut close to the river, not far from your home. It was late last Wednesday evening, a week ago tonight. You were talking together for some time. You were seen by a water bailiff who was on the lookout for poachers.'

Beaumont thought carefully before he replied. 'I'm sure it must have been dark, Mr. Evans. Your witness is mistaken. In fact I'm certain he is.'

'Can you offer an explanation as to how the deceased Marcus Payne could have been in possession of a Ronson cigarette lighter inscribed with the initials M. P.?' Jeff asked.

'His own initials, you mean? Hardly unusual is it?'

'No, it was Medwyn Parry's lighter, the lighter that was used to intimidate Emily Parry. The one that was used in conjunction with a tape recording of Prokofiev's 'Peter And The Wolf' in an attempt to make her believe that her son had returned. Something that would frighten her enough to make her want to leave Hendre Fawr or perhaps even kill her.'

Beaumont's mind flashed back to his last sight of the lighter as it plunged into the depths of the Irish Sea. 'And pray tell me, Mr. Evans, where is your evidence that any such lighter exists?'

'Here it is.' Jeff replied, emptying the contents of a labelled exhibit bag onto the table between them.

It was the first occasion on which Jeff had noted any change in Beaumont's demeanour. He was clearly taken aback.

'We've traced the man who sold it to Mrs. Parry. The same man who engraved it and the same man who, only yesterday identified his very own engraving on it.'

It took Beaumont a second or two to regain his composure.

'And how is that lighter linked to me?' he asked.

'I'm asking you if you can provide an explanation as to how a man such as Marcus Payne, who had no connection with Llanglanaber, could have come by that lighter and also the knowledge that Medwyn Parry was so fond of 'Peter And The Wolf'?'

'If that's true, then someone must have told him,' he replied.

'Someone who knew Medwyn perhaps?' suggested Jeff.

Beaumont was silent.

'Obviously someone who knew Payne,' Jeff added. You knew Medwyn, didn't you?' It was Jeff who was leaning forward now.

'You have no realistic evidence that I knew this Mr. Payne,' Beaumont insisted.

'You sold him a car didn't you, in nineteen eighty-seven, in exchange for antique furniture. That car was used to pick up a girl in Halifax. She was murdered shortly afterwards. Marcus Payne was responsible for that murder.'

'I made my statement to the police at the time. There isn't a shred of evidence that I sold the car to this Payne fellow, or that it was used at the time of that murder in Halifax. They only had a part number and the police were canvassing thousands of motorists.'

'Still a coincidence,' replied Jeff.

'But you don't have any evidence, do you?'

'Don't I?' asked Jeff. 'Bear with me, Mr. Beaumont. I haven't finished yet. Do you recall telling me the last time we met, that you hadn't seen or spoken to Mr. Renton since the press conference on Thursday last?'

'Yes, that's correct.' Beaumont was becoming a little unsettled now; uncomfortable because he didn't know what was coming next.

Jeff looked directly into his eyes. 'That was a lie, wasn't it?'

There was no response from Beaumont.

'We've obtained a printout of all calls recently made from Mr. Renton's mobile and also from yours,' he continued. 'Marvellous thing technology, isn't it?' Jeff paused, making him wait. The more Beaumont obviously disliked it, the longer Jeff made him wait. 'He called you on Saturday afternoon, didn't he?'

'If he did so, then I don't remember it,' replied Beaumont, showing signs of pressure now.

'Perhaps you are suffering from a convenient loss of memory, because you telephoned him back later that evening, didn't you?'

'If you say so. Like I said, I don't recall. Are you sure that you can prove it was me?' Beaumont was a little unsure of himself now, but his mind was racing ahead in an attempt to deliver a credible explanation.

'And between those calls you made one other call, remember?'

'Get to the point, Mr. Evans.' Beaumont was bluffing – trying to draw him into a position whereby his line of questioning would collapse.

'That call was made to another mobile. That number corresponds to a mobile found on Payne's body. In fact you've made a total of twenty-seven calls to Marcus Payne's mobile 'phone during the last three months or so.'

Beaumont didn't reply.

'When you made that second call to Mr. Renton on Saturday evening, Mr. Beaumont, where were you?'

'I didn't make it, so how can I recall where it was made from? I haven't made any calls to Mr. Payne's phone either, Mr. Evans. My phone was either lost or stolen some time ago. If any such calls were made, I did not make them and neither did I receive any calls from Alex Renton or anyone else on Saturday. Do you understand me?'

'Your phone was not lost or stolen during the relevant time. Other calls using it were made to and from your home, to and from the council offices and several to and from Edwin James as well as Payne and Mr. Renton. I'm asking you specifically about that second call to Mr. Renton on Saturday evening because when you made it, you were close to Hendre Fawr Farm. You see, Mr. Beaumont, technology is such these days that every mobile 'phone acts as a beacon that transmits its location to the 'phone company at all times. It doesn't even have to be in use. Your mobile was detected in exactly the same spot as Payne's phone when the water-bailiff saw you by the river that night. They have been detected together on several occasions over recent weeks, so don't tell me you haven't met him or spoken to him.'

David Beaumont did not reply.

It was important to keep up the pressure. 'Like I said, wonderful thing, technology!' he continued. 'These telephone company masts record a direction from which any mobile phone is carried. When you have two masts or more that pick up the phone's signal, you can pinpoint its location. Clever, isn't it?' Jeff enjoyed being cynical occasionally, but seldom as much as he did at that moment.

'What if I didn't have my 'phone with me on those days? And in any event, I sometimes pass Hendre Fawr on my way home.' He tried to cover all options. He thought it unwise to deny that he had been in the vicinity of the farm in case the police had found someone who had seen him close by.

'You mean the scenic route, just past the place where a double murder was committed? It's hardly the route you would normally take home, is it?'

You have nothing to connect me to Hendre Fawr Farm on Saturday evening or those deaths, Mr. Evans and you know it.' He was gambling that he would have introduced any such evidence by then, had it been available.

'What we do have, Mr. Beaumont, is a clear indication that there was someone else present when those murders took place. An examination of Mr. Renton's body indicated that the weapon was fired by a right-handed person and Mr. Renton was…'

'Left-handed, I know,' Beaumont interrupted. 'I've played golf with him on hundreds of occasions,' he added, recalling with disbelief that he hadn't taken account of that factor.

'Which is your dominant hand, Mr. Beaumont?'

'The right, Mr. Evans, same as the vast majority of people.'

'It's also interesting that the only fingerprints of Mr. Renton's on the gun were bloodstained, indicating that the gun had been placed in his hands after he was injured or killed.'

'What does that have to do with me?' Beaumont asked. 'My presence there is a figment of your imagination.'

'Precisely this,' began Jeff. 'When all that was taking place, records held by Orange, Vodafone and O2 show that mobiles belonging to all three you, yes, Payne, Mr. Renton and you, were together at Hendre Fawr.'

'That's unreliable information,' replied Beaumont. 'I know it is. Even if my 'phone was there, I certainly wasn't. It still doesn't connect me with the incident, nor indeed does anything you have put to me this morning. I have been wrongly detained. I must warn you that I will use every means at my disposal to seek retribution for your unprofessional behaviour. I want you to know that I'll be coming after you personally with a lawsuit and the Chief Constable too. You haven't got an ounce of evidence which justifies my detention and questioning in this manner.'

On this occasion, his solicitor spoke for the first time.

'Yes, officer, I must add my deepest concern at the lack of credible evidence you appear to have against my client. If you have nothing further to add, I intend making representations to the custody sergeant to ensure my client's release at the earliest opportunity.'

Jeff Evans brought the interview to a close, knowing that the evidence available was lacking in many respects. His only hope now was that other officers had found more incriminating evidence elsewhere. He was banking that Beaumont's fingerprints would be found in Payne's 'Jaguar'. He had given the interview his best shot and though it had made its impact, he felt saddened that if nothing else turned up, Beaumont might walk.

He took Beaumont before the custody sergeant and outlined the basis on which the interview had proceeded. Beaumont's solicitor insisted that he wanted to make full representations once he'd had an opportunity of speaking privately with his client. They were led away into a detention room for that purpose.

Once they had departed, Jeff Evans was told that the A.C.C. wanted to see him urgently the minute he had emerged from the interview room. Apparently, Mr. Eric Edwards hadn't seemed too pleased about something.

Jeff Evans knocked on the door, waited for the invitation and entered.

'Sit down, D.C. Evans,' said Edwards in a more formal manner than Jeff had been addressed by him in recent days. 'You have got some explaining to do.'

Once inside the door, Jeff glanced to his right and saw that there was someone else present. It was Dr. Brian Poole from the forensic laboratory. His face was expressionless but for a hint of a wink using the eye that was to Edwards's blind side. Jeff felt his gut tightening, but he wanted confirmation.

'Have we got a result?' he asked.

The doctor nodded.

'You'll have to accept my apologies, Mr. Edwards,' he turned to the A.C.C. 'It wasn't that I was attempting to keep anything deliberately away from you,' he continued. 'It's just that I thought this line of enquiry might be seen as ridiculous, and when I decided to look at it, Mr. Renton was still in charge and making life difficult for me. I did agree with Dr. Poole that any positive result would be directed to you first and not to me. I hope that serves to indicate that my intentions were sincere.'

'You've just saved your arse, Jeff,' said Edwards. 'Here's Dr. Poole's statement detailing his findings. You'd better read it before going back downstairs.'

By the time Jeff arrived back at the custody block, David Beaumont and his solicitor were standing next to the counter, impatiently waiting to address the sergeant.

'Ah, here's the officer now,' said the solicitor turning towards

Jeff. 'I'm about to make my representations for Mr. Beaumont's immediate release from custody.'

Beaumont raised his chin arrogantly as he looked at Jeff Evans, but he noted a slight difference in the detective's demeanour. Clearly, Jeff possessed an air of confidence that wasn't there a few minutes earlier. Beaumont's self-assurance suddenly faded.

'Before you start, I have something to say that might alter your plans,' said Jeff, speaking to the solicitor without taking his eyes away from Beaumont's gaze.

'It had better be good,' said Beaumont. His eyes were fixed on Jeff's as if both men were prizefighters ready to begin a championship bout. Beaumont's mind was still searching for possibilities, but he remained confident that none of the other enquiries that were taking place that morning would serve to endanger his position further.

Jeff Evans stepped back. He was speaking slowly and clearly.

'I am arresting you for the rape and murder of Diane Smith in Llanglanaber on the fifteenth of September, nineteen seventy-six.' And then he cautioned him.

David Beaumont's mouth dropped and his startled eyes looked for comfort in the direction of his solicitor who was equally stunned. Beads of sweat developed on his forehead, which quickly ran into tiny streams down his grey-coloured face. Suddenly, Beaumont collapsed.

It was an hour before a doctor certified that he was fit for a second interview, but this was not the same David Beaumont. He was a different person from the one who had been seated at the same table earlier that day, a man whose spirit had been crushed by a terrible sin he had managed to keep secret for thirty years – until now. Councillor David Beaumont's world had gone forever. Suddenly, he was a man who was afraid of the future.

The tapes rolled and the interview began.

'Semen found on internal swabs taken from the body of Diane Smith matches your D.N.A. The chance of it being someone else's is a thousand million to one.'

Beaumont remained silent, his eyes filling with moisture.

'Skin samples from beneath her nails match up with your D.N.A. too.'

Jeff waited, giving him time to respond. When he did so, it was as if another person was now speaking.

'For thirty years I've had to live with this. Can you imagine what it's been like to have been in that position?'

'No, tell me,' replied Jeff.

There was another pause.

'I didn't mean to kill her. It started out as a bit of fun. I got carried away. She was fighting and I was squeezing and suddenly,' he paused, 'she wasn't fighting any more.'

'Tell me what happened, from the beginning, Mr. Beaumont. All of it; tell me about Medwyn too.' Jeff waited again, passing Beaumont a paper cup, half-filled with water.

'Yes, Medwyn too,' he agreed. 'I was passing the bridge when I heard the girl giggling and I went beneath it to see what was going on. I watched them for a while – after a bit, my eyes got used to the dark. They didn't know I was there. They were kissing. She was taking the lead. She opened her blouse and put his hand inside. I doubt that Medwyn had ever been in that position before.'

'Were you becoming aroused?' asked Jeff.

'What do you think? I was nineteen, of course I was. But then they saw me and I must have startled them. Medwyn had no idea what he was doing and I thought she wanted it, so I got hold of him and pushed him away.'

'What did he do?'

'Nothing. He cowered away, holding his cap in both of his fists. He thought that he'd been caught doing something he shouldn't, because that's the kind of boy he was.'

'And what did she do?' 'Jeff asked.

'I couldn't understand why she wanted him and didn't want me touching her. I couldn't understand why she was struggling so much. I was inside her then. She was making too much noise and so I hit her and I gagged her with her own knickers, but she still screamed. I wake up at night, you know. To this day, I remember clearly how I squeezed her throat. I squeezed and I squeezed and I squeezed. With these hands,' he said, holding his palms in front of his face.

Beaumont's tears were flowing now.

'What happened when it was over?' Jeff asked, softly.

'I realised that I'd killed her and I didn't know what to do. Medwyn was going to call an ambulance or something, but I convinced him not to do it. I took his cap and hit him about the face with it, just to bring him back to his senses, but before we left, I put the cap in the girl's hand.'

'Where did you go?'

'I told Medwyn I needed somewhere to hide and he took me to his secret place down in the tunnel at Hendre Fawr. I'd been there before, but I could never have found the way myself. I knew what I had to do. He would have been sure to tell someone that I'd killed her. He'd never told a lie in his life, you see, it wasn't in his character. I had to kill him.'

'What happened then, Mr. Beaumont?'

'He called it his den. He lit the candles with his lighter and that's when I saw the iron bar. I had to do it. I had no choice.'

'How many times?' Jeff asked.

'How many times did I hit him, do you mean? Two or three at least, maybe more. I had to be sure you see. Sure that he was dead.' Beaumont's hands were shaking now, spilling water from the cup as he brought it to his mouth. 'Then I hid his body inside some sacking and I left him. His cigarette lighter and a candle were the only means of light I had to find my way out again. The next day, I left for college.'

'And you gave Marcus Payne the lighter to intimidate Emily Parry?'

'Yes.' Beaumont replied. 'But I didn't know what lengths he'd go to. I had no idea he would kill her.'

'When did you know that he had?'

'He told me the following morning. That's when I told Alex to delay the car's examination. Payne said that he could put things right in the meantime, hide whatever he'd done to the brakes. Alex was in it up to his neck you know.' He sounded pleased to be able to incriminate him.

'But things went wrong when Payne killed Donna Marie Murphy, didn't they?' suggested Jeff. 'That's when Alex Renton found that his loyalties were divided.'

'Yes, bringing Payne in to persuade the old lady was my biggest mistake.'

'Is that why you had Mr. Renton killed?'

"Yes. I couldn't trust him any more. He wanted to arrest Payne and I couldn't afford to let that happen.'

'Who killed Marcus Payne?'

'I did. Foolishly, I thought all my troubles would be over then.'

'Making it look as if Mr. Renton was responsible?'

'Yes, but failing miserably by all accounts.'

'What were you wearing at the time?'

'That's of no consequence now, Mr. Evans. I burnt all my

clothing that night. You see, I was conscious of forensic.'

'A bit late by all accounts, Mr. Beaumont,' said Jeff. 'I have one last question. Why did you have the Thomas boy kidnapped?' he asked.

'I didn't. I just told Payne to get the lighter back from Elen Thomas at any cost.'

'Was that when you met Payne at the river bank?'

'Yes, but something strange happened. Someone delivered an identical lighter to my house. I thought it was Medwyn's lighter and that I was safe once I disposed of it by throwing it into the sea.'

'I can't help you there, Mr. Beaumont.' Jeff Evans replied, drawing the interview to a close.

'Holland, you're a son of a bitch!' he thought.

Chapter Nineteen

There were two funerals in Llanglanaber on Friday of the following week. The first was for Donna Marie Murphy and the second for Medwyn Parry. They had been two people connected by sinister events – murdered, thirty years apart. It seemed that the whole town had been brought together in grief. There wasn't a shop open in Llanglanaber that morning and no one was eager to engage in his or her daily routine. The streets were empty.

For Medwyn's funeral, the grave had been opened a second time in just three weeks. It was the place where Emily Parry had been put to rest along side her husband, Huw. After thirty long years, the family was together again – their souls united in peace.

Some of those in attendance had known both families. Many did not, but it didn't seem to matter now. For thirty years, the people of Llanglanaber had been caught on one side or the other of an immense divide. There had been those who believed that Medwyn Parry had been responsible for the murder of Diane Smith and those who thought otherwise. Today they stood together in grief. Some of them felt the guilt of having wrongly blamed Medwyn, but foremost in all their minds was the shock left by the events of the past weeks. Uppermost in the thoughts of this small community was a sense of disbelief that their civic leader, David Beaumont, had been responsible, in one way or another, for both the events that had brought them there. Maybe Diane Smith would rest more easily now too.

Llanglanaber Cemetery had never seen so many grieving people, but there were only two bearers alongside Medwyn's coffin – Michael Holland and Jeffrey Evans. There were no graveside hymns. They had already been sung in the chapel. Elen had decided that there was only the one piece of music that could pay the kind of tribute that was appropriate for Medwyn – Prokofiev's 'Peter And The Wolf' – a playful tune that, on this occasion, brought tears to many eyes.

Detective Constable Jeff Evans and Assistant Chief Constable Eric Edwards stood at the gate afterwards watching people as they departed. Amongst the mourners was one woman who didn't look as if she was dressed for a funeral, but it didn't seem to matter. She stopped next to them for a moment, but didn't say a word. She just smiled at Jeff who returned it with a wink of his eye that was noted by Edwards.

'Who was that?' the A.C.C. asked Jeff.

'Her name is Mary. I call her 'Midnight Mary'. Today, she's just another mourner,' he replied.

'That reminds me,' Eric Edwards said. 'I've got a message for you from the Chief Constable. He's surprised that in the nine years since you've been qualified, you've never applied for promotion.'

'I've had other things on my mind, Sir.'

'The message is that he's promoting you to the rank of Detective Sergeant with immediate effect. He wants you to work from Headquarters Projects Department for twelve months or so on a special assignment.'

Jeff paused in thought before replying, but only for a moment or two.

'Please tell the Chief Constable that I'm very grateful, but I feel that my place is here, in Llanglanaber, putting villains behind bars. It's what I know best.'

'Shame,' replied Edwards. 'You'd be working nine until five with weekends off, which would give you more time to spend with your wife. Oh, I should mention that the special project he had in mind was to carry out research for him on behalf of the Association of Chief Police Officers Crime Committee. He wants a detailed paper from a police perspective on legalising the use of cannabis for medical treatments such as Multiple Sclerosis.'

Jeff was stunned momentarily as he looked at 'Midnight Mary' walking away in the crowd, but then he turned his head towards Eric Edwards and replied.

'In that case, Sir, please tell the Chief Constable that I accept.'

Elen Thomas and Michael Holland were among the last to leave.

'Michael,' she said, turning to face him. 'I'm so grateful for everything you've done. I don't know how to thank you.'

'You can accept this if you like,' he replied, producing an envelope from within his suit pocket. 'I hadn't figured on giving it to you here, but being as you've asked.'

The envelope contained three tickets to Mauritius, flying from Manchester at the end of the following week.

She gave him a huge smile.

'Three?' she asked.

'We're not going anywhere without Geraint, now, are we?' he replied.

She turned, held him and kissed him tenderly on his mouth.

'Not here, my darling,' he said, as his eyes swivelled, watching others leaving the cemetery.

Four months later David Beaumont stood in the dock at Chester Crown Court charged with murdering Diane Smith, Emily Parry, Medwyn Parry, Marcus Payne and Alex Renton, Conspiracy To Abduct Geraint Thomas and Perverting The Course Of Justice. The indictment was read out before a courtroom packed with members of the public and media.

To each charge, he replied 'Not guilty.'